RARE ENCOUNTER

RARE ENCOUNTER
A War Novel

J.K. Hall

WINDAGE & ELEVATION PRESS
MINNEAPOLIS

Published in the United States by Windage & Elevation Press / Wind Waltz Pictures LLC, Minneapolis, Minnesota

www.jkhallauthor.com

Book and jacket design by Kiersten Armstrong

Library of Congress Cataloguing-in-Publication Data
Names: Hall, J. K., 1948— author
Title: Rare Encounter : A War Novel / J.K. Hall

1. Soldiers—World War Two—Fictions. 2. Mothers—Fathers—Death—Fictions. 3. American Universities—Seminary—Fictions. 4. Battle of the Bulge—Ardennes Forest—Fictions. 5. Vietnam War—Twentieth Century—Fictions. 6. Dust Bowl—Great Depression—Fictions. 7. Historical Fiction—Literary. 8. Outlaws—Fiction. 9. Blood Sport—Fiction. 10. Family Saga—Fiction.

Description: First American Edition | Minneapolis: J.K. Hall

Identifiers: LCCN 2021915813 (print)
ISBN 978-1-7375687-0-4 (hardcover) | ISBN 978-1-7375687-1-1 (paperback)

Printed in the United States

1 3 5 7 9 10 8 6 4 2

First American Edition

ACKNOWLEDGEMENTS

The author gratefully acknowledges, among others, Dr. Beth Shinn and Carol
Wheeler for insights into their father, Dr. Roger Lincoln Shinn.
He also acknowledges his wife
Lou Ann for her invaluable advice and fortitude;
Gene Hall and Richard Hall for their support and wisdom;
and Susan T. Hall
for her critical and perceptive eye.

The author also thanks Carolyn V. Bratnober and Columbia University's Burke
Library at Union Theological Seminary, New York City; Preus Library at Luther
College and Decorah Public Library, Decorah, Iowa; and Hennepin County
Libraries, Minneapolis, Minnesota, without which this work could not have been
completed.

As well, the author gratefully acknowledges help from the following
books and newspaper:
The United States Army in World War II: The Ardennes: Battle of the Bulge
by Hugh M. Cole
Office of the Chief of Military History,
Department of the Army, Washington, D.C.
Wars and Rumors of Wars
by Roger Lincoln Shinn
Abington Press
An Indigenous People's History of the United States
by Roxanne Dunbar-Ortiz
Beacon Press
Avalanche-Journal
Lubbock, Texas

To Lou Ann

CONTENTS

A candle in a night of storms,
Blown back and choked with rain,
Holds longer than the mounting forms
That ride time's hurricane. ...

— Maxwell Anderson, 1888-1959

PART I

DUST BOWL BOY

To know the man one must know the child, he said. Then he read from Whitman,

My tongue, every atom of my blood, form'd from this soil, this air, / Born here of parents born here of parents the same, and their / parents the same...

What followed was a story from decades earlier. The class wondered why the great Professor Shinn would begin there? With a farm boy from the Dust Bowl of Oklahoma? And where was the professor taking them?

Chapter 1

INKLINGS

No sound the boy heard was alien to his space. Not the rolling conversations of scarlet tanagers or the low moan of cattle at first light. Not the rasping interventions of insects or the morning's buoyant gait of a faraway horse that took residence in the tall room of his memory.

Like exiles assembled on a rise in eastern Oklahoma, a cluster of trees stood dignified but vulnerable. Under one, John William Hall at the northern edge of thirteen rested just after the moment of daybreak in April, 1929. Unnoticed was the shudder of leaves whose motion led to more, never the same. The boy's wheat-colored hair crudely shorn on the sides but left tumultuous on top had begun to darken. As vivid a blue as a glacial lake his eyes swept over the family farm, its undulant lines, its serrated, arbitrary horizon: his birthplace north and east of Durant, the terminus of the Trail of Tears's Choctaw diaspora and the Treaty of Dancing Rabbit Creek where the unequivocal light of the new and ancient sun washed through the boy's vision like the first water of Eden.

Standing, the boy took a final survey of the tableau, his family's forty acres of plot and curve, meager but fertile if the rains visited and sequenced among more prosperous homesteads. The Hall acreage with its overflowing of bobwhite quail, cunning trout, cultivars of pears and beans, okra and squash was sanctuary. He felt his body was of this clay and places beyond it peculiar, hostile even. For he had seen outside Bryant County.

A year earlier, his father, Arnold Munro Hall, had taken him to Lawton, one-hundred-and-forty blistering Oklahoma miles west, where Arnold tried to dicker a land deal that would never materialize. The massive stretch of ferric wasteland between Durant and their destination, much of it farmed into extinction, consumed the boy.

"This is freakish country, Pa," he allowed as he squirmed in the oven of summer. "It gives nothin' back." The old truck that carried them spewed fumes from its rusty undercarriage, making John queasy. He thrust his hand out the window trying to direct moving air onto his green and broiling face. After a long spell empty of words John spoke again, "This ground's like an old floorboard. Flat 'n dead with little to provoke its routine."

This annoyed his father and Arnold Hall replied. "Hell's bells, I know this ain't the prettiest part a' the world, boy."

Tall, pole-thin, taciturn and humorless he sat squashed up in the driver's seat. On his head as always rested a mud-brown fedora with a capacious brim to block the sun and a tall crown with a deep crease like a dry arroyo down its center. Its wide Petersham band masked sweat stains at the rim. The ribbon culminated in a bow where once a small feather had peeked up like a wary bird in the bush. But Arnold had removed the feather. He replaced it with a silver-certificate dollar bill neatly folded into a triangle, its green filagreed pinnacle emerging from under the ribbon announcing his perceived station in life.

"But this land smells 'a money, boy. North'n west 'a Lawton, up in the panhandle of Oklahomy, is the great western prairie, North America's most magnif-y-cent high plains grassland. It's so fertile they say yew can plant an agate in it and it'll grow! Farmers, even them who ain't made it anywheres, have been a' movin' in fer years. They are 'a breakin' up that prairie, easy as crackin' wishbones."

John's father imagined soaring wheat prices lasting for decades, making landowners and merchants in west Oklahoma and Texas rich as Croesus. "And I wanna be in on it!" John's father yelped. His voice raked across the dry flatland as he pounded the scalding black steering wheel in a burst of euphoria.

To the boy little except the railroad interrupted this land's leaden monotony. The parallel filaments caught the sun and bore hypnotic trains along flashing threads of silver.

When the rails followed the road, John listened for their enduring rhythm. This was the cadence of dominion over time and space and he watched with fascination the boxcars and flatbeds racing across the expanse in close sequence. Loaded with cotton bales and wheat flour and oil-well riggings and automobiles from Detroit the color of midnight, the trains betraying no end trumpeted America's long and perpetual prosperity. And then there were the legions of ploughs with twisted moldboards stacked on a dozen uncovered railcars ready to open up the veins of virgin prairie, prime it for cash crops and offer up its deep black humus in sacrifice to the god of quick money. Inside the boxcars were kitchen appliances and gewgaws from Sears catalogues and crates of soft goods and fashions from the East that the gentlemen and ladies of Lawton and Boise City and Amarillo prized. Beyond the railway, mystical armies of perpetually blowing wads of rootless Russian thistle and wind witch tumbled hysterically across the plains seeking resting places that didn't exist.

****

His memory ending, John reclined against the tree again and closed his eyes to absorb the present before obligations took him. The reverberation of hooves grew louder and stopped. A younger boy dismounted a Tennessee Walking Horse that radiated a sheen of chestnut and carbon.

"What the Sam Hill you doin' up here, John William?"

"Fishin'!"

"For sure no stream up here!" Leo Graham declared.

"Castin' my line in the prettiest water you ever did see," John said, his eyes still closed. "Where'd ya get that steed, Leo?"

"Got her for the week," the visitor, two years younger and three inches shorter than his curious friend, sparkled. "From my uncle on my mama's side."

"I'd say she's clean in the bone with a nice tah-rrruuuue four-beat gait," John warbled as he wove his fingers behind his head. "Anyway, I'm really up here pondering my own existence."

The mare cocked forward her ears.

Opening his eyes, John peered up at the canopy as if seeking counsel. But today the meandering branches were mute. Other days they looked like alphabets, codes to be deciphered. Now they were but scorched lines on the sky. "Wayward inklings," he thought and a discordance came over him like a child secure in the womb realizing it was about to be let into the universe. The next years would substantiate the boy's apprehension. And then the world, and he, would be at war.

****

John took a last glance at the vista and stepped over to Leo's horse.

"Where you gallopin' to next?" John asked as he stroked the animal's withers.

Leo sidestepped the question. "What have you been daydreaming about?" he asked.

"Travellin' west to Lawton with Pa across ugly land."

"It's why the Oklahoma State Flower is *flora moribunda*," Leo quipped and waited for John to follow his deprecating joke. He didn't.

"Well, gotta go back home and help Ma clean windows," Leo huffed.

John wanted to know if his friend would come back tomorrow afternoon. And bring his baseball glove. Leo grinned.

"Since it's Sunday I get to play," John said as he swung an invisible bat. "After the stupid sermon, that is. We can take turns hittin' and pitchin'. The old barn is a good backstop. Jack'll play. Maybe A.M., too. Then we could do teams. Them against us. Lucille'll roam the outfield. We'll slaughter 'em! A.M.'s big, but I know how to strike him out!"

"Dang right!" Leo shouted. "Tomorrow!" He reined his horse and was off.

John slipped his work shoes back on and returned to the corral where he tended a few cattle and a pair of sorrel mules. Afterwards, he would finish cultivating his mother's acre-and-a-half garden, then patch the surrounding fence. Finally he would draw cold well water for evening baths and feed grain to the pullets and the cockerel before being called for supper. During his labors, the recollection of last year's journey into the barrens with his father stuck in his mind.

Chapter 2

NOTHING DIMMED HER

Preparing the soil of Lucy Lee's garden was an annual ritual entrusted to John. This gave him pride. His mother would bring life and provide much of the family's yearly sustenance from the ground he fertilized, tilled, and smoothed. The plot lay near the house where Arnold and Lucy Lee Hall's eight children were born of blended blood—English, Scottish, French, Irish, Baptist and Methodist, vulgarian and saint, poor and poorer. Each of them carried the distinguishing mark of the Hall family line. Where the bridge of the nose dips just before swooping up to meet the forehead, at the spot equidistant between the eyes, a diminutive bump states its presence, as if someone had inserted a small pearl just beneath the skin.

By this time, three of John's siblings were of an age to earn their own living and, at the insistence of their father, left the nest. Marion Irving, nicknamed M.I., and Robert E. Lee were out in the vast universe of Bryant County, Oklahoma. Roy was a hundred fifty miles away at Ft. Sill, a sprawling military base and home of the Army's artillery school. Built following the Civil War as a defensive redoubt, the fort incubated white soldiers to fight the Comanche, Kiowa, and Wichita tribes.

Nineteen-year-old Helen Hall would leave the household within a year to marry a merchant in Tishomingo. Her name and those of their mother and sister Lucille would be stenciled onto John's Sherman tanks as he entered the Second World War.

Remaining in the clapboard and stone roost held together largely by their forty-six-year-old mother, Lucy Lee, was A.M, the tall sixteen-year-old quail-hunting virtuoso, along with Jack, ten; Lucille, seven; and John. Arnold, a Mississippian in turn, was a resolute force who shunted physical labor off to others. He preferred the more recumbent life of sole-proprietor-ship keeping an office on the second story of a building whose main floor housed the Durant Mercantile. A self-employed commodities broker, Arnold the elder bought and sold fields of long-staple "Oklahoma Triumph" and one or two other cotton varieties usually at preferential margins. To fashion his cotton into mountainous bales for transport on rail and ship, Hall contracted with local ginners and compressors. His brokerage provided him with not only a living but freed him to move around the region's money centers at will and maintain a flexible personal program away from family and homestead and the birthing of animals. Though he knew little of the mineral and real estate businesses, the self-confident patriarch also bought a minor interest in an oil lease and dabbled in land speculation and other fulfillments.

****

Gloved and kneeling, John's mother had already devoted an hour's diligence to planting when John arrived. Lucy Lee Hall was seeding Kentucky Wonders, a pole bean her younger children loved with hot buttered cornbread at evening meals. It was half past seven in the morning, still cool and pleasant, and a diffident rising sun continued its gentle hold of the Hall homestead.

"I see you're 'a wearing some 'new' clothes," his mother noted as John approached leading a mule by a rope. "Where d'you get that blue twill shirt and striped overalls?"

Vigilant when his parents probed his thoughts or actions, John kept mute as he lifted the harness around the mule's neck.

"You look like you're about to run off to work on the railroad," she said eyeing his ill-fitting clothes. "I know they're not store-bought. And I sure didn't make 'em."

Like Oklahoma roads the boy was more length than breadth. Though he rarely failed to reach his destination, the hems of his garments never seemed to reach theirs. His garb was old and had lost much of its color like grass too long under a bucket. Worn earlier by others they had lost their original shape. John showed no concern for what he wore. Unless in the company of girls.

"Pa bought 'em cheap from a Union Pacific gandy dancer turned railroad brakeman," the kid said finally.

"Trouser legs are too short," Lucy Lee scoffed. "And why you have the them rolled up so high?"

One reason outdistanced the others: comfort. He liked cool air moving around his ankles and legs. But rolling them up had other benefits.

"Gotta have big cuffs, Mama! They catch dirt and gravel. Can't let 'em get into my work shoes. They'll torture the delicate soles of my feet!" John smiled at his own exaggeration. "And they catch wayward coins, Ma. Can't drop a penny and have it roll underneath store cabinets! Gotta catch it in my big cuffs so I can buy two spirals of black licorice for me and Lucille."

His mother shook her head. "You got the Brown Jerseys tended, John William?" She knew he had, but wanted to remind him of her continuing attentiveness.

"As you asked."

"Where's your younger brother?"

"Jack's down at the creek." He turned so she couldn't see his grimace.

"Why now?" she inquired with feigned surprise.

"Uh, must've seen 'em jumpin', I guess. He'll land a trout or two for supper, I bet," John said covering for his brother, who was swimming in a deep pool.

Lucy Lee in no mood for nonsense looked up with a knowing glare. "Hmmm, don't you think that boy's a little young for us to rely on for supper? We'll need him up here directly."

She stood with a groan, aware her son saw her struggling.

"It's nothin', Sugar. Kneeling too long."

After the cultivating John worked on the garden fence. "Got to get this right, Mama. If it doesn't shut out the deer and rabbits, and if the dogs don't discourage those infernal raccoons, our family meals are gonna be sorry affairs."

Taking a lengthy breath and another stretch, Lucy Lee removed her cloth gloves, patched and sewn to eke out another year's service. With bare hands she pushed seed potato fragments into the ground, eyes skyward. Her garden's cool red soil accepted them as a mother would a nursing child. For her, planting was sacred work. Every encounter with the soil, with each touch of fertile garden and field, Lucy Lee felt alive.

John looked over at his mother. Though the lines in her face were deeper now, her frame more stooped than a few years ago and her lips thinner, this slender woman seemed to glow in the mercurial Southern warmth.

Shy by nature and preferring to keep her own company, except for family, Lucy Lee Thompson descended from poor Scottish stock. Yet to strangers she was welcoming whether she sought them out or they came to her. To those arriving at her door out of the blue she would say, "Come and sit a spell."

Though she always reserved judgment of others, except when it came to drink and the Commandments, Lucy Lee could be flinty if crossed. Her stern kerosene eyes were misleading for they could become tender the moment they met another's. Family and acquaintances knew, however, her gaze could perforate any facade: woman, man, or child's. She stowed away all that she divined about people not for malice, but as warranty to support the footings essential for a selfless mother and wife.

Twenty feet from where John stretched wire around hickory posts, a hundred petite yellow flowers dyed onto the blue expanse of his mother's bonnet winked at him. He watched when without warning an impudent

Oklahoma gust tried to loosen its ties and turn her garden cap into a banderole waving to the prairie as if signaling the surrender of a lost cause. But the calico wrap endured, continuing to protect her face: rabbit brown, gale-and-birth-beaten, the poetry of its former youth struggling not to be utterly extinguished.

John and his mother talked little. But when a question leapt into his mind, he would stop, wipe his forehead, and ask it. "You ever want to live in town, Mama, just to be closer to everything?"

"This is my element, child: the beauty, the music of the earth. Plenty of nice folks in town, I am sure. But after a while I'd feel packed in like eggs in a basket."

Anytime her son spoke, Lucy Lee would use the opportunity to shepherd the boy toward good ends. And she would learn more about his leanings and aspirations. When home, her husband commanded John's time and she feared the imbalance.

"How about you, John William? You ever wanted to live in town?"

The sun warmed his back. He considered the question she had redirected to him. Towns, in his estimation, were places to visit not to live in.

"You can't farm in town, and ya can't shoot," he said. "Farmin' seems like a glorious life. If I could have some hired hands. I don't find dawn-to-dusk labor any more agreeable than dawn-to-dusk talkin.'"

"But people take to you, John William. And that ready sense of humor of yours? You carry it around like a sack 'a hard candy handing morsels out to anybody and everybody."

"I like plenty of folks, Ma, but sometimes my sense of humor lands me in hot water.

The boy put his work gloves on and returned to the fence, careful not to cut himself on the barbed wire he stretched between posts.

"Just be careful not to use humor to belittle," his mother warned with a tiny smile of her own. She had cautioned him before about "that straightforward tongue you own."

"You'll not want to sound harsh," she said. "It can set people off like match to tinder."

He put up his defense. "Don't mean to rile anybody. I just wanna set 'em straight."

His mother was pointed. "Well, at thirteen I'm not sure you warrant such authority."

Lucy Lee stood and dusted off her long cotton dress and field apron before returning to the first subject. "As for you farming, yes, it might make a man a living and a decent life." She had seen three generations of her family work farms and knew it would produce for her son erratic security and happiness. "But you know nothing *but* farming. How do you reckon at your age what you will want the rest of your days?"

Her response intrigued him. The boy studied her to see if she would disclose more. But she left for another part of the garden.

✱✱✱✱✱✱✱✱✱✱✱✱✱✱✱✱

This old young mother sat on a water pail and straightened her back. Her gaze transitioned from the worked-up garden plot to the wood line that stretched along the homestead's western perimeter where her own mortal destiny stopped. For all its raw beauty this was wilderness still and at its core the hard reality of peril and uncertainty. But the trees, for her, stood outside of this. Brought into the world at some unknown hour she could not divine, they assembled as if guardians with claws in the earth—like heraldic griffins but with a thousand quivering wings. Lucy Lee watched these forms catch the light as she felt the warm ensemble of prairie winds blowing across the field. No matter how immersed in her station, she, like Ruth the Moabite, never failed to look beyond her toil. For there was the fabled carnival. Its momentary orange and green and pink huzzahs flashed in a harmony that brought time and earth into balance below a cerulean-blue sky she adored. In these moments Lucy Lee Hall did not ponder the precariousness of meagre fortune, nor the rich prairie soil being sucked from a million foul-tilled rainless furrows due west destined to fill lungs and abrade eyes with dead earth from Oklahoma to Maine. Nor did she consider the ever-risky cotton crop—the substance of bone-colored wedding veils and thread for mending dresses and stiff collars worn by the minor barons of Durant business and industry, which they needed for income. Neither did she worry about other cash crops that fueled the towns but were unsustainable within the deviant marriage of politics and greed. Not at that moment would she meditate over any of this. Nor did the diminutive ache forming in Lucy Lee's uterus get so much as a thought. Or that strange vulnerability that had awakened at her center in the night. No room for these worries existed when her god's luminosity emerged before her eyes drawing in her perfect comprehension.

****

Lucy Lee's namesake was her youngest, seven-year-old Lucille. In back of her the child scuttered barefoot between the fragrant pear orchard and the yellow jonquils that had sprung up in silly asymmetrical choruses circling the house like celebrants.

John had realized that for one so young Lucille was especially steadfast. Nothing dimmed her, as if she had been born with memories of other histories. Conquests she led across millennia. New lands discovered. Fierce enemies subsumed.

"Mama, I am ready for A.M. and Jack to finish their field work and get back here with Papa. I'm hungry. And I have places to go," Lucille announced, having appeared at her mother's side, though she had no real place to go.

Lucy Lee, brought back from her reverie, rose, wiped the sweat running down her face and the clay from her hands onto a long white apron.

"They'll be leavin' the pasture soon and be along directly. I'll fry the salt pork, child."

Chapter 3

FATHER'S LIGHTNING

John William arrived first for breakfast. Though weathered around the edges the family home beamed for him in the morning light as if it were welcoming a beloved child.

"Dad and the boys are just behind me. I'm starvin'! So I doubt there will be enough food for them anyway!" he joked as he sat on a stool inside the entrance to remove his work shoes. The screen door swung open and A.M. and Jack, weary from their chores, and finally their father entered the house. Helen, winsome and luminescent, looked up from cleaning the floor with lye soap and a coarse pig-bristle scrubber. "Kindly reserve your shoes and boots to the mat," she said in her refined plantation English. Her voice was as mellow as coffee with sweet cream.

A.M. and John had already removed their dirt-encrusted boots when Helen spoke. But their irascible father, not partial to women, family or otherwise, giving him instruction, made his way to the breakfast table, eyes blazing at his daughter with his boots strapped on. Onto her newly scrubbed floor they deposited prairie and viscous remnants of hog wallow.

At the exact moment Arnold sat at the table Lucy Lee placed a Royal Delft Blue porcelain plate before him. On it: biscuits, fried salt pork, and two beautiful eggs swimming in an attenuated pool of fragrant grease in which they had been gently basted. Helen washed, joined the gathering, and the Hall children passed the food. Their father watched as they spooned modest portions onto metal plates handed down from the Thompson family that already had accommodated thousands of meals. Before Lucy Lee said grace, they heard a rap at the door. The Graham boy, thin, smiling, impish, cracked it open.

"Oh, sorry. Didn't know you were havin' breakfast," he apologized meekly but hopeful.

"Thought you were helping your ma in town, Leo," John called out.

"Come on in, honey, and sit yourself down. We'll set you a place," Lucy Lee responded. "How's your mamma doing?"

"She's fine, Ma'am."

"Any word from your pa?"

"Far as we know, he's still on the high seas."

"When you all expect him back?"

"Not sure, but should be soon. Been better 'n two years now since he sailed out of Nantucket."

Lucy Lee served Leo a healthy portion before putting a half biscuit on her saucer and pouring herself a cup of tea. She blessed the food and forks were lifted.

Everyone ate in silence. This made the young visitor uncomfortable even though he had eaten at their table many times. Hall progeny were not to speak at the table, even the nearly nineteen-year-old Helen, unless first addressed by their parents.

John William pushed a pat of butter around in a spoonful of dark sorghum molasses and loaded the pungent confection onto a buttermilk biscuit. Annoyed with only hearing people chew, he broke the quiet with the same finesse as if he had thrown his plate of food against the kitchen wall.

"Mama, will you make us some pear preserves this fall?" he blurted out in an overt act of resistance to authority and boredom. Everyone except Lucy Lee glanced at Arnold. She placed her bread on her plate and looked over at him. The boy continued, "The pear trees are full of blossoms. We'll have a full harvest!"

"You shall have it," his mother whispered, peeking at her husband. "I'll put up a dozen jars," she promised. Her eyes carried an abiding affection for John as well as uneasiness. She knew her son's impatience could outmaneuver him. But he had a certain quality, a stranger's deep scrutiny, something his other siblings did not possess. Yet her fear for him was not misplaced. His stubborn, sometimes defiant streak, which he deployed like a field general on a suicide mission, often led to rocky consequences.

As Arnold cut into his second egg, he barked, "Leave the table and unharness the mules!" His voice was as rough as quarry stones shaken in a tin can. John stood, gave his mother a furtive smile, and marched outside.

The mules were tethered to the hitching post near the corral. As John worked to unhitch the team, he decided on a second act of defiance.

"When I'm done here, I'm gonna return to the house and reclaim the food on my plate," he connived. But his labors and his scheming left John distracted and he failed to hear his father's approach from behind. With his lips hardened until they were white, Arnold stood behind his son for a few seconds then swiftly launched the flat of his hand against the side of the boy's head.

The blow produced a sharp crack that startled the animals. John landed heavy on the ground. When he came to his senses, the right side of his face felt as if it were covered in red ants and his mouth throbbed. A sharp ache spiked in his head. When he opened his eyes, he was staring at the mule's underbelly. Turning on his side he watched his father stomp into the house. But he heard no footsteps, only an internal siren screaming in his ear.

Within minutes Helen approached John carrying a pan of warm water and a cloth. He greeted her. "Hi-dee," he groaned as he sat up. Leo had left the commotion inside to watch from the porch. Helen asked her brother to sit on a bucket. She sang as she wiped blood, dirt, and mule products from his face.

> *The wrath of King Arnold Munro Hall*
> *Comes flailing out with the mornin' dew*

And hammers his lad with terrible gall
Til he's black 'n blue with shit to chew.

Howls of laughter squeezed through John's swollen lips.

"Seems like father's lightning always strikes in the same place every time—right where you are standing, John William."

"I reckon," he groaned.

"Wish I could predict the horses at the Hot Springs race track with the same perfection I can foretell your beatings. I'd be a rich girl."

"I reckon."

"Time for you to smarten up, young fella. Your brothers know how to keep father's lightning away. Why don't you? And don't you love your dad? Why do you test his resolve?"

"I seek to avoid him, Helen!" The boy realized his voice was loud when he heard it echo, and he lowered it.

"But, yeah, I love him, and I try to show respect. Don't like him much. Guess it shows." John rose to his feet and whispered in his sister's ear, "Like him about as much as a coyote likes the iron trap."

She tossed the cloth into the basin of brownish-pink water. "Strike some distance between yourself and that man," she warned. "Break out of here, boy, just as soon as circumstances allow."

He nodded and returned to tending the mules. After lifting the harness onto the fence, the boy held his hand to his ear, trying to subdue the pain. "Pa isn't much help here and I'm not about to walk out on Mama, Jack, and Lucille."

Running away now was not what Helen was implying.

"People come out of who they are and what they see. And you have seen too little of life here. Hang around too long and this minor spit of the world is all you'll ever know. You will never become anything. You'll not grow past these fence rows."

"I love Durant, Helen, always have…."

"But what are you gonna do with yourself?"

"I'm gonna do somethin' no one else can do."

"Well, what is that?" Helen asked.

"Dunno. I'm still a kid!"

John paused and gazed at his sister. "But I have to wonder, Helen. After what you've said, why are you still in Durant and on the farm?"

"See, you ask smart questions. It is a quality I admire but threatens our daddy."

She placed both hands on his shoulders.

"My answer, same as yours. Mamma couldn't do all this herself. But the time has come for me. Likely gettin' married to Jimmy in the fall."

"I'm happy for you, Helen!" John smiled warmly.

"I think he's a decent fella. Hope I know what I'm getting into." She tipped her head down and looked down at her shoes. "Sometimes wonder."

"Meanin' what?"

"Well, don't you ever ponder why Mama married Pa? He doesn't hold a candle to her. Did he change over time? I can't imagine he possessed that foul temperament when they were sparking. In twenty years will I be scratching my head about why I wed the man I did? Will I be asking why I committed myself to a lifetime of washing clothes and boiling cabbage?"

Her statement surprised John. He had not considered women taking paths other than the household.

"You go on over to the house now," Helen nudged him. Leo's a good friend and he is still on the porch looking over here. He's worried about you, John William. As if he doesn't have enough to worry about. Let him know you'll be fine. And fetch him another biscuit."

John wobbled through the yard, removed his work shoes, swung open the screen door, and rushed inside the house. Before the door could slam behind him, he darted out of the kitchen holding a clean folded dish towel in his hand. Sitting on the stoop's edge next to Leo, he opened the cloth protecting two biscuits and two pieces of fried salt pork.

"Thanks, John William," Leo intoned. He examined John's bloody, ballooning face and grimaced. "Damn it!" he whispered in disgust.

"Are you up for going to the cave and looking for arrowheads?" Leo asked after he swallowed the last morsel of biscuit.

John pressed his handkerchief to his bleeding ear. "When it's winter, I can't wait for spring and summer," he said instead of replying to Leo's appeal.

"Now that it's nearly summer, I think about fall."

"Why is that?" Leo exclaimed in disbelief.

"Well, for one, I love to watch the seasons change. Powerful, the turning of green to yellow and red. And I can eat as many apples and pears as I want. Then after the frost stings us, the persimmons are sweet…"

The Hall brothers leaving the house and returning to the field interrupted the conversation.

"Myself, I don't want summer to end," Leo resumed. "The swimming the fishing the firecrackers the scorchin' days and cool watermelon evenings. Besides autumn is when Pa left and…." He did not finish the sentence.

After another awkward silence, John picked up his thread. "And with autumn, Leo, pheasant and quail are back on the dinner table thanks to A.M., Pa, and myself. I don't know, maybe I like to feel the seasons change because I need a feeling of motion, that things aren't like an ox sitting forever in the middle of the road. That things'll get better in time."

John heard the door open and the clomp of his father's boots on the porch. The boy didn't look up. Without a word Arnold made his way down the steps, proceeded to his automobile, cranked it, and drove away.

"Or maybe it is that fall means my dawn-to-dusk field work eases off," John continued. He carefully removed the handkerchief from his head. The bleeding had stopped and the ear was purple now and buckled.

Chapter 4

ARBITERS OF EARTH AND SKY

T he fall came. When he could steal away, John lay under the shade and ate apples, plums, and pears that he gathered from the orchard. After the leaves had fallen, he would climb the great oak that dominated a rise on the Hall property. Here he was, out of sight. A waxwing had settled on a limb near him. Within the architecture of oak branches and far above the nonsense of the world below, he would watch the clouds and try to discern their shapes. Resting in the crook of a large branch, he watched the sun dropping in the West like a ripe yellow melon handed gently to a child. Leo Graham, mounted on the Tennessee Walking Horse, rode out to the oak from town.

"I don't think any of those clouds are up there by chance, Leo," John yelled as his friend dismounted. He was thirty-feet high, drawing the spicy, molasses-like resin from a sweet gum twig. "I don't know where they come from, Peru maybe, but they all have a purpose. Those two high ones over yonder movin' faster than the ones below, those are you and me. Steeds feeling the wind in their nostrils. The slower ones, the ones with the sad eyes, they are gypsy palm readers."

The Hall boy climbed down closer to the ground.

"Your Pa isn't right, John William!" Leo inserted into John's monologue.

"Clouds are fortune tellers don't you think, Leo?"

"Your Pa isn't right," Leo repeated more forcefully. "And the blue yonder doesn't give a damn about us."

"But we have to figure 'em out," John continued unabated. He pointed to others that reminded him of memories. "See those two airy ones to the right? That's the Ojibwe warrior Hiawatha. He's 'a chasing Minnehaha!" The kid smiled at his fanciful decoding.

Graham smirked. Then he gazed skyward himself.

"Don't know where or when I first looked long into the sky, Leo. We watch the earth and it tells of all kind of tales. But if we don't read the yonder we'll get only half the picture. Don't you think?"

"Those over there above the rim of the far hills? Reminds me of Achilles raising his shield." Now Leo had gotten into the game.

"Course we must pay attention to the high birds—the hawks, the eagles, the geese, and the scissor-tails—that swoop out from the woods...."

"What are you talking about?"

"Birds! They are the only ones that communicate between the two realms. Nothin' else does. They see ever'thing that goes on down here and up there. They are our arbiters, 'ya know, between heaven and us."

Looking up into the tree Leo's eyes already were speaking.

"All I know right now is that we got to talk about earthly matters."

As he crawled out of the oak John asked, "What earthly matters?"

"I gotta tell you...I am sorry to say it...but somebody must keep your pa from messin' you up." Leo had remained worried for months about what he witnessed in the spring. "Your pa's gotta streak 'a bad in him. And it will have a bad end—for you."

"You're not talkin' about that tussle durin' breakfast way back, are you?" John moaned. "That didn't mean a thing. Not worth a hill 'a beans."

Surprised that his friend even remembered the incident, he asked him if he didn't get the same treatment before his father left.

"No! Nothing like what your pa did!" Leo gasped, his cheeks and the skin around his eyes flushing pink. "And not for stupid stuff like talkin' during a meal about canning pears. Damn it all!" The adolescent boy who was ready always to drop a tactical swear had come to the fork in the road and had to explain piteous reality to his friend. John, he determined, would not recognize his father was crazy by himself.

"You may not divine it in the clouds, John William, but only a coward comes up from behind and hits his own kid along side of his face!"

John was having none of it. "My pa has a lot 'a good in him, Leo."

"Greek fathers prized their sons above all else, John William. Odysseus, Priam…."

Dorothy Graham's only child had been reading Greek fables for two years. They had come tucked inside the saddlebags strapped to the hind-quarters of the horse his uncle lent him. The adventures of gods and heroes conquering enemies and slaying monsters ensnared Leo. As did tales that told of honor and bravery.

"Greek mythology!" John didn't like being outflanked by a surprise attack. "What does that have to do with anything? And since when do twelve-year-olds spout on about ancient Greece!"

Regardless of his feigned outrage, John absorbed everything his friend said. He considered him wise. Leo had one blue eye and one hazel with a sliver of emerald at one o'clock. John said Leo's eyes confirmed that his friend was an oracle of sorts.

"I don't mean to be disrespectful, but your Pa doesn't measure up, not even to fathers from the long ago," he said.

"Don't think ya need ta worry about him, Leo. I see beyond Pa now. Can't carry him with me all my days like other sons do their kin. I won't." John pointed high and to the east. "Me, I got important places to go."

"I worry about your Ma, too…." John's companion stopped, fearing he had gone too far, and climbed back on his horse.

"Whatayasay we go do some fishing?" John asked before Leo could ride away. "Throw our bobs in the water and take in that cool air comin' off the river? Catch us some goggle-eyes."

"Late enough in the day, they oughta be bitin', I guess," Graham sighed, somewhat purged of his anger but not his fear. "I brought some earthworms."

Chapter 5

SINS OF THE FATHERS

Johns father, like many fathers, for better or worse, was the fulcrum of his family's destiny. Bread winner, role model, shaper of young minds, symbol of family virtues and failings, and self-appointed historian. Born in Mississippi, Arnold Munro Hall's life unfolded like a soiled map. At nineteen he fled the state, which by and large was its own preserve and sovereign by its own fictions, and would never return.

At the time of his birth, Mississippi, not factoring in the four years of secession, had been a constituent but unruly state of the Union for sixty-three years though, like Arnold, it really didn't pay much attention to relationships outside of itself and likewise the obligations that came with sustaining relationships.

Arnold's entry into the world on June 19, 1880, was possible only because of the meticulous and loving attention of a black midwife and family servant who tended the long, difficult labor, cut and tied the umbilical and buried the placenta with its accompanying tissues that had surrounded the frail newborn of five-and-three-quarter pounds. In the ensuing years, Arnold rarely uttered a word to the woman who delivered him.

From the time he was six to the age of thirteen, when he finally ran off from home, Arnold Hall was bound to the dawn-to-dusk labor his tenant-farm father required of him. The work assured the boy of food, clothing, shelter, a backyard toilet dusted weekly with lime, and the daily dose of cod liver oil necessary, his parents believed, to ward off infirmities and keep their child in the field.

If anything diverted young Hall from his father's sway and his own raw instincts, it was the serenity he felt when fishing the languid Blue Mountain River on Sundays at dusk. And leaving the house late at night to gaze at the heavens.

On the first of February 1893, while the rest of the family slept, the wispy boy left the Hall homestead near Blue Mountain with all his worldly belongings neatly arranged in an old Confederate haversack that his uncle had carried in the war. Arnold was headed for Oxford, Mississippi, some fifty miles away. "The town has opportunities for good-paying labor in cotton operations," Arnold told his brother, Terrill, the night before, "and in a crazy new industry, manufactured ice."

In the ensuing six years, Hall, vexatious by nature, failed to find meaningful employment in the frozen water business, which required a measure of amity with retail customers. But in commodities he worked his way up from day laborer—receiving cotton and preparing it for transport—to overseer. His promotion gave him power over a four-man team in charge of lading. And he liked having power over men and the rewards that ensued.

Shortly after his good fortune, in April, Arnold Hall, then nineteen, had a proposal for his friend, Thomas Paedric O'Byrne, age eighteen, sometimes referred to as "O", an endearing fair-skinned moon-faced youth. The graceful distribution of tiny moles on his face like black pepper dusted gently onto a fried egg enhanced his charm.

"Friday let's take the Mississippi Central from Oxford Depot, O, and head over to Tuscaloosa where we can spend the weekend. Yew think your ma and pa will give you leave?" Arnold asked with a contemptuous snort.

"My dad's in Vicksburg for three days tryin' to put together a business deal. Mother's gonna do what she does every end of week— entertaining. She doesn't want me around."

The idea appealed to O'Byrne but he wanted to be sure what his friend had in mind. "I've never been outside Mississippi. What's there for us over in 'Bama, Arn?"

Hall had it all planned. "Bein' men for once, O, bein' men! We'll go to one 'a them crazy cockerel fights, take in some winnings and drink a glass or three of busthead whiskey," Arnold rhapsodized.

Tuscaloosa County was notorious for cockfighting, a game where specially bred rooster chickens fought to the death. Few Tuscaloosans considered their passion for Jesus, love of fairs and Sunday socials, and revelry in blood sport to be contradictory. As for Hall and O'Byrne the thought of seeing gamecocks maul each other in mortal combat intrigued them, though for different reasons.

"A lot 'a money at cockfights, I hear tell," Arnold puffed, "and there's a favorable chance we'll meet some fetchin' young swans in town, if ya' follow me, O." Deep down Thomas wanted most to rebel against his absentee parents. Thus the decision was ratified.

****

Hall and O'Byrne sat in the train station waiting for the 4:40 bound for Tuscaloosa. "It's about time I see the world, isn't it, Arn? Drink it dry and wake snakes?" the nervous, well-scrubbed O asked his friend. While chattering he chiseled the red Mississippi clay from the welts of his fine leather boots. When they were clean, O'Byrne grabbed a broom and dustpan that hung in the lobby and cleaned up his mess.

Arnold Hall, even at this young age, was conservative in his financial affairs and a fastidious saver. However, he had a weakness for gambling, which he had acquired at a tender age. When Arnold was a boy, his father, Uriah X. Hall, a tall, gray-eyed man with a high scratchy voice like a razor being stropped on a wide leather belt, took him deep into the Mississippi woods one steamy July night. Carved out of dense Mississippi pines was a large makeshift amphitheater. At its center, a boxing ring. Four taut evenly spaced horizontal ropes resembling giant tourniquets wrapped around the ring. Wooden poles stood like totems anchoring them at the corners. Great numbers of torches and hurricane lamps made the space burn bright and, to a lesser extent, the area where the observing audience quaffed overpriced ale and rum.

Here the kid witnessed an event that would reach underneath his already encrusting sensibilities and bedazzle him: a vicious bare-knuckle boxing match filled with adroit ringside gamblers gathering up lucrative winnings from the inebriated and the unwary. It looked to Arnold as easy as picking up gold coins strewn on the forest floor. In ensuing years he would tell this story over and over to children born to him.

"I've never seen such beautiful lights, Pa," the nine-year-old Arnold yelled through rough and calloused hands cupped around his mouth trying to project his tiny voice above the clamor. "But cain't hardly see the celestial canopy. Where's the stars? The planets?"

"They're a float'n and dance'n up thar, boy, jes' like at Blue Mountain," his father, John William's grandfather, returned coldly. "But the real show is right in front of 'yer face and 'bout to start. So pay attention to whut matters!"

Covering the boxing platform was stretched canvas bespeckled with stains where vassals had tried to remove its history of sweat, blood and stomach contents with lye soap and hog-bristle brushes. At its center were the words "John L. Sullivan/Boston Strong Boy."

"That's him!" Arnold's father exclaimed stiffly, nudging the boy as the muscular Irishman stepped into the ring. "That's Sullivan! The most celebrated bare-knuckle fist fighter of all time!" The kid would watch this man knock senseless the brawny New Yorker Jake Kilrain, who had won the World Championship Title two years earlier in a 106-round pasting of a highly ranked opponent.

Tonight Kilrain hoping for an extravagant $1,500 purse would hit the canvas in round seventy-five of a scheduled eighty-round match. When he did, the roar of the crowd would vibrate through the woods for miles and burrow into the boy's essence where it remained for the rest of his life.

Even more than the outlawed contest itself, the furious exchange of money from fist to hand amongst the hundreds upon hundreds of spectators mesmerized Arnold. They had expended no toil. Just easy money, he concluded, as his father had done that night. From that day forward Arnold Hall had a passion for high-risk brutal sport. Especially if it could provide him with quick paper.

****

Arnold Hall and Thomas O'Byrne arrived at the Tuscaloosa train station late into the night. They saw shadows stumbling in the dark. An empty bottle thrown against a stone building released a high angry cry. Despite the hour, the boys were ready to join the hurly burley. Above them, a thunder broke flashes into the distance. Moaning brays rose from the livestock yards.

Finding a rank saloon at the city's edge the artless youth washed the soot and dust from their mouths with ferrous drink. After an intemperate night at this squalid divot playing poker and drinking beer, followed by whiskey cut with river water, the two spent the following day in bed on its second story. By nightfall they felt well enough to bet on the cockerels. Uriah X. Hall's teenage son fearlessly bet his not-insignificant savings. Deploying an eye for superior gamecocks he would come out ahead though he would secure no fortune. O, diminished and leaning on Arnold, would board the Sunday train for home broke. Gamblers had stripped him of money and beat him senseless. The night before, his nose caught the elbow and boot of a beefy Tuscaloosa cracker after a luckless exchange of unpleasantries between cockfights. The cartilage and part of the bone of O'Byrne's nose had been disengaged from their moorings and moved southwest on his face. Seeing the altercation, his friend ran to him, "Christ-a-mighty, O!" Arnold stared at the carnage both in horror and morbid curiosity.

"I am gonna wash away as much blood and grit as I can from your wound with sour mash whiskey," Hall shouted above the din at the nearly comatose boy. O'Byrne came to life when Arnold began repositioning the nose to the center of his face. The screaming was so intense that it momentarily attracted the attention of bettors girdling the ring.

Arnold dragged the bleeding Irish lad away from the pandemonium, then put a partially depleted pint of sour mash in Thomas's hand.

"Take a pull when the pain worsens, O," Arnold instructed his now incoherent companion and he departed to resume his betting.

The next day Arnold, slumped and bilious, peered at his friend in the Tuscaloosa station. As they awaited the train, both squirmed on hard wooden benches fashioned with severe contours. Arnold suspected the station's owner, Southern Railway, had saved money by employing executioners rather than furniture builders to design the benches. The lobby clock gonged on the hour and distracted Arnold from his bother. As he stretched, he caught at the edge of his bleary eyes the contour of a youthful woman. Silhouetted against the windows she cut a striking form. Clad in a plain cotton dress and apron she mopped up trails of dirt and fecal residue left mainly by the boots of Alabama cattlemen. As she walked out of the glare, the young woman, years Arnold's junior, paused to gape at O'Byrne. She left her mop in the bucket and sat beside the semi-collapsed boy. Boldly lifting the corner of the blood-soaked kerchief that covered his face, she glimpsed the damage underneath. O, lost in soporific misery, his wounds encrusted with dried blood, didn't reconcile her presence.

"He gotta boot in the face last night," Arnold grunted. "I'mma gittin' him home."

"Where's that," the young woman demanded, not taking her eyes from the blood and revolting liquid still oozing up through the surface of the bandana.

"Oxford, Mississippi, ma'am."

"Sweet Jesus, boy. With stops, that's near a five-hour ride!" she warned. Again the inquisitive character peered at O's wound before turning to face Arnold. "You got time to take him to Doc Wilwers before the train leaves.

His bandage, or whatever this is, stinks of toad in the throes of putrefaction."

"No money," Arnold lied.

She stood towering over the slouching visitor. "I have a mind to take him myself— what's your Christian name, boy?"

"Arn. Arnold. Arnold Munro Hall. Admirers call me Mister Hall."

"Your friend's in trouble. He's half dead. Haven't you figured that out yet, Arnold. Munro. Hall?"

She reached into her apron pocket and pulled out a vial of a shimmering reddish-purple substance. "After the train leaves the station, secure some menfolk to hold your friend down," she dictated. "Then pull off this stinking bandage and toss it toward your worst enemy. Before you put on a clean one, wash his face in warm green tea. They have it in the dining car. Then spread what's in this container over every inch of the wound. Don't get any in his eyes!"

The attractive medicine handler also cautioned Arnold to isolate O from passengers before applying the medicine. "He's gonna howl like a Jesuit chained to hell's half acre."

When they'd arrive home, she instructed him to take the suffering boy to a doctor. "You got doctors in Mississipp'?" she glared.

"What is that in the vial?"

"Mecur-ee-chrome. Use it all the time to treat my cuts and wounds," she said as she picked up her bucket and mop. "It'll purge the infection; got mercury in it they say but it'll also stain your friend's face something fierce. I guess in his torn-up condition, well, it won't perturb him any."

Arnold nodded and faced away.

"Hey, what's your name…miss?" he asked.

"Lucy Lee Thompson, if'n ya please."

To avoid staring, he looked down at his shoes. After a pause and trying to make conversation, he asked, "You a Scot or…?" But she was gone.

Chapter 6

SHORT ARM OF THE LAW

Not four months after the cotton firm promoted him to over-seer and following his recent frolic in Alabama, Arnold welcomed Terrill Hall, his older brother, to stay with him in Oxford.

Of even temperament, Terrill was a docile man. Unless he was drinking. His entire being seemed an epic battle between two demon polarities inherited from unfortunate progenitors: one a fumbling and dangerous alcohol-sodden misfire, the other an indolent fop.

Arnold recalled one mid-day when their father noticed a strange indentation in a field of bluebells carpeting the woodland bordering their shanty. Curious, he approached it thinking this was the sanctuary of an injured white tail. Coming closer he spied Terrill lying on his back admiring his long neatly trimmed fingernails.

"I'll be goddamn!" his father bellowed. "It is the sloth!" Removing the belt from his breeches for a whip, the old man beat the lad until crimson-blue welts rose on his back, ribs, and face like raw oysters from a red tide. Terrill let out high-pitched screeches like a rabbit being torn apart by a lynx. Grabbing the belt from his father's fist and throwing it far up into a tree, his brother ended the beating, an act for which Uriah slapped Arnold into next week. The leather strap hung on high branches like a waiting snake.

A few years after settling in Oxford Arnold learned from Blue Mountain friends that his brother was in a bad way. Looking out for Terrill, his senior by three years, had been Arnold's self-imposed duty since before he could remember.

Miserable working under their father, Terrill drank nightly and dried out in the town jail. Worried that his brother's empty life was at the corner of everlasting drift and wanting to atone in some way for the misery he brought on his friend O'Byrne, Arnold pulled strings at the Oxford cotton warehouse where he worked, wangling a job for his brother, one which required no savvy and little native ability. Arnold sent a letter informing his brother that he would extricate him from their father's bondage and set him up with employment, but only if Terrill agreed to "withdraw his foot from the brass rail and harness his purpose." Terrill agreed, moved to Oxford, and was fired within two weeks.

When he heard the news and having vouched for his brother to the company foreman, Arnold had trouble restraining his fury. Fearing the episode had smeared his reputation, Arnold concluded further advancement at the cotton firm would be impossible. His poor judgment and misplaced faith in Terrill had ruined his future. A match fell into the tinder three weeks later.

By happenstance Arnold ran into Terrill one night at Talbott's Tavern, a secluded seamy watering hole between Oxford and Thaxton.

Terrill was sitting at a table with two other men talking big. The barmaid had poured him his fifth or sixth whiskey when Arnold came in, spotted his brother, and walked over to exchange unpleasantries.

"Where'd yew git the money for spirits, brother?" Arnold snorted. "Didn't think worthless indigents had coin. How long yew been here?"

Terrill peered up at him with eyelids unable to open more than half way. "Why am I a' gettin' peppered with all these pearly questions, brother. Trying to have a g-g-g-ood time hyar and leave behind me mentals."

People in the tavern quieted to hear the boil rise between the two.

"Well, thought you'd have come by my place and apologize after yew got fired—and tell me why ya washed out the job I gotchee. Seen neither hide nor hair of my older brother, so I'mma askin' yew now, goddamn it!"

Terrill laid both hands on the barroom table and pushed himself up uneasily, like a colt on new legs, to a standing position. He staggered close to Arnold and, jabbing his finger into his guardian brother's chest, berated him in an incoherent slobber. This vexed Arnold. With bile coming out his pores, he slapped Terrill away, "Yew better get your ass back to Blue Mountain first thing tomorrow, Terrill Hall. Go back to work fer pa. Got no interest in seeing yore goddamn face around here no more!"

Moving toward the disruption, the tavern owner halted when Arnold headed for the door. Then Terrill, his cheek stinging, heaved a half-drunk glass of brown liquor at his fuming kin, hitting him at the base of the skull with a crack and spraying whiskey onto two blue-nosed inebriates close by.

Arnold dropped to his knees. Terrill howled with glee, picked up another man's drink from a table and crudely splashed its remainder down his throat as if celebrating his brilliant aim and newfound superiority. Then he pitched the glass into the mirror above the bar shattering it. With that, a younger man named Asa Zemuly, an off-duty deputy sheriff from the neighboring district trying to enjoy a drink where the good citizens of Pontotoc County couldn't pick up his scent, interceded.

Zemuly approached Terrill to affect calm and return to his drink without further disturbance. When Zemuly pulled his badge from his pocket, Terrill in a state of drunken baseless panic pulled a revolver from under his shirt. Even in his blissful inebriation the deputy regarded this as a dangerous encroachment and tried and failed to wrestle the weapon away. Terrill began to pistol whip the stunned and floundering Zemuly before the bleeding constable could skin his unwieldy Colt dragoon. The third blow from Terrill was a wicked cross hand. His pistol raked viciously over the deputy's right cheek drawing blood and fracturing his cheekbone. The impact caused his weapon to discharge. In an instant, scalding gas and burning powder, trailing the fat lead bullet out of the barrel, cauterized a large section Zemuly's face. The bullet found harbor near the center of Talbott's oak bar but only after it severed Zemuly's right ear and passed through the neck of a barmaid running for safety.

A four-foot cord of blood streamed from the hole in the young woman's throat. "Gawd a'mighty!" Terrill cried. Aghast at what he'd done, his body began to shake like a squirrel in the grip of death. He looked down at the deputy writhing on the tavern floor holding his head trying to stanch the bleeding and sickening pain. Revived from the shock to his skull, Arnold seized his brother by the collar and yanked him from the tavern.

As they sprinted to their horses, Arnold yelled, "Gawd damn yew, Terrill! Gawd damn yew!" As they mounted and took flight, the tavern owner bolted after them. At a full run he fired both barrels of his 10-gauge shotgun toward the two shadows, catching Terrill's back and shoulder with six pellets.

Terrill howled in agony as if being drawn and quartered. But the distant shot barely penetrated three layers of clothing so the wounds were superficial at worst. Suffering little loss of blood and hell-bent on avoiding the hangman's noose, Terrill rode through the night close behind Arnold. The brothers stopped at a remote tavern outside Taylor, Mississippi and took an upstairs room where they had a clear view of the road and easy egress.

"My back is hurtin'! What's our plan, brother?" Terrill whimpered.

Before dawn they would ride to the Mississippi River and take a ferry at nightfall and cross into Arkansas. "To throw off any law on our tail, we'll zig-zag west until we reach the river," Arnold snapped curtly. "Cross it and head toward Indian Territory whar U.S. law got no jurisdiction." Then he told his brother to remove his shirt. Arnold would have one pleasure that day. "Now I'm gonna yank that buckshot outta yer hide."

Slowed by tavern visits where both drank and Arnold won money, the two brothers were in Arkansas five weeks before reaching eastern Oklahoma Territory, the domain of the Choctaw Nation. On New Year's Eve they arrived at a mid-size crossroads town founded in the mid-1800s by a Choctaw-French family named DuRant. Out of jurisdictional reach of Mississippi constabularies, the two brothers found jobs in Durant Station, as it was called then,

Arnold as a laborer on a cotton gin, and Terrill working the manure fork in a livery. The year the two fugitives arrived, Durant Station was already a stop on the Missouri–Kansas–Texas Railway, which cut like a blade into Indian and Mexican territories, current and former, along with other rail lines ordained to divide up that part of the hemisphere into semi-congruous but thriving zones of white man's commercial enterprise.

The railroads' substantial and growing presence in Durant would be prescient for Arnold Munro Hall and his family to come.

Two years later Arnold stepped into a Durant mercantile. As he approached the counter it was as if harmonies existed in a discordant universe, and he gasped. With hair black as cracked pepper and skin the color of pale moonstone, the young woman taking payments and marking credit obligations into the mercantile's thick ledger stepped right out of Arnold's past.

"Hello, miss," Arnold greeted her politely. "I'd like two pounds of salt pork, three of flour and pinto beans, a jar of sorghum molasses and a tin of Clabber Girl baking powder. Thankin' yew kindly, Miss Thompson."

"Do I know you?"

"My name's Arnold Munro Hall. Arn to friends. Admirers call me Mister Hall."

"Who?"

"From the Tuscaloosa train station."

The clerk frowned. "Oh. Yeah," she said figuring his bill. "Did your friend, the one with the face danced on by a team of mules, did he survive?"

"Yes, ma'am! Healed up nicely. But, sure as I'm standin' here, he got pickled one Easter. The ol' boy fell in a sty and the hogs ate 'em." A stunned silence came over her. Lucy Lee Thompson stared in horror at Hall until he betrayed a flash in his eye. The two broke into laughter. She gathered Hall's provisions from shelving painted clinical white and placed them into the wooden crate Arnold had placed on the counter.

"He healed up pretty well, Miss Thompson," Hall continued in a more serious tone. "O took a degree at the University of Mississippi and has done gone up North to lawyer school in Philadelphia. What yew doin' in Doo-rant, Miss Thompson?"

"I needed my space, Mr. Hall. Me and my sister Pinky decided to go west. We have an aunt here."

"Haven't heard that name 'afore."

Two more customers entered the mercantile.

"Her real name is Penelope. We call her Pinky 'cause she's got reddish hair and cheeks like the Damask rose. How 'bout you, Mr. Hall. You got business here in Indian territory?"

"Me and Terrill, he's my older brother, we jes' keeping a step ahead 'o the law, that's all." They laughed for different reasons. And the incident at Talbott's Tavern flashed in his memory. He had never learned the fate of the barmaid and deputy Terrill shot.

The two older customers had lined up behind Hall and were beginning to grumble. Lucy Lee pushed Arnold's crate of supplies toward him.

In this coarse and alien land beyond the reach of comfort and nuance and crossroaded by strange men like brush wolves seeking quarry, the thin tendril that connected the histories of Arnold Hall and Lucy Lee Thompson provided them the bridge to matrimony. They were married in 1904 in Indian Territory. He was twenty-three, she nineteen. Her older brother Tam travelled from Alabama to give her away.

In common turn, Terrill wed Pinky.

In June 1916 John William Hall was born to Arnold and Lucy Lee Hall in Durant, Oklahoma. He was their sixth with two more to come. Of the children, John William would be the only one to see war.

Chapter 7

PROVIDE, PROVIDE!

Lucy Lee's summer's garden of 1929 at the Hall homestead was beyond all expectations, portending abundance on the winter and spring dinner tables. The farm animals were fattened and ready to provide their substance. Best of all, Arnold had had seven consecutive years of accumulating income from his commodity brokering in Durant, which had grown into a significant commercial intersection west of the Mississippi for sales and distribution of cotton and wheat and to a lesser extent peanuts. To Arnold, the financial uneasiness on the East Coast was a thin and insignificant cry on the horizon.

Having flung tracks deep into Oklahoma and established robust schedules to Texas and Louisiana for transporting commodities, the railroads were strategic to the elder Hall's business. He would stack his bundled exports on these immense iron pack animals that would carry them at the speed of Thoroughbreds to coastal shipping lanes. Cotton was the fiber that would make the most cunning country brokers rich. Like Hall brokers bought not by the pound or the ton but by the mountain. They saw to its ginning, compression, and wrapping. These tremendous bales laid in wait upon acres of field lots like vast white buffalo herds asleep on the plains. Hall sold his bales to nervous central-market buyers in major cities where more risk meant higher reward. From Durant he railed his product to the great ports in Houston and New Orleans from where merchant freighters would transport them to mills in the east and across oceans.

For eighty-four straight months, demand was high, sales fulsome.

Despite the fat years, however, Arnold added only slightly to the family's comforts. Rather than presentable clothes, work-saving appliances like a foot-pedal sewing machine, or paying down the mortgages and reducing other obligations, the irascible cotton man cycled his profits into speculative endeavors he believed to be foolproof and which would secure for him effortless consequential wealth.

Hall leveraged his family assets to buy stock shares on margin and speculate on land. In one of these schemes he borrowed heavily to secure a plot of agricultural property in Grayson County between Pottsboro and Sherman, Texas, roughly thirty-five miles southwest of Durant, where he would raise and broker his own cotton and then sell the land years later at a grossly inflated price.

As frugal as he was, Arnold could devote substantial sums to himself. He made a large down payment and took a $500 lien on a Model A Ford. Delivered to him with great fanfare by rail from its assembly plant in Chicago, the magnificent black touring automobile rolled off the freight car where half the town of Durant gathered to see some dazzle come to the dreary but turgid community.

Hall also bought a handcrafted Winterhalder grandfather clock manufactured in Neustadt Baden, Germany. It had a long polished pendulum that in the afternoons would throw the western sun around the great room like lightning. Besides the status the instrument bestowed on him, Arnold believed its precision and the pendulum's perpetual motion would be fortuitous. He imagined the meticulous clockworks would mystically influence the beneficial rhythms of his own body.

"I do believe the clock's ceaseless movement means a long life for all of us," Arnold told sons Irving, A.M., and Jack soon after its arrival. "And its accuracy will mean good business fer me and eventually a bigger share of God's prosperity fer the family."

As for the exquisite sounds resonating from the clock and its ethereal gong, Arnold Hall considered them not at all. Lucy Lee, however, found them a joy. And initially, she could not resist the thrill of the automobile: its mystifying engine and the emblem of success it conferred on the family. But her excitement quickly waned.

Given Arnold's nature, money for the household and for his wife and children was spare. The surprise purchase of the Model A served as an epiphany for Lucy Lee. It troubled her for a long time before she spoke directly about it.

"Pray, where did you get the coin for an automobile?" she challenged her husband a month after it arrived. "Don't I have a right to know the particulars of where our monies come from?"

Arnold's responded as if he was spitting out tainted meat. "My financial affairs are a private matter and not that of any woman, child, or person other than my banker and stock broker," he stormed. "I will provide fer the family with my money. I alone will control how it is spent. That is the Bible's charge. There'll be no frivolous spendin' in this here house!"

Unintimidated, Lucy Lee followed Arnold out the door to where he sat down on an old kitchen stool under a shade tree next to the cellar. It was in that deep dug-out orifice whose berm allowed for an inside cool in the summer and warm in the winter that his wife stored her prodigious output of canning: shelf upon shelf of vegetables, jams, fruits, and meat.

"I am going to re-victual this fruit cellar and we're gonna have a full larder," Lucy Lee explained to her husband as if he were a schoolboy. "There are still seven stomachs to fortify from this year with my preserves. But, husband, my canning won't survive the winter 'cause this rickety thing is about to collapse. We need repointing mortar, lumber, shingles…."

Arnold cut her off.

"We don't have cash fer that, wife," he huffed while fiddling with a lantern wick.

"Well, that doesn't sound like a solution does it!" she mocked. Her husband weighed her words lightly though he knew he had put little or no money into the house or cellar since Jack was born ten years ago that coming December.

"Can't do anything right now. All our money is 'a tied up in investments. Good investments. Growin' a solid future. That's all yew need to know!"

Lucy Lee guffawed.

"Our 'solid' future is a figment of your own contemptible ego!" she rasped. "What has there been for the rest of us…for a better life now? And what for the children! Everything you talk about husband is as thin as pauper's burial gauze. Excep' for that fancy car you drive around town and to Texas in."

Sometimes, when she had had enough of her station and the brittleness of male covenants, scales fell from her eyes and the hellion in Lucy Lee Hall emerged. At these moments venturing beyond convention and even the rigid scriptural jurisdiction that bound her, her mind would light. She pondered if these aging men had any actual use at all. Her own husband, once carefree, full of humor and aggressively amorous, was now inert—a dour, barely civil, bloodless appliance devoted to moneymaking. Silver the family never saw, much less enjoyed. Her intelligence roamed like a hawk on the wing and she contemplated in high positive terms the instincts of female arachnids who disposed of their tiresome mates after conception by simply eating them. Lucy Lee snickered out loud at nature's perfection; Arnold didn't respond.

Her ears hot and crimson with disgust, Lucy Lee bent at the waist and put her hands firmly on the tiny bench where her husband fumbled with his repairs. Her face was close to his.

"I'm uneasy, husband, just so you know," she whispered, crafting her words and delivery to bore into Arnold's thick, virile carapace. "Worried down to my core. My mettle is under siege and that is something you ought to be well-advised to consider."

She drew closer. Her mouth almost touching his ear. "Seems you have not a notion that our little star is out of kilter with our rightful purpose. Diverting the earth's charity is like forcing new wine into old wineskins. Willfully or not, you are purblind to where your course will lead us. Most of all," Lucy Lee gently pulled on his ear as if to open it wider for her words, "I smell the odor of nefarious intentions. And I'm bettin' your secret notions of what is best for our family are lame as last year's goose."

Arnold slammed the lantern shut without repairing the wick. He wiped the dust and soot from it then hammered it onto the table breaking the globe into scores of shards that punctured the air.

"A man's job is to provide. His and his alone," he replied, not looking up from his mess. Lucy Lee stood over him and watched the muscles in his jaw flex.

The last word was her's. "You fool! A man's *job* is not to betray his wife and family!"

Chapter 8

'HERE YOU WILL PASS AMONG THE FALLEN'

On the morning of Sunday, Oct. 27, 1929, Arnold packed a small traveling bag. He would drive from Durant to Pottsboro, Texas early the next day though he wished he could leave immediately. At 9 A.M. the Hall family attended services at Durant's Logos Baptist Church, as always, joining celebrants from around Bryant County.

Under a short, diminutive steeple that grasped skyward toward a blanket of gray sat this plain, white wooden box. This was the expeditious low-cost remedy for the lonesome, fearful and obligated. Arnold and Lucy Lee with children Helen, A.M., John William, Jack, and Lucille joined dozens of congregants clustered around two entrance doors talking before the two-and-a-half hour service. All were dressed in faces and clothes deemed appropriate for souls about to be in the company of King Jesus.

As the Halls climbed the painted steps, John, at the back of the line, whispered into his brother's ear. "Wearin' these clothes makes me feel like I'm hog-tied in hell." A.M. covered John's mouth with his hand to muffle the giggles.

A large window, squat and toad like, dominated the front of the church. The shape was grotesquely unlike the narrow, graceful European antecedents that the church builders tried to replicate. Grievously, this main window, which should have been equidistant from the two entryways, was closer to one than the other. Once inside, congregants sensed that the awkward window provided more light to one side of the congregation than the other, oddly symbolizing for some that the Lord of Hosts shed His divine luster on people in unequal portions. Adding to the church's peculiar nature, the point section of the front window, which occupied almost a third of the space, was not glass at all but peeling wood planking more suggestive of an old animal hide than transcendence. Helen had told John that what should have been a window of all glass was a casualty of weak tithes and offerings, though she pointed no fingers.

Irrespective of its unfortunate design, the spartan inner sanctuary on Sunday mornings was a wonder of sound, Biblical poetry, fire, rhythm, and fervor.

Of the Hall family attending that day, religion had taken root only in Lucy Lee and Helen. But the shape-note "Sacred Harp" singing that filled the sacrarium with its rhythmic storm and near-perfect harmonies moved them all, save for Arnold.

After the gathering the seven boarded their Model A Ford and motored to the homestead for a prayer and the premier meal of their week. When they arrived, Leo Graham was waiting on the porch step.

"Hey, John William!" he shouted. "The fish are biting. Thought we should go down to the creek."

As she stepped onto the porch, Lucy Lee spoke to Leo, who had washed his face, though his fingernails looked as if he had been digging for worms. "Come in, honey, and sit with us for noon dinner. Fried chicken and turnip greens and baking powder biscuits to start. Then if you're not too puffy, there'll be a sweet rice pudding with nutmeg."

"Love to. Thank you, Miss Hall," Leo chirped.

They served food according to ritual. A blessing was said and plates passed. The young appeared happy with the meal. Any gathering that included a guest had the feel of a special occasion to all but Arnold. Lucy Lee, wishing to keep even sparse conversation away from her family matters, took an interest in the Graham household.

"Anything new with you or your mama, Leo?" Lucy Lee asked as she always did. The boy halted his biscuit buttering to answer.

"Well, Ma heard from her brother, the one that lives in Ft. Smith. Got a letter the other day. He used to work cattle on a ranch east of there."

"How's he getting along? Don't think I've seen him since the day you were born."

"Not so good. A steer gored him. Punctured his stomach and liver. Not worked for three months. Ma says he's in a bad way."

John looked over at Leo wanting to say something, but thought the better of it.

"Well, uh, Leo, do you think you'll be a ranch hand someday?" Lucy Lee asked not knowing exactly how to exit this dinner-table topic gracefully.

"Oh, no, Miss Hall," he answered.

Estranged from this sibling, Leo's mother was gratified that he lived far away. The sorry fellow became a reverse object lesson in Leo's upbringing.

"Ma told me that I wasn't to be like him, my uncle," the boy explained. "Nor does she want me to be around him much at all. 'There is no benefit to listening to people who have no spark,' she has surely advised me."

Leo spooned some sorghum molasses onto his last bite of biscuit, smiled, swallowed, and took a sip of milk before he went on.

"'They'll drag you down to their level,' Ma said. 'Pretty soon you think that *dull* and *mediocre* are all you can accomplish in life. In that state if you have a noble idea, you'll talk yourself out of doing it," the boy pronounced as if he was giving a sermon himself. "And I believe her, Miss Hall and, uh, Mr. Hall. I read about human flaws frequently—in my books 'bout the yesteryear Greeks."

When all had finished dinner, Lucy Lee bid the children to take their leave. She turned to Arnold after the last had left the room.

"When can we expect you back from Pottsboro?" Lucy Lee asked sharply, as if the wealth of Christian charity she had absorbed from Pastor Stubblefield's sermon less than an hour ago had been washed away by the cup of hot orange pekoe tea she sipped with her meal.

"I'll be back on All Hallows Eve. Gonna have a good long gander at my cotton fields and the harvest which now should be near eighty percent," Arnold replied coldly, uncomfortable saying as much as he did. "Afterwards I'll get wages for the men at the Sherman Bank, meet with Eli, and negotiate hard with the ginner while I'm in the neighborhood."

Arnold got up from the table and pulled a tobacco pouch from his back pocket. Before preparing his smoke, he thought his wife needed a reminder of his prowess. 'Spect real profitable things outta my harvest again this year. As for the boys, A.M., Jack, and John William already know what I require of 'em while I'm away."

The trip to Pottsboro on Monday was long. The thirty-one mile trip on rutted dirt roads and detours around unattended washouts that occurred nearly two years earlier took Arnold Hall three hours. En route he stopped the Model A because it overheated, then spent seventy minutes fiddling with the ignition in Henry Ford's "miracle machine" before it would start again.

Tuesday morning, after sleeping Monday night in his automobile, which he had parked off the road by his land, Hall briefly surveyed his cotton fields. Afterwards, acting like an overbearing train conductor on a tight schedule, he met with his foreman. Eli Waters was in charge of workers tasked with harvesting the crop and transporting it to the railhead. "I want nothin' short a' the best thoroughness, care, and speed for handlin' this crop, Eli," Hall bellowed.

The foreman had seen twenty-nine years and had supervised farm labor for Hall since the Oklahoman bought the Texas farmland three years earlier. Eli's work had always pleased his boss.

Having just taken a wife and with thoughts moving toward securing a level of prosperity nowhere near him now but meticulously imagined, Waters was hell bent to spend more time with his boss in hopes of learning the ins-and-outs of the brokerage business.

As he walked the fields, Hall scrutinized the pickers and loaders like he was overseeing black slaves in need of the whip, while Eli reviewed with him the upcoming transaction. This would occur at the railhead in Sherman where the cotton would be delivered following compression and wrapping then loaded onto the freight train.

"Yew sure you're 'a gettin' ever'thing outta these men, Eli?" Hall challenged, chewing his lip.

"We're gonna come in real nice with our profit margins, sir, real nice," Waters assured him.

Before Eli returned to his work, he stuttered, "Mr. Hall, kin you, uh, kin you tell me a bit about the brokerage business? I'm mighty interested in…."

"Yew want ta go in competition with me, Eli, goddamnit?" Hall interrupted.

"No, sir, not at all. I jes' gotta wife who's expectin' and am thinkin' I gotta earn more. Yew know, fer her and the babe."

Hall eyed him for a long time, still chewing his lip. If he could turn this into a business deal, he felt he might come out the better for it.

"Well, there are a lotta brokers around. So one more won't matter much, I'm a guessin'. Yew jes' stay outta my territory and maybe we can work together somehow."

Hall spit on the dry ground.

"First thing, unless you gotta lot of coin squirreled away yew inherited from a rich uncle, get a partner with some money who wants to make more," Hall began. "Draw up the partner contract yourse'f, with yer lawyer, so you start under yer own terms. It'll cost ya somethin', but worth it."

Hall rolled and lit a cigarette. The two men sat down on the Model A's runner. "Then what I did was rent an office on the second story of the building nearest the telegraph office. Yew cain't do nothing without the telegraph."

He went through point-by-point the critical aspects of setting up a business, establishing accounting methods, and subscribing to reports coming out of New Orleans and New York cotton futures exchanges. "Ever' thirty minutes you'll get a report over the telegraph of what country market brokers, that's us, are paying farmers for their cotton."

Waters knew a master was tutoring him. Hall was putting on quite a show.

"Then you gotta develop 'the sixth sense', Eli. In other words a varmint's cunning for what the other guy is thinkin' and what his next move is. Then yew gather a lot a' ripe information from others on when to buy and sell. Find farmers you know and can work with. Sniff tha air; put yer goddamn nose ta the ground."

Making friends and business connections was the mother lode of an independent commodity broker. This was where Hall gathered intelligence, got tips, and learned how to be agile in a changing market. Timing for him was everything.

"You'll want to make a few points on either side a' the market. At the beginning, act fast to try to take advantage of fleetin', small, up and down movements. But don't do nothin' big till yew know what yer doin'. Start slow. Use a little caution while yer learnin'. Got questions?"

"Uh, why the second floor?" Waters asked.

"Hell, Eli, the rent on the bottom floor's too damn expensive. That storefront real estate is fer lawyers, medicine men and dry goods swindlers. And none of your older customers'll want to climb all three stories 'a steps where the rent is cheapest. Unless there is a trollop waitin' for 'em up there, which, now to think of it, might be considered."

On Tuesday, after reviewing the progress and satisfied with the delivery schedule, Hall walked to a shed. From it he removed an old chair. When exposed to the prairie wind its yellow paint flew off its dry wooden skeleton-like sparks from a welder's torch. When he set the chair down in the center of his hundred acres, it shed another multitude of colored flakes onto the ground. That chair was one slight mark of yellow in what looked like an ocean of floating white dumplings being picked by a score of black and brown forms. It was 3 p.m. and Hall wanted only to sit in repose and enjoy the aroma of his money being made.

His mind traced his five-hundred-pound bales of silver fleece from Sherman where it would be packed onto Southwestern Railway's "Cotton Belt" train, whisked to the port of Galveston, and offloaded onto a steamer. Hall's bounty would traverse the Gulf of Mexico, sweep around the tip of Florida like a baleen whale in pursuit of krill, and move up the Atlantic coast until it docked in Wilmington, North Carolina. There, half was to be inspected, unloaded, and moved to the Cone Mills. Boston was the destination for the rest. What started with his February purchase of seed would end by Dec. 31 of that year. His check would reflect the rampant commodities market and arrive by mid-January 1930. Or so he had arranged.

As he sat in his chair, the yellow flakes on the ground around him now looked like confetti fallen from a Wall Street parade. Hall had a lot running through his mind. He tried to foretell any last-minute hitches and develop alternate solutions. But when this fall afternoon washed its warm sunlight over his face, he drifted away from matters of business. Instead he contemplated *una fiesta loca*, the wild nightlife in Sherman, Texas's red-light, beer and brown liquor district, just a forty-minute drive south and east from where he sat watching his cotton being picked. Hall estimated that he would be in the middle of raucous festivities in only three hours, and he rubbed his palms together in anticipation.

Arnold Hall knew people in Sherman, though only a few. That was by his purpose. Fewer acquaintances meant less worry that unsavory gossip with his name attached would cross the Texas-Oklahoma border. Unless some scoundrel killed an Okie in Texas or an Oklahoma white woman disappeared in the Lone Star State, not much had currency in terms of sordid tittle-tattle.

"If I'm kerful," Arnold had confessed to his peeling chair, "I should have no worries that the wife'll hear stories of my drinkin' and entertainments down here. Can't have nothin' poisoning her high opinion of me. Or worse, gettin' more pigheaded about what I expect of her."

Lucy Lee was intolerant of strong waters. Intoxicants of any kind were not to cross the lips of her husband and especially those of her children no matter what their adult age. There would be no "alkie-hawlicks" in the Hall family. Requiring an ironclad assurance, the wife and mother, fearing vulnerabilities exploited by the devil, demanded that her eight offspring and husband sign their name to the ornate temperance pledge in the family Bible. It was a solemn, prayerful ceremony. Adding to its presumed impact, each of the signatories noted that above their autographs hovered a color picture of Lucifer, lost in barely reserved crimson delight, towering over men drinking ale in a tavern.

Even with this "assurance," Lucy Lee was ever vigilant for brown bottles hidden in the homestead's remotest places and telltale fumes expelled from the lungs of her males.

Little besides Arnold's business trips gave him relief from what he considered the Holy rigor of the Baptist girdle. So he craved Sherman's anonymity. There the law turned a blind eye to man's "most necessary vices" and, for whites, it did not enforce Prohibition. Hall also found pleasure in the Klan presence. For like Durant, Sherman was a sundown town. According to ordinance, "coloreds, including Mexicans, are not allowed in the municipality after nightfall as the city's amenities have been reserved for the exclusive use of white persons." Those who disobeyed this warrant faced harsh penalties.

Sherman being a town of growing wealth and attraction also was to Hall's liking. It assured him of lots of saloons and amiable night women. Faro games that could yield a sharp player winnings enough for a two-day stint of drink and iniquity were available around the clock.

****

As the cotton broker sat below the magnificent orange and blue Texas firmament thinking about the night he was about to enjoy, an eerie chill came upon him and interfered with his coarse reverie. Opening his eyes ever so slightly, he saw a tiny figure dashing towards him about half a mile away.

The blotch continued its approach and when it was nearly upon him, Arnold sat up, his back straight and tight.

"What the hell, Crispian!" Arnold sputtered.

A lengthy pause hung motionless in the Texas breeze, like a Cooper's hawk eyeing a dying rodent. Crispian Grimes, forties, too fat to be running, wearing a starched white shirt with a short wide floral wind-whipped tie and dark gray gabardine trousers held up at the waist by prodigious green and black suspenders with embroidered dollar signs, stopped. His stooped, winded figure shadowed Arnold from the sun. He gazed at his feet then straightened to look out over the field and catch his breath. Grimes had a lot to say that late afternoon but the only utterance Hall's stockbroker could muster was, "I fear, sir, you are broke."

The unvarnished delivery of these six catastrophic monosyllables stupefied Hall, and he wheezed like a bagpipe. Never had he considered his business acumen vulnerable to calamity. Hall did not look at the messenger. Covering his head with his arms he screamed until his lungs ached. Crispian Grimes frozen in place stared at the collapsed figure.

When the cotton man finally stood, he kicked the chair away. Arnold had decided to garrote his broker with barbed wire and would wait no longer. Seeing none he reached behind him, unhooked the strap on the holster securing his revolver, removed the weapon, and pointed it at Grimes.

"I'm gonna kill you where you stand, Crispian, and bury yer goddamn worthless corpse in this here now worthless ground where a stampede of goddamn worms'll turn you into shite!" he sputtered.

Hall was shaking and soaked in sweat. He cocked the weapon and aimed at Grimes's heart. The stockbroker, pale as the belly of a field mouse and having trouble retaining his toilet, dropped to his knees.

"Don't do this, Arnold," he pleaded softly as if afraid to disturb the universe. He watched the quivering gun barrel move away from him and onto Hall's temple.

Grimes snapped. "Put the goddamn gun down, Arnold! Down! Jesus! Jesus!"

Ruin would bring certain disgrace to the cotton man. Just the thought staggered him. But more terrified of the unknown, the beyond, Hall took the weapon from his head, thrust it into the air and fired it with an ear-splitting crack. The shot caused an infinite torrent of birds to flee their repose in the field and dart into the clouds as if to deliver their god a hundred warning dispatches. The disoriented man holstered the gun. In unalloyed defeat, he stood in place on the empty unforgiving plain for a time. Then, as the sun dimmed, sucked away by the insistence of a rotating planet seeking blindness, Hall wobbled to his satchel. He pulled out a half-full bottle of rye whiskey and two glasses. He poured, and after Grimes had cleaned himself, the pair completed the beaker's contents in near silence.

Deep into the night Arnold stumbled into his car and motored home.

Chapter 9

JUDGEMENT DAY

H elen and Lucy Lee had prepared breakfast. October thirtieth was bright but cool. Before anyone left the house that morning, they wanted to serve a hot breakfast. No one noticed Arnold on the edge of the porch. Not until John William, Jack, and A.M. stepped out into the morning on their way to chores.

Their father sat on the stoop, his legs drooped over it. He was in a strange state, mumbling to himself. A hand-rolled cigarette made with stale King Albert shag hung from his lips. Whenever he muttered, it wiggled up and down. Through the blue haze of tobacco smoke he eyed a gathering of fat rooks, judge-like in tight dark robes flashing streaks of indigo and bristling with self-importance. Intermittently their beaks opened like scissors and cawed at him from their roost in a leafless tree. So unyielding was their gaze through those tiny inscrutable black pearls that it seemed to further undo the teetering patriarch.

"I'll be damned if those aren't the priests of the realm, boys," he laughed as his eyes rolled backwards briefly into his head, "waiting to record my sins and bend me toward the fires."

Lucy Lee, Helen, and Lucille joined everyone on the porch. A cow mooed in the roiling distance as if to remind them of their burdensome existence.

"Thought you wouldn't be home until All Hallow's," Lucy Lee said sharply, detecting menace in the air.

Arnold pulled a lung-full of smoke from the now shortened cigarette and stared at the horizon.

She pursued her questions. "Well? How's our Texas crop doing?"

"Crispian got a telegram dated October 29, 1929, yesterday. He read it and flew to me on the wings of Pegasus." Hall appeared amused, as he crushed the still-burning cigarette into his left palm as if extinguishing a half-lived life. "The Great 'Ol Herbert Hoover bull done stampeded off the cliff," Crispian tells me." Nearby, a meadowlark interjected a joyous anthem to the rippling grass, giving Arnold's lamentation an incongruent score. He failed to notice. The family went silent.

"If there are any banks left by year's end, they'll be coming to seize most of what we own. Including our back teeth." Her husband gave her a nervous smile before spitting into the empty tobacco tin. "If not them, individual creditors will come here and circle their quarry. Know, wife, that I have buried enough tender to keep making payments on the homestead for some months at least. Other than that, prepare for God's reckoning."

Silence gripped the cosmos. Finally, Lucy Lee spoke. "This isn't God's reckoning, this is on you. It is you who have failed the family. You hear me! It isn't Hoover. It isn't the bankers. It isn't God. It isn't Crispian Grimes. It's you! Arnold Munro Hall. Have the backbone to admit it!"

Lucy Lee glanced at her children, who had gathered around trying to grasp what this meant.

"Where's the revenues from this great crop of cotton you promised?" she scowled. "Your mystery stocks, you know, the ones that are gonna 'secure our future?' They aren't all worthless. Cash 'em in and get us some money to live on! While you're at it, sell that peacock of a car!"

"Cotton prices are falling like a fat stone off a great wall," Arnold sighed. "And anythin' I get for ma cotton'll go to creditors. Bought a lotta stocks and bonds with loans, so they'll divide my securities among themselves. Signed the car as collateral, so they'll take that, too. Unless I can hide it."

He assured his wife they were not alone in going under. "Many will be in our shoes." But his voice was so weak he couldn't even convince himself that he and his family had not joined the ranks of the precariat permanently. Or in his words, "the damned."

"Yeah, but you're Arnold Munro Hall! 'Oklahoma's smartest businessman,'" Lucy Lee spit. "You can imagine that we are a little surprised that you, of all the great mercantile poobahs, are the same as all those other quick-money clods without the brains to pour piss out of a boot."

Looking far into the distance, which is where he wanted to be, the head of the household sat inert.

"If you had shared your dull-witted intentions maybe I could have saved us and the children from your disasters!"

The Hall young had never seen their mother in this state. "We're disgraced, husband, and will be living off other folks' throwaways." As her anger mutated into a loathing pity, she paused. and watched her husband, reduced to speechlessness, limp into the shed.

"Men are such pathetic creatures," Lucy Lee said to Helen as they went into the house. "Tedious. Visionless as cave lizards. They have no staying power. Not in love, certainly. Not in compassion. Not in anything other than taking care of themselves. And we got one that's failed at that." She took a breath. "I'm praying it's gonna be better for you, honey."

Chapter 10

IN CLEARING, MUCH WILL
BE REVEALED

Uncertainty gripped the household in ever-larger proportion over the next weeks. But everyone tried to lessen the trauma they all knew was coming. Arnold attempted to call in his chits, recent and ancient. He got some day-labor work in Durant. And though he rarely went home to avoid creditors, he completed repairs that would save the food cellar. Lucy Lee took in laundry. Helen and Lucille did most of the canning. A.M., John William, and Jack tended cattle and the farm. Occasionally, Roy sent a banknote to his mother.

On a mid-November Saturday morning John had finished milking and was washing his face. He dipped his hands in cold water reserved in a steel pan and contemplated its coolness when a rapping startled him. The time was 6:50. Walking to the door, drying his hands, he found a strange man smoking a cigar.

"Hi-dee," John said politely.

"Yo' pappy at home, kid?" the voice demanded, the words sliding over the tongue of an armadillo-shaped dwarf. He wore a pork pie hat and vested suit that fit tightly around his waist. John could see roach-colored wax seeping from his ears. Another man was in the front yard about twenty feet from the door. He was tall with a face that looked to have a permanent smirk chiseled in it. His eyes held a snake's gaze. On the cover of John's milking bucket he had propped a foot.

"He's not here. And who, sir, are you?"

The intruder drew within two feet of the boy. John took a step back when he smelled the fat man's breath.

"Tell ma friend, Arnold Munro, that Doke Carns stopped to say 'hello'—and to collect on his debt."

John's face broke into a scowl.

"But if'n yew don't, it'll make me no nevermind," Carns said. He grinned and pulled back his left lapel just enough so that John could see the firearm holstered under his wet and stinking armpit. "Unless I hear back this comin' week, I'll return with hell's bells on. I'm sure we can work somethin' out."

"You the law?" the boy shouted to him as he waddled away.

"Jes' tell him, kid!" Doke and his companion climbed in the car and sped away but not before the tall man in the passenger seat discharged his revolver from the open window. His three shots put three holes in John's bucket. Fresh milk streamed onto the ground.

John retreated to the kitchen. The arrival of these men, but more his being caught unready, chilled the fifteen-year-old. John determined to treat any future encounters with rogues frankly and harshly. He walked outside to chop wood for the stove and clear his mind. According to scripture he remembered, in clearing dead wood from the wilderness, "much would be revealed."

His thin work gloves lay on the stump. He threaded his fingers into them and began splitting firewood with a heavy stroke. His body coiled and the axe dropped with alarming force, cleaving the wood at an eerily steady pace as if by metronome. Tempo: largo. Rage and anxiety left him and took residence in the instrument. At each blow, split logs jumped into the air like rabbits from a prairie blaze.

Roy Hall was seven years John's senior. He had secured a three-day pass from training at Ft. Sill to join the family for Thanksgiving. Sipping hot tea on the porch he watched his brother carrying wood for the fireplace.

"Too airish out here, John William," Roy said. "I'm goin' in." As the two entered the house, Roy wished to divert John's attention from the catastrophes that had befallen them.

"How long you been doin' the choppin', John William?" Roy asked, feeling his brother's shoulders.

"Couple years now."

His shoulders and upper back surprised Roy. His wrists were like beams. "You've got a lumberjack's upper body, kid, and fast legs. Hell, you could be a boxer. Maybe it's your ticket outta hard times."

Arnold entered from another room. "Nobody in this house knows boxing but me," he grunted. "And I'm tellin' y'all now, the only people with a future at a boxing arena are the ones outside the ring. That's where the money is made and you can keep your brains and face intact."

"I'll show you how to box," Irving, who John disliked, jeered after their father departed. "I need someone I know to bet on. Or against."

Chapter 11

THE FIGHT

As he did everyday through the school year, Leo Graham sat on his porch reading and waiting for the Hall brood to walk by on their way to "lessons." A.M. Hall had abandoned, of his own accord, the formalities of school in eighth grade. But Jack, Lucille, and John passed by daily and Leo would run to join them.

"Mama made cinnamon sweet rolls this morning," he exclaimed. "Here, split this among you."

John took the large, warm, thickly frosted spiral of the yeasty stuff, divided it into three and handed one chunk to Lucille and one to Jack, who fumbled it, dropping it on the ground.

"No!" Jack screamed. John picked it up, picked off a few blades of grass and handed it back to his brother.

"No harm," John said. Jack stuffed the entire portion into his mouth leaving notes of frosting on his nose and chin.

Leo, always happy and deeply curious about how the universe was being formed around him, eagerly awaited the news from John's life.

"Anything goin' on at your spread, John William?" Leo began as they trudged down the dusty street. Jack, who was the same age as Leo and two years behind John, was still trying to recover all the sweetness from his face with his tongue and fingers.

"Not much, Leo, we're in a terr-bul state with Pa losin' ever'thing in the Crash. I try to keep Lucille and myself away from the house much as possible. Irvin' has been teachin' me to box." Leo glanced at his friend's shoulders. To him they looked as big as hams.

Wagons moved up and down the street and shopkeepers had opened their doors. Lucille and Jack were slightly ahead of the two boys now, which is where John wanted them. He could monitor the two and talk to Leo and drag his foot on the road making diminutive valleys and mountain ranges in the red dust. John stopped when he caught a glimpse of two figures on the shadow side of the bank building.

"What's goin' on over there, Leo?" John asked.

"Looks like Laura Fields is having trouble again with Dun."

"I know about him," John scowled.

John had connected once with Dunton Cardamon two years before. It had not been an agreeable meeting. Arnold Hall had driven in to meet with Taylor Cardamon, a well-to-do Durant real estate broker, about a land deal and took his son with him. As the men talked on the porch, young Hall spotted Cardamon's son in the backyard.

"What kinda rifle is that?" John asked after hearing it made almost no sound.

"Daisy air gun," came Dun's reply. "Haven't you seen a BB gun before?"

"Nope."

He threw John a package of the small copper-colored beads.

"Looks like birdshot," John said.

"Shush!" Cardamon whispered, then pulled the trigger. John heard a puff of air and then saw a bluebird twenty feet away drop to the ground and shake. Dun walked over and picked the bird up by its feet.

"What are you shootin' songbirds for?" John questioned in a confrontational tone.

"Why not? It's fun. I'm starting a collection."

John followed the boy to outside the family carriage house where he threw the bird onto a heap of other kills.

"Here's my hobby!" Cardamon said admiring himself.

There Hall saw a stack of dead birds nearly three-feet high. The sight disgusted him. Those on the bottom and midsection of the pile were black and soupy from decay. The smell of the dead creatures was sickening. At the top of the heap, and still distinguishable, John could see robins, sparrows, a white-throated swift, flycatchers, a cedar waxwing, two sapsuckers, and now an iridescent female bluebird.

"Wanna add to my collection? Bet you can't hit that one in the tree," Dun taunted John as he held out the gun.

"The only thing I would add to this is your sorry ass," he replied in a distant tone before returning to his father's Model A.

****

On the alley side of the bank Dun had pinned Laura and was trying without success to kiss her.

"Are you in trouble here?" John asked the girl, who he barely knew. She gave him a frightened glance. Dun, keeping Laura's right arm in his grip, set about to walk to a more secluded location. Then he looked at Hall and assessed his challenger's size. Using a vulgarity, he told John to mind his own business.

"Well, I'm gonna follow you two to school," John replied.

Dun, in a fury, released Laura's arm and threw a sweeping left-handed haymaker at Hall's face. John stepped back to avoid it. Dun telegraphed another sweeping punch from his right side, which John dodged.

"Enough!" John shouted.

The larger, older Dun had confidence he could knock senseless this kid who had slighted him at his own home. When he came flailing again, John brought his fists up. Leaning his body into the punch, he catapulted his right fist into Dun's face. The elder boy's head snapped back and his body collapsed into the alleyway rubbish. Bluish-red blood flowed from his nose and mouth.

Worse, Dun had failed to set his jaw before taking the punch. The tip of his tongue had been clamped between his teeth when the blow landed.

John walked away from the bleeding assailant to follow Laura to school as he had promised and Leo stayed with him.

Dun climbed to his feet, yelled "coward!" and John halted.

"Don't go back there!" Leo shouted at him. "He's not worth it." But John had drifted wildly and headed back toward his victim.

"This is serious, John William. You could really hurt him. And what for? He's not gonna torment Laura anymore."

John stopped, blew out a long hot breath, put his hands on his knees, and let his temper cool. "Yeah, guess you're right, Leo. Can't be hurtin' folks. Even skunks like him. If you don't have to."

Chapter 12

THE TASK AHEAD

John, submerged in a book, marked the page with his thumb when he heard boots moving through the grass.

"You readin'? What is it?"

"'Riders of the Purple Sage'. It's a western."

Roy Hall stood above his brother. John had aspirations and begged Roy for months to teach him to shoot.

The elder Hall was wearing his Oklahoma National Guard uniform. On his right shoulder was a thirty-ought-six Springfield M1903 rifle, and it caused John's eyes to widen.

"What's it about," Roy asked as he kneeled to peer at the book gripped in his brother's hand.

"It's a story about a fast draw and a woman who doesn't want to get married," John replied.

"Why don't she wanna get hitched?"

"Some old man in the church wants to marry her. But he's already got nine wives. She's not interested in being number ten. Besides, he smells bad and doesn't drink." They broke into a wicked laugh.

The time had come. "Let's go," Roy grinned.

They marched down the hill to level ground where Roy had established a shooting station with a target mounted on a log a hundred feet down range.

"First I'm gonna teach yew sight picture," Roy explained. "How the target is suppose'ta look through this here iron sight when yew wanna score a bullseye. This Springfield has what they call curved leg sevens for the rear sight with volley notch and small dished windage and elevation knobs." Roy pointed to all the components as he explained how to set and use them. John was getting his first lesson in marksmanship. Actual shooting, however, was down the road.

"After today you'll know the hissin' truth of shootin', John William."

This was the high point of his life. The juncture at which John first stepped into manhood, his first stride toward a future. With it he gathered with his ancestors that vine of old blood that for centuries provided and sustained, the rootstock and grafts that refused to perish. John was chasing perfection. And in it, he knew, lay the hallowed ceremony of life and death.

For Roy shooting merited more than mechanics. It deserved the philosophical. To John's older brother no more serious transaction existed, outside of sustaining human bonds, than the proper usage of a firearm.

"Learn to shoot, and do it well, John William, you'll never go hungry," he said solemnly. "Not as long as there is game to be had. And with large caliber rifles and the mastery of their use, yew can take down the wild boar, the bear. If you're ever called upon to protect yerself, yer kith, kin and country, the lessons yew are 'bout to learn here'll ready yer bones for that, too." Roy's words were freighted with meaning. "That is the task ahead."

"Now, look. Look at this beauty!" the older brother exclaimed, losing his frown and beaming as if the borrowed rifle were his own. "This Springfield is what helped us win The Great War, John William. And there's still nothin' better fer sharpshootin' sons-a-bitches."

With starch in his words, Roy tutored his brother. No longer the loving sibling, he assumed the rigor of a drill sergeant. "Tighten yer sling. Drop gradual-like to yer knees. Put the rifle's butt to the ground and use the weapon fer support as ya ease yerse'f into the prone position," he charged.

Still grinning with delight, the boy lowered himself until he was flat on the ground with the rifle barrel pointed down range. Seeing his legs were too close together, Roy kicked his brother's boots apart to where they belonged.

"Listen, John William. Yew gotta do the basics right 'til it's so natural you don't even know you're a'doin' it," he cried.

John focused; Roy proceeded.

"Feet now shoulder width apart. Point yer toes out to steady yer whole physical domain. Cradle the rifle's stock softly in your left palm. The weight of this honey should be even on both sides and directly over that left elbow." John followed every command.

"The butt's gotta be tucked securely into that flesh pocket in yer shoulder. Comfy-cozy." Roy reached down to move the rifle into the spot he wanted it. Gun oil got on his hand.

"That's right. Feel it!" The guardsman grinned. "Now plant that feelin' in yer brain. Feel the yewn-verse come inta balance. Come back to it ever' time. Same spot. Same feel. Same comfort. Same position. Same. Same. Same."

Roy rubbed the gun oil into his hands' thick yellow calluses. "Got it?" he growled abruptly.

"Got it," John answered.

"Good. *Now*, we kin begin," Roy said.

Chapter 13

A PRICK OF THE HEART

The summer of 1930 had been hotter and drier than the past few years. The yard was the color of corn husks. Barrenness circled the garden, an oasis of wonders and luxuriant green, as if desiring to overtake it. Lucille, Jack, and John dug Sibley potatoes with a garden fork while Lucy Lee sat on a bucket nearby shucking corn for the night's supper. When she finished, John carried the corn to the kitchen for her, and they talked.

"I want to be a boxer," he said to his mother. "Irving has taught me a lot."

This was Lucy Lee's moment. "I'm sure he has," she replied as if spitting out an orange rind. Neither John nor his mother thought much of the untrustworthy oldest son. "You really want a get in a boxing match and have some thick-necked cracker beat you around the head all night? Dull your bright blue eyes!"

"I'm fast; they aren't gonna hit me much. And I hit hard, too." He danced around her throwing mock punches.

"In boxin' there's always someone bigger, faster, stronger, better. Be smart, boy. Follow your own mind, not Irving's or anyone else's. Except'n mine, 'a course," his mother smiled into his eyes. "You'll soon know what feels right for you."

They reached the porch, and she rested there before going inside. "You are not like your brothers, John William. You know it. And I think you also know to be wary of your oldest brother."

She sighed and her eyes drank in the golden sheen of the fat ears of sweet corn John carried. "You have a curiosity the others don't have. And a sense of what matters." Not sure of his mother's references, the boy shrugged his shoulders.

Lucy Lee would use this moment. Her son had to be "moved along" in awareness of himself. Qualities mixed into his marrow before birth, she counseled, would be part of him always. "And 'a course you got gumption, boy. A bucket full. So I know that whatever course in life you choose, it will be the right one. And you will have to outshine all others or you'll never be at peace. So you might as well realize it now. That's what I expect. And that is what is in your bones."

His mother's eyes twinkled. "I am sure you got it from the Thompson side."

"There's times when I feel powerless. Caged. I can't get beyond Pa's edicts to where I want to be headed."

"I know this," she affirmed as they moved into the kitchen. No one was more aware of the trouble that lay ahead for her family. But Lucy Lee knew her son would dance to his own tune. "You'll survive it; so will little Lucille with your help and mine. You'll endure whatever life throws at you, son. Because you can shepherd even a strong horse from a bad well."

Ending her meditation, she rested on a kitchen chair. "My love runs deep as a river for you, child." John swallowed hard. His mother's response to his taking a boxing career mystified him. And he had never heard her open up like this. It was as if a small door appeared in the eternal wall that separates mother and child, elder and novice.

"Go on, now. Hurry and finish your chores a'fore supper," Lucy Lee laughed oddly.

Before turning away, John noticed rivulets of blood twisting down her brown ankles and pooling onto the floor. His mother frowned and dipped an old rag into a bucket containing the morning's dishwater. John was mute as his mother dabbed her legs. When she began to wash the blood from the floor, he exclaimed, "What is that!"

"This isn't anything," she said brushing the incident aside.

"Let me help you into bed. Helen and I will fix supper."

"No, run along, honey. I'm fine."

She could not expunge the stain from the wood. Its pink remains had formed a near-perfect circle.

Chapter 14

THE PURSUIT

John's older brother Roy threw open the door. "Let's go!" he hooted at John William. "I got the Springfield again! And some cartridges!"

The sight of his brother in his starched National Guard uniform caused a rush in John. He left his breakfast unfinished and followed Roy to the flat plot a half-mile north of the house. A.M. and Jack would arrive at the makeshift range shortly thereafter to see what all the commotion was about. And witness the expertise of their uniformed brother.

Roy and John paced off one hundred yards and fixed a target four feet up on a rough plank secured between two Sycamore logs.

To John the rifle was the Holy Grail. With a brazen gray-cobalt sheen the barrel had a special allure and fit with perfection into the oiled walnut stock. Its leather sling was tourniquet-tight around his arm, just as he liked it.

"I went through some of this the last time I saw ya, but we're gonna get deep down in it now," Roy drawled.

"Over the next year, you'll learn whut you need to know to be the best." The first order of business was showing the novice how to clean the bore.

"Yew gotta clean out any goddamn dirt, left over gunpowder, and other residue." Roy warned John that an unclean bore would "screw up the course" of the bullet.

"How many shots I get to take today, Roy?"

"One."

John was dumbfounded.

"Only got an hour to learn ya more of the fundamental stuff, Johnny. You'll understand when we're done," Roy assured him.

"Now, what is one of the most important things in target shooting?"

"Same exact position ever' time? Sight picture...?" John fished.

The Guardsman cut him off. "Note taking."

"Come on!" the boy moaned.

Tracking the details of practice-shooting was Roy's secret to mastery. It was the way to perfection for a competitive rifleman. Logging one's settings for bullseyes at different distances, wind speeds, and other variables made all the difference.

"You won't be able to compete without recordin' yer settings," Roy scoffed. "I can hear the announcer now: 'After Round One, John William Hall bolos out. He'll have the pleasure 'o watchin' the rest of the match from the stands because he didn't know how to log his shots and learn from them. Poor ol' Johnny.'"

"Roy, you know I can't spell anything. And what is a 'bolo'?" Annoyance had seeped into the boy's reply.

"It's a term we use for losers." The short slender Guardsman who had a twenty-eight-inch waist laid his warnings on thickly. He was resolute in preparing his brother for the reality of competition. Roy would help John avoid traps he himself had stepped into during training. He had seen men humiliated for failing the night reconnaissance test or being unsuccessful field stripping their Springfield and reassembling it blindfolded. And promising troops were drummed out of the Guard for failing to qualify as a "marksman."

"You bolo something in the Guard, John William, you'll find the ninth ring of hell more hospitable than your own barracks. Soldiers can heap a lot a' scorn on a body."

Roy strutted as he assured the boy that if he listened and performed as trained, the chance of bolo-ing his rifle qualification was nil. "Not with ol'

Roy teachin' ya."

"So the 'marksman' medal doesn't pertain to the best shooters?" John asked anxiously.

"Hell, no. It's the worst you can do 'n still qualify fer the Guard. 'Sharp-shooter' is second best 'n they award 'Expert' only to those with the very top elite scores. Ninety-eight, ninety-nine, or one hun-durd."

"Okay then, Roy, teach me how to be an expert!"

Roy set his jaw. "Okay, let's get down to bidness."

During his instruction, John became blind and deaf to all distraction. This was how he would absorb and retain every gesture, every image, every word, every vowel, every sensation related to a weapon and its use. He was told to check the front sight post at the end of the barrel. If it or the front sight had had been altered from one rifle match to the next, he would be defeated quickly if he didn't deduce the problem and re-adjust the sights. "Not doing this would be like fergettin' to open yer fly before takin' a piss," Roy drawled.

"Check the front sight with a micrometer before *every* match, kid. Record the height in your log book so you don't forget, and make goddamn sure it is the exact same every time."

Each charge vibrated with consequence.

"Then we gotta eliminate all glare from sun because it will compromise yer focus on the front sight," Roy continued in a sequence of orders.

"See this here? It's a carbide lamp, the kind they use up in the Picher lead 'n zinc mines near Tar Creek. Miners attach them to their hard hats. Throws a brilliant light in the tunnels. We use 'em to blacken front sights to keep the durn glare off 'em."

Roy held up the copper-colored "smoker" and lit it. The narrow fire from the lamp grew to about an inch and threw off a fierce sooty char. John found its acrid metallic odor unnatural. Putting the flame near the front sight for three seconds gave it a powdery black scorch, dark and dense like the inside of a long cave.

"Here you can take account of windage 'n elevation," Roy said, "Test the play of wind and distance on your bullet. You'll record yer sight settings…"

John interrupted, "Hey, I've already read this stuff in the manuals you gave me."

"I know it! But I'm gonna go through it all in my own way to make sure you didn't misunderstand, misinterpret, or glide over a goddamn thing. And so I can put the proper emphasis where it needs to be!"

With his time and patience limited Roy was reluctant to field complaints. "So if yew want to be the very best someday, then reduce yer jawin' and listen," Roy said.

Roy, intense, dark browed, loving, and pre-alcoholic, sat like a saint on a stone going over fundamentals of competitive shooting with his brother in his own proprietary sequence. Compensating for wind speed and variation. Determining precise distance and how to focus the dominant eye on the front sight. Getting the perfect sight picture. Forming the weld between the cheek and the rifle stock. Using the sling to minimize sway. Diagnosing which ammunition was smooth, unblemished and uniform. Last, for Roy, the foundation of civilization: breathing and trigger squeeze.

After fifty-three minutes of tutelage, John fired his one round. The copper and zinc thirty-ought-six bullet left the barrel with a head-splitting clap. It put a hole at the southwest corner of the target half a lifetime away from the bullseye.

Chapter 15

PANIC

Before first light on a wintry February in 1931, Jack, A.M., and John William followed their father into the kitchen after tending the livestock. The boys warmed their hands over the wood-burning stove, washed, grabbed napkins made from fabric odds-and-ends, and gathered at the breakfast table. Lucille was now old enough to prepare eggs, grits, and salt pork. She served her father first on his porcelain dish as her mother had always done. The boys received their portions on steel plates.

At one end of the Great Room was the kitchen. Cupboards, a shallow pan in a dry sink for washing dishes, the stove as black as midnight and a wood counter inhabited it. As did a long dining table surrounded by ten chairs. At the opposite end of the room, a flame jumped in an open stone fireplace. The floor was a mixture of sturdy planked hardwoods cut and milled from Hall-property timber. It was thick but worn. So well scrubbed was it that the labor of women's hands to keep it bright over the years had become a proportion of it and locked into its character.

John William, ignoring family table etiquette, asked where his mother was.

"She's a' layin' down. In the bedroom," their father replied between bites, his words leached of emotion.

"Ma got the fever?" A.M. pursued. "Or is it all the creditors bangin' at the door a'wearin' her down?"

"Mama's got no fever, no cough. She's in pain. And there's blood...," Lucille interjected betraying a child's panic.

"It's been comin' and goin' for some time now. I've called for the doctor," Arnold said with impatience.

"Has anyone heard from Helen," Jack asked.

"She's puttin' in fourteen-hour days at the millinery shop in Tishomingo," Arnold answered and pushed his plate away. "She likes it, or so she says. Dudn't matter. Your sister is lucky to be a workin'. I 'spect we'll see her come Sunday. Now get a move on."

Lucille cleared the dishes and A.M. marched to the well to draw water. His feet crunched the frozen grass. John William and Jack put on clean shirts for school that Lucille had ironed the night before.

The Hall children were walking together the three miles to school when Dr. Atkinson passed them. He was in his worn and feeble buggy on his way to see their mother and signaling the horse with the sharp sound of his whip to persist in a vigorous canter. When she realized the doctor's frenzied hurtle, Lucille wept.

As they made their way home together that afternoon, John told Jack and Lucille that he would not start chores until he got the truth about his mother's condition.

"Same with me," Lucille proclaimed. Jack threw them a look of caution. Their father was in the stable binding the shank of their mare when they found him. When he glanced up, Arnold saw that Jack, A.M., John, and little Lucille had surrounded him. He finished wrapping the leg and slapped the mare on her rump. She tried to bolt, but a strong tether prevented her escape.

"Git to yer chores. No need hanging around me," their father growled.

"Tell us what the doctor said," John demanded.

"I'll tell you after chores; we'll go over it at the dinner table," Arnold snapped.

None of the children moved. Then Jack turned, began to walk away, and halted before facing his father again.

"I am obliged to hear 'bout it now before I do anything, sir," John announced. "Can't work without knowing."

Arnold, who looked drained, spat and softened.

"Atkinson thinks your ma has a cancer," he said as he wiped dirt and manure off his hands. "Womb cancer."

"What's that?" Lucille cried.

"Can he make her well?" Jack asked.

"There's no need yer frettin' now," their father said evenly, trying to comfort his children. "Your mother is feeling better already. Up and around the house. Now go on about yer chores. Won't know anythin' more until next week."

Atkinson made another visit six days later while the children were in school, but Arnold said nothing more to them. At home Lucy Lee seemed almost back to normal.

Chapter 16

RABBIT FEVER

B y May of the new year, John had matured as a shooter of game. After school, finding no meat in the larder for Monday dinner, he walked to the fields and shot two large rabbits. Because of his training and practice with Roy, he was feeling a slow but ascending mastery of the smaller .22 rifle as well. He flung the game over his shoulder and hurried home.

To prepare for the meal, he dressed the rabbits outside, seasoned them in the kitchen with salt, pepper, and a sprinkling of sage, added dried celery leaves to the pot, and stewed them with dumplings that rose to perfection. Adding to the feast in which his mother, Lucille, Jack, and Leo Graham shared, John cooked buttery crowder peas plus mustard greens boiled with a smoked, richly marrowed ham bone.

John was ecstatic about the kill, not only because he hit both targets but that it took only one shot each. And both rabbits were struck near the eye where he had placed his sight picture. The generally taciturn boy talked freely during the meal that night, his father being away in Texas.

"I got my first rifle match comin' up Saturday," he announced, looking at Leo Graham. His mother, weakened now, moved like a torpid Alabama river denied summer rains. Yet she managed a smile at John's delight on display.

"You got what it takes to go up against all those old farts, John William?" Leo poked. He spun around to Lucy Lee. "Uh, sorry ma'am, that word slipped out."

"It's over on the Pernell Dubois ranch eight miles east a' Durant. Roy is lendin' me a Springfield he's 'borrowing' from the Guard. Dubois is providin' ammunition, targets and cleanin' supplies for those without. Gotta give it a try."

After dinner, Lucy Lee limped to her room leaning on Jack. In the kitchen John boasted of his daring to Leo and Lucille.

"Shooters from all over creation will be there. If I do well at this match and a few others, I reckon it will open the door for me."

Lucille scoffed, "Open the door to what?"

"To get into the National Guard."

"Wowza!" Leo chirped, wide-eyed at John's daring.

"No Guard worth its salt will let a sixteen-year-old stripling with no hair into its ranks!" Lucille sneered before gurgling with laughter.

"If I'm good enough, they won't even check my age. What 'a they gonna do, march down and comb through the birth certificates at the courthouse?" John argued. "Besides, you oughta be more supportive, honey. The Guard pays. We need money. All I gotta do is get in, go to a few meetings and train on the weekends. Saturday, I'm hittin' the road to a bigger life!"

Early in the morning, three days later, and before his walk to school, John was on his own makeshift firing range. He was studying the Guard manuals Roy had lent him and practicing no-bullet "dry-shooting."

That night John started to cough. A pain in his chest was sharp. By midday Thursday breathing was hard. He felt like a grown sow was lying on his chest. His temperature jumped and he went into sinking worry. Roy was due the next day to help him practice for the match. The Guard's Springfield rifle and some ammunition were coming with him.

When Roy arrived at noon Friday, John was worse. A skin ulcer had invaded John's neck and right shoulder. Swollen, burning lymph glands in his collar and right armpit worsened the misery. Despite his brother's protests, Roy sent for Atkinson. The doctor arrived late Friday night, near exhaustion. An hour earlier he had tended a teenage Choctaw woman who delivered into his hands a stillborn child.

Atkinson always dressed in a white shirt with a four-in-hand polka-dot tie, and a black suit with a matching vest. A black bag swung at the end of his arm like a bob on a weakly functioning pendulum. In it he had carefully packed medicaments, bandages, and diagnostic paraphernalia along with flesh-cutting instruments. One of them donned a sinister razor at its fore the shape of a crescent moon and frightened many a child in Durant over the years. When deployed it sent pain like a dose of electricity through the tissue of adults and the young alike. The device was used to lance boils and carbuncles that failed to drain.

"What's the matter, son?" the doctor asked as he stood over the sick boy.

Cleveland Emory Atkinson was in his sixties but looked older. Trained in the east before settling in St. Louis to practice medicine, the doctor had dark fitful hair, a closely trimmed beard, and was gifted with supple steady hands and long fingers perfectly formed for surgery.

Having spent eleven years making rounds and treating patients, simultaneously at the infirmary at the St. Louis Department of Public Welfare and the Evangelical Lutheran Hospital and Asylum, along with treating female indigents and outcasts at St. Louis County Social Evil Hospital, Atkinson left for Durant to start his own medical practice.

The small Oklahoma town was never one to eschew rumors. The gossip about the doctor, in reality, a highly capable physician but occasional feather-ruffler, was that the Missouri river city had expelled him for malpractice. Durant gossip assigned the doctor to misdiagnosing the disease of a state senator's wife who passed out during a dressage tourney. While in the Lutheran Hospital and under Dr. Atkinson's care she supposedly developed unsightly paralysis of the left side of her face.

Yet another rumor claimed that he was fired because a fellow doctor accused Atkinson of having "Negro blood."

The Durant doctor's naturally warm countenance indeed had become more severe over the years, though not because of the prattle surrounding him, to which he gave no quarter. Rather it was the defeats he suffered in his battle against sickness and death that scratched away at his once unalloyed hopefulness.

Yet when the doctor entered the space or consciousness of the sick, he was always smiling, tender, almost buoyant. To assure the ill that their doctor had confidence that the best outcome would be forthcoming from the affliction he was about to challenge.

Arnold Hall's Winterhalder clock struck eleven times as Atkinson began his examination. He felt the boy's scarlet cheek and sat next to the bed, which was illuminated with candlelight and a single hurricane lamp. John's body was in riot. Though partially delusional, John recognized the doctor. He gripped his hand not out of fear of reckoning but in relief that now what could be done would be.

Diarrhea and nausea had played mercilessly in the boy's gut all afternoon. Yet to Atkinson the room had the scent of coyote skulls. Lucy Lee sat motionless in the dark corner watching the stooped physician clamp tarnished pince-nez spectacles on his nose. He leaned forward and pushed on her son's troubled stomach and throat. Lucille brought cool cloths, laying them on her brother's forehead and neck.

When through with the examination, Atkinson leaned back in the chair and sighed as if a respite could reverse his diagnosis; he stroked his chin and looked blankly past the miserable boy and into the picture on the wall above him. Partly illuminated by the lamp on John's nightstand was a painting Atkinson had seen in Europe.

"I'll be damned! 'Judith Slaying Holofernes.' When I saw the original in Florence, it brought me to my knees," Atkinson reminisced excitedly to no one, though John and Lucy Lee heard his whisperings. "Took a ship to Italy after medical school. On borrowed money. Had no job. Artemisia Gentileschi. Even at twenty-three she could see into the human heart. The silly men… could not abide a female painter."

Minutes of silence passed.

"He's not going to like this. We've got to get his fever down, and quickly," the doctor said at last to Lucy Lee.

"Jack, A.M., put warm water in the bath basin. We'll lower him into it. Then add cold water continuously until it slowly reaches a chill he can hardly tolerate."

A.M. carried a lantern with him to ready his brother's bath. It would be in a rough zinc-galvanized tin washtub conveniently near the cog-geared hand pump at the corral. He hitched a chute to the pump's lip so water could be channeled down into the tub. Its four-and-a-half foot diameter was as good for washing clothes as it was for cleansing the Hall males in warm weather.

The pump drew frigid water from a well four-hundred feet deep. A.M. tempered the cold draws with water heated in a black caldron nearby. Dipping one sick with a fever into a bath at almost any temperature was agonizing.

In the tub, A.M. mixed the waters so that it was warm to the touch. Then he and Jack carried John from the house and gently lowered the already shivering boy into the bath. He tolerated it until his ribs met the water line. His scream echoed off the hills.

"Ahhh, I can't stand this! I'm freezin'!" the naked boy wailed. "Let me out! Let me out!" His two brothers finished immersing him, and then held him down as well as they could; John jerked about like a thresher victim having his arm amputated.

After only a minute, Atkinson came. "We are going to add the chilly stuff now, John. Your body is adjusting to the shock. It shouldn't be as painful from here, but we have to arrest the fever."

"The cold is piercing my organs!" John yelled, his teeth chattering.

In what looked like a ritual washing below a waning moon, A.M. scooped out a bucketful of warm water and threw it on the ground as Jack put in a cold one from a fresh well draw. John folded into himself. He groaned, grabbed his legs, brought them to his chest. Only his shoulders and head, which he rested on his knees, poked above the waterline. He uttered not another sound as the temperature of his bath was lowered to near that of the well water. He clenched his teeth, fighting off the misery. His only solace was that the frigid liquid drawn from the deep might save him.

John was in the water fourteen minutes when Atkinson instructed A.M. and Jack to remove him from the basin. The doctor placed a blanket around him and the brothers carried their brother inside to his bed. Atkinson gave John aspirin to take with cold tea, closed the door, and made his way into the kitchen. It was past midnight and he sat with the family over hot tea and milk.

"He has tularemia."

John's mother gasped. "Rabbit fever." Her translation was immediate for she had to drive from her mind the petrifying medical term she could not reckon with.

"We all ate the rabbits!" A.M. blurted. "Why none of the rest of us sick?"

"Your brother got the disease from handling wild game, son, not from eating it. Must have been well-cooked. Otherwise could have been more of you in his state."

The doctor laid blame on a flea from the rabbits John killed. "Probably bit him on the neck and shoulder where the ulcers emerged. That's where the sickness entered his bloodstream.

"What will become of him, Dr. Atkinson?" was all Lucy Lee could manage to utter.

"Treated eight cases in the past three years, Miss Hall. Half died. It is a kind of plague. Veiled in the beginning, then ferocious. None of those that passed was as strong as John William." Atkinson, knowing the family's perils, was perhaps more optimistic in his prognosis with Lucy Lee, telling her if he pulls through the next few days his recovery should be a full one. Though he would have permanent scarification where the ulcers were. "I think we got the fever down in time, Miss Hall. Fevers like his if they burn too long, well, I've seen 'em permanently dull minds and weaken the kidneys."

Rising from his chair and as if he were the man of the house, the doctor instructed A.M. to follow him to town. He would send him back with syrup for John with strict instructions on dosage.

"Now, Miss Hall, please make sure he gets no more than what I prescribe. It's got an arsenic base. We want to poison the disease, not the boy."

As he left, Atkinson asked Lucy Lee, "Where's Mr. Hall, ma'am?"

"Said he was goin' to Lawton. Then Texas." She trailed off, "On business."

Chapter 17

A SLENDER MARGIN

Three days later John's fever broke. On the fourth day in the afternoon he plodded to the porch, blanketed in the heat, and remained there until after the day lost its light. He thought about little, though a hushed sense of triumph spread through his body where the disease had lived.

The boy's recovery took four weeks, after which he felt almost like himself though routine chores wore on him. Then, in early July, he started shooting again. He had three weeks to re-acquaint himself with the rifle. In late July, John would board an open-backed Army truck dispatched by the Oklahoma National Guard. He would be one of fourteen traveling the hot, dirty, alkaline hours to Ft. Sill where they would be field-tested on the Springfield thirty-ought-six rifle. John saw qualifying on the weapon as the door to his future. Sensing the consequence of the event, Lucy Lee and Lucille travelled into downtown Durant where they waited with the anxious teen until the carrier arrived.

A weakened Lucy Lee hugged her son in front of the mercantile in a gesture of confidence as much as love. When he put his arms around her, John realized she was light as a cobweb. No longer did she smell of sweet rose and lavender but of musty cloth. The other young men milling about the thoroughfare smirked at the sight of affection.

When John boarded the rear of the military truck and took a seat, he noticed how much older the thirteen others looked. But before day's end John and eight others had qualified at the "Marksman" level. Only two others scored higher.

On August 1, 1931, at sixteen years and one-and-a-half months, the Hall boy entered the Oklahoma National Guard by claiming to be eighteen. No one checked his birth records, as he had predicted. He had competed in no organized rifle matches and claimed none. But despite his slender margin of success on the range, John's solid interview convinced the board of his potential.

When he stepped off the truck upon his return to Durant, Roy was the only greeter. Seeing the beam radiating from his brother's face, Roy knew the results before a word was spoken.

Chapter 18

BITTER SCENT

Arnold Hall sat at the dinner table in the late night darkness. It was mid-January 1932. He lit another candle to illuminate more of the table's surface. His face was pale and empty.

Bent, drained, and inert, Arnold surveyed the papers spread before him. Bills, claims, summonses, writs, and menacing handwritten correspondence stared up from across the wide dinner table. At its edge was his Delft plate from dinner. Left on it, an untouched biscuit, cold and covered in red-eye gravy now clotted with cold yellow fat and the remains of a morsel of sugar-cured ham. The father of eight had the frightened look of a roped dog eyeing the figure about to euthanize him. Picking up a stub of a pencil, Arnold tallied. Then erased. Tallied and erased again. The candlelight flickered back and forth, animating the sinkholes in his cheeks and the age lines carved into his face. Arnold's facial creases were so mercenary now they could remind those closest to him, of whom there were few, of the dry estuaries that disfigured the Oklahoma landscape.

From a bottle retrieved from under the back porch remained one finger of Monongahela rye whiskey. Arnold tipped it into a glass and sipped it tenderly. He had always considered it a reliable intoxicant and flavorful pour. Even had his wife been in the room, she would have been too sick to notice his sin.

From the bed in the far corner of the room, John had been watching.

He remembered when his father possessed the look and comportment of an English king. Tall, stoic, avaricious, arrogant with the sharply cleaved features of a storybook noble. Tonight he was different. Tonight his father looked more like serf than patrician.

"Pa never works late," he thought to himself. "The king's domain has not withstood the siege."

Arnold Hall's winter nighttime hours normally were spent in front of the hearth smoking, usually a pipe with a cheap yet aromatic tobacco. He would read the newspaper or play an occasional game of chess with one of his sons. He would carve. He would listen to the farm radio shaped like a thick tombstone, connected to dry cell batteries and taken it in trade from an Arkansas client and peanut farmer short on cash.

If none of these, the father would sit watching the fire dance off the hardwoods burning in the fireplace. John knew not what flames licking the dark stirred in his father's imagination. Though he often wondered.

Alarmed by the late-night anomaly of his father's drinking, John got out of bed. Never had his father brought whiskey into the house. John was present when Arnold signed the pledge in the Bible. He never imagined his father would go back on his word.

John stepped to where his father was trying to manipulate numbers. He sat down beyond the diminishing reach of the candle's illumination. A few minutes passed before the elder Hall appeared to speak to the paper he had been figuring on. "Why don't you add up, damn it…don't balance…this ain't gonna work. God a' mercy!" His quiet voice shook with alarm.

John flinched. Lucy Lee forbad cursing. Oaths were never uttered in the house. The young man felt pity for his father as he whispered on. "Shorted fifty bales on speculation. Now price risin'! It's the New Orleans Exchange, not me, that's vexed."

Arnold glanced past the darkness where his son was sitting motionless as if the shade of a lost child had returned to witness the moment of generational dénouement. The muscles in his father's jaw clenched like a fist.

Veins in his forehead protruded like aggrieved snakes.

"Never should have done this. Times ain't what they used to be," he said looking down at the stub of a pencil between his fingers. John saw in his father more anger than lamentation, and he was curious if the old fellow cared that his choices had deepened the family's vulnerability. The young man did not want to see the Hall patriarch drown. Rather he hoped to witness a man of substance humble and rising from defeat. He yearned for Arnold Hall to be a family man, not an oaf concerned that his name had been expunged from the cornerstone of illusory greatness in the sovereign universe of Durant society.

Arnold gripped a telegram received eight hours earlier from "R.N. Gourdin Smith, Cotton Broker, New Orleans, Associate Member Southhampton Cotton Exchange." It offered him $28.30 for each of another thirty-eight low middling bales under Hall's ownership. It carried a side note, "Mr Hall, Southhampton market at bottom now AND STILL IN TURMOIL stop India, Egypt offering fancy long fiber cotton for just cents above middling stop Advise forthwith of your decision stop".

"Sweet Jesus!" Arnold gasped. "I got nearly forty-eight dollars in each of them ginned bales. They're sittin' down in the Durant cotton yard right now wrapped so poorly by those bastards in Ardmore they're a' sufferin' wind and moisture damage. Five year ago for the purdiest wrapped bales you ever did see, woulda got damn near sixty-five apiece."

"I'll be bringing home ten dollars a month from my weekends in the Guard," John interjected into the muck of his father's delirium. "That will help."

Arnold looked up with a start and realized his son was with him. The aging man tilted his head like a pup curious as to what his master was saying. "You better get to bed, son," he said with uncharacteristic softness.

Chapter 19

THE DOOR

John William leaned forward on an old armchair pulled near his mother's bed. His forearms rested on his knees as he watched over the nearly comatose figure. It was a tumultuous morning in March 1932. A faraway storm sent dry thunder and troubled winds like a Greek chorus bearing revelation and it sang through the cracks and seams of the Hall dwelling.

Two days earlier, Lucy Lee had felt a pain that tore through her viscera. Her suffering became so relentless for such long periods that her children broke down at the sound of her cries. In short measures they would leave the horror behind for the refuge of outdoors to gather themselves.

The first day the pain had subsided for an hour or two before spiking back into her. A day later Lucy Lee had few hours of respite. Throughout, her face alternated between crimson and ashen.

"I know it's been difficult for you." Lucy Lee's hoarse voice broke out from her stillness and startled her son. "Your daddy moved you to a distant place in his life, honey, just as he did me." She tried in vain to moisten her lips with her tongue. "No matter how close we stood to him, we were far away. Hard…when the people we love do this."

Her lids drifted over dry eyes; her cracked lips bled. But Lucy Lee was resolute in conveying her mind.

"We are different, you and I, yes? Nothing wrong with that! But hurt takes residence in this earthly conflict, baby. Not sure your father knows what love means anymore. Maybe not his fault. Maybe. Don't want you to worry. That you're not like him. Didn't fit into his life. Or you let him down. You've done right." Lucy Lee traveled back into unconsciousness.

As he looked into her face, John wondered who his mother really was, this once and forever Alabama farmer's daughter. At 49, she seemed so old and worn down. How did she come to be, this woman who birthed eight children and never lost a one, this once tireless bulwark who nursed and raised them all and, despite her lack of formal education, had a vivid mind? From native memory she taught her daughters of a hundred plant species, exotic for such a forlorn land. Forsythia, floribunda, japonica. She could recognize them even from a distance inside a moving buggy. Verbena, passiflora, spirea, caryopteris. She declaimed them like a poet. Hydrangea, viburnum, eulalia. His mother's second language. Her prowess at gardening was astonishing. Her knowledge of canning was so precise, so consummate, that not once did he remember seeing so much as a dot of mold under any lid of a newly opened jar, much less a spoiled jar of fruit, vegetables, or meat. John's family, unlike so many others, found their winters secure in abundance because of her.

He thought of her mystical religion. Its music, scripture, and frightening spirituality gave her at once an almost unyielding optimism and unquenchable drive even as it tried to suppress her fullness through fear and its code of obedience.

John realized he had come too late to this. The door had closed on him. He would not solve the mystery of this complex woman who brought him onto this earth, even if he had the capacity to form the crucial questions and the strength to endure the answers. Her time was at hand.

On the third day Atkinson arrived. John had left her side and A.M. was with her. She was wailing with pain. The doctor carried opiates he had ordered from Tulsa. At his arrival, well after nightfall, he asked Helen, who had returned from Tishomingo to be with her mother, to fetch him a bowl of cool water, two clean soft cloths, some bread and butter, a spoonful of plum jelly, and a cup of strong black tea. She gathered it all and placed it on Lucy Lee's night table.

Sitting at her bedside, Atkinson positioned a moistened cloth on Lucy Lee's face and administered two drugs. Two blinking kerosene lamps softened the room's darkness. At the point his patient calmed, the doctor buttered his bread, spooned on the jelly which Lucy Lee had canned in the fall, and ate while he sipped the tea, for he had not eaten since breakfast. He was barely cognizant of the Hall children silently moving in and out.

When Lucy Lee's agony returned, the doctor positioned the remaining cloth, which he had wound into a small braid, between her teeth. Atkinson's cautious doses of laudanum and morphine initially mitigated the intensity and frequency of the mother's pain. Her anguish would fall for short periods, then rise again with a renewed ferocity that lasted for nearly half an hour. Later, incrementally larger doses of the two opiates proved ineffective at easing her misery. After some hours of this, Atkinson saw that Lucy Lee would not be coming back to any form of comfort, much less recover even a particle of her former self.

He waited for her to calm. Wistful and seated but a few inches from her, Atkinson eased his head into his hands and asked the family to leave the room. Arnold kissed his wife's hand and was the last to leave.

When the door shut, Atkinson whispered to Lucy Lee. "I think it's time, don't you, honey?" She uttered no words, but her eyes turned to him and softened. He dabbed a jot of plum jelly on his finger and put it on her tongue, and she grinned.

Before another bitter cry from a pain he could not imagine, no matter how many dying cancer patients he had been with, the doctor tenderly, as if performing a kind of sacrament, administered heroin into a vein in Lucy Lee's left arm, the dosage ample enough to dull her senses without inducing outright unconsciousness.

Atkinson then moved his omniscient gaze to her. As she watched him, he smiled warmly upon her and gently stroked her forehead. Gratitude and love radiated from her eyes. Undoing the braided cloth she had held in her teeth, Atkinson quarter folded it, placing it loosely over the stricken mother's mouth and nose. He put a surgical mask over his face and began squeezing pearls of ether, aromatic but resolute, onto her cloth. Drop by drop the anesthetic seeped through the cloth that Lucy Lee had used nightly for years to dry and polish her dishes. After a time, the ether, its vapors coursing though her lungs and into her blood, slowed her breathing, then brought it to an end; Lucy Lee Hall, the devoted mother and wife, was, after a long and terrible odyssey, at ease.

The man of science, remedies, and last remaining hopes sat by her side. Time passed. Atkinson felt something lingering near the body just after death. And he did not want it to be alone.

They came for her body by wagon at daybreak. Later, weakened by grief, John retreated to a swell overlooking an expanse of his preserve. He watched as a tempest of dust advanced under a sky as dull as galvanized tin. It rolled in like a primitive thing relentlessly crossing the desiccated landscape, its jaws gorging on everything—clapboard homes, farm animals, clothes hanging on bent lines, storefronts, steeples, sod shanties, buckboard wagons loaded and unloaded, and all other manners of human dross. The gale tore scrub from its roots. Trees genuflected, then fell and disappeared. Felt hats were whipped from the heads of men and hurled through the sky like black comets.

Newspapers snapped, then spun like dervishes. Chips and planks from porches and outbuildings littered the ground storm. The duster moved faster now as if its charge had been trumpeted. On the hillock the young man could scarcely stand against the torrent. Yet he remained, locked in his sadness but consumed by the storm's spellbinding otherworldly dimension, its titanic force. As if its purpose was to inflict a terrible retribution, the storm swallowed the boy standing against it and he, as did the entire realm, disappeared inside the billowing grit and wreckage.

A day after the storm, relatives and friends gathered for the funeral of Lucy Lee Hall. It was short. She never respected undertaking in general and had no fondness for certain undertakers in particular. At her long-understood request they were excluded from her death. No casket, no embalming fluids, no public gawking at her corpse. Two days after her passing, her soul swaddled in the breath of trees and her body wrapped in a soft brilliant quilt her mother made for her in a time gone by from clothes her kin wore in life, she was lowered into her grave by her four eldest boys with heavy cord braided from Thompson tartan. Words of the Baptist service of the dead floated over her resting place, songs were sung, remembrances uttered by friends. Just as she had wanted it. And that was that.

Chapter 20
"YORE GONNA STAY"

Days after, John still found his mother's death overpowering. Nonetheless, he left the house to begin the livestock tending and field work intolerant of hiatus. The sunrise was the color of iodine. Its jaundiced light rode the ground fog spread out over the dusty purlieu like a shroud. While at the barn, he caught sight of his oldest brother and pondered why he had left town in the middle of the week. Irving was as an on-again, off-again haberdasher and evening card dealer. John assumed he was more off-again than anything.

Irving stood on the porch as his younger brother approached. John rarely saw his oldest brother and tried to avoid conversation when he did. Leaning on the peeling porch column, Irving puffed himself up like a prairie chicken for all the livestock to ignore. He wore the same soiled blue suit every time John saw him, though now it appeared to be a size or two too small. He looked like a paunched Billy Sunday without the elan. John noticed that his brother's suit-sleeves had frayed at the wrists, exposing their white underlayment. They appeared as dirty crowns above his hands.

Arnold Hall's oldest was smoking a contemptible cigar. Its hot orange disc created an effluvium akin to an outhouse fire. Something a merchant would give away to a third-tier customer for purchasing a gunny of soon-to-spoil feed. Or maybe a used chair with a hole for a seat, John thought. But Irving would never part with a cent, so he must have stolen the thing.

His brother's hair, long on top and cut to the skin on the sides, was dotted with white flakes secured by oil and combed front to back. Fat was collecting at his temples and surrounding his eyes, making them appear small and vole-like. His mouth was small. His teeth were the color of lead and arranged like leaning gravestones. At his feet was a beat-up suitcase, fully packed, once owned by an itinerant brassiere salesman. One latch was gone and a trouser belt circumnavigated the box to hold its tired cardboard jaws together. John, wondering what was going on, sat down on the stoop next to him.

"Look at that goddamn sunrise!" Irving crowed. "It's as if the prairie is vomiting up all that Indian blood and bile that soaked into her long ago," he said grinning. "I guess it don't want it either."

"Ma hasn't been dead but a few days and here you are fouling up her home with curses," John berated him.

Oblivious, the eldest brother continued, "You know about the Battle o' Wash-tah River, Johnny Cakes?"

John's brother was no scholar. He loathed school and the schoolmasters who pushed him, with abject failure, to apply himself. He was smart to be sure. But his intelligence showed itself as a kind of low order of animal scheming. Irving loved "history," that narrow excavation of cowboy lore that sang of whites conquering Indians, subduing the African and the Mexican, and having dominion over the land. Backgrounding it all was righteous Old Testament thunder and cavalry trumpets resounding gloriously over the whole western trauma.

"Yep, it wasn't but about two-hunur'd-fifty mile up air'n west of us, near Elk City, Oklahoma, John William, that 'ol Custer and hiz Seventh Cal-ver-ee caught Chief Black Kettle, hiz squaw and his band of Cheyenne cutthroats sleepin' like babies. He and hiz men made quick work of their hides. Kilt the tribe's pony and mule herd, too. Nearly eight hunur'd head of livestock cut down and left to rot. Damn, that must have been a sight!"

"Charge of the Light Yellow-Hair Brigade," John scoffed, twisting Tennyson. "Was it your fearless Custer that cut through the Indian women and children, too, at Washita, Irvin'?" John spat.

"Yeah, more'n a hun-durd of 'em. But hellfire, what of it! Red skins were never meant to survive, Johnny Cakes. Not in God's grand scheme 'a things. Ever'body knows that!"

Depleted by his brother's presence, John pivoted, "Just what are you doing here, Irvin'? It's not like you to be up this early."

"Not a jot in Doo-rant worth a damn to me now. None of us, really. Pa and me are roundin' up Lee, A.M. and Jack. We are leavin' tud-ay fer west Texas." Irving's announcement was bizarre. "We gonna start over, make some coin!"

To John, his brother was spouting twisted blessings over him as if he were dead. "Yore stayin' right here: tend the homestead and look after Lucille. And keep yer mouth shut about ar whereabouts! With Helen marryin' that grocer and Roy headin' out to Ft. Silly, we think this is best."

"We! I haven't any say in it. Why Lucille and I being left behind, *Marion*?" John snapped using his brother's first name, which he loathed. Fearing violence, Irving gave himself another step's distance from his younger brother's reach.

"Times ain't what they used ta be, John William," his brother whined, unsettled by John's challenge to his seniority.

Arnold had wanted someone in the family to stay with the farm, pay the mortgage, and keep squatters out. Irving was the delivery boy of bad tidings.

"We'll send yew money fer payments," he said, trying to sooth the situation. "Otherwise the bank'll foreclose, and we won't get a dime. Gotta keep our place until the real estate market fires up. Then we'll sell it, Pa says. You 'n Lucille can come to Lubbock then."

At this point John wouldn't give a dead man's farthing for his father's promises or his eldest's happy talk.

"Pa runnin' away from Doke Carns, I suppose. He'd rather beat cheeks to Texas than face up to his obligations. To us and his lenders," John William chided, not hiding his spite.

"Doke Carns ain't no banker, John William! Fer chrissake, he ain't even high enough in the *vegetable* kingdom to outrank a turnip," Irving gargled. "Besides, Pa not worried one bit about that oily sidewinder."

"Why not?"

"Uncle Terrill took care of him," Irving said in a low matter-of-fact voice. "You know, like he dun with that thar deputy in Mississipp'."

"In Texas, I'mma gonna eat rich food, drink good whiskey, smoke five ceegars a day, and have a different woman ever' night."

John scoffed. "Hard times are in the West Texas Dust Bowl just like they are here in Durant, Irvin', and the women just as particular." He wondered out loud how his brother was to come by money to fuel his adventures.

"Hell, I don't know yet, goddamn it!" Irving said. "But I'll get it. Don't yew bet against me, kid! All I know is I'm gonna fleece ever' redskin, ever' Mexican, ever' blackamoor in Lubbock. And when I'm done with them, I'll go after the whites. You show up in Lubbock, I'll fleece you, too, John William. You'd be easy pickins'!" He spat big, but most of it landed on his shoes.

"You're gonna starve to death, Irvin'."

"Why's that?"

"Swindlers gotta be at least half as smart as the people they're tryin' to swindle," he snorted.

Irving's face reddened. "So, what you *gonna* do with yersef, Johnny Cakes?" he chirped.

The boy felt it was time to school his brother on the realities that should have been obvious. "Well, sounds like I'll be looking after Lucille for the foreseeable, doesn't it! So that is what I will be 'doing with myself,' *Marion*, making sure she gets an education in a strong and womanly manner. And no mischief befalls her. And she's fed well. And properly dressed, 'specially on Sundays."

Besides his newfound commitment to the household, John had determined to hone his shooting skills on the range until no one could beat him. And be ready for the next war.

"Ha! War is for goobers, Johnny Cakes," Irving sneered. "Straight outta Gumtown. "You're gonna go to Europe or god-knows-where the next one is and attack some stupid country with rifles, artillery and high moral intent. But yew go right ahead. And I'll do my part," Irving bleated, his voice dripping with sarcasm. "I'll visit your grave once or twice and hang a cheery lil' American flag out every fuckin' Fourth of Jooly."

At nowhere in time had these two personalities looked so starkly dissimilar. Two brothers raised under the same roof suckled by the same mother, schooled by the same teachers, and disciplined by the same father. Though Irving had been living outside the house for eight years, John was startled by how little he knew him.

"Me, I'm gonna do somethin' that pays off," he continued his screed. "Not that army shit. I am gonna attack them goddamn Texicans, though, but in their pocketbook. With my keen sales abilities, I'll come up with all kinda' schemes, Johnny! I'll become fat, rich, and famous. The dames'll be flocking 'ta my wiener."

"I think I've heard enough," John barked as the news of his family leaving consumed him. But Irving was like a defective clock whose alarm couldn't be silenced.

"But you, brother, you'll be dead. Or come home with your face blowed off. And ol' Herbert Fucking Hoover won't know you or what you did for him from an outhouse hole. And no amount of target practice is gonna save you from a goddamn early grave."

His lecturing halted momentarily so he could, thinking it would add gravitas to his words, take a few puffs on his cigar. Blowing the smoke through his teeth, he wondered if John remembered the story their mother had told them of Uncle Josiah, who'd fought in the Civil War. At the Battle of Antietam he was, the story went, shot in the crotch with a Minié ball.

Irving explained in a low, morbid tone, "Ma said the musket ball didn't kill him; it was the gangrene down there. Yew think about what that felt like!"

"When you all leavin' for Lubbock, Irvin'?" John asked.

His brother ignored the question and proceeded with another story to build his case. Their father's cousin, considered the most intelligent of that generation of Halls, had noticed a poster on the post office wall provoking him to enlist in the Army at Camp Logan in south Texas.

"Some colonel assigned him to the Red Diamonds!" Irving crowed. "Fought in the Argonne. Came back home without a scratch. Yew, remember? But, thereafter, could hold nary a job or know a woman! Then he went and set that preacher on fire."

"Never heard this story either, Marion," the boy sighed.

"I do believe he's still in the Texas loony asylum down in Austin. Why don't yew go down there an' ask him yersef what it's like to be a goddamn war hero."

John was becoming unnerved, but he hid it. He would never allow his oldest sibling to think he had gotten the upper hand.

"Sounds to me like you're makin' excuses for yourself, brother, rather than admit you don't have the hair to sign up to serve your country," he tossed back. "Why, you're just flat afraid, brother! Hoppin' scared of gettin' your little nuts blown off. But I guess that'd keep you a virgin."

"Well, you do jes' as you want, Johnny Cakes," his brother fumed. "But don't come to me cryin' for help."

The automobile appeared out of nowhere. John hadn't known where his father kept it hidden. Arnold shoved A.M., Lee and Jack into the back seat with their belonging. They were ready to leave and Irving made his way toward it. When he was out of earshot, John whispered, "Now I know why mama said you were 'one of God's smallest productions.'"

The oldest brother threw his suitcase in the automobile and took the front passenger seat. Arnold smiled, swept the brim of his fedora, waved to John without saying a word, put his Model A in gear, and gave it enough throttle to break the inertia of the farmstead gravity.

As he looked down the drive, the Hall patriarch pondered his release from Oklahoma and its gossip. His failure as a businessman and Durant society's disdain for him were about to vanish from his mind. In the mirror, the son he left behind was chasing the car. Arnold shifted the transmission and stepped on the accelerator to avoid hearing John's screams.

"You're a coward, Pa!" John yelled as he ran toward the grinding vehicle. "You wore Ma down till she died! You rotted our futures. Now you've split the family. And you're throwin' me and Lucille away. We're like carp flung up on the river bank to suffocate!"

Chapter 21

FATHOMLESS PULL

That night Lucille and John were alone in the old home and considered their fate. She watched the child. Not really a child, of course, her brother. Sixteen, seven years her senior. The boy-man's contour was motionless against the hearth fire transfixing him.

The diminutive Lucille, her mother's "Little Comet," lay still. She was in a bed in the great room under a piece-work quilt Lucy Lee finished for her just before she was born.

The girl was a mole pushing up a tiny mound of brightly colored linen, charadarie, and cotton-calico in a garden of exquisite geometries. For her John had tamed the terrible cold—bizarre for late March—that had galloped with outward intent out of Canada southward across the plains and into their home, unannounced and unfettered from out of the blue-black maw of the Oklahoma night just as death had come for their young mother.

Exotic perfume from oak and mesquite burning in the hearth settled into her nose with an elegance that soothed her and appeased her sorrow. The wind sang in the chimney's throat and traveled down into the fireplace. Lucille thought of her great-greats from centuries past: those who gathered around mysterious fires, just as her brother and she did tonight. Cuddling their children. Telling stories. Considering the vast unknown. Then an emptiness seeped in and her imaginings darkened.

She peered from under the quilt. "What will become of us, John William?"

Her new guardian rose from the hearth, walked to the pine-wash stand, lifted the pitcher, and slowly poured water into a Choctaw clay bowl. He dipped his hands into the liquid then brought it to his face as if he were washing away the soot and sin of the past.

"You are the one that matters, Little Comet," John said. "To me you are the crest of the night sky. It took Mama eight tries to birth perfection, but she did it."

He smiled at her and turned on the radio, which none of the Hall children had been allowed to touch.

It wailed as he rolled the tuning needle through mysterious static and alien sounds until it landed on what he wanted. This chosen frequency, its volume waxing and waning with wanton unpredictability, delivered dance bands pumping wild euphoria blended with the wind song from outside and into their space. Deaf to the furies circling their lives, John and Lucille danced to the crackling, thumping beats, the jubilation that annulled all else.

"What are we doin', John William?" she shouted.

"We're wind waltzin', honey!" he replied never stopping.

They roared and shimmied to The Charleston. Tiger Rag. and King Porter Stomp. Deep into the night.

John woke at sunrise. He loaded the old iron stove with wood and ignited it. Water was boiled and coffee made, weaker than usual since he wanted Lucille to enjoy some. His mother's caution that a cup of coffee would stunt growth in children was a tale John never believed, figuring adults made it up long ago, reluctant to share their morning luxury with the young. While eggs cooked and three large biscuits baked in the oven, he awakened Lucille. As she stepped into the aroma-laden scullery in the robe her mother wore, John immediately knew that the reality of their new existence had re-entered his sister's mind like a dangerous animal.

"We're on our own adventure now, Comet," he said brightly as he poured fresh cream into Lucille's steaming coffee, for she now was the woman of the house. "I'm gonna take care of you just as good as mama did. Maybe better."

Knowing that his soon-to-be-ten sister would bristle at being coddled or robbed of her independence, he added in a serious tone, "Of course, you must do the same for me." She smiled and nodded her assurance.

With the meal over John removed the dishes from the table, placed them in a pan of soapy water and spoke. "If you'll finish getting ready, we'll leave for school in about twenty minutes. I'm goin' outside for a bit and will be back by then."

He hurried up the hill and leaned against a redbud tree. Yesterday's events haunted him. The uncontrollable rage that overtook his body had settled in him as profound sadness. Pushing it into a remote corner of his mind, John looked around the land then closed his eyes. His lungs drew in the sweet breath of the Oklahoma plains, his ears its invocations, and in his veins he still felt the blood and pulse Arnold and Lucy Lee Hall had bequeathed him as had generations of Halls and Thompsons and Taylors and Barlows and Ballous and Donnellys and Livermores and Attaingnants before them. He divined the near fathomless pull of kin living and dead and the affirmation absorbed from long-held tales of being part of an honorable sequence. But as he had grown and learned of his father and his father's mark, the young man felt the ghosts of the past would be best left to the past, and, seeking to escape his father's still formidable gravity, he would attempt to form his own significance.

END OF PART I

ENTR'ACTE

5 March 1945; Hall, John W., captain; statement before U.S. Army Reconnaissance liaison, London, England

I don't remember where I first met Cap'n Shinn, though I got to know him on our row across the Atlantic en route to our appointment with the devil. The world was at war. As if we didn't get our fill of the last one. Shinn was an Ohio boy who lived in New York City before joining up. I was from Durant, Oklahoma, where I served in the National Guard before joining the Army. Our unit, Shinn's and mine, Ninth Armored Division, 60th Armored Infantry Battalion, was headin' east northeast, would land in England and get combat orders. All of us allowed that we would be assigned a post in Northern Europe, thinking that in no time we'd be fighting the Krauts on their home soil.

Ike had pushed the bastards out of France, most of it anyway, with D-Day. The Brits had been fighting since the beginning and were worn down like a pencil eraser that had tried for years to scrub a tragic ending from a book being written by the damn German and Italian Nazis. The French army was finished, corralled like calves by the Nazi army, though the guerrilla warfare against the Krauts by the Resistance was heroic and damn effective. Our boys were primed for a full-scale offensive, which I thought, wrongly, I am damn sorry to report, would come just about the moment our boots touched continental soil.

Me? I wanted the pleasure of dogging the infernal German army all the way back to Berlin and giving 'em a heavy dose of the misery they had dished out to others. We would mess up the Fatherland until we brought the Kraut hoard to its knees and put that mustached bastard, goose step and all, on ice. None of us, if we were still alive, wounded or not, Shinn included, would ever have considered goin' home until the enemy had experienced our ill temper. And we had ended their shit show for good.

Few of us had seen combat, but no matter. We were ready, or, rather we thought we were ready. Myself, I came down with a bad case of what my old friend Leo Graham called 'hubris' as I waited for orders to go after the Hun. Over-estimating myself and underestimating the Germans poisoned my thinking and gave me a false sense of security. It affected the readiness of my command, a mistake I worried I could never make up for. Our generals, at least some of 'em, speculated before the attack that the Germans were probably on their last legs. I am amazed at what little we knew. And how I went along with that thinking, despite my periods of uneasiness, as our months of waiting for battle dragged on like a life sentence in solitary.

Shinn was tough to figure out. Graduated college and enlisted as a private in the army. Then after a couple years, he volunteered for Officer School and earned his commission. He already had a preacher's degree and could have served in the Chaplain Corps, which meant he probably would get out of the war in one piece. But the guy wanted to be a combat infantry-man! Helluva thing! Pick ten guys in their twenties random off the street and line 'em up with Shinn. Then pick three you think most likely to be a combat soldier. No one would have picked Shinn. Shaking his hand was like gripping a fresh cow pie. He was a skinny feller, looked like a malnourished librarian.

He wasn't one. Though to his credit he did know his books. If you don't look below the finish, you never know the quality of the timber. No soldier in our battalion, officer or enlisted, had more guts than the vicar. At the same time he lit a path for us and warned that war perverts. And changes all destinies.

Part II

THE VOYAGE

Who, constructing the house of himself or herself, not for a day but for all
time, sees races, eras, dates, generations,
The past, the future, dwelling there, like space, inseparable
      together.
                      —Walt Whitman, 1819-1892

Chapter 1

THE CAPTAINS

The current issue of the *New York Herald Tribune*, dated Jan. 5, 1965, under the arm of a lone figure, flapped in the wind. The newspaper carried reports of the death of T.S. Eliot on page one and a brief report on page eleven of a Viet Cong military offensive in South Vietnam. According to the four-inch article, the battle inflicted heavy casualties in the town of Binh Gia. The figure, hunched and wearing a coffee-colored beret, inched forward against the blowing snow. To prevent the winter's gale from breaching his dark, boiled-wool overcoat, he gripped its collar in a near stranglehold around his neck. Having decamped at 6:41 A.M. from the bus at West 120th St and Amsterdam Avenue in Manhattan's Morningside Heights neighborhood, he continued his journey, straining toward an edifice that echoed the transcendent gothic structures of France and England. Its imposing exterior dwarfed him. In his left hand the man gripped a worn leather satchel of a dusty chestnut brown that held his personal files from the Second World War, the day's lecture notes, and a small tortoise-shell plastic comb.

A gust caught him head on. Quicker now, he marched through the campus of Columbia University, crossed Broadway and veered toward a sign that read "Union Theological Seminary" where he left the blizzard and entered the building, appearing to be the first on site. Inside the rotunda he paused to wipe his raw nose and slippery upper lip with a handkerchief.

He pressed his palms against frigid ears, removed his overcoat and a tawny scarf, which he stuffed into a coat sleeve. This trim fellow of medium stature was in his late 40s. His dark brown suit, horn-rimmed glasses and thinning hair, oiled so it lay close to his scalp, contributed to a look of bland resoluteness. From a distance, Roger Lincoln Shinn, professor of philosophy and religion, could have been mistaken for a Manhattan insurance actuary or a Madison Avenue comptroller tracking margins on breakfast food advertising for a top national brand.

Before opening the door to a suite of small offices on the seminary's second floor, the professor punctured the tranquility by stomping the last of the snow from his rubber boots, the sound like a low faraway cannon, which echoed through the building's august granite and limestone cavity. He picked up the boots and entered.

"You're here early, professor!" A disembodied voice jumped out from behind a desk lit by a solitary lamp. It carried an edge not unlike the wind he just left.

Looking up, he saw Eve Spektor, his academic secretary of ten years. She was deep into scheduling for midterm exams. There was a cake doughnut beside her, mostly gone. "Any hot tea?" he pleaded with feigned anxiety. "And good morning, Eve! Yes, uh, I am altering my plan for spring term, so I have a lot of work to do."

Holding in one hand a cup of orange pekoe black tea that Eve gave him, and his overcoat in the other, the shivering academic undertook to turn the doorknob to his office. Lettered on the door window, in formal black typography, "Roger Lincoln Shinn" above, in smaller letters, "Reinhold Niebuhr Professor of Social Ethics." His hand slipped off the brass doorknob dumping the hot liquid onto his shoes. "Damn!"

"What is your research on, professor, 'Vulgarities in Mid-Century Academia'?" Eve chided as if the word poisoned her ears.

"No, in the original scriptures," Shinn deadpanned as he backed into the office using his body to push open the door.

Eve stared at him. "In the Gnostic Gospels, no doubt," she answered, returning to her doughnut and test scheduling.

"War is the topic, Eve. War, the curse of Cain, 'the maker of men.' I am about to loose the dogs of war. On my class!"

He ended his theatrical flourish murmuring, "Once more into the breach…." The professor closed the door.

"What the hell does he know about war?" Eve whispered under her breath.

Roger Shinn, who earned his Ph.D. at Columbia University just a block from his office, sat down at his desk in an unlit room. He pulled the cord on a desk lamp with an emerald glass shade. Then he removed his shoes and socks, drew another folded cotton handkerchief from his pocket, and wiped dry his bare feet. Still amused at Eve's mild rebuke and his display of clumsiness, he tossed the wet socks onto the radiator. They sizzled, and he took a sip of tea. "Ugh, too weak," he mumbled. "Angel piss as our GIs would say."

Taking a deep breath the professor pulled a ratty olive-drab accordion folder from his satchel. He paused and stared at it before loosening the string that had held its musty contents from the world for so many years. As he began to open the flap he halted, again. Maybe it is too soon, Shinn thought. Without looking inside he gently laid the folder back on his desk as he would a creature he feared to wake. He put his feet on the desk and closed his eyes. A minute or two had passed when Shinn's office door opened with a jolt.

Emeritus Professor of Philosophy Eberhard Dagg, senescent, rheumatic, owly, early eighties, looking as if his wife had fed him a stone for breakfast, began, "Professor Shhhh…" When his one good eye caught Shinn's pale white feet propped on the desk he stopped. "I'll come back when you're dressed," Dagg sniffed.

Without giving his colleague a thought, Shinn reached for the folder and slowly removed its contents, laying it all out before him. Military maps, yellowed rosters, reports, copies of orders, letters, two diaries and a collection of black and white photos. The professor had begun his exhumation of his time, his being, his ordeal in battle as an officer in the Second World War.

He held two creased photographs up to the early morning light. Though looking as if little more than wisps of smoke, they drew him into a past he had long avoided. Feared, even, to remember. One of the photos was of himself. Dressed in a crisp Army uniform, he stood on the shore of the English Channel looking with delight into the camera. With him was another officer. The second photo he took himself. It was of the same officer balancing precariously on a high cliff bordering Luxembourg and Germany.

The dawn gathered in Shinn's office like flares in a gem and the cold-violet interior warmed to ochre and orange. "Time that you address my class, Captain Hall, from wherever you are," he whispered.

The professor opened a brown folder marked with a "War Department" imprimatur. His left index finger ran down a list of names mimeographed in black onto sheets of thick newsprint now brittle as winter leaves. Carefully, he touched each name as if trying to memorize grains of sand without disturbing them. Eve opened the door.

"Would you like another cup, Roger?"

Shinn did not hear.

"How about a glazed doughnut up your nose?"

No response. She left.

Deep in concentration the professor reviewed twenty-year-old battalion morning reports from the war. Now, years later, they were speaking to him again: the day's manpower numbers, action in battle, casualties including those from his unit, Company C, 60th Armored Infantry Battalion, 9th Armored Division. He picked up one of his war diaries. Oblivious to the sigh that escaped his throat, he set the journal aside. Like it was Pandora's mythical box. Or a reliquary.

Notes Shinn scribbled frantically after the war while in a field hospital in Brandenburg an der Havel and later at the Convalescent Hospital in London were now before him: recollections of action in the Ardennes Forest and elsewhere which he sharpened, adding detail, on his return trip home. He felt a compulsion to get his thoughts down for he feared time would blunt and distort recall. Or his conscious being would partition his memory, making the actuality of experience irretrievable, even if he wanted to resurrect it.

"I had to get it all down," he remembered. "I could not leave anything to reminiscence."

The former Army officer rose from his chair, stretched and leaned on the thick stone sill below a tall, reticulated gothic window that swooped up to its apex as if pointing all eyes away from earth. Snow and a winter gale attacked the panes. It sounded to him like the crack of electricity. Shinn expelled the present from his lungs. His breathing came forward and the war charged through his mind like a wild boar. At first, the crispness of his recall shook his equilibrium. Then a strange insistence overcame him and he was ready to allow the serenity and the tempest from decades past to inform the present.

From out of his office window the balding professor gazed through the membrane of time. Images flashed and shimmered like clips scissored from a 16-millimeter home movie. A dropped fly ball, his lost dog. Bees in hollyhocks. A broken pitcher. His triumphant role as Laertes in college. His correspondence with Albert Einstein. Reinhold Niebuhr's Windsor knots. Turgenev's novel left on the staircase. Chalkboard scratchings on the nature of existence. His courtship of Katharine Cole. And finally a field of brass casings.

Outside, the snow and ice storm worsened.

Beyond where trees lined the panoramic Columbia University commons, a few dark forms appeared. Then hundreds. Then thousands dashed toward his keep. On their heads steel helmets, German Stahlhelms with their distinctive coal-scuttle contour, which provoked in him a cellular fear. In the invaders' arms were Walther combat rifles superior to the carbine he carried.

The mass moved closer. Revenants. Silent. Virgin snow exploded from under their bootfalls almost erasing their forms. In this boreal wildness behind the stampeding Volksgrenadier infantrymen, Nazi Panzers, the lethal German tank, crawled from the woods, iron beasts seeking alien hearts. The reckoning force spread and surrounded him; this colossal Teutonic drama, fearless and flanking, seemed beyond mortal conception. Above it all the professor heard a single gunshot from another time and place, and he flinched. A stripling, mid-teens in farm clothes lay motionless on the campus green below him. A summer sun emerged from above lead-colored hills. Gnats and stoneflies raked the boy's face, which was flushed by heat and veined with perspiration. A man knelt beside him.

The inert boy moved.

Removal of the Springfield rifle from its weld on his cheek was unrushed. The youth peered into a pocked military telescope carried at the Battle of the Argonne by a lost relative who watched the quick become acquainted with the dead. Only then did the kid release his breath.

The round had cut the wind with thunder and whistle and burrowed into the intimate space of two other black holes, like tiny bruises that marked the white paper target. A Winged Liberty silver dime, had he owned one, would have covered all the punctures. The man beside the boy stood up. He was in uniform. And he clapped.

The teenage shooter peeked up at the standing figure and grinned.

From his window perch the professor whispered, "Good shooting, Captain Hall."

Chapter 2

GORDIAN KNOT

Prof. Shinn heard a knock on his office door and turned.

"Hi, Roger. You okay, old thing?" came a voice from a head peeking in the entrance. "Eve says you're damn near catatonic and refused a doughnut. That's not like you. So I thought I'd see if I should call an ambulance or the coroner."

"Come on in, Phil. Need a cup? Who you callin' old?"

"Eve poured me one, thanks," he replied.

Professor of Biblical Languages, Philip Sekou Chikelu, late thirties, stood in the doorway. The crown of his head was less than six inches from the top of the seven-foot threshold. He wore, as he often did, a body shirt made in southern Nigeria, this one black with native fauna and flying birds in yellow and blue.

"So to what do I owe the pleasure of a visit from our university's esteemed authority on ancient Aramaic semi-colons?"

His colleague laughed at the tease.

"Something of the highest importance, Roger, I assure you. Or I wouldn't bother you," Sekou Chikelu grinned, his face as dark and luminous as a black opal. "Saw your light was on, so I thought I would stop in before class. Just curious if our trip to Walden Pond is still on for this summer. It's gonna be loaded with small-mouth bass!"

"I am looking forward to it, Phil, even though I'm not much of a fisherman. Been rough inside these walls and out. And my next few months probably won't be any better."

Shinn waxed eloquent on the serenity of nature. And catching "smallies."

"Speaking of rough going, are you aware that the Imperious One is out for blood? Your blood," Phil interjected.

"Dr. Dagg popped in earlier this morning. Just said he wanted to talk sometime and left."

"Not sure if it warrants your concern, but His Eminence is upset with your off-duty witchcraft, you know, advising conscientious objectors, going to anti-war rallies, and, uh, maybe not coming to work fully dressed."

Shinn giggled. "Three strikes, it looks like."

"I think he considers COs and rabble-rousers all self-absorbed cowards."

"Time for him to crush dissent," Shinn sighed. "You know all about that, Phil. Same ol' story. Test the tensile properties of liberal acquiescence and hope it doesn't snap into doing something."

"He's rattling the cages of Union donors and alumni." His friend had a troubled frown. He took a sip of coffee and pulled up a chair. A lot of Dagg's umbrage "is bouncing around Union's hallowed hallways," he informed his friend.

"Beneath it, I think he's concerned about positions you've taken on the global rights of women, or their lack thereof," Sekou Chikelu continued, "and your work with the UN. But on the surface, the old boy is challenging your patriotism, Roger."

"I'm nowhere in the vicinity of worrying about him, my friend. Eb has been pedaling backwards for some time."

Shinn handed Sekou Chikelu his folder from the Second World War. Phil pulled out black and white images of Shinn and the soldiers in his unit.

"I'm tackling some heady stuff this term. But I'll meet with him, if he has the vapors," Shinn said, breaking the gravity of the conversation with the slight and a grin.

"'Heady stuff,' indeed," the biblical scholar murmured. He reviewed an image of a burning American tank.

"World War Two. Humanity and ethics. Relating actual battle experiences and my capture by the Nazis to the conundrum of moral decision-making versus accomplishing a mission. That's code for 'how the hell can we take part in war and not lose our minds. And our innermost self?'"

Sekou Chikelu looked up from the photograph with a start. "Whoa! You have always been reluctant to talk about your past, Roger. Not even your friends, me included, know what the hell went on over there. Why now? And with your students?"

"For a long time I wanted my war years to be my gone years." But the once infantry captain had contemplated for months talking about his former life with students of social ethics. "I feel the moment has come." Shinn looked out on the gathering daylight. "It's like Thomas Wolfe's charge to open the window of time."

Phil stroked his chin. "Sounds like you are stepping into historian's shoes."

"Nah," the professor scoffed. "I'm no historian. Nor am I interested in a historical reconstruction of the Second World War. I will present a story. A personal experience. It may allow my students to better grip the sweep of it all, of war, the interior and exterior of...."

"How the past stirs the present," Sekou Chikelu interjected.

The fastidious reader of newspapers, journals, playwrights' scripts, books, and matchbook covers set his cup on the windowsill. "Young American men aren't the only ones facing today's killing fields, are they?" Shinn mused looking out at the campus and recalling an earlier discussion. "You said the Igbo people are facing it in Africa. Biafra, you said, will go to war for independence."

Sekou Chikelu nodded slowly. "Killing humans may be simple for some, but the moral geometry is complicated," he muttered with unfocused eyes.

"As a Gordian Knot," Shinn replied.

The African shifted in his chair. "I assume soldiers must consider their actions every time they fix bayonets or post a blockade or activate a missile?"

A smirk popped from Shinn's throat. "In war death quickly becomes routine. Most GIs do not struggle to unravel the Gordian Knot of morality," the former soldier laughed. "We just teach them 'kill or be killed.' Victory above all else. Yes, simple."

"Then it sounds to me less like a Gordian Knot and more like the Schwarzschild Radius…"

"Ha!" Shinn interrupted. "You mean the cosmological threshold from which nothing escapes and nothing returns? I had forgotten you were a quantum physics guy before you became a language guy. But…."

Surprised his colleague knew the term, Sekou Chikelu briefly interrupted with an unreserved roar.

"… maybe a better definition is, 'from whose bourn no traveler returns,'" Shinn, the old thespian, quoted from *Hamlet*.

Sekou Chikelu's repartee with this esteemed and unassuming philosopher of ethics in his sanctuary of coffee, tea and books was always pleasure, even in argument.

"I guess I can understand the 'kill or be killed' thing, Roger," Sekou Chikelu lamented. "Though I won't cheer for it." His expression skewed and facial lines emerged like invisible ink under a candle. "What I cannot comprehend is the public, and why it commits its sons and daughters to such savagery with so little hesitation."

Shinn nodded and shifted the conversation as he prepared his satchel. "My focus will be on another captain. An unorthodox soldier and the headquarters company commander in my battalion."

Removing now-dry socks from the radiator, Shinn slipped them on with routine precision. Their warmth revived his chilled feet. "Normal contours of battle didn't seem to interfere with what he had to do." The professor tied his shoes. "Some looked up to him. Others thought he should have been court-martialed. A few considered him an outright traitor."

"How do you know enough about this man to recount his story, Roger?"

"Got to know him on the ship taking us to the European front. Then I was with him at the beginning of Battle of the Bulge. Until I was captured."

Sekou Chikelu's eyes widen.

"And I chatted with soldiers in our unit after the war." Shinn talked as he collected his material for class. "On the troopship returning us to the states. About the fabled Capt. Hall."

Phil made a face, took the last sip of coffee, and lighted his pipe. "You're right, Roger. Come summer you will need a lot of pond time." He closed the door quietly and left.

Chapter 3

AND WHAT DO YOU KNOW ABOUT WAR?

T he professor posed a question to his class. "Can we as human beings be lethal *and* ethical? If our destinies are no one's responsibility but our own, are we able to take lives and keep possession of our self-worth? Our integrity? Our personal identity?"

Shinn was reputed to be a hard grader and rigorous questioner. When he announced cutting much of the reading list from the semester's syllabus and focusing on a personal story from what "military historians have called the greatest single battle" the U.S. Army ever fought, the students were slack-jawed. They had expected a mountain of reading.

He took out his notes and cleared his throat.

"We will discuss the moral implications of the Ardennes Forest Campaign in the Second World War. You probably know it as the 'Battle of the Bulge,' named by someone with an alliteration fetish." Shinn winked at the class but got no response. Outlining the German offensive that began without warning on December 16, 1944, and in the space of days left eighty thousand American dead and wounded in its wake, the professor set the scene.

"Within hours of the German attack, which most never dreamed possible and launched after five years of war, the American Army was in chaos," he admitted. "As late as the day before the onslaught, American generals thought Adolf Hitler and the Third Reich were finished. Forty-eight hours later the same people feared the war would go in the wrong direction."

Shinn scanned a few faces. He saw a uniform look of quandary. This pleased him. Inchoate dilemma is where he preferred to begin.

"I would like to bring you into battle as a witness. And use this experience for our exploration of ethics…"

Ariel Jeffers, a history major from Mill Valley, California, addressed the slightly built academic as if he were a trespasser. "Doctor Shinn, please, what do you know about war?" She removed her glasses and glared at the professor. "My father fought in one. And he…he gave his life at Luzon." Expressions of shock filled the room. Jeffers' face flushed. The professor didn't respond to her missile but finished his opening thought.

"By the end of term I want you all to appreciate that the phenomenon of human warfare—its majesty, its ridiculousness, its carnage, its insufferable longevity, its monumentality, its vacantness—will challenge you to the edge of your comprehension."

A brassy student returned to the thread. "I too wonder about Jeffers's point. What does an Ivy-League professor know about the killing fields of war? Nothing! Though I am not sure trusting a military man to talk about ethics is a good move either, Ariel," Brooklyner Robert Newman stated bluntly, asserting that "third-hand accounts," "nationalist doggerel and patriotic bon mots" from old generals would "lard the class with nonsense."

As the two rested on their promontories, the professor deferred to others.

Another student stated she was wary of prejudging the class or the professor. Mia Rivera peered down at the desk where her fingers surveyed its surface before turning to Jeffers and Newman with a contemptuous glare. "Nor do I believe any of us want our time interrupted every two sentences with commentary."

Her rebuke brought loud condemnations from Jeffers and Newman and other students joined in the fray with their opinions. All spoke at once and the class broke into a frenzy.

After getting the students to calm down, the professor squeezed in four more sentences. "You are about to get a view of war, through my eyes and those of a captain I knew. A farm kid who had joined the Oklahoma National Guard. After the Japanese attacked Pearl, he put in for Army Officer Candidate School. The man was a committed soldier, but wayward, one might say." As the students exited the room, the uproar arose again.

Chapter 4

BURNING CARD

The late-afternoon winter sky was dark as a clowder of inky cats. It was a time of enjambed melancholy seeping around the city lights. As Prof. Shinn made his way from Columbia University toward St. James Methodist Episcopal Church on 126th in East Harlem, it snowed. The flakes appeared dirty to him as they coursed through the forever twilight of street lamps and joined the exhaust of the city. To the weary professor the haze reminded him of smoke and fume, murky and acrid, pouring from the muzzles of field cannons. A student protest rally at the St. James prompted Shinn to delay dinner with his family. He had to hear what those at the gathering would say about Vietnam.

By the time he arrived, people had packed the sanctuary. The professor was tired and preferred not to stand. Taking one of the few remaining seats, he positioned himself in a spot that provided a graceful exit should he wish to leave mid-rally.

At least eighty percent of the gathering was under thirty years of age. He recognized some older faces, faculty mostly: Dreyfus of Barnard College, Gibbons and Velychenko from Union and Grondin who taught art history at Columbia. The room was too warm and radiators clanged as if there were prisoners inside them striking the bars with tin plates. The professor closed his eyes. He is in a Nazi interrogation cell. Standing above him, surreal and vivid, is a German SS officer in a pitch-colored uniform. His mouth is distorted in a silent scream. Shinn jerked and his eyes opened when the minister of the church, a small black man with a deep baritone voice, awakened the crowd while a tall man moved into the pew next to the professor.

"Did I see you snoozing," Philip Sekou Chikelu teased as he shoe-horned himself next his friend.

"Just gathering my wits, professor," Shinn whispered. "Good to see you out and about, Phil."

The St. James minister introduced the first speaker, a young black man in jeans, long-sleeved tee shirt, and a vest. A colorful band circled his head. He held the floor for about eight minutes. His mastery of speaking directly to students fired up the assembly. When he raised the question of "why poor black Americans and poor white Americans and poor brown and red Americans should kill poor Vietnamese" on the far side of an "ocean whose name means peace," the crowd erupted in shouts and applause. Shinn noticed a few along the sides of the sanctuary were as unmoved as corpses. One of them was Eberhard Dagg. The professor assumed the others were J. Edgar Hoover's eyes and ears.

The next speaker condemned the draft and the American bombing of North Vietnam. The crowd turned frenetic. Shinn, feeling that he had absorbed all he could, rose to leave. His wife Katharine had promised fried chicken.

The reverend announced, "Please welcome Robert Newman, a gradu-ate student at Columbia. He will speak on the delusions of violence."

Shinn re-took his seat.

"War. We all know what war is." A fury climbed from Newman's throat. "Except we forget it at the most important hour: when politicians first rattle their swords, talk about an evil about to destroy us, and demand we preserve the nation's so-called 'honor.' They tell us America cannot appear 'weak,' as if diplomacy enfeebles and killing people in other places is power."

The crowd was quiet, listening. Phil nudged his friend in the ribs. "This guy has skills," he whispered.

"We are told America is a moral nation, therefore our actions are virtuous. And we capitulate to this fantasy. We become worshipers of Mars. The trumpets addle our reason. We are dizzied by the callow drama of drums. The chevrons. The braided fourragères. The spangles. The joyful cries of children on the parade route. Do you hear them?" Newman took a drink of water as if to flush away any inhibitions that might have restrained his tongue. "Then there are the anthems. Glorious colors 'a flyin' in the wind! Hands over the hearts! How wonderful the feet marching to America's delusion of self-eminence!"

The audience stirred and encouraged the orator like Pentecostals rallying to a quaking minister. Individual voices rose like fish to surface. "You tell it." "Amen." "Speak it, brother!"

Newman's homily reached a crescendo when he asserted that generations return to war out of ignorance and emotion.

"We critique nothing, remember nothing. Nothing that matters," he closed. "In the beginning, we never think. We just salute. That, my friends, is about to change!"

On the way home, Shinn thought about the gathering at St. James Church. The falling snow now seemed to glitter in the night air. He contemplated war, the precariousness of the twentieth century, the escalating intolerance of dissent. His rubber boots blemished the snow's satiny accumulation. Seeing people huddled in an alley triggered a memory of a disheveled teen from the Catholic Worker Movement. A few months earlier the young man had been photographed burning his draft card at the Armed Forces Induction Center on Whitehall Street. City police arrested him soon after. Shinn knew that for many such an act of defiance, the refusal to fight in an American war, would have been a rank betrayal in 1941. Tonight the youth's flaming card was like a lamp in the professor's mind.

Chapter 5

THE FIRE AS LAMP

Two days after his first class erupted in disorder, Prof. Roger Lincoln Shinn, faculty at Union Theological Seminary and Columbia University, ethicist, philosopher, author, public intellectual, and a leader in the Protestant ecumenical movement; born in Germantown, Ohio, January 6, 1917, son of Reverend Henderson L. V. Shinn and Carrie Margaret Shinn; B.A., Heidelberg College, Tiffin, Ohio, 1938; Master of Divinity, summa cum laude, Union Theological Seminary 1941; doctorate, Columbia University, 1949; ordained in the United Church of Christ, stood again in front of his class unsure of himself. For today he was to unearth, publicly, the unquiet elements from his past.

As students from Union and Columbia entered, the professor had an uncommon awareness of the details and scents of this familiar place. Men and women settled behind walnut and iron furniture bolted to an oak floor. He observed the desks. Once aligned in precise columns, they now were a shade off center and years of accumulated scars and marks, as if from the crossfire of competing ideas and whipsaw of changing attitudes, stood visible across their surfaces.

Today aromatic juniper filled the room. Someone had plucked a sprig and massaged it between their fingers. Its perfume replaced the odor of veneration and the professor smiled weakly as he arranged on the lectern his sparse notes hand-written on two recipe cards the color of the Eucharist.

This course was aridly named: "20th-Century Ethical Challenges." Only Katharine, the professor's wife, had heard the story Shinn was about to tell, and then only a part of it.

Images of his days in the Second World War was moored for years in the remote harbors of the former infantryman's mind, flickering, fading, crystallizing and ultimately blurring.

The class waited. He filled his lungs with air and released to ready himself to speak again. Except for the clock's pricking of the silence, hardly a sound existed. Shinn's uneasiness was palpable and transferred itself to the students in front of him who were unaccustomed to anything from him but self-assurance. Though often a renegade, a contrarian, a dissenter, a pusher of ecumenical boundaries in the so-called Golden Epoch of American Protestantism at odds with the world's Age of Anxiety, nothing ever appeared to disturb his cosmos. From a distance he was as even and proportionate as his wardrobe: a conservative blue suit crafted with precision to his narrow-gauged contour. He had threaded a skinny prosaic belt through six loops of worsted wool trousers and balanced horn-rimmed glasses on his nose like the scales of justice. Yet a closer review of the professor's attire mirrored his penchant for dissent, his lack of interest in what he called the inconsequential. Men's fashion, for instance. Emerging from under his starched collar was a shockingly brazen tie, a decade out of fashion. It was tightly knotted as if a clench could hold a splintered world in place. Clipped to it an understated silver clasp threw reflected flares around the room. Shinn's time-worn black brogues partially hid unmatched socks. The early morning trill of juncos outside his bedroom window had taken his focus from dressing. He hadn't noticed his gaucherie, nor would he have cared.

No one could have suspected that this man had been a predator in combat. Every gesture, every utterance evinced a gentleman who had devoted his existence and career to the life of the mind and the centrality of his liberal faith. The professor looked out at the kaleidoscopic assembly: multifarious, keen-eyed, a whirlwind of disparate attitudes, ethnicities, aspirations, circumstances and torments, students seeking to fulfill purpose through religion, philosophy, mathematics, political science, history, humanities, anthropology, and diplomacy. Besides youth, the one common ingredient was restlessness. Shinn earlier had observed that the churn of recent events had dislodged them from complacency. Dissatisfaction, he believed, was an asset in life and the door to human progress. In no small measure the professor felt an obligation to the ethical and intellectual husbandry of the future, which included poking holes in students' circumscribed notions of reality.

"I should like to begin with an excerpt from a poem by Thomas Hardy," the professor finally announced, offering no context.

To know what? questioned I.
To know how things have been going on earth and below it:
It is clear he must know some day.
I thereon asked them why....

Willing at times to walk away from neatly interconnected transitions, Shinn pivoted to a former teacher and what he called "the furniture" of power. "German theologian Dietrich Bonhoeffer taught students of Columbia University and Union Theological Seminary, including me, using this podium," Shinn told the class.

Bonhoeffer, a mythic figure even then, was a kind of research chemist of heaven and earth. From behind round, wire-rimmed glasses peered an intellect that excited audiences on both sides of the Atlantic when he spoke of something as obscure as a rabbi from two millennia past, or any other subject. But the astonishing theologian stepped out of the ancient world and forever into the present when, while in Germany, he publicly challenged Adolf Hitler and became a force pushing societies to reconsider the purpose of organized religion. Why, he asked, did the German Protestant church and other denominations fail to stand up to the storm of fascism?

"From the moment he entered a room people quieted, time paused, and all stopped to hear him," Shinn remembered.

In 1939 after the Nazi Wehrmacht invaded Poland, Bonhoeffer left Union to return to Germany. He was not to see his fortieth birthday. "Determined to end the regime of Adolf Hitler, he worked with the German Resistance and was party to the attempt on the Führer's life at the Wolf's Lair bunker," the professor confessed. The room was silent in astonishment.

The Reich imprisoned and tortured Bonhoeffer before hanging him days before the war ended.

"Bonhoeffer the teacher, thinker, and student of language and the political subversive illuminated my path. He challenged my understanding of 'reality' and altered my course in life." In the frame of a second, Shinn saw the German theologian in front of his class and tears gathered in his eyes.

Clearing his throat, the teacher peered over his glasses. Steadier now, and feeling a rush of adrenaline, he set the stage. A new American offensive on foreign soil, following two world wars and an undeclared war on the Korean peninsula—all in the same century—became his backdrop.

"It is time for us to look into the red-eyed dogs of war," he announced. "Confronting the moral paradox of state-sponsored killing in pursuit of political ends will cap our examination of twentieth-century ethics."

The professor asked if anyone knew the origin of the phrase, "dogs of war."

A response from the rear of the classroom, "Marc Antony in Shakespeare's *Julius Caesar*."

"Thank you, Mister Newman. You a theater major as an undergraduate?" Shinn responded, knowing the answer.

"Mathematics," Newman replied. The walls shook with laughter.

"Ahh, a universal man," Shinn anointed him and moved to the lectern's side.

"The dogs of war. Why dogs?"

Students' eyes migrated from note taking and the windows to him.

"For the Roman general, Marc Antony, 'dog' was an apt metaphor, don't you think? Feral. Tribal. Savage in pursuit of prey. They appear, they destroy, they eat, they move to another kill. What better symbol for the reality of war?"

Jeffers raised her hand. But before Shinn acknowledged her she throws down her challenge. "War is more complicated than this."

"Is it?" he probed. "Before we tackle that, let me ask this: predatory pack dogs, they appear in an instant, out of nowhere, then inflict havoc on the living. Same for war, Mr. Newman? Ms. Jeffers? Ms. Rivera? Anyone?"

"Hardly," Newman answered. "When war breaks out, it is no surprise to those who are awake in the world. War is the result of a long line of blunders. Spears and bullets fly from an aged swamp of miscalculations and misdeeds."

"Not all wars arise from 'blunders,'" Jeffers threw back. "You cannot support that position!"

Shinn scanned the class. "Ms. Jeffers, point aside, were the seeds of yesterday's Boer War in Africa, for example, and today's conflict in Southeast Asia, planted before they sprouted, as Mr. Newman suggests?"

"We will never get rid of war," another student moaned. "It is not an abnormality at all."

"So the 'dogs' are a metaphor for human nature," the professor summarized. "'Red-eyed' because they never sleep. Never retreat to the cave? If this is the case, then why do we bother getting all worked up over it," he asked as the class processed the conundrum, "if armed conflict is nothing more than a natural human appetite for someone else's blood, trinkets and territory?"

The professor complicated the quandary. "Do we have the right to pass judgment on human nature? Do individual soldiers who fight on behalf of their country and its collective instincts warrant society's condemnation?"

Having posed these challenges, the former infantry officer stood and studied the room of forty-one students who were wrestling with these questions. No one spoke until Rivera threw a bomb.

"Perhaps war is organic only to patriarchies. For most women, love is the instinct above all others, the love and protection of children, preserving the family. Not killing. Wars continue because our gender has no power."

Shinn guided his hands into his pockets and walked to the right of the stage. He waited. Like a grand master expecting his opponent's next chess move. Several young men appeared eager to counter Rivera's pronouncement. But they chose not to pursue it.

"Ms. Rivera brings forward an important point," the professor remarked, breaking the stalemate. "I know that a lot of American and German, French, Italian, Polish, Japanese, English, and Ethiopian soldiers did not want or need the Second World War."

The class stirred.

"For mothers who see husbands and sons off to war," Jeffers countered, voice raised, "theirs is a sacrifice of love, the love of country, the love for future generations whom they are protecting."

Newman scoffed and shoved his books to the floor. The concussion caused the class to jump.

Rivera turned and glared at Jeffers. "That may be how women rationalize their compliance. But they don't believe it, not if they are honest with themselves."

"The lecture has become a battlefield," Álvaro Belloc laughed.

Newman was having none of it. "Let's cut the levity! The question is this: Should we pass judgment on countries who take up arms? The answer is yes, even if warfare is a basic human instinct."

"Why?" Shinn asked neutrally.

Newman responded as if addressing a jury. "We must subjugate our destructive instincts! We know in our hearts that war and virtue are on opposite ends of the moral spectrum!"

"How can you be so sure, Robert?" Shinn asked calmly.

"How can you not be sure, professor!"

Hearing raised voices, people in the hallway stopped and peered into the classroom.

"The premise is flawed," Newman charged. "And it does not change reality!"

"And to which reality are you referring, Mr. Newman?"

"The reality that war by definition is unethical! Immoral! Brainless! The reality that , uh, bellico-centric cultures must endure. It is pure game— of negative numbers! Except if you're in business selling to the military."

"Just gonna wish war away, Newman?" Jeffers chided. "Why didn't anyone think of that?"

Newman said nothing.

"What's the matter, Robert? Got an inexpressible truth stuck in your throat?" Rivera added.

Newman shook his head and the room settled.

"One point, er, query." The professor smiled as he made his way to the podium and the paradox. "Am I goading anyone to enlist or march in the parade?"

Shinn moved to the front of the stage. "Let's return to Ms. Jeffers' earlier thought. Should we consider, as she said, that 'war is more complicated' than common notions of it?" He looked at Newman, then down, advanced a few steps rightward without a word as if searching for resolutions that might rise from the floorboards and float into his students' minds. Drawing his gaze back to the class, he answered his own question. "Yes, I think we should."

Chapter 6

SHADOW PEOPLE

What followed four days later began differently. The students had mostly enjoyed the previous hurley-burley and hoped this session would be as lively.

"A number of important ethical questions were raised in the previous class," the professor started. "Is war unethical by definition? Is fighting an aggressor country an act of hate or, at least, partially, love? Is reality a concept shared by all? Or is it a manufactured state created by each of us individually? Are those who continue to fight our wars immoral, duped into service?"

Something was always roiling Shinn, his "cavalry of stampeding thoughts." And he decided before this session to begin at the actual beginning. "We cannot comprehend soldiers at war in a moral context if we don't begin well before they step into battle," Shinn submitted.

"All new trainees are forced to cross a threshold from one world, from one so-called reality, into another," the professor asserted. "I crossed it when I took my Army physical, which every American male must endure whether or not they go into the service. So let's begin there."

Shinn glanced at his notes and coughed. The professor's anxiety appeared to have left him. His suit coat wrapped the back of an empty first-row chair as if warming the shoulders of a child.

"Glimpses from the raw experiences of others, as Bonhoeffer might say, can re-orient our understanding. I believe mine can play such a role." And he began his recollection of his Army physical to the class.

On the twenty-first of December 1941, snow fell on and off all night. At 5:45 a.m. men were shoveling the parking lot at the Jefferson Bus station in Tiffin, Ohio. Heidelberg College senior Roger Shinn arrived, purchased his ticket and sat on the last seat in the waiting room, a hard, uncomfortable space between a toothless elderly white woman who was snoring and a large black man smoking a hand-rolled cigarette. The bench moved slightly when young Shinn sat despite its being fastened to the cement floor. The begrimed room was vacuous, illuminated by only three forlorn bulbs suspended by sticky tar-colored electrical cables dropped from jagged holes in the tin ceiling. Dead flies from summers past, unable to break free from the mysterious goo coating the wires, lay in state. At 6:11 a.m., young Shinn and thirty-nine other males from corners unknown boarded a bus at the town's dark perimeter. The marquee above the bus's front window read, "Fort Hayes."

Once every fortnight men between the ages of sixteen and thirty-nine from all over Ohio took their army physical at the compound. When called, attendance was mandatory, the round trip and examination stealing a Saturday from them. However, in 1941, the Great Depression having had its way with both blue and white-collar families, Saturdays did not differ much from any other day. It was a day without. Unlike Shinn, many on the Jefferson Bus Line longed for a good meal and relief from joblessness. "All imma lookin' for is somethin' close to a stable life," a new recruit with a leaking nose whispered in Shinn's ear. For many, the military offered escape, if, in their words, they were "fortunate enough" to be accepted into its ranks.

"Soon after three hundred souls arrived at Ft. Hayes," Shinn said, "we laid our clothes in front of our feet and stood naked at attention in ten regimental lines inside a military garage the size of an airport hangar."

Men of every sort were side by side under towering ceilings, patrician with coal miner; Catholic with Protestant, Muslim with Hindu, Jew with Quaker; the illiterate with the lettered; the healthy with the diseased and malformed; the bathed with the filthy.

"The smell appalled me," Shinn told the class. "I had never witnessed such a thing. The odor from the bodies and the clothes they removed. The fetid breath, rotting teeth. And, ashamed to say, I was staggered by the human forms around me. The extreme physical and social affliction life levies on so many shattered my naïve illusion that I knew what was going on in the land of men. At that moment, I understood that I didn't know a damn thing about humanity or the society I inhabited." Shinn was nearly twenty-two years old.

Framed by the towering space, a staggering number of figures were physically grotesque, "dwellers of eternal night."

"I knew nothing about them. They were different, disgusting. My immaturity crowded out all empathy I should have had for these naked wretches among their brothers of privilege. All splayed out for processing in an industrial asylum built to house guns massive as the fear that created them."

The Columbus sun rushed through tall windows into the vast emptiness. "I was not seeing men made in God's image but tragically forlorn figures where perfect American bodies should have been standing. Here I had expected to see the future Army of the Republic—superior, whole, invincible."

Pale. Quavering. Bent. Those stood out in their rows like diseased husks to be culled. One had dark sockets and his hollow face made his protruding eyes look even more extreme. An immense veined purple goiter was at his throat. From the rectum of another boy hung a long intestinal abnormality.

Some had teeth the color of licorice. A few had a sightless eye. Others tremendous scars and lesions. Two youths had hydrocephaly, a condition that enlarged the head.

"A teen in the row ahead of me carried a reddish birthmark on his ochre skin. Shaped like a Balkan sea, the naevus invaded a quarter of his upper body. Where it entered his face the flesh ballooned out. He had the lip of a camel, one ear resembled a sailor's fist. To his left, a jaundiced, febrile youth had a sunken chest resembling an old grave."

Young Shinn wondered what god made these shadows. And why? Were these what the primordials allowed the jackals to delete from their tribe? Or did they anoint them shamans?

"Like twitching birds six military doctors jumped in to inspect lines of men. They examined all, the healthy and the infirm, scribbling fiercely as if into the Book of the Damned. 'Gentlemen,' they squealed with laughable seriousness, 'bend over and spread yore cheeks!' I peeked up and watched doctors in white coats whizzing by, shining their flashlights into hundreds of anuses."

Reaction from students to this macabre, carnal vision was disbelief.

"They peered at our joints and tendons. Feet and elbows, skin and scalp. Septa and lobes and scrota. Wearing lab tunics, like meat inspectors or eugenicists calculating heritage, they interrogated every orifice. Every scar. Every visible aberration. Every lesion and boil. While all of us watched and shivered."

"As you waited for the bus to take you to Fort Hayes, were you frightened?" Rivera asked. "It sounds dystopian. And I'm sure you realized this was a prelude to armed service. Forced or otherwise."

"No, I was eager," Shinn replied.

That night at his home in the upper east side Shinn entered his study, turned on the lamps and opened a drawer containing more photographs from the war: the RMS Queen Mary which transported him and his unit to Europe; a line of troops loading onto the vessel; shooting lessons on the deck. Then his eyes moved to images from a dance party thrown by the USO the day before the liner docked in Southampton, England.

Chapter 7
THE GRAY GHOST

His greeting each day varied little. "Good morning, Eve. Any hot tea?" Prof. Shinn pleaded. She would nod, sparking his march to the tea pot to fill a cup. Today she grimaced.

"Roger, we all know how smitten you are of Katharine," Eve began.

"I confess every time I am with her I melt like a starry-eyed high schooler, even after nearly twenty-five years," he acknowledged. "But why bring up my wife this morning?

"Now would be a good time to turn around and spend the day with her, have lunch at the Russian Tea Room," Eve suggested cheerfully. But her grimace returned. "Eberhard Dagg has already been in looking for you and he means you no good. We all know the man's trying to ruin your reputation." She threw a wadded paper into her waste basket. "He doesn't teach anymore so I don't know why he is hanging around. He's like a skin tag. Just thought—"

"Oh, the good professor is just trying to stay engaged, Eve," Shinn responded. "I will take K. to lunch soon, though at the Oyster Bar at Grand Central She practically inhales the Rappahannocks—" Shinn entered his office with his mind running in multiple directions and closed the door before Eve could hear the end of his sentence. A sigh escaped him and he began rummaging through his war files for class. He removed some photos taken of his voyage on the Queen Mary. One is a picture of himself with Capt. Hall on the deck. Both men were in khaki uniforms. Captain's double silver bars glimmer on both their stiff collars.

"My god, we look great!" the professor exclaimed out loud. "Just two days earlier we had vomited our damn guts out."

As Shinn did the final prep for class, Sekou Chikelu stepped into the outer office. "Good morning, Eve," he trilled having taken the pipe from his lips. "Roger in?"

"Hunkered down at his desk, Phil. I think he's playing cowboys and fascists. Go on in," Shinn's assistant responded before blowing her nose.

"Coming down with something, Eve?"

"Just a garden variety cold. It came to me special delivery a couple days ago from my fifth grader. I'll probably leave early, go home, get under the covers, drink a gallon of jasmine tea, and finish my book."

"What's the book?"

"*Life with Picasso.*"

"Ha!" Sekou Chikelu snorts. "They say books by French mistresses are pre-ordained."

"What?"

"You know, to be best sellers," he sniffed.

"Françoise Gilot has a brilliant mind and is a superb artist herself, Philip." Eve unleashed a wanton gesture making fun of Phil's comment. "No wonder ol' Pablo couldn't hang on to her!" She blows a mocking goodbye kiss to the jilted Picasso.

"Come on in, Phil," Shinn called to his friend. "What did you think of the rally at St. James?"

"A lot of bile pumped into the atmosphere. I kept picturing a whale spewing vapor though its blowhole. Hope they got whatever it was outta their systems. I didn't see much else that was positive."

"But some truth in what the speakers said, don't you think, professor?"

"Yes, but...."

"You seem unsure."

"No, I am sure they made eloquent noise."

"But no idea how to leverage their anger into a solution?" Shinn asked.

"Yep, exactly." Sekou Chikelu points at his friend showing he nailed it. "Any of your students attend, Rog?"

"One from Ethics spoke. You remember, Robert Newman."

"His words scorched the hair on my arms. Good luck with that one, Rog. Well, I'll leave you to it." The biblical languages scholar stepped toward the door.

"I've got a minute. What's on your mind?" Shinn asked.

Sekou Chikelu returned to his seat. His face was serious. "Just want to know about your ethics class."

"I am worried. Not sure whether students will engage. Get the connections, you know. The story gets raw. Intricate. Surreal. Are they ready to support or *create* alternatives to war? Are we prepared as a university? As a nation?" Shinn has pinned a frozen smile on his face. "Going back—back to the battlefield is queer, Phil. It is like I'm in the theater watching an unfamiliar incomprehensible tragedy. Sometimes roles are reversed and I am acting in the production. But there is no plot. The audience miniscule. Doesn't matter, really. My words, my knowledge, my gestures can't escape the gravity of the stage. I cannot even reach the senses of the audience. I stand naked between words inside a single line like some nonentity in a John Hawkes novel."

Phil shudders. "Why not assign them readings instead? There is a profusion of...."

"*Nein!*" Shinn yelped with amused dread. "The real war will *never* get in the books, Phil, if you remember your Whitman. Those on the front lines know the scenery. That's what civilians need now: the closest reality of our violent commotion at the grunt level. The reality of the meat grinder. Yeah, I understand that few vets talk about their experiences. And never all of it. But I can do it now. Whether my story impacts them is...." He halted. Peered out the window. "You know, Phil, the first German I saw drop from a round I fired—it gave me a feeling, I am ashamed to say—of power. Thankfully, he was too far away for me to see his face...but—I—I actually was proud of myself."

Shinn walked down the granite hallway toward the empty classroom, passing a raucous bulletin board that shouted times and dates of concerts, readings, and rallies from makeshift flyers and handbills, but he gave it no glance. Arriving in the room, the scholar set recipe cards containing his day's notes onto the lectern, removed his suit jacket, and watched the students file in like a jury. They appeared restless even as he launched into his remembrance.

"I want to tell you about the voyage," Shinn began. "In 1944, a British troopship pulled away from New York harbor near where we sit today. After having crossed the Atlantic Ocean in six days and offloading thousands of American troops onto England's shore, it would turn around, set its course for New York and more fresh soldiers."

From England scores of landing craft would take Shinn's unit toward the European front lines.

Belloc interrupted. "How do you know all of this, professor? Were you living in New York at the time?"

"I was on that ship."

Jeffers covered her face with her hands and a few gasps were heard. It was as if Prof. Shinn had removed the sheet from over a dead body.

****

These students had been in diapers when Infantry Captain Shinn boarded the Queen Mary heading for war. As the professor continued, he seemed to wrap students into the story as if history were rolling through them—most of them—like a resuscitated spirit.

In massive numbers, newly trained American soldiers sailed to Europe to support depleted allies, destroy Nazi resistance, retake occupied territory, and to drive the Germans deep into their "Fatherland" and oblige their surrender.

"We came late and were now the only fresh meat," the professor explained. "It was a tall order for us."

Before the war, The RMS Queen Mary had hosted people of wealth on voyages between England, Cherbourg, France and New York. However, when Shinn boarded her the English Navy had converted her from a rose to a sow's ear. Gone were the chandeliers, the chef's kitchens, the cherry wood paneled bars, the glorious dining rooms, the comfortable suites. Gutted and redone she could haul fifteen thousand GIs rather than two thousand from the echelons of privilege. Bare eating arenas—the Army called them mess halls for a reason—and massive open areas with thousands of hammocks swinging from naked ceiling framework and bunks secured to the floor and a few spartan officers' quarters were what had become of her.

"It was hot and overcast when this once grand British liner docked in New York harbor. She weighed in at nearly eighty-five thousand tons so she was almost as heavy as Boss Tweed after a big meal," Shinn cracked, but few got the joke. "A casualty of war some might say, but we were happy to be on a ship so large, so powerful, and so fast."

The ship's distinctive exterior, once a two-tone black and white hull with magnificent triple smokestacks of black and red, was now gray, an otherworldly hue like the ash of a forest fire. The vessel had become a gauzy, almost imperceptible silhouette against a gunmetal sea and sky.

"For German U-boats and fighter planes on search-and-destroy missions, she was all but a phantom, a ghost." Shinn was seeing the scene in the harbor and not the faces of his students.

"It took three full days to load us onto the ship. The human cargo included battlefield medical personnel. Nurses. Doctors. Surgeons. Orderlies."

For security reasons all communications regarding the ship's schedule were restricted. Even those boarding her were unsure of the time or date of their departure. There were no brass bands, champagne toasts, or relatives waving goodbye to loved ones. One night, the Queen Mary dropped her cables, lifted anchor, and departed quietly out of the harbor like a cast-off child, unloved and un-feted.

Shinn circled around the lectern, which he rarely used. The morning light was streaming through the windows. "Before the ship pulled out of New York harbor, I walked past recruits lying about the deck. Some joked around. Some played cards and threw dice. A few sang and many prayed. But the number that wept ached in me. Homesickness already had taken hold. They yearned for the place they left and, I suppose, were scared witless of the place they were going."

Three-quarters of them were new draftees. And, like Shinn, had not seen combat. Before this many hadn't traveled more than an hour from where they were born.

"They all were headed 'straight into the jaws of hell.' They knew that they were to be strangers in a strange land, a changed land, a land where people wanted to kill them, to deny their return home. They were at the nexus of two shadows. Though officer training supposedly hardened me, I was filled with sadness for them."

Shinn moved to the back of the stage, picked up a folding chair and sat in front of the class smiling.

"The first days on the open sea seemed like an eternity. The Queen was better than other troop ships. But this was no graceful cruise."

The vessel's engines operated at high speeds and the massive ocean liner zig-zagged mercilessly to evade detection. Seasickness was everywhere. Because of her prowess moving enemy troops to the battlefield, Hitler offered a bounty to any U-Boat captain who sank her: a quarter of a million Deutschmarks and the Iron Cross with an oak leaf. To keep on schedule and avoid being a sitting duck, the ship averaged between twenty-seven and twenty-eight knots on the trip, but would hit over thirty knots at her peak.

"The Queen, bless her, shook almost continually. The propellers were ill suited to the ship and caused her to vibrate. After launch, as she built power in calm waters, the vessel shuddered like an earthquake," Shinn said as he leaned forward in the chair. It creaked whenever he moved. "The waves reached a height of thirty to forty feet from trough to crest. Even those who didn't get seasick heaved for hours because the food was vile and the smell worse."

Shinn and the other officers suspected that much of the meat had already spoiled by the time the Army quartermaster secured it for the voyage. From the beginning, the odor of diarrhea, tainted pork, and warm vomit invaded the ship. After two days in the heat, the bouquet was indescribable. No one could bear going near a toilet. So the aroma of gastro-intestinal distress was spread about the decks.

"This, ladies and gentlemen, was when all of us realized we were married to the U.S. Army, and this was our damn honeymoon!" Shinn rose smiling from the creaking chair amidst a riot of laughter.

"It was on this voyage I got acquainted with another captain in my unit named Hall. A peculiar mix of by-the-book commander—when it suited him—and unruly, instinctual subordinate—when it did not. I stumbled onto John William Hall on the morning of the third day at sea. I came to consider him the best of officers. It is his story which I believe will give us insight into our topic."

Chapter 8
KINDNESS NOT FORGOTTEN

Rising early. Prof. Shinn took breakfast of a soft egg, toast and a pad of butter that melted into the bread's recesses. He caught the 6:20 bus. By 6:50 a.m. he was climbing the Union stairs. Though he taught no classes that day, his committee on new admissions met at ten o'clock and his office hours for students began at eleven.

With his arrival he retreated into his sanctuary and pulled his war diary and photographs in their silver sleeves from out of a cabinet. The first images were of destroyed Sherman tanks that once protected his battalion. They sit wan and helpless on a snowy plain. An American half-track used for transporting troops that caught a bazooka rocket in 1944 is still burning, its tires melting into the earth on a sub-zero day. He looked at his maps of troop positions around Savelborn, Beaufort, and Christnach, Luxembourg. Arcane military iconography overlays the combat zone's topographical eddies and currents. Erased pencil marks show how his unit's command post lurched from place to place during the German onslaught of Dec. 16-19, like a young hare fleeing a hungry owl.

The professor squinted again at the photo he took of Hall, the captain balancing on the gorge's edge, and moved on. Working feverishly on lecture notes for the next day's class, Shinn plotted the outline on the recipe cards before packing files of student applications into his satchel and leaving for his first meeting.

As he reached for the doorknob, Shinn spied Eberhard Dagg through the window. Dagg was waiting in the hallway. The professor hesitated; perhaps his nemesis would move on. He didn't, Shinn exited his office and was intercepted in the hall.

"Professor. I am relieved to finally catch you," Dagg said as he walked Shinn back into his office, closing the door.

"I have an appointment in ten," Shinn told him, though Dagg knew this. "Can we discuss what is on your mind when I am not so cramped for time?"

"Some faculty and alumni aren't happy with you, I am sorry to say—"

Shinn interrupted. "I asked if this could wait for a better—"

"We are at war to spread democracy to other nations," Dagg continued. "But you are counseling students on how to avoid their obligation on so-called 'moral grounds'—"

"I really am in a hurry, Eb," Shinn cut in, losing his patience. "But still understand that you are wrong. The faculty is either supportive of or blithely indifferent to my affairs off-campus." He removed his glasses. "As for our situation in Indochina, perhaps you should cut open this Vietnam-conflict thing yourself and examine its entrails. Something is not right with this fish. Have you seen a declaration of war, Eb? Maybe I missed it. Now I need—"

Dagg cut him off. "Well there has been talk and *I* am letting you know. We can't abandon our country or any other to the communists, Prof. Shinn. Some think what you are doing borders on treason, and your interpretation of scripture heresy. 'We have not come to bring peace, but a sword.'"

The younger professor took a deep breath, not willing to let Dagg's ambush slide.

"Heresy!" he sniffed." With respect, the teachings of Jesus are tuned to a political situation of two thousand years ago! They are metaphorical. Jesus of Nazareth was a dramatist! Neither his words nor the Bible make up an unabridged system of ethics or social policy—or even intelligent inquiry."

"I beg your pardon."

Shinn decided to take off the gloves. "The New Testament was written to disturb, Eb, awaken new styles of human awareness. It's not meant to dispense hardened social remedies like over-the-counter pills you pick up at our corner drug."

"Clergy and congregations all across the nation would take issue—"

"What's happened to you! We are not in the camp that regards the Texts as some infallible code of dos and do nots. But I am more than a bit surprised to see my old friend sitting around that old fire. Do you really think our faith should be a cluster of ossified creeds? Doesn't its presence, rather, move us toward unrealized possibilities of justice?"

As if putting on silver weave and grabbing his combat lance, the elder professor repeated that he is taking this issue and the "problem of raised voices" in Shinn's class to the Union president. "Nothing personal," he sneered.

He stared at Dagg in disbelief. "What is this 'raised voices' thing you have grabbed out of the blue?"

"You have lost control of your students."

"Yes, tensions have emerged," Shinn admitted, though he wanted to tell Dagg to cease his meddling. "But we're talking about war, Eb, not what kind of breakfast food we eat."

Shinn paused, checked his watch and worried about hurting his colleague.

"I will never forget your kindness, Eb, to both Katharine and me when we first came to Union. Our gratitude to you is unwavering. But please understand that what you call 'disloyalty' is just my donation to a healthy democracy."

"I fear we are at odds over this, Roger."

Shinn gasped. As he walked down the hall, he completed his point. "Washington and the Pentagon can't snap their fingers and, no matter what the particulars, expect us to line up for a merry caper in the killing fields. Not how our republic works, Eb. Nor our faith. We cannot abide such totalitarianism. We're not damned fascists!"

★★★★★★★★★★★★★★★★

At the close of a charged workday, the professor was ready for home. When he arrived, Katharine was sitting in the living room reading. She put down her book. "You look drained."

"Busy schedule, I guess. Meetings. Talking with students. And had a testy run-in with Eb today," he replied as he hung his coat in the entryway. "Guess that swallowed me up this morning and haven't gotten over it."

"Still going after you about Vietnam," Katharine divined.

"He's acting a little off, and I don't want to mistreat him. He came to my rescue, as did you, when I went into that dark room after the war."

"He was a veteran and a man of God. That made him a good confidant," Katharine said. Her hand moved to his shoulder. The other nipped his rear. He jumped and howled. "You were in a pinch, darling."

"The crusty old bastard." Shinn's face lightened. "He stuck by me. Defended my absences. Went eye-to-eye with the provost."

Chapter 9

DISPARATE CREATURES

Some memories go dormant. Some stay as vivid as the day they were logged. Those often are the bad ones. Other recollections decay and get bounced around between dreams and illusions of reality, where they get hung up somewhere like forlorn tumbleweeds caught on a barbed-wire claw on the Oklahoma plains, and then move on. I don't recall when I—with my divinity degree secured and my captain's bars on my lapel—first crossed paths with Captain Hall. However, I remember when we formally introduced ourselves. We were on the deck of the Queen Mary.

Hall had had a troubled relationship with his father, an imperious sort, and his oldest brother. With the death of his mother when he was a teenager, John was left alone to care for his young sister. In Depression-Era America this was hardly a unique story, something hardly worth telling but for Hall's long struggle to break free of his family saga and the centripetal forces of patriarchy. For him a particular ambition became a liberating force.

On the deck Hall had his head buried in a book. Giant swells from days before had subsided and the green sea was peacefully rocking the vessel as if it was its cradle and we were its brood. I deduced the ocean wanted to gift us at least a few hours of peace before our time of mortal reckoning.

So I came up to him. "What are you reading?" He closed his book, stood up straight and stuck out his hand. The elements had weathered his skin to a walnut brown, but you could see at his shirt lines he was as fair as a newborn.

The captain's hair was dark. Strange scar tissue on his neck about the size of a silver dollar was partially hidden by his collar. It had the look of coarse sandpaper. He had immaculate teeth. Square jaw. So close shaven his skin shined. Definitely a military man. "Hall. John William Hall. *The Call of the Wild.*"

I shook his hand. "Roger, Roger Lincoln Shinn." He didn't say it—Hall seemed the sort who wouldn't want to hurt feelings. You know, an officer and a gentleman. But I could tell by his body language he considered my handshake too soft for a captain in the U.S. Army.

Months earlier, we had trained in the same unit, first in the sands of the California desert and later at Fort Riley, Kansas, a wilderness of a different kind. Ninth Armored Division made up of thirteen battalions and miscellaneous units had nearly ten thousand men. Hall and I had crossed paths on maneuvers somewhere. I remembered him from training, and I believed he had a recollection of me. Didn't matter.

I had heard scuttlebutt about this youthful captain for months, a sharpshooter's sharpshooter they said. And since we'd be together a lot during our European "vacation" as company commanders in the same battalion in the same war, thought we should get acquainted. But within a few seconds I sensed no friendship would develop between us. Hall seemed the kind of taciturn fellow who would have little to say when off duty beyond the particulars of soldiering, which probably was about all he knew: developing a kill zone, amusing anecdotes about training oddities, enfilade fire, successful flanking maneuvers. The stuff one tires of quickly, like brackish water. But somewhere between the New York harbor and the western coast of England I found he had wit and a story. And he seemed interested in mine, which he concluded was even harder to believe.

Hall and I were disparate creatures, and yet we weren't. Hall was an outlier, no doubt. Saw no use for custom if it blocked his doorways, hampered his purpose. This got him in trouble. So did his disposition for risk. His personality showed itself right away. When we arrived at our combat post in Luxembourg, he asked me to take a picture of him standing on a precipice. It was windy! Hall walked over to bluff's edge above the Saar River Valley. His back was to Germany. The great, brutal, beautiful Teutonic nation spread out before us from horizon to horizon. He stood on the rim of the abyss, then shuffled back a few inches further so the heels of his combat boots hung over the damn edge of the cliff, in midair. If he had sneezed, he would have dropped like a canon ball hundreds of feet to certain death. "Shinn, snap my picture!" he bellowed. Before I could take the photo he was standing on his tiptoes! It was as if he was daring the German gods to kill him. It made my scrotum ache.

We came from different circumstances. I had a college education; Hall's family had no interest and made no provision for their children. If they finished high school, it was because the child had the gumption to do it on their own. I spent my formative years in a modest—very modest—but stable, tightly laced household in the Ohio River Valley. At no part of my childhood did I experience raw poverty. My family never came apart. No one beat me with a strap, a hand, a school marm's ferule, nothing. My surroundings didn't suffer from man's catastrophic abuse of nature. As divergent as our backgrounds, Hall and I shared the need to engage this Great Churning, this thing that visits itself on nations with such persistence. I had to inhabit the core of war. There I would lock horns with malevolence. And there, too, would I come face-to-face with the ambiguities of morality.

For Hall, here was his purpose. During the voyage the captain dwelled on Nazi Germany, its misadventure and its maliciousness. Whatever it was, from wherever it came, he thought he could beat it "But only if I address it on my own terms," he said.

Both of us were quiet but assured in different respects. Hall was wary of over confidence. He feared not death but failure. He believed arrogance was blindness and forced otherwise worthy men outside the command of events.

Every other one of us, myself included, feared for our own skins. So we thought long and hard about survival for in short order we all would fight the fascist "super men." Their reputation preceded them, of course, and took root in our minds. The killing fields would be an abstraction no longer. And none of us had seen warfare. That was a helluva thing to deal with when you're in your late teens and twenties.

When the battle began both Hall and I walked straight into the cavernous maw of it. One day, the sun illuminated the universe, the next day it set it on fire. The more the fire spread, the greater the darkness.

This Oklahoma Dust Bowl stray did shocking things on the battlefield. Some in our unit considered him an anti-hero or the anti-Christ for what he did and refused to do. He took a lot of "shit" in army speak.

Even before we had stepped onto the field and into the first days of the German slaughter we had changed one another. Hall had weaned me away from pure moral philosophy in the field. I would cause him to re-consider how best to view his path to victory.

Nonetheless, I still didn't know where this guy came from? It seemed he could not have sprung from his family line and circumstance. Hall appeared to come from somewhere else altogether.

Chapter 10

BIT OF A HELLION

O n the third day of the voyage, the August sun rose over the
Atlantic, its governance over the firmament unchallenged.
The miraculous blue had kidnapped the heretofore omnipresent clouds and ransomed them all to places unknown and unseen.
On every deck, troops streamed forth after breakfast like anxious fugitives
escaping solitary confinement. Most wore a military jacket and wrapped
themselves in coarse olive drab blankets out of respect for the morning
chill and the desire to enjoy in comfort the sparkling sea air, the pirouetting
spume, and the butter-colored sun. Hall was sprawled in a canvas chair, a
rough weather-beaten refugee of many storms, reading. Swabbies were all
around mopping every surface of the Queen as if to sanitize the colossus
for surgery. Hall, ashen and drained, didn't look up as Shinn approached.

"The library on two legs. How are you today, Captain Hall?" Shinn
asked. The reclining figure looked up from his pages and into the glare
where the infantryman was standing.

"Still havin' a helluva time with sea sickness, Shinn," he grunted as he
shaded his eyes.

But for one incident, Hall addressed Captain Shinn by his surname
as he did with almost everyone, except his superior officers. Even then he
sometimes slipped.

"Got a weak stomach. The medicine from the infirmary takin' effect, though," he gasped.

"And what are you reading? Still Jack London?"

"Yep, should finish it today," he replied as concisely as before.

"There are many reasons I like books," Shinn said. "One of them is that they respect my freedom. They don't dictate my pace and sequence."

Hall looked at the infantry captain curiously. "Yeah, never thought of it that way."

****

Before dusk some nine hours later, Shinn walked to the rear of the deck. Not yet ready to eat in the mess hall, he had picked up a couple slices of white bread and a scoop of peanut butter from the mess sergeant. He leaned onto the cold gray railing eating. The ocean rested, its surface barely rippling. The atmosphere was a blood orange and sparkled over the sea's fractured mirror as far as his vision would reach.

"I can't eat that shit in there, either," Hall muttered as he came up to Shinn from some hidden corner. "Just the smell of it…" He felt he didn't need to complete the sentence.

"Know what you mean," the infantryman replied. "The air out here is pure. A lot better than that stuff we breathe in New York City. And a relief from what was in the hold."

"Hard to believe this ol' gal carried the world's richest folks around in aristocratic luxury all her life, until now," Hall remarked, trying to characterize the ship's opulent past. "How you come to be here, captain? I thought all preachers went into the Army Chaplain's Corps where they could travel First Class."

Avoiding his trap, Shinn recited his ten-second autobiography: bachelor's degree from Heidelberg College in Ohio; graduated from Union Theological Seminary in New York City; the same year the Japanese bombed Pearl he received his divinity diploma.

"Union is a remarkable place, captain," he continued. "They turn out more doers than dreamers."

"I am not that familiar with colleges or seminaries. Nor the people who attend them."

"Well, at Union most students want to cure injustice, misery, ignorance, spiritual depletion. Though understand, I have nothing against dreamers."

"Not sure there is a 'cure' for injustice," Hall sniffed.

"I had a teacher at Union. Brilliant fellow. Native of Germany. Helping the persecuted was a passion."

"Sounds like he lived a frustrated life."

"He left Union for Germany when Hitler invaded Poland," Shinn replied.

"The week of the invasion I was competin' on the rifle range."

"He told us Nazism had soiled his country, polluted it, and he wouldn't sit on his hands in America while it spread."

"So you followed in his footsteps," Hall surmised.

"Yes, I grabbed my Bible, tucked it under my wing, and volunteered. I felt the infantry was where I should be. I was sure God believed more justice was present in a democracy than in Nazism."

Hall let out a deep breath, the kind a sheriff expels just before he informs a young woman she is a widow.

"I'm glad you're here, Shinn. I hope ya make it through. We'll take on those damn murderin' book-burners together."

As he patted his olive-colored trouser pockets checking for a pack of cigarettes, Hall asked, "What happened to your teacher?"

"We think he's somewhere in the German military prison system. The Nazis found documents linking him to an attempt on Hitler's life. God knows what will happen to him."

Hall didn't betray what he was thinking. His fingers found a nearly depleted pack of Lucky Strikes in his jacket pocket and offered Shinn one, which he declined. Hall lit his, flicked the match overboard, and observed its prolonged, vertiginous descent to the ocean surface.

"You got guts, vicar," Hall remarked after a moment. "I hope you've got a sense of humor, too."

Shinn asked why, but his colleague made no reply.

"How long were you a private?" Hall asked.

Shinn told him it wasn't long. The Army commissioned him a second lieutenant after graduating Officer Candidate School at Ft. Benning, Georgia. Within six months he was on maneuvers with the Ninth Armored Division at the California Desert Training Center that George Patton built.

"I'm sure by that time you were there, too," Shinn surmised.

"Yeah, went there after tank trainin' at Ft. Knox and learnin' the Louisiana Maneuvers at Ft. Polk," Hall said. "Hot'ern a goddamn sauna in hell." He took a long draw on his cigarette and blew smoke rings that ran away in the wind. "Before I went in the Army, I spent about eight years in the Guard. Snuck in when I was sixteen," Hall bragged under a wide grin.

"What a coincidence, Hall! That's the same age the Maid of Orléans convinced the dauphin that she could lead the French army and save France from English domination. You must be John of Arc!"

"Always had a likin' for France: its goose liver on toast and Armagnac," Hall said as he flicked off the New Yorker's mockery with a cracked smile. "But let's get back to bidness, Shinn. I remember you in some of the colonel's briefings at Ft. Riley. You're straight infantry. I'm a tank guy. You'll head up Charlie Company, am I wrong?"

Shinn continued to goad the captain. "I'll be out in front where the action is whereas you, as commander of Headquarters Company, will be sitting behind the lines safe as a child in bunting sucking mother's milk and warning us over the field phone not to shoot ourselves."

"John of Arc is never behind the lines, parson," Hall snorted. "And when he drinks, it'll be French cognac."

There was a lengthy pause while Hall struck another match. "I 'm startin' to like you, vicar," he said stone-faced.

The sun dipped low on the horizon. Hall and his companion buttoned their collars. "Don't want to embarrass you," Hall said getting ready to depart, "but my grandmother on my mother's side was a Shinn. Born in Tennessee. Henrietta Shinn. I never met her, but Ma said Henny was a hellion."

"Bet she was good soul," Shinn said, tossing away the ribbing.

"Religion never took to her, at least that was what Ma allowed," Hall, who liked to talk about anomalies, replied. "But Ma loved Henny. Thought the sun rose and set in her. My mother got her Baptist flame from her daddy, though, John Jefferson Thompson, he a farmer and part-time travelin' preacher."

"How was she baptized, your mother?" Shinn asked, curious of the Southern ritual.

"Ma wasn't baptized until she turned twelve. Her paw-paw, as she called him, pushed her deep under the swift waters of the Tellico River like he was drowning a bag 'a cats. When she came up sputterin' to the surface, Ma, both her original and earthly sin discharged, as she told it, was a new person. She said she had 'travelled to the River Jordan and back on a wave of celestial rapture.'" Hall paused again. " Guess we're a helluva lot different from ya'all up north."

"All told, not so much," Shinn reasoned.

With the last of their daylight perishing, all on deck had departed to quarters except the two captains. "Why did you become an officer?" Hall wanted to know.

"Bit of a 'hellion' myself, I guess," Shinn said. "I'm not a gung-ho recruiter, though. I don't lose my senses when I hear the band play. Don't have delusions about glory. Or the inborn superiority of Britain and America."

"America is a pretty fine place, captain," Hall replied, looking at Shinn.

"Yes, it is. But inside, no matter where they live, people aren't that much different. Every country will have their saints and their sinners. I am here as an officer to hinder the tyrants, the Hitlers, the Tôjôs and the poison of nationalism. Despots are scorpions. They rot the universe. It becomes a place where laughing is forbidden except at the oppressor's jokes, where love is weakness and dissent is a sentence to hang."

Shinn halted, realizing his answer was turning into a sermon.

"You'll do well, captain," Hall replied as he looked into the drowning sun and felt the sea wind moving softly over the deck.

Finally Shinn asked wearily, "How do the enemies of humanity like Hitler rally such a mass following, John? What is the great appeal of raw hatred stacked like kindling on top of counterfeit promises?"

"The longest lines, they say, form for the thinnest gruel," was all Hall offered.

Chapter 11

REBELLION

Robert Newman poked his head into Prof. Shinn's office. "Dr. Shinn, good afternoon."

"Hello," the professor responded hiding his amazement.

"I'd like to talk with you…about the class." He spoke deferentially.

"Anything in particular?"

The student looked tired and anxious as he sat facing Shinn. His sizable frame made the chair he rested in look like a child's.

"Where you from, Robert?" Shinn asked before the student could speak.

He answered the question quickly, wanting to get it out of the way. "Oh, all over. Born in Brooklyn moved to Connecticut then Atlanta then back to New York."

"What are your career plans—

Newman, back in character, interrupted. "I just want to say I am not getting much from this class. I, uh, think it is a joke, to be honest."

The professor sat in silence. Newman detected a minute frown as Shinn reached down to close an open drawer. He then leaned forward and put his hands on the desk.

"I see," he said, betraying no antagonism to the student. "Do you want to drop the class? It is well past the deadline for that, but perhaps the dean would make an except—"

"The credits are necessary for me to graduate, unfortunately, so I can't drop the course."

"What do you wish to talk about?"

"Thought you might hear me out."

Holding his gaze, Shinn nodded.

"I don't care about the tonnage of ocean-going troopships or if some military automaton likes goose liver. But your narrative about the misery soldiers endured, even before arriving at the battlefield where they were killed or wounded, does nothing but support my point."

The person of letters filled in the conclusion he thought this disquieted critic was about to make. "That war is ugly, immoral business, and we shouldn't get involved?"

"We should not be part of fighting, killing, maiming!" Newman exclaimed, punching his right index finger into the professor's desk as if vicariously poking him in the chest.

He spoke so forcefully that Shinn felt points of cool where spit droplets sprayed onto his hand. The professor noted a slight tremble in the unnerved man.

"Why?" the student asked rhetorically. "Because wars in our day and age should be junked! Because armed conflict, as a method, as a tool of American foreign policy, is really nothing but a ruse and a failure. A failure of diplomacy, assuming they even seek amicable settlements."

Newman lectured his professor on the American war machine when Shinn interrupted him.

"Robert!" Shinn interjected abruptly. "You make some relevant points. But I know what your position is. You don't have to repeat the St. James speech. I was there."

Having concluded that his student was twisting the substance of the class to make room for his propagandizing, the professor asked Newman to speak to what was troubling him.

"You are throwing stones at the wrong bird, Robert," Shinn exhaled. "I am not painting wars as virtuous enterprises."

"More than that, war is *unethical*, professor! Any other conclusion is a fantasy, a deception," he responded talking around his professor's point.

"I am not offering conclusions, Robert. This academic gathering of young scholars is offering no unassailable verdict. It can only provide you and the others with an unmediated first-hand account. Add it to your knowledge of history, government, the human comedy, whatever, and make your own judgment. But, please, only after you've penetrated beyond the surface of the dilemma."

Newman, unsatisfied with the conversation, stood.

"Before you go, Robert, can I ask *you* something? Are Tobias and Ben Newman relatives of yours?"

"Yes."

"I've been acquainted with them, through their writings on conscientious objection and the views they held, for some time."

"The press turned them into pariahs," Newman said. "They trivialized and demonized their work. Laughed at them. Scorned them. Whipped up hate. From there it was easy for the government to prosecute."

"They were as brave as any soldier. Champions. Heroes."

Newman responded bitterly. "And they got a real American heroes' welcome. Threats to their lives, their *children's* lives, abuse on the street, shunned at their place of worship, stones through their windows, evaporating friendships, failure, financial ruin, disrepute. And a bunch of hospital bills they couldn't pay. This land of freedom and free speech are highly intolerant of freedom and free speech when they don't toe the party line."

"Courageous people who paid a heavy price for their convictions," Shinn lamented. "But regarding our class, I still am not sure what you are asking of me."

Newman's face was blank as if his head was sorting out a crossword puzzle in Chinese. He glanced down, moved his head from side to side, attempting to loosen his neck, and left.

At 5:40 p.m. the professor bundled up for the chill he was about to endure, gripped his satchel, and walked through the dark along the north edge of the Columbia University campus. His left hand held his coat collar around his neck. When he arrived at the Amsterdam and 120th bus stop he joined other uncomfortable-looking figures exhaling puffs of white steam as if they each had just announced a new pope.

Shinn jittered in place struggling to generate enough body heat to survive until the six-o'clock bus arrived. When it did, the chilled academic saw that the windows on the southbound were heavily fogged, meaning its seats were fully occupied. The professor trailed in with eight others knowing he would wobble around the aisle for the duration of his trip home.

"Good evening, Josh," Shinn greeted the bus driver as he moved up the slippery steps.

"Watch your step, professor," the smiling man said. "I don't want to deliver you to Katharine all shook up."

The bus roared off, leaving a trail of black soot.

For Shinn the mangled colors from lights and signs dancing on the windows' clammy grimed translucence was a welcome diversion. The hues of this hypnotic urban Morse code smeared and blipped and nebulized past him as unreadable beautiful fractured pools, an alien syntax reborn each night and sequenced beyond his comprehension.

Undaunted by the cold and still-falling snow they had just escaped, the shoulder-to-shoulder quarters, and the almost airless cabin seasoned with burning cigarettes and a ubiquitous fart, nearly every passenger seemed cheery. And the professor had left behind his vaulted arches and book-weighted world to be captivated by a chorus of buoyant voices bouncing around this dirty steel container. Here, sounds gathered into a bright clot of languages hyphenated by punchlines and hilarity. Then he was home.

Chapter 12

ISLAND OF COMMONALITIES

She heard him open and close the door and felt the draft on her legs. Once her husband breached the entryway to their New York apartment, Katharine listened as he peeled off his coat and scarf and struggled to remove his rubber boots. This moment always gave her a notion of what lay ahead in the evening.

The weary academic continued with his rite of winter by replacing his shoes with wool slippers and his suit coat with a heavy cardigan that hung conveniently in the front closet. The tie stayed.

"Keeps the gale from running down my neck, but I take it off before bed," Shinn repeated anytime he was asked about his affair with ties.

"Welcome home, Roger," Katharine cheered from somewhere.

The Shinns lived in a modest brownstone with tall windows and creaking 1930s plumbing. The walls were a sequence of walnut trim and smooth painted plaster. Hardwoods enveloped the study and covered the floor. A Persian runner in the corridor and a matching rug in the living room added color and an exotic note to the traditional surroundings.

In the study, the reading lamp illuminated the space and carved shadows in the floor-to-ceiling bookcase. The base of the lamp from which Roger Shinn read each night was a glazed porcelain urn from China. Depicted upon its surface were Tang warriors riding white and red stallions into battle. In their grip were long sabers with jade handles and shields festooned with creatures. Beside them were peasants in uniform flying ominous declaratory flags and diviners who read omens and the celestial circle. The acute angles of the horses' legs and necks and the pennon poles and the arms of the spearmen waving to the heavens imbued everlasting energy to the changeless scene.

Katharine was in the kitchen where her husband greeted her with a kiss on the ear, before washing his hands at the sink, grabbing a handful of salted almonds, and rushing to the living room to turn on the network news.

Roger's wife, the former Katharine Cole, had a penetrating intellect and an entrepreneur's vigor from an early age. When she met Roger Lincoln Shinn in tryouts for Shakespeare's *Twelfth Night* at Tiffin High, she already was intent on a literary publishing career in Chicago or New York after college. Katharine's stage presence, a silky waterfall of waist-length hair and eloquent hazel eyes along with a voice as clear, smooth, and resonant as a heralding trumpet, earned her the female lead in the theatrical event of the year. Classmate Roger badly wanted to perform as this enchantress's suitor in the comedy, but it was not to be. The director cast him in the role of her uncle, Sir Toby Belch. Shaking off what to him were a humiliation and an interruption of destiny, young Shinn would pursue Katharine Cole for five years, eventually proposing to her under the famed bronze statue, "The Indian Maiden," on Frost Parkway in Tiffin. She accepted and, ever confident, wed him shortly before the newly minted captain left for war in Europe.

Roger reached for the left knob on the blond, nearly decade-old television that had rested blankly the full day as if awaiting a command. He turned the knob and black, white, and gray snow invaded the screen along with the soft crackle of static.

"It's the High-Frequency Electromagnetic Apocalypse Show!" her husband announced from afar. A turn of another control brought him a wooly picture. In a few seconds, as the set's vacuum tubes warmed, a voice emerged and a form materialized. The bluish dazzle from the diode-ray screen pirouetted around the wallpaper like an apparition seeking escape.

The professor leaned forward in his chair. Sounds from Katharine's work in the kitchen faded as the expansive, obsessive, driving second movement of Beethoven's Ninth Symphony filled the room. The theme music of the network news declared the broadcast's opening with gravitas.

"Good evening from New York…"

The after-burn of President Lyndon Johnson's announced bombing of North Vietnam a few days earlier was white hot. The network had aired Defense Department footage of bombs dropped from B-52s on suspected enemy positions. Tonight, updated coverage was the first story and came with the announcement that more American troops were being sent to war. "Near Da Nang, another contingent of U.S. Marines has landed on South Vietnamese beaches," the newscaster reported. "American combat strength in Vietnam continues to grow." Film from a shaking camera shows U.S. Marines exiting a landing craft and charging through shallow waters washing in from the South China Sea. The hunched shapes scurry to establish a beachhead perimeter as if an enemy were present. The sound of boats hitting the shore, gates dropping, and boots splashing in the sea accompany the images. No hostile or friendly fire occurs. Nothing attends the martial noise but white sand, a forgiving tide, and ocean winds rustling the seaside grasses.

"The tiger," Shinn muttered, "is miles away sleeping in the jungle. And the Marines know it."

A brief interview with the Secretary of State follows. His lips are thin as steel blades. His eyes as black as targets. Dean Rusk's few and measured words are blank as stones. Shinn clicked the television off before the secretary's comments were finished.

"I fear for the future," Katharine said as Roger entered the kitchen. "I see a horse about to go lame. And years of political mythology surrounding this disease about to be sung."

She felt her husband enclosing her waist with his arms. "Our nation is riding that horse off a high cliff, honey," Roger lamented. "And without a thought to the landing. But I don't worry. With you, at least our family is in excellent hands."

Katharine's eyes mist.

"Speaking of excellence, how are our amazing daughters?"

"Carol reports all is well at boarding school and she's looking forward to holiday. Beth is at play practice."

"What is the play?"

"You know, Ionesco's *Rhinoceros*"

"Perfect!" Roger exclaimed as he grabbed more almonds and two plates. "There is no better time to re-visit the meaning and obligations of human existence."

"You didn't stay with the television news long."

"Hard to watch it, K.," Roger huffed as he placed the dishes they have had since the early fifties, pink as lawn flamingos, onto the small table. "The sound, the images. Violence all bound up in a neatly wrapped package surrounded by motor oil and cigarette commercials. Think I'll have to follow this war as it unfolds on newsprint."

Sensing her husband is moving one foot in the quicksand of remembered experience as he sometimes does to ill effect, Katharine changed the subject. "I put tonight's *Herald-Tribune* on your desk. It's got a news story on some kid from the University of Alabama signing with the Jets for four hundred thousand dollars. Quarterback, I think….Sugar, is it too late for you to monetize your football skills? "she teased her hundred-and-forty pound mate.

"You know I never played," the table setter, now distant, replied seriously not catching Katharine's overture to engage in light banter.

"Yeah. Everything else all right? You seemed upset when you got home. How is your 'Experiment' going?"

"Just chewing on that, K."

"Before dinner!" she jabbed.

"Sometimes I think I should have pursued a career in baked goods."

"Not football? It's far more lucrative!" Katharine continued to poke him.

"Ha!" Roger cried and came back to life. "No, just making honeyed apricot danishes in the wee hours, which a short while later would put joy in the mouths of every mortal who eats one. No people-worries. No emeritus academic drones hanging around with their stingers out ready to punish younger worker bees. And no students to act bored and contrary when I tell my personal stories."

"Drone bees don't sting, Roger," Katharine schooled her doctor of philosophy as she plated baked salmon.

"Someone from ethics class came into my office today. Said he thought my course was a waste of his time. A 'joke.' His eyes dripped with resentment. Though I also detected a touch of fear."

"Frightened of you?"

"More likely panicked by his draft board. I should have invited him for tea at Estelle's."

Katharine asked why a student upset with class worried him. "You've always said that if all the women and men liked your course, then it was too easy or didn't challenge their prejudices enough," she quipped as she closed the oven door.

"The nastiness in Indochina occupies the region of their minds devoted to repulsing trauma. That is the real war for them and no other. It seems nothing else matters. Well, except for *amour*, of course."

"Oh, yes!" Katharine beamed. "Love can drive almost anything else from the mind of a twenty-something."

"I must make sure they see how Hall's experiences in the war, and mine, bear on what is going on now."

Katharine nodded. She handed her husband a dish to place on the dining table. "Your approach to teaching is not flawed," she declared.

"It isn't flawed if it grips the students. And stimulates interest in enquiry. If it blows up unexamined conformity," Roger acknowledged before saying more about his most outspoken critic. "Robert Warren Newman declared my class a farce. He is a precocious Brooklyner who is eager for the grist to bake his political bread."

"Then I admire his 'crust.' He is arguing for what he believes, Roger. Kind of reminds me of you!"

"And me of you," Roger whispered in her ear.

"Though I enjoy solid rebuttals to my ideas, I bristle sometimes at Newman's condescension," he added.

"You think he's comfortable only in the shallows of his own making?" Katharine probed.

"Maybe," her husband replied with a note of sadness.

"Well, he had the wherewithal to talk to you face to face, love."

"I'm still not sure why."

"I've surveyed the evidence," Katharine said with a comedienne's flourish. "Mr. Newman senses that he has commonalities with you and with Capt. Hall. You are all three islands, sort of, in the same archipelago. He simply cannot accept the reality of it. Or the irony. Not yet." She passed food back to him. "But you have opened a portal for him. And, perhaps, he is opening one for you, Roger."

Chapter 13

UP TO OUR NECKS

Capt. Hall, curious to know about this preacher turned soldier, looked for Shinn the next day in the mess hall, which was now close to a normal operation.

Men eating breakfast filled the tables. Hall had gone through the line and a modest portion of warmed army chow was spooned onto his tray by the cook's assistants. Dried eggs boiled in a little water and grease to make them look freshly scrambled, two strips of nearly raw bacon, and a small, cohesive mound of oatmeal, the texture of clotted blood, looked up at him with menace as he walked to where Shinn and a lieutenant in his company, James Ruder, were comparing history museums in New York.

"Mind if I sit?" Hall asked.

"Not at all," Shinn responded gesturing to the open seat.

"As I stood in the chow line, one fella loadin' the trays told me he was a vet's assistant in civilian life," Hall said. "Prior to becoming a cook he shaved the fur off cats and dogs to get 'em ready for surgery."

Ruder laughed. Shinn didn't know if his fellow soldier was being serious or silly.

Hall took a bite of egg. "Hey, but the food is great." He pushed the tray of uneaten food to the far side of the table and poured himself coffee. His airy complaining masked lingering seasickness and nausea.

"Like to fish, vicar?"

"Oh, yeah." The captain loved to fish but had done little of it.

After taking a drag from his cigarette, Hall told the two officers he would walk to the river most evenings after supper and fish until dark. When night set in, he'd fire up the kerosene lantern, wade into the shallows, and look for nice amber soft-shell crawdads under flat rocks. He'd keep them in a bucket of cool water and use them for bait the next day.

"I had to be quick, though; they have strong tails. The bastards can launch their bodies lickety split into the unlit waters where you can't see 'em," he said. "Only creature I ever saw that propels itself backwards. Well, except for humans who are almost always goin' the wrong direction." Hall laughed at his own joke.

"Lantern helped me spot water moccasins, too, so I could avoid all correspondence with them. Oklahoma pit vipers never liked me much."

"We'll all be up to our necks in vipers soon," Shinn chided Hall, hoping Wehrmacht soldiers were easier to spot than night snakes.

Ruder, who once had stepped on a copperhead and survived, grimaced. "Our odds are better fighting Germans."

"Let's get some air on deck before the staff meeting," Shinn recommended as he wiped his mouth with a brown paper towel. Ruder excused himself to check on Headquarters Company platoon.

The morning was bright. The ship, steaming toward an English port at thirty knots, kicked up fine spray onto the lower decks. In a day and a half, the ship would dock in Southampton. The sentimental part of Hall wished he could travel to his mother's ancestral home, drink Scottish spirits, and find a lady in Glasgow instead of running through protocols and paperwork with the 60th in Hampshire.

"What do you think is gonna happen over there?" Shinn asked Hall as he gazed eastward toward Europe. Hall took a minute to respond.

"We'll soon be preparin' for our landing in France and movin' up to the front. I hear Quartermaster Corps is still recovering the bodies of American troops we lost at Normandy on D-Day. The sea keeps giving 'em up."

Shinn reached for the book sticking out of Hall's pocket. "What are you reading?" Before Hall could answer, Shinn responded to his own inquiry, "Ah, Robert Graves." He selected a passage from an earmarked page. "'What, then, was war? No mere discord of flags, but an infection of the common sky that sagged ominously upon the earth... and we, oppressed, thrust out boastful tongue, clenched fist and valiant yard. Natural infirmaries were out of mode....'"

Hall completed the phrase. "... for death was young again."

Shinn handed the book back to Hall. "Why are you reading that!" he exclaimed.

"Hell, I read what I can get my hands on. A sergeant loaned it to me."

"Try comedy next time," Shinn deadpanned.

Recounting the scolding Irving gave him years ago, Hall said plaintively, "My brother gave me the same message, sort of."

"And what was that?"

"War is a fool's errand, said he," Hall replied.

The sea threw more spume onto the deck and droplets put dark spots on the captains' fatigues.

"Much as I hate to admit it, some of what he spouted may be true," Hall added. "Though I still disagree with his conclusion."

"And what was his conclusion?

"Turn a blind eye to the world's problems. They don't affect us. Pass by the saber rattlers and the two-legged timber rattlers wearin' fancy campaign ribbons. They're all frauds. 'Avoid service, kid,' he warned me. Told me to spend my time 'wisely.' Make money. Chase women. Smoke cigars. Cavort."

"You think war is a 'fool's errand,' Capt. Hall?" Shinn asked.

"Men are fools, Captain Shinn."

"All of them!" Shinn exclaimed.

Hall had no doubt the clergyman had seen the soiled, mutilated edges of humankind. "The planet is full of wonderful, able, hard-working folks, parson, whose purpose is to do right unto others. At least I've seen it in the small corners I know."

Both captains caught sea mist thrown up by the monster ship racing east. But neither retreated from their place on the balustrade.

"But the human clan taken as a whole, Captain Shinn, we're a curious lot. Too many of us are followin' swindlers into rigged games of faro and the P.T. Barnums into their tents of manufactured freaks."

"Those who find solace in tyrants are a strange lot, if that's what you mean," Shinn replied.

People with influence too often were willing to let the destinies of others rot for their own gain, Hall lamented.

"In America, Hall?"

"Therein floats a tale, captain," he quipped.

President Hoover's decision to deploy the U.S. Army to squelch protests by First World War veterans set the dye for Hall. It solidified his suspicion of authority, whether governmental or big business or craven kinfolk.

"You mean the Army Bonus Marchers?" Shinn asked in disbelief. "The vets who wanted Congress to pass that bill in '32 so they could collect their bonuses early? They had no right...."

Shinn saw red spots appear on the captain's face.

"The War to End All Wars ended in '18. The damn government wasn't gonna pay the vets their bonuses until 1948, for Christ's sake." Hall spit and checked his watch.

"Those vets just wanted to feed their families, buy some damn cigarettes," Hall said. "These were our guys, parson! The ones who fought the war in the stinkin' trenches. Suffered mustard gas and phosgene! Trench foot rotted them alive! Yet they won the war!"

Nonplused by his recollection and the indignation that surfaced, Shinn stopped him. "Yeah, I know. Hoover used infantry, tanks, and machine guns to maintain control, otherwise...."

Hall cut in. "And arsenic gas. Some of our vets were killed, a thousand injured and hundreds thrown in jail. Damn MacArthur was doing Hoover's shit." He looked at his watch again. Seven minutes to battalion staff meeting.

"So why did you join the Army?" Shinn turned to lighten the mood. "You one of the gullibles?"

"Certainly wasn't blind trust! How long you been so prickly, Shinn? Ever since your circumcision, I suppose."

Hall continued. "I got obligations. For myself, and for others. And I believe I belong in this infernal war. Hitler's in this to prove to himself that he's God, even though he knows deep inside he's nothin' but a Bavarian cur. You and I are here to give him a dose of reality."

Shinn watched Hall light another cigarette. "My thoughts in recent years have gone the way of glorifying the severe and heroic life," Shinn confessed.

Hall turned, put a hand in his trouser pocket, and looked at Shinn. "I am sorry to butt in, parson, but I believe only victory matters. Not heroes. Definitely not glory. And why do you want to go outta your way to make this life any more 'severe' than it already is?"

The infantryman appeared tolerant as Hall preached.

"You want 'severe'? You're about to step deep into the middle of it. Unlike the easy life we just left—a pair of dry socks, worm-less food, a day without death, a laugh—will soon be gone *tout de suite.*"

"You've been in a war?" Shinn poked even though he knew Hall was laying out the terms of participation.

Hall groaned, exaggerating his Oklahoma drawl, as if he was telling his friend something he didn't already know. "Hells bells, captain. I've talked to vets. Soon we'll think a cup of warm weak tea is a king's feast."

"I think we are on earth for a purpose, Captain Hall," Shinn changed course and tone. "Our efforts are necessary to bring about justice. The religious indifference that infects the country and which thrives in the Army hinders that purpose."

"Hmm," Hall mused. "You got mules in Ohio?"

"I am sure we do." Shinn sighed.

"We had mules," Hall said. "The beasts were essential to farm work in

Oklahoma. Though difficult to manage, survival often depended on them. "Their contrariness is worst of all creatures. You pull the reins on a mule to go left, they'll fart and move right."

"We better get to the briefing," Shinn moaned.

"Some folks, Shinn, they're like mules. They don't like religion yokin' them up to make 'em go a certain direction, 'specially if it pulls against their natural grain. Preachers give these folks a stiff yank to the left with the 'holy' reins. Damned if we don't turn right. If preachers want people to stop doin' something like drinkin' the fruit of the vine or going fishin' Sunday for bluegills instead of sittin' in pews, they'll yank those poor bastards' heads back hard with their straps forged from hard scripture."

An oath escaped from Shinn's mouth, "Damn! How long are you gonna torture this metaphor?"

"We'll bray 'n step up our pace and keep movin' where we wanna go and, just like a mule, lift up our tails and let another one in your face."

"You said it yourself, John, 'men are fools.' A lot of wisdom is woven into scripture if we have the courage to seek it out. Men'll destroy themselves and others around them without it," Shinn stated, his fist clenched to the rail

"I'm not sayin' we should be free to do whatever we want. If you're tryin' to bring justice and a better life for people, parson, I am with 'ya. I've read the Sermon on the Mount."

"You know your Bible?" Shinn mocked.

"Hell, ever' body in Oklahoma knows their Bible, captain!" Hall spouted. "That's not the point!"

"What is your point?"

"The harder you preachers try to pull people in the direction of your rules 'n decrees, your creeds and shalt-nots, the more they're gonna yank in the other direction when they shouldn't be turnin' at all."

"Really," Shinn replied skeptically, his temper starting to fray.

"Good people should be followin' their own course," Hall continued, his voice high and overly emphatic and nose within eight inches of Shinn's. "It ain't working, religion tryin' to put people into straight jackets, arresting their motion. You gotta try a novel approach. If heroism exists in people, it comes from inside our bellies. Problem is, churches don't have faith in people."

"We're going to be late," Shinn exhaled.

"Religion should be the same as why you like reading, Captain Shinn."

"What!"

"Because it shouldn't 'dictate our pace and sequence.'" Hall lit a cigarette, patted his friend on the shoulder and said in a kindly voice. "We gotta go."

Chapter 14

THE TROPHY EVERY SHOOTER WANTED

The eve before the Queen Mary was to dock in a protected bay on the southern coast of England and to discharge the troops, the captain of the ship held a party in the ballroom for officers and nurses. When she was an ocean liner before the war, the Queen's lights would shimmer out into the night thousands strong. Now her portals were blacked out, her eyes by all outward appearances deadened. To accommodate the festivities, gone were the soldier's cots, their burdensome canvas haversacks, the oscillating military hammocks attached to the ceiling's vast metal framework, which was now alive with red, blue, and white lights. A half hour before the party was to begin, a well-stocked bar was operational at the ballroom's stern.

Many men arrived early. They wore pressed khaki uniforms so rigid with starch and flexing in such few places they looked cartilaginous. Matching khaki ties were knotted around necks and woven khaki belts circumnavigated firm lean waists. A line of thirsty soldiers meandered from the ballroom's entry to the bar. Finn Dunbar, a lieutenant in Hall's company, walked into the line where his commander stood.

"Evenin', Captain Hall," Dunbar said brightly.

"How are things below, lieutenant?"

"The men are having a rousing and agreeable time, sir. Not having any beer since we left New York port, they are really enjoying it. Their minds are in a better place, uh, you know...."

"Have Sergeant Paz alert you of any out-of-control mischief," Hall directed. "Then come back and enjoy yourself, Dunbar."

The captain ordered a glass of Kentucky straight bourbon whiskey, spotted a table surrounded by other captains from the 60th, and danced over to them as if he had a partner in his arms. He approached commanders of Alpha and Bravo Companies, Armato ("Armie") Rossetti and Ira ("Bones") Lazarus.

"Where the hell is Lamb?" Hall asked.

"To his misfortune and ours, Captain Alter Lamb, our esteemed Delta Company leader and expert in the arts of childcare, was assigned division guard duty. He will spend the night in command of the guardians of our safety, drinking cold coffee, and enduring the odor of two dozen privates first class in close quarters," Lazarus declaimed with mock concern. "We *must* make it up to him somehow."

Seeing Shinn enter the ballroom, Hall shouted, "Cap'n Shinn!" as he waved to him. "Mind if we join you gentlemen?"

"As long as you don't want us to play poker with you, Hall," Rossetti growled.

In minutes, Shinn came over carrying a wine glass. It contained one untouched sip of Bordeaux. He swirled it gracefully around the sides, releasing its fragrance.

"That ain't enough lubricant to even get your tongue wet, Roger, 'ma friend," one of the officers whined.

"Not much of a drinker, gentlemen," he replied. "This is more sacrament than intoxicant."

Hall thought humans as a lot were fearful creatures. They panicked over the unknown, death, strangers, the great reckoning, other peoples' sex lives. Just about everything unfamiliar. For protestant ministers and their flock, God in heaven was the balm to fear. To others less certain of a benevolent omnipresent deity, a more foolproof palliate was readily available.

"To Captain Roger Shinn, Charlie Company's alpha male," Lazarus raised a toast; and the men clinked their glasses together.

The clergyman returned the tribute. "To you all and Captain Lamb, the Four Horsemen of the Apocalypse. Nothing will save the Nazis now." Again the glasses touched, radiating a sound of ice falling from winter trees.

"When do the dames get here?" Rossetti broke in.

"The nurses will be fashionably late, no doubt," Shinn predicted.

"Hall, I understand you were a crack shot. What are you doing in an armored division?" Bones asked looking to kill time.

"My tank'll shoot, Lazarus."

"I put some buckshot in a half-crippled wild turkey once, only game I could ever kill," Rossetti laughed.

Lazarus couldn't help himself and rose to mock his colleague. "Great! I can hear the Germans now, 'Here comes Armato the Dreadful. Don't worry, there's nothing to fear! He can't hit anything.'"

"Those stories of you winning shooting championships and beating George Patton's rifle team a load of horse shit like we all think?" Rossetti nudged Hall.

"Not a word 'o truth in any of it, but the guy I had to convince to bestow my Army commission swallowed it whole," he assured them. The captains laughed and drank around the throaty ever-present rumble of engines below them.

On many evenings after supper, Hall's parents told stories of the Hall and Thompson families around the hearth. John William was a soul of few words but he loved to summon the past through the oral tradition.

"Hell, I was a dumb kid," Hall began, taking a sip of bourbon. It was the spring of '38, he recalled, and he'd just made master sergeant. "For three years I'd competed in the Oklahoma National Guard Rifle Tournament. The contest drew the best shooters. Those active in the Army, Marines, Guard or a veteran could compete. They may have let some hot-shot law enforcement types in, too," Hall said.

"They let the Blues join in!" Lazarus scoffed. "They are no competition, Hall. All the police know is drinkin' coffee and shootin' at cans."

"Watch yer mouth, Bones," Rossetti flared with fake outrage. "I got two uncles in the New York City police force."

Lazarus held up his glass, "To the Rossettis in the NYPD!" Glasses clicked as laughter rose from the table.

"The winnowing started on Friday," the storyteller continued, "and the two who survived all those earlier competitions and a shoot-off would have a rifle match on Sunday to determine the top dog."

Hall took another sip and stared across the room. It was lit up like a carnival.

A lot of medals were conferred during the competition to top shooters, he told them. "Even I won some of them."

"You must have had a ringer standing in for ya, John," Lazarus howled.

The trophy every shooter wanted was the gold Rifle Championship Medal, awarded after the final round. "I thought it would be quite a feelin' to stand up on the top platform and let the Oklahoma breeze cool ya off," Hall said, "and have a bigwig pin a medal on your pocket."

For three years Hall had watched the championship round from hard benches along side other shooters who didn't make the cut. "Each year I gaped at the tournament's premier sharpshooter," he reminisced. "The crowd cheered as if the winner was the last gladiator standing in the final battle in the world's grandest coliseum."

A military man of high rank or former champion awarded the solid, 18-carat gold medal to the victor whose name was engraved on the back along with the year of the match. "Don't know why, but I jes' knew 1938 was my year to be the champion," Hall mused as he finished his drink.

"The weather was perfect. Blue skies, not too hot, not too windy. Now all I had to do was beat one of those old men who made it to the final day; I had the best feeling. It was my time."

He paused and looked across the room again as if he was present in 1938.

"Nothing, gentlemen, could stop me," the captain noted after coming back from his trance. "Nothin'. Except myself."

"Damn it!" Lazarus almost shouted.

Rossetti said Hall's winning five medals at the tournament should have been enough to satisfy him.

"It came down to me and one other fella, a Marine Captain with an odd name, D. Orlie Dillsugar. The 'D' stood for Daniel. But they called him 'Hawk.' Must have been because of his eyesight. Or maybe it was his feathers. Late thirties, early forties. California boy. Fought in the Great War. He and I were about to face off in the blood bout, shootin' prone, which is my favorite position and where I do my best work."

Hall, who had just turned twenty-two, stood on the raised line, facing the last shooter he had to beat. Before the range officer signaled the beginning of the final match, Hall decided to wish his opponent well.

"My self-confidence runneth over," he confessed. "So I walked over to Dillsugar. He thought this was just a show of arrogance on my part. Likely it was. But that was the beginning of the end for me."

"Seems like a handshake would be a normal thing to do," Shinn exclaimed.

"I stuck out my hand to wish him good luck and saw right away he had the eyes of an assassin," Hall laughed before his face fell and he gritted his teeth. "He just glared at me—wouldn't take my hand—then huffed, turned to his left, and spat his chaw onto the ground. I couldn't cleanse myself of the humiliation. He had knocked me off balance; my head went 'round and I broke into a sweat. I went behind the ammo shack where the crowd couldn't see me and emptied my stomach."

His rhythm gone, Hall lost the match.

"I shot pretty well, but wasn't close to beating him," he confessed. "For the first time a fear that I could never be the best grabbed me. It was like the panic of an animal caught in a trap knowing it couldn't escape its fate."

Chapter 15

SWEET OIL

The story cast a momentary shadow on the table. The captains returned to the bar. The ballroom started to fill. Included in the arriving entourage was their commanding officer, a lieutenant colonel, Corbin Collier. They had already seen he had iron in his backbone. Even his forehead looked spit polished. Men feared Collier. His look could change the course of rivers. At his arrival, top brass from Ninth Armored led by a major general greeted him.

"You ever meet up with the 'Hawk' again?" Shinn asked Hall as they returned to their seats. Cigarette smoke hung in the air like it was a party ornament. The natter of a couple of hundred officers at voyage's end overwhelmed the grumble of the ship's engines.

"The next year, in fact, at the same tournament," the captain answered loudly to cut through the clamor. "Except that year the match landed in early fall, for reasons I don't remember, and the weather was scorchin' hot." Hall let out a sigh and leaned forward, his forearms resting on the table. "It was so dry. Dust and grit nested in everyone's ears and eyes. So dry the ticks couldn't draw blood meals outta' their withered hosts. Seemed like the year of the insect. Peculiar how the clicking and buzzing were ever'where."

On the last day in the concluding contest, a high and irregular cross current swirled around the range, capricious and insolent. Worst for the shooters, the closing match was offhand, not prone. Dillsugar and Hall would stand straight up like sails in the wind where the gale would collide with their bodies and try to jigger their rifles off target.

"So it came down to this," Hall recollected. "Dillsugar and me. Again. This time it is 1939, and I'm doin' the dance, contendin' for the championship and the gold medal that had dangled in my dreams for four long years."

The other captains at the table, as if choreographed, took a simultaneous swallow of whiskey.

"It was a strange day. You know how those feel. Something momentous is in the air. But you don't know what." Just before the match Hall had walked by the stands. People shining like sequins in the sun packed the seats. The sweet smell of pipe tobacco filled Hall's nostrils. The men smoked and read newspapers. As he walked by them Hall glimpsed front-page headlines: "Hitler Invades Poland!"

"I gave it little thought, though it filled me with an unsettlin' feelin' like I had as a kid."

With the match about to start, Dillsugar and Hall drifted to their shooting stations on the line. The wind whipped their shooting coats, trying to tear them off and send them into the sky like untethered kites.

"I glance over at Dillsugar. He's the same, but I am not."

"Bet you didn't go over to shake his hand and wish him *bon appétit* this time," Lazarus laughed.

"Hell, I did exactly that," Hall replied.

This stupefied the other captains.

"I decided after my defeat in '38 that I would never reach the damn summit unless I took control of the goddamned circumstances, and most of all myself. So this time I'd try swayin' conditions to my advantage because the unexpected is a given, you know. Whether it is a sudden storm, a sniper in a church window, or a Kraut in tart's clothes hidin' a stiletto."

Hall said he felt his opponent would throw his spitefulness over to him one way or another. But this time he would bend it.

"Yeah, I was scared. But I start to walk over to ol' Orlie. He looks up and sees me coming. And he gives me the most bewildered look! I can almost hear his mind churning, 'What's this dumb Guardsman coming over here for again?'"

Hall stuck out his hand to wish his adversary good luck. Instead of looking cheery and self-important, as in 1938, the young sergeant wore a serious face but with a smile of confidence. "It was more a grin that said 'This ain't the same as last year, Dillsugar.'"

The announcer called the shooters to their stations. "Then I walk up closer and get my face tight on his, like a boxer in the ring staring into his opponent's eyes before the first bell. I'm taking his wherewithal and plantin' doubt. Givin' him the unexpected for a change. In ol' Hawk's eyes I see that somethin's gurgling inside him. Lookin' closer, I'll be damned if his eyeballs aren't movin' fast from side to side, but so minutely you almost couldn't detect it, as if they were 'a tryin' to survey danger and signal the brain to fight or take flight."

With a jerk and a scoff the Marine stepped away, refusing to shake Hall's hand. Then he spit, "Get the hell outta my station, sergeant."

"I point my finger at him, hold my grin, turn, and walk away. When my back is to him, I let the grin fall quickly as it is hurting my face."

Like the year before the tension set Hall's head spinning. He walked as evenly as possible to the ammo shed. He squatted on an old wooden stool. "It's like I am alone on the shadow side of the moon," he said. "I convulse and heave. Then for a minute I close my eyes and take some breaths. 'This can't be happening again,' I whisper to myself."

"Jesus, Hall," Rossetti exclaimed.

Leo Graham from Durant was at the tournament to watch his friend shoot in competition. Spotting his friend as he walked to the stands, he diverted his route. Graham bent over to scrutinize the pupils in his friend's eyes. "You're pale as a snow goose and sweating like a field hand, John William."

Just the presence of Graham helped Hall steady himself. "Leo, glad you're here. Everything is under control."

Graham gave him a canteen of water. Hall pulled a salt tablet out of his duffle and washed it down with a couple of long swigs. He sat for another two minutes, composing himself. Hall walked back up to his station overlooking the range.

"Unlike the year before, I cleared everything out of my head, secured my spiritual reserves, and ignored the battle goin' on in my gut. Then I saw an image in my mind of Leo's worried look, and I kind of laughed. And I thought about how I put The Hawk on the ropes. Then I forgot he existed."

Everything looked bright down range. He scanned the landscape, his eye taking in every detail.

"I'm a batter seein' every individual seam on a baseball as it whizzes into my strike zone." He rotated the index finger on his right hand emulating the spin on a baseball. Then he pointed to a spot on the ceiling across the ballroom. "The banner above the firing range is whippin' in the wind; it's 'a ballyhoo-in' '1939 Oklahoma State Rifle Championship.'"

The turnout was especially large that day. People from Lawton and surrounding communities brought picnic lunches and spent the day socializing, playing games, and trying to fly kites in the rippling wind between matches. When the stands filled to watch Dillsugar and Hall, it was a mass of soldiers in khaki and men, women, and children from the towns in white.

"Marine Capt. Daniel Orlie Dillsugar of Yorba Linda, California, formerly of Seminole, Oklahoma, will shoot first," the announcer broadcast through the speaker as the crowd stilled. When they introduced him as the 1938 Oklahoma champion, the gallery erupted in a clamor. It hushed as the defending champion took his position and readied to shoot.

"I paid no attention to this," Hall told the other captains as he took a drag from his cigarette. "I am focused on the only world that existed, the space surrounding me, my rifle and the range.

After Dillsugar fired his last round, the announcer spoke and the loud speakers crackled. His booming words echoed around the hills.

"Our final shooter is John William Hall of Doo-rant. At age twenty-two,

Hall, a sergeant in the Guard, is the youngest competitor to make the finals, which he has done two years in succession."

Then the announcer pulled the binoculars from his eyes. The crowd heard him say, "Young Sergeant Hall will need a mighty tight pattern near the bull to defeat our current champion." The throng roared and the major doffed his Marine's cap in acknowledgment of his supremacy.

In the ballroom, Hall picked up his glass of bourbon and looked into the moiling liquid. "To me, ever'thin' was far-off noise, damn-near silence."

He moved three steps to the line. His breathing was slow and even now. "My Springfield rifle feels in perfect balance, a part of my body. I pull up some grass and fling it toward the clouds as my brother Roy had taught me. The breeze whisks the blades away sharply. I make a slight adjustment to my rear sight. Then the rifle seems to move itself up to my shoulder pocket. I am one with it and smell the sweet oil on her. At that moment, I hear no sound. My sight picture is brilliant, my hold stone steady. I squeeze and fire and am surprised when the rifle erupts."

The announcer was at the scoring table with three judges. They raised their binoculars and peered downrange. The announcer listened and picked up the microphone, "Bulls-eye!"

"Right then I was in my element," Hall said leaning forward on the table. "I feel of this world and apart from it, all at the same time.

"After the event, Leo Graham told me that the shooters from previous matches got closer and closer to where I was standing. Then the military folks in the stands left their seats to get closer."

Hall fired.

"Near on top of it," the announcer declared.

The competition would end after Hall made one more shot. He moved into his shooting position, took a deep breath, then a shallower one, let it out half way, and aimed.

"As I fix on the target for that last shot, I want nothing ta' interfere with my concentration. Even so, I had to take the Springfield from my shoulder. The damn wind is gusting, kickin' up sand and shoving me and my rifle around like we are windsocks. My sight picture is movin' all over the place, so I take a step back, breathe, and close my eyes to keep the sand from getting in them."

The stands hushed.

After a few seconds, when the gale had calmed to what Hall considered manageable, he opened his eyes, wiped away rivulets of perspiration that stung them, and stepped back to the line. He looked again out over the range, raised his rifle again, and secured the butt plate firmly in his shoulder's pocket. Breathe. Hold. Aim.

"Despite the sweltering day, my hands are cool and dry." Hall held his hands out in front of him and gazed at them in astonishment. "My senses are alive. At the third and final shot my trigger squeeze is undetectable. I feel no nudge of the recoil when the firing pin ignites the primer and the bullet flies."

Looking up from his hands to those around the table, Hall smiled. "My ears fixed on the report of the rifle. The sound was clean and echoed like the high whistle of a father signaling his boy to come home; it jumped off the hills around the range and was gone."

Minutes passed before the announcer spoke into the microphone. "Either that missed or it passed through one of the same holes. Marker, bring the target."

Hall placed his Springfield into a holder on the firing line as gently as if he was stabling a prize thoroughbred.

"While the judges were doing their work, I look over at ol' Hawk, who is still at his station," Hall said, gesturing with his hand. "He appears real tense. I offer him no gloating gesture. I don't know the outcome. No wise-ass grin, just the respectful look of one shooter to another."

The marker had carefully grabbed Hall's target from its stanchion and secured it in a stiff cardboard folder.

"This old guy ran the target up to the judges, holding it as tenderly as if it was the damn Magna Carta," Hall chuckled.

All three examined the paper, turned it over and felt the holes. Everyone could see them talking. After a few seconds, they nodded in agreement to the announcer, now on his parapet.

"The crowd is humming when the judge in his white shirt, bow tie, and suspenders announces, 'Ladies and gents, we have a new Oklahoma State Rifle Champion!'" Hall told them. "At that point I see a couple hundred hats and bonnets fly into the air. Leo told me later the roar could have been heard all the way to Yorba Linda. I don't even think I heard it."

Shinn looked at Hall. "And life turns," he undertoned.

After the ceremony his brother Roy and Leo Graham approached him. "That old son of a bitch was tough!" Hall said to them.

"But ol' Daniel didn't survive the lion's den!" Shinn quipped and the captains whoop and pound the table. "Now, what about the tournament where you defeated George Patton's team?" Rossetti gurgled.

"Uh, the nurses are starting to come in," Hall said checking the ballroom. "When the music plays, I'm headin' over yonder." The captains turn their gaze to the women's tables.

"About this Patton thing," Hall started. "It's more of a love story."

With one eye on the nurses tables, the captain begins. "It is 1941 and I'm in a Jefferson bus, one of those long silver beauties travelin' from Oklahoma City to Ohio. All expenses paid by the Guard. The long trip gives me time to read my book on Wyatt Earp and ruminate on the match."

The rifle competition excited him. Attracting some of the best on the continent.

"I would be shooting at targets ten football fields away. With iron sights. No Lyman or any other scopes allowed." Hall took a drag from his cigarette. If telescopic sights had been used, "I would not have competed." He refused to train with them.

"Too fragile and prone to get knocked out of adjustment if you're in combat. And they take the sport out of competition," the captain said.

"Anyway, I've been on this bus for prob'ly ten hours…"

"I want to hear about the match at Camp Perry," Rossetti interrupted.

"This part is better," Hall snapped. The bus had stopped at Fort Wayne, Indiana with three-quarters of its seats full. Hall looked up from his book as three young women boarded the bus.

"They hand their tickets to the driver and head back looking for empty seats," Hall said. "Two of 'em sit together, and I'll be damned if the third doesn't take the empty seat next to me."

"She tappin' the floor with one of those canes?" Lazarus mocked as Shinn and Rossetti howled.

"She was attractive, had spark, Samantha something. I mean real winsome. Waterford. Long dark hair, eyes the color of mahogany. Talkative, but yet a little standoffish," Hall said biting his lip. "Definitely the best part of the trip. So when I arrive at Camp Perry..."

"Wait, what happened with you and this Samantha? You get her address?" Rossetti interrupted again.

The woman had been visiting her brother in St. Louis from where she travelled to Indiana to rendezvous with two of her college friends. They were traveling to Cleveland, Ohio, to begin nursing school.

"My first love, ever since I was a little girl, is horses," Waterford told Hall soon after she took her seat. "I had Arabians. They are graceful creatures, powerful, gentle, astute." Then she laughed, "Beautiful without being self-absorbed."

Hall did more listening than talking. "I was not about to tell her about our mules," he said to the captains and winked at Shinn.

"Where are you off to, John William Hall?" she asked. "Do you wear that uniform everywhere you go?"

"No, just when I'm on task for the Oklahoma National Guard," he said, trying to calculate what might interest a Greek goddess. She was a faraway but alluring creature. As with her Arabian horses she had grace, intelligence, and gamesmanship, he thought.

"My destination is Camp Perry, Ohio," the National Guard sergeant continued.

"And what is in Camp Perry for you? Are you being re-assigned?"

"I will compete in a shootin' match," Hall boasted, as he turned slightly toward her, wishing to add a dash of swagger to his thin biography. "The Camp Perry matches are the grandest in the country. I can win—"

Waterford waved her hand; Hall stopped talking. He noticed that her skin was flushed. "I hate guns," she said bluntly. "And I better not see patients in my ward shot up by you!"

Hall ended his story and looked over at the table of captains. "Helluva thing," he said scratching his head. "She clammed up the rest of the journey. Must say, I liked her anyway."

"Yeah, you stepped in it, Hall. But did you get her address?" Rossetti whined.

"Not much to say about the match at Camp Perry...." Hall said as he got up.

"Come on, Hall," Shinn urged. But the Oklahoma captain's attentions were across the room.

Chapter 16

BEFORE WE GO

Abrill-white line of nurses curled single-file into the ballroom, bringing a certain luminosity to the space. Following them, the ship's renowned but aging captain, Commodore Roland Spencer, strawberry-faced and sporting his dress uniform, stepped to the fore of the stage. Had there not been war with Germany, one could imagine the commodore introducing an Austrian orchestra to begin the festivities with a grand waltz at the Liechtenstein Palace. Instead he lifted his voice in greeting.

"As a stand-in for His Majesty George the Sixth I welcome you all to tonight's event and I send His Majesty's gratitude on behalf of the entire English Empire for your interdiction and your charge to the service of justice and freedom. May God be with you all."

At the stage's edge the commodore stood at attention while 78-rpm recordings played "Rule, Britannia!" followed by the "Star-Spangled Banner." As the final note of America's national anthem faded, he twirled his hand. A recording of Benny Goodman and his swing band emerged from the Queen Mary's electronic speakers and dance music filled the ballroom. Lieutenants, captains, and majors surrounded the nurses. And the dancing couples took off like race cars.

Hall left for the bar and Shinn asked the round of bleary captains if an accomplished dancer existed among them.

"I can't dance but I won't let that hinder me," Lazarus asserted with gesture of certainty. He pushed himself up from the table and strode toward the nurses' tables. Shinn remained.

While the bartender poured Hall another drink, the captain glimpsed a willowy dark-haired army nurse. A spellbinding presence, she appeared to have just stepped out of Araby. The soldier walked through a maze of officers who hovered around her table.

"Excuse me. Aren't you Katharine Hepburn?" Hall butted in. His demeanor was serious, though he was visibly delighted by this encounter.

The radiant woman peered at the figure standing above her. "No, but you must be Oliver Hardy?" she quipped, assigning him the role of the imbecilic, bumbling character in Hal Roach comedies. "And where is Mr. Laurel?"

The soldier drew closer, searched her eyes, and followed the jest. "I am Captain John Hall, and you are the very first lady to mistake me for Mr. Hardy, for, you see, I dance like Fred Astaire."

"Ahh, the sharpshooting soldier from the bus," she responded.

"I wasn't sure you would, uh, recognize me, Miss Waterford."

"Call me Sam," she said curtly. "When they start the next number, I'll see how you do on the dance floor, Fred." Hall took a chair and the other soldiers diverted themselves to other prospects.

"So, here we are, captain. Off to war. Here is a toast to guns," Waterford raised her glass mocking her suitor. Hall wondered why she was throwing a fast ball at his head this early in the game. Not wanting anything to distract from this opportunity, he flashed a big smile.

"To guns," another nurse at the table chimed in with derision, "long and hard."

"Let me introduce you to my friends. This is Ann St. Vincent, Nessa Stone, and Nanaiya Trethewey. Everyone calls her 'Anya.'"

"A pleasure," Hall remarked as he saluted them with two fingers to his brow. "I am grateful you are here."

"We're here to do what women have always done, captain," Stone put forward.

Hall glanced at Waterford wondering what he had stepped into. "Well, I wish it weren't so—"

St. Vincent interrupted him. "You should consult the women in all these testosterone over-dosed countries before your war machine cranks out more of this fucking madness?"

Hall's face dropped. He clenched his jaw, causing the muscles to ripple. His eyes pierced into the women's stare; they began to giggle.

"Lighten up, captain," Waterford interceded. "I told them about you when you were at the bar. We're baiting you. It's all in fun."

"Not all of it!" St. Vincent interjected as everyone else laughed.

"You sound like you're from south of the Mason-Dixon," St. Vincent said.

"Oklahoma, born and raised."

"Where is that, exactly?" Trethewey asked.

"Somewhere between paradise and the Inferno."

"More like north of Texas, south of Kansas, and west of Arkansas?" Trethewey countered.

"Yeah, just like I said…" Hall responded, curious as to why the nurse asked since she already knew.

"My great-grandmother was part Choctaw and lived in Oklahoma when it was Indian Nation." She wasn't smiling.

"Hey, this set is over, blue eyes. Wish they'd play some Duke Ellington." You like the Duke, captain?" Waterford asked.

"It don't mean a thing if'n it ain't got that swing," the captain replied, messing up an Ellington title.

"Come on, Hall!" She took his hand.

Instead of heading to the dance floor, he moved her towards his friends' table. As they passed, he motioned to them and mouthed, "This is the girl!"

The detour confused the nurse. "What was that about, captain?"

"I told my buddies about you. The truth is I haven't been able to get you off my mind since I met you on the bus," Hall confessed.

"That was nearly three years ago! Did I fail to get your letters?"

"I knew deep down I'd be going to war, Sam," he said as they sat at a remote table. "And I guess I was avoiding life until I got back."

"Now you are on your way to war. Seems ironic that—"

"Yeah, and I'm prepared for it."

Waterford rolled her eyes. "Don't get ahead for yourself, general. You're ready to take on the great German legions having practiced all your life on unarmed paper targets? According to you, your trigger squeeze is so gradual it requires three years to fire a round."

He mounted his defense in his Oklahoma slow-speaking trot, "Hell, Sam, I've shot rabbits on the run!" he drawled before taking a drag from his cigarette to settle himself. His hiatus allowed her to charge in.

"Do you think you could move your Lucky Strike out of your mouth long enough to even shoot an enemy, captain? Or get lucky?" she chided, trying to hide her smile.

Her kidding threw him off guard. She was a champion fencer, while he was a novice, one unfamiliar with her style.

He crushed his cigarette in an ashtray that carried the Union Jack emblem and stared into her eyes.

The nurse cocked her head.

Reaching over and taking her hand, the captain could almost feel her implacable core fighting off anxiety. "Though I am worried about what you will witness, I know you'll storm through this...."

Waterford squeezed his hand. "Before we go to war shall we dance, John? Shall we give it a go?" Her words were silver coins floating in the air.

Chapter 17

HAUNTED ARIA

At midnight, the last dance over and voices receding, Commodore Spencer wished his guests a good night and the curfew fell like a cleaver. First to exit were the nurses, escorted to their quarters by members of the Women's Army Corps. Next, the male officers departed for their bunks.

Captain Shinn fell asleep quickly. But soon his slumber became afflicted by whiteness, a haze of ghosts in pallid uniforms in pale rooms where he sat alone and immovable inside a colorless jacket and under bright lights. His hands were white as if dusted with lye. Bleached gauzy faces peered at him, like curious children, from behind chalk casements.

Three doors down, Hall laid in his bunk. Unable to sleep, he smoked and surveyed the netting above him. It supported a thin mattress where a twitching man slept. This was the cocoon of an orb weaver spun around a gigantic paralyzed grasshopper suddenly terrified by his destiny. With the gathering stupor of night, Hall floated back to when Leo Graham rode up the hill on his shimmering Morgan as John lay in reverie. Out of nowhere, an ominous buzzing invaded his psyche. His body relaxed and spasmed. Lights from the evening's gala flickered in his mind like fireflies above a river. He materialized in a dim colorless room with the mysterious sibyl. Venetian blinds against the summer sun created black and white lanes that mutated into chevrons as they bent around the floor and walls and embraced the two of them. Sam looked up at him as he released the thin straps of her dress down around her shoulders. The fragrance of her body saturated him. Her clothes, light as music, floated down toward her feet. He stood against her. Her warmth and affection seeped into his body. Then he was running alone in the woods far from the ship and beneath the Northern Lights that drew near him like titanic shards of glass. Lit by the cold full moon he dashed naked through the forest. His bare feet throbbed with pain. Gray wolves sang a haunted aria to the planets. The creatures' eyes burned with moonlight and he was powerless to focus or follow their movements. His only clothing was a belt with a pistol holstered to it. The wolves heard his scent and inhaled his footfalls. The warrior was on their ground and they rushed to him from all directions. Though the cold had nearly paralyzed his hands he unholstered the pistol, drew a bead on attacking the wolf, and pulled the trigger. Empty, the gun uttered a click and turned to dust. A wolf leapt. He twirled, but the animal's jaws found his throat. As he fell, he saw his men, their faces white as larvae; they lay in the corporeal polar night feeding the snow with their blood. Standing above each of the dying forms was a faceless SS officer in black firing a round into their hearts. A deep loneliness entered John's body. The cognition of defeat. He bled from his neck. The wolves vanished and a phalanx of Nazi soldiers waited a few yards distant behind a German SS officer who now stood above him. The captain rose to look into his face. From treetops, Hall watched the German point a pistol and shoot him in the chest. The force thrust the captain backwards across the plain. Stunned by this impossible turn of events, he called to a woman on horseback flashing noiselessly through the forest then attempted to stand to rally his dead men. But an incomprehensible reckoning force disabled him. Above him the aurora borealis rippled in a frenzied state. The German moved to him and fired again into his head.

Hall opened his eyes, lit a cigarette, and stared into the dark.

Chapter 18

THE FALLACY OF ARMOR

"**A**mazing night last night," Capt. Shinn said to his colleague as he joined him on the front deck just after dawn. Staring east into the sun and trying to wake up, Hall was cheered that he could see no land.

"Where did you pick up your ballroom skills, John?"

"Older sister Helen gave me lessons after Friday suppers. Knew I had to do sumpin' ta make headway with the ladies, you know, so I asked her to teach me. She'd been to dances in Tulsa and Oklahoma City with her girl's club." He turned away from his survey of the horizon and peered at Shinn. "You didn't venture onto the dance floor last night."

"Oh, I am not much of a dancer. And my partner is in New York."

"Yeah," Hall sighs.

"You have more courage than I, reverend," Hall remarked. "Not sure I could face battle…." He halted abruptly realizing he was about to wound his friend.

"I think I know what you mean…"

Hall recoiled. "*I* don't even know myself what I mean."

Shinn moved to another topic. "You don't worry about anything, do you, captain?"

"That's where you're wrong, vicar. I fret all the time. At least about the important stuff."

Finding this statement hard to believe, Shinn pressed him. "Like what?"

"You know, important stuff, religious stuff," Hall said looking out at the ocean.

"Okay, give me an example," Shinn followed, wanting to wring something substantive out of the man.

"Adam and Eve, the Garden of Eden."

"What about it?" Shinn prodded.

"If Eden was really paradise, how could they get baseball teams together with just two people," Hall deadpanned, ribbing his friend. "I worry about that all the time."

"Hell of an ecclesiastical issue, captain," Shinn replied and broke out in laughter. "I can see you losing sleep over it."

After a pause, Hall pointed eastward. "In a couple hours land will appear over there. Then it won't be long until we can do what we've come here to do."

Shinn took a deep breath. He thinks he glimpsed some gulls near the eastern horizon.

"Yeah, we're close. Besides kicking the stuffing out of the Wehrmacht, why are *we* here?" Shinn asked his essential question.

"Kill Germans," Hall replied, tightening his lips.

"You hate Germans?" Shinn asked bluntly.

"Nope, I don't."

"Our mission is more complicated than killing Germans, isn't it captain?" The infantryman's voice was sharp. "Are we just ethnic assassins?"

"It is the only means there is."

"At any cost?"

"I didn't say that, but at the cost required. No more, no less."

"How do you know? How are you, Captain John W. Hall, able to comprehend what you dish out isn't going to be too much or too little?"

"I know because of who I am."

"Well, if you believe just 'killing Germans' is your mission here, I doubt seriously you know who you are."

Hall absorbs this for a moment. "I've never been in combat, Shinn. To be direct, I worry about it. And yet, I cannot wait to wade into the fight, to take a'hold of it and control it on my own terms."

"We are all fearful of death."

"It's not death that chills me, man! My fear is that I could make a mistake."

"A mistake!" Shinn blurts. "Mistakes are part of war!"

"A miscalculation. A blunder. Somethin' that fails my men, puts 'em in harm's way." Hall gestured emphatically. "I know myself. I am not, by any stretch, perfect. Made lots 'a errors in my life. But the battlefield definitely is not where I can screw up."

The notion perplexed Shinn.

"You just told me that your goal is to kill Germans. They are going to fire back. They are not your paper targets anymore. Your men will die because of it. As may you."

"If I am unprepared, stupid and needlessly put those under my command—or anyone—in jeopardy, yeah, I am accountable."

"Few officers wring their hands over the inevitable; the 'best' think little about it, Hall. Soldiers aren't supposed to think, just follow orders."

"You're coverin' old ground, my friend," Hall stated with a snort. "Yeah, I've heard it over and over and over. Had it shouted in my ear ever' day in officer trainin'. But both you and I will be giving orders...."

Shinn cut him off. "We aren't 'allowed' to let death, or the possibility of it, impede victory. Nor high-minded philosophies during battle."

"You're misinterpretin' ma intentions, parson!" Hall scolded. "High-minded or not, those who survive this war will have to live with themselves the rest of their lives. We won't tolerate defeat by the hun or anyone else. But what will we tolerate in ourselves when our dark instincts come out to play?" Hall glared at Shinn, waiting for a response that didn't come. "Will we true-out our own construction or will we assume the design of the enemy we face? If we're not steady, we'll go ravin' mad, Cap'n Shinn. End up in a white room with people lookin' through windows."

"You know, Hall, I didn't think you had all this rust on your armor."

Hall thought Shinn was teasing him so he dusted off the infantryman's assertion like lint on a lapel. "Shhhiiittt, I got so many flaws I can't even count 'em. My spellin' is the worst. Don't think I ever spelled a word the same way twice. Then there's my singin'..."

"I am not referring to that."

Hall returned to his serious side. "If I am alive at battle's end, I don't want to bury myself in life, Shinn. But that is what I would do if I corrupted myself. Because I couldn't stand the stain of me."

Shinn said, "Ah, I see. The *im*mortal wound."

Out of packaged cigarettes, Hall rolled his own with loose tobacco from a pouch then cupped his hands around it. With his back to the wind, he struck the match with his thumbnail. It flamed, and he touched the roll up to the fire and took a long drag and released the smoke slowly through his nostrils. A gust quickly cleansed the air of it.

"That aside, Cap'n Shinn, I figgur I have 'ta kick the hell out of the Germans. We all do. In your lingo, we're goin' to do a whole lotta smitin'. We're gonna drive those bastards back into the sewer where they came from and put a concrete lid on it. One way or t'other."

"We have our work cut out for us," Shinn asserted.

"But we can't fail our men doin' it. That's my nightmare. Not the grave."

Shinn squinted at him, "Avoiding mistakes and leading with competence is all good, captain. But win or lose, live or die, I'm here acting out of personal responsibility. I believe you are too. Our cause is right. But defeating Germany and Japan may not be a sure thing."

Chapter 19

A THOUSAND YEARS

The passengers on the Queen Mary found the last lunch spare: white beans, a few bites of some sort of dried meat, milk re-animated from powder, coffee. Shinn, Lazarus, Rossetti, and Lamb sat at a table pondering what lay ahead when the ship set anchor on the shores of Southampton. It was the 26th of August 1944.

After organizing their units, Ninth Armored would muster and board trains for Weymouth, England on the 28th. There, battalion commanders would receive their orders and brief their subordinates. The men would load into landing crafts, cross the English Channel, and disembark on the now secure Normandy Beach, proceeding through northern France en route to southern Luxembourg and Belgium. Anxiety at lunch was palpable. Shinn, burying his own apprehensions, tried to improve the mood.

"I doubt we will see much action, gentlemen, other than shooting the Jerries in the butt as they flee to Berlin," Shinn said somewhat disingenuously. Capt. Hall, having just left a discussion with a battalion commander, sat down at the table, cigarette in one hand, coffee in the other.

Shinn continued playing the optimistic war sage and giving his colleagues palliative care. "D-Day knocked the Germans silly, boys; radio dispatches say that, two days ago, General De Gaulle marched into a liberated Paris, thanks to us and the French Resistance. We beat up the Germans in North Africa and our troops there are now on their way to reinforce us in Europe."

"I think you're right, Rog," Lamb, nervous and pale, nodded in agreement. "My bottom dollar says we're in for more clean-up action than an all-out offensive."

With his hand cupped to his ear, glowing with an orange-pink translucence as it caught the mid-day light, Shinn crooned, "I'm hearing the Third Reich's death rattle. The signs point to the war soon being over."

"Yeah, the Jerries are fighting on two fronts and German civilians are now part of the carnage inside the Fatherland," Rossetti chimed in to reinforce Shinn's prediction. "Allied bombing has turned Kraut cities into rubble. I bet the German people are ready to put Hitler's head on a stick."

A pause settled over the soothsaying before Hall, who had seemed not to be listening, set his coffee cup on the tabletop. A look of disgust crossed his face. "Gentlemen, this goddamn war won't be over for a thousand years."

"John William goin' crazy on us?" Lamb asked his colleagues after Hall had walked out of earshot. "Bones, you know him pretty well."

"I think his mind is in a lot of places, bad and good. Mostly bad, I'm afraid." Lazarus watched Hall go over to the restricted area where the nurses had just arrived. "Just like us."

The captain approached the Women's Army Corps guard at the entry of the nurses' dining area. Hall talked and the surly gatekeeper seemed to give off static. Hall pulled a matchbook from his pocket, flipped it open and appeared to read something written on the inside flap to the guard. The now-fuming WAC summoned a nurse from a back table. Lazarus watched the captain leave the mess hall with Samantha Waterford. *I see what you're up to, Hall*, Lazarus thought to himself.

"We are not supposed to be with men, Captain Hall," Waterford said as they made their way to the deck.

"Hi-dee, Miss Waterford. I wanted to spare you from having to eat that slop."

"What was written on the matchbook?"

"Nothin'. I told her Brigadier General Rhodes wanted to see you, and

I would escort you to the conference room. If she had a problem with that she could talk to him herself. And that I had his room number on the matchbook."

"Is that true?" Waterford asked with skepticism.

"Hell, no. There's not even a General Rhodes on the ship."

Hall took her to the aft deck opposite where the crew was off-loading cargo. They were alone. She removed her cap. Her black hair danced in the wind. The two figures, dwarfed by the ship, stood motionless in contrast to the pandemonium beyond their view. This woman, an astonishing beauty whose presence veiled her delicate form, had captivated the young captain. Still somewhat an impish kid he had decided that certain protocols did not apply to him.

"Thought we needed to talk," he said. "Who could be with you even for a moment without wanting to be with you forever?"

Waterford drew close and peered into his eyes as if to divine his purpose.

"I want to see you on the voyage back to New York, Sam. Then I think we should drive to the Florida Keys and drink in life." Their arms wrapped around each other. The captain gave her a long kiss.

Chapter 20

TO LUXEMBOURG

The Ninth Armored, including the 60th Armored Infantry Battalion, landed on the beaches of France on a rainy fall day. Over the next week, the battalion, with captains Shinn, Lamb, Rossetti, Lazarus, and Hall, moved to Rouen, France, then Amiens, St-Quentin, through Charleville-Mézières, and finally to their combat positions in southwest Luxembourg.

The pitiful residue of war lay everywhere. But the affliction of German occupation was no longer etched on the faces of the liberated. The people cheered that the Americans had driven the Nazis from their soil, yet retained the trepidation that the misery of battle might again be visited on their lives.

As the Americans moved through northern France, Hall saw no squalor even amidst the wreckage of violence and privation. No one seemed neglected, cast aside, or shunned, save for a few Nazi sympathizers and consorts. And he was surprised, for he had seen in peacetime many a forsaken soul in Oklahoma, especially when he travelled into Indian communities or through what some whites including his father and brothers and he himself called "Nigger Towns." At age twenty-one he had journeyed to Chicago to pursue a foolish self-centered dream of a Golden Gloves trophy and where on the second day proceeded to South Chicago for the match. There, a black man named Joe Barrow defeated him and he would remember it always. But more powerful was his memory of desperate conditions on the South Side, and the squalid tenements inhabited only by ebony families whose grandfathers, fathers, and sons worked the stockyards and kill floors and foundries and railroads.

Chapter 21

WOUNDS TO THE CONSCIENCE

A sub-zero February encased the New York and the entire Eastern seaboard. Columbia and Union Theological students moved briskly between classes. In the windless morning, exhaust from taxis and buses froze and hung in the air like clouds pinned on clotheslines. Nineteen sixty-five had begun with the escalation of war in Indochina. Inside Columbia's Knox Hall, Eberhard Dagg stood in the hallway watching as women and men carrying notebooks entered Roger Shinn's ethics class. When the corridor emptied, the emeritus scholar, who walked with a carved walnut cane from his native Germany, moved haltingly to a window overlooking the room. As the students shed their coats and took their seats, Dagg sensed tension.

Shinn had finished his account of the voyage to Europe and was ready to shift the focus to human reckoning in time of war. But first he wanted to take the students' temperature.

The melancholy the group brought in with them did not surprised him, and he called out with an ironic cheeriness as he cleaned his glasses, "You all must have read the morning papers." An inarticulate din of grunts, sighs, groans, and prickly syllables of anger took over the room.

"We're bombing North Vietnam," a female student finally ventured. "Another wave of American troops has landed in South Vietnam," another said. "I graduate in May and my on-the-ball draft board in Blue Earth,

Minnesota, has already, shall we say, been in touch."

The professor spotted Dagg peering through the glass into his pedagogical fishbowl.

"A rally tomorrow afternoon at Riverside Church has been confirmed," Shinn announced. "It will address the American intervention in Southeast Asia. Riverside Church, as you may know, not only is close to Union geographically, but spiritually. Since it was built in 1930, it has been a force of international justice and civil rights. Martin Luther King, Jr. spoke from its pulpit many times. Theologians Paul Tillich and Reinhold Niebuhr firmly planted bold new ideas there on human meaning. Tomorrow, I will stand on the shoulders of giants and speak, but don't let that hinder you from coming."

****

How does possible death at, say, twenty-two affect a draftee's desire to fulfill his life's purpose? How should soldiers be judged? Shinn had asked himself these questions for months and again on his way to work. Now he would insist the class turn those questions on themselves. For him it wasn't as troubling when he went into the army. It wasn't a career move, certainly. And he didn't join, as others had, to keep from starving. And when he heard, as a green soldier, the first enemy shell fly by him, his confidence endured that he would survive not only the next shot but the entire war. He had faith that he would return to his wife. *Was that naive?* he often asked himself. The search for understanding was his passion.

Shinn would never shortchange the mission or duck a fight to save himself. Never. Nor as an infantry captain did he worry of letting others down. *Just stupid overconfidence?* he wondered. *I don't think it was.*

The professor thought about Hall, his seasoned but agitated counterpart and the irony at play. The self-assured, self-reliant Oklahoma sharpshooter fretting over unforeseeable command decisions that lay weeks and probably months in the future.

"I worry only about wounds of conscience," Hall had told Shinn on the voyage to England. "Physical injuries, they'll bleed but can heal. But wounds to the conscience, they bleed forever." And when Shinn saw that Hall was smitten by the nurse on the Queen Mary, that she had tattooed stars in his eyes, he pondered then if the Oklahoma sharpshooter would become more cautious, increasingly protective of himself in battle.

After relaying Hall's conversation to the class, the theology scholar continued to lay out conundrums like a buffet of infectious diseases before med students. "How do you 'judge' men in the spring of their lives—serving in Vietnam, or any war—who exist in the shadow of imminent mortality? Human beings who might think more of their own safety than that of other soldiers? Perhaps they have hopes of returning to their wife or sweetheart at war's end or a lucrative job. Or warriors to whom the success of the mission rises above all else including morality—and humanity? And, then, how should we consider the ethical dimension of those who contemplate a prison sentence or fleeing the country to avoid going to war, leaving someone else to fight in their stead in the jungles of Indochina or somewhere else?"

Shinn looked toward the window into the hallway. Dagg had left. "On the other hand some in the public, and I, suspect some in this class condemn draftees and others who would serve in the country's wars. Perhaps we discuss this in light of Ariel Jeffers' caution that war is far more complex than we realize"?

Chapter 22

CONVOCATION OF VULTURES

A week later and a half hour before his class, Prof. Shinn stood again at his office window looking out and remembering Sept. 1944 when his battalion moved across northern France through the forest of Compiègne, within a few kilometers of Verdun, upon whose soil humanity had been sustained for millennia and had secured, in turn, the blood of the wounded and innumerable corpses of soldiers slain through centuries of wars and where a kinship quivered in his bones.

Once at their posts in Luxembourg, above where the Saar waterway emptied into the Our River, American servicemen of the 60th viewed soldiers of the German Third Reich fidget harmlessly in their camps behind the Siegfried Line. They looked busy in their dull routines, Shinn recollected, and were close enough that their body heat seemed capable of warming the air around those across the river they hoped to kill.

The Germans lobbed a few artillery shells into the American zone from time to time and American howitzers returned fire tit for tat. The 60th recorded no casualties from these obligatory exchanges. Hall complained, exaggerating the lack of activity, "We just sat and waited. Waited for orders. Marched in place so long we started to rot." Waiting dominated the time during the nearly four months before the two forces collided, though drills were conducted daily, inspections weekly. Shinn opened his diary to Nov. 14, 1944:

"We keep our gear dry and our weapons in good working order. The men continue to dig foxholes. They play gin rummy and wash their clothes. Some travel to Paris on leave. Some of us journey to town to distribute chocolate to the children. This helps keep their spirits high. But we've been dormant here for months and having so little to do to win the war is wearing on the GIs. The officers as well. Letter writing has helped."

✶✶✶✶✶✶✶✶✶✶✶✶✶✶✶✶

A call from Union's provost almost caused Prof. Shinn to be late for class. The conversation, centering on Eberhardt Dagg, upset him. But he was unsure why. "Dagg is annoying some faculty and not a few alumni," the provost told him. "Now he's pressing for your censure."

"And my removal to a correctional institution," Shinn interjected throwing an elbow.

"...and possibly your tenure."

"My tenure!" Shinn exclaimed with amusement.

"Not likely, of course, that he can succeed," the provost continued, "but the proceedings could get ugly. I've heard from some of the faculty, some of those he has contacted."

"Well, what are they saying?" Shinn asked, somewhat perturbed.

"To boil it down, they are, to a person, informing Prof. Dagg that he was in the wrong lane and now with this possible tenure-challenge nonsense he has plunged off the road."

"Somehow I don't see a problem then."

"The problem is that Eb articulates his grievance well, is spreading it to more and more alumni, and is insistent. Not to mention he has brought it to the president's attention."

"Excellent. The president is the one to deal with it if the executive VP won't. He can cut this off in five seconds...."

"The president wants you to use your championship debating chops to convince Prof. Dagg he needs to drop his crusade and take up card sharking or something."

"Eb and I go back a long way...."

"That's why we think you are the person to put the quietus on this. Keep the president, his lieutenants, and the trustees out of it and prevent this from spreading like a pool of dinosaur vomit on the dining room marble. Dagg's attacks on you are ludicrous, we all know this. And ironically, there are any number of faculty he could go after with the same rancor. So 'why you?' is anybody's guess. That aside, we don't want this to become an item. We don't want him stirring up more ...."

"Eb is not a dinosaur, if that is what you are implying."

"Bad analogy. Sorry," the provost said.

Shinn rushed to his waiting students. As he proceeded to the front of the room while unbuckling his satchel and straightening his tie, he spoke. "I am sorry to be late. Little prevents me from getting where I want to be. Other than amoebic dysentery or faculty politics. Both share equally in their capacity to inflict misery. But, today, my lateness is due to the latter."

Shinn continued, "I want to relate something, something about soldiers waiting to go to battle, and the crazy desire to get it over with despite its probable, tragic consequences. Unlike us in the infantry, the armored guys had more to do during the quiet before the storm, like practicing their maneuvers and perfecting their tank skills."

Sherman tanks were hard to navigate and operate. The professor preferred to draw an ethical analogy surrounding war preparation. He knew it was a convoluted parallel, but he liked the story.

"Excuse me, why is this important to us?" a student interrupted.

"What should we expect from human beings in war in terms of moral code, Mr. Bushnell? Do the circumstances of the actors and their predicament matter? I think we'll find that the application of ethics in war shows a consistency and, therefore, will happen in unusual places."

"But tank drills!" Bushnell questioned. "Is there a moral dimension to tank drills, professor?"

"No!" Newman sniffed.

Shinn pointed towards a heavily varnished wood door on the west side of the room. It was the entrance to a small but tall closet with space to hang a dozen coats and stack supplies.

"The volume in that closet is just short of what you would find in the interior of the Army's Sherman M4 tanks, tanks our battalion depended on to lead us infantry into battle," Shinn said. "The equivalent of that space housed five men."

In terms of capability, he explained, the tank crew located the enemy, navigated the tank, calculated range and loaded, aimed, and fired one 105mm howitzer. A couple of .30 caliber machine guns and one .50 caliber machine gun lent support.

"The roar from the big gun deafened and rattled the teeth of the crew inside," Shinn said. "Firing the weapons filled the cabin with soot and gases. One naive infantryman called it an iron womb, because, I suppose, he thought it a protective habitat. But when the hatches were closed and the tank buttoned up, it felt like a tomb."

Most American tanks ran on gasoline, which unlike the diesel fueling German Panzers, was highly flammable. Shinn noted the Sherman's armor was thin and not engineered well to deflect enemy fire. German tank and anti-tank guns could penetrate her shell with a solid hit. If a shell or grenade or rocket didn't kill the men inside the tank, they would likely burn to death when unspent ammo and gasoline ignited. Although the Sherman had advantages over the German tanks, sturdiness under fire wasn't one of them.

A doleful Shinn questioned the class, "Anyone ever heard of a 'Ronson?'"

"I use a Ronson lighter to light my weed," a student in the back said inducing a volcano of laughter.

"In the 60th we called our tanks Ronsons after the lighter company's slogan 'lights up every time.' Or something like that."

"Knowing the Sherman's penchant to catch fire if hit, Hall drilled his tank team so mercilessly in exiting protocols that his men could escape 'the womb' and death—faster than anyone."

Hall would yell, "Abandon tank" to the men inside a buttoned up Sherman and it was evident that, after relentless practice, the crew's flawless, swift-as-greased-lightning response had become second nature. The drill even included moving wounded soldiers out of the tank. It took them only seconds to disengage, lift the wounded through the iron maze, and exit.

"We actually found this fun to watch," the professor smiled. "Like an Olympic event combining the sprint competition with gymnastics inside a coat closet. Set it all to Scarlatti and it would have looked like, well, ballet."

Other commanders did not drill their men so relentlessly, so Shinn and others heard grumbling from Hall's tank crew.

"Oddly, soldiers who haven't seen battle don't know what is good for them," Shinn said, gesturing with his hands to emphasize the point. "Even when their lives are at stake!"

The professor stilled before continuing. "A lot of American boys burned to death inside their Shermans. None of Hall's did, even though most of his tanks were destroyed by enemy fire. You might call this the captain's 'ethics of foresight,' Mr. Bushnell. Or in plain language, 'giving a shit.'"

Winter came and everything changed. "I had felt the longer we waited to engage the German army, the worse it would be for us," Shinn lamented, taking a deep breath and releasing it. Gathering his note cards and slipping them into the inside pocket of his jacket, he examined the class. "Nor did I believe that the Nazis were spent as some up the command chain had claimed."

What happened in the week before Christmas, 1944, to American forces in Luxembourg and Belgium was one of the most remarkable military surprises of all time.

"The war came to us, and, in all my years, it has remained my most profound contact with the unknown. I realized at that moment my ignorance of heaven and earth, and now I inhabited that invisible, inscrutable white-hot dominion between the head of a lighted match and where its blue flame declares its presence. Yet I came back out of war somehow and with the understanding that there is more than nothing here. And more than nothing beyond."

Moving to the front of the lectern the veteran lifted his left arm upward drawing a sphere in the air.

"For Captain Hall, in that same instant, like a convocation of vultures, or the circling of dogs, his great foreboding came down upon him. And its intention was to simply destroy the man and his troops in their entirety."

END OF PART II

ENTR'ACTE

Hdq.Co-60th Arm. Inf. Bn.
U.S. Army-A.P.O. #464
NYC

Lucille Hall
123 Uvalde St.
Lubbock 2, Texas
USA

Dear Lucille,

It is Thanksgiving eve. Here's hoping you are enjoying the good earth's bounty. I had a helluva terrific dinner. Duck and a kind of stuffing made out of a coarse meal, oats, and sage. So lucky to be invited into a family's home, sis. They don't celebrate Thanksgiving here, but made the meal out of respect for us. I am sure they used their best ingredients. Also had cheese, a hard sausage, bread, olives, and pudding. The whole thing lasted over three hours! A good amount of French wine throughout, and lots of talk. (I am learning some German and French; many here speak English.) Had a tasty Armagnac to top it all off! Such good people here in Luxembourg and everywhere we've come through. What the Nazis have done to them makes me sick to my stomach.

The villages around here have kept their historical nature despite it all. Some of the buildings lining the streets were here before Washington and the French beat Cornwallis at Yorktown. The people made the big outdoor markets in the fall joyful affairs even though food is scarce and the fear that the Nazis will return to wipe them out is abundant. The people of Luxembourg and Belgium feel the need to create their own reality now. On the street I saw juggling by a woman in full jester's costume while riding a bike with only one wheel! A hurdy-gurdy cranked out tunes that buzzed in the outdoor market and seemed to cheer everybody's spirits. Children flock around American soldiers laughing and jumping for joy. Some march with us in parade.

Happy to hear you are going to Texas Tech. This will give you spurs. You will open the stable doors and bolt towards a better life. I hear, too, you are working for Irving. Tell him from me he better treat you right, or dead or alive, I will come after him.

So little to do here, Lucille. I am living with officers in a fancy medieval castle that is too good for me. I can actually see the Krauts in the valley beyond the river from where I sit writing this letter. But nothing happens. Ike won't let us attack! Germans must be licking their wounds from D-Day over there waiting for a miracle. Well, in my opinion, they are getting their miracle. It is a miracle we don't march over there and kick their asses up between their ears. As for me, I am beginning to think Hitler may be done for. Hell of a thing that I come over here sit around and blow wind like a mule with hay belly for 4 months while the U.S. wins the damn war without me even taking a shot!

Seriously, this place rips me in two, Lucille. I'm caught between terrible excitement wanting to take on the Nazi sons-a-bitches and my heartbreak seeing the destruction visited on this land and these people. Villages in

Luxembourg are filled with people many of whom are barely surviving. London has been totally destroyed in some places. When we landed at Normandy in Sept., they still were retrieving bodies of our dead from D-Day months earlier that had washed up on shore! This war is a damn disgrace, honey. We have to be here to put an end to this sickness, which we are right in doing, and will do, so help me. But that we let our world come to this is a damn sorry predicament.

Can't think about it much out of fear for what it tells me, that we're wandering alone and blind and going nowhere inside the blackest duster, forever facing windward always windward.

Write soon.
Watch out for Irving.
Love, your devoted brother and the best damn shot in the world,

John William Hall

P.S. What do you think of my perfect spelling! To be honest I had a buddy fix it before I put the final version to paper. He's an Artillery officer. I check his math. Even trade.

PART III

I WILL BE WITH YOU

There's a certain slant of light,
  On winter afternoons,
  That oppresses, like the weight
  Of cathedral tunes.

Heavenly hurt it gives us;
We can find no scar,
But internal difference
Where the meanings are....
          — Emily Dickinson, 1830-1886

Chapter 1

THE HORNET'S NEST

The ancient fortress, mortared to a promontory at the eastern perimeter of Luxembourg, seemed to be only a stone's throw from the German border. For hundreds of years Baron-Vervoy Castle's limestone, shale and sandstone presence. its high battlements and colossal metal portcullis, which would lower in response to imminent threat, protected local nobility and their tenants against foreign invaders and contrary neighbors. In December 1944, it surrounded officers of the American 60th Armored Infantry Battalion, anxious gladiators waiting release to face the great Germanic lion.

On a clear day, from anywhere on its circular parapet, or towers rising from the earth like vertical cannons, Capt. John William Hall could see shards of Adolf Hitler's magnificent Wehrmacht, the remnants of cataclysmic lost battles And yet the Wehrmacht was still the army of the Third Reich and it lay in wait for him on Germany's western terminus. Hall and his spotters had watched them day-in and day-out for over a hundred days, seeking evidence, omens, even, of their intentions. To do him, his troops, and his country harm, they nested, these dark hornets, along the Siegfried Line, the German defensive bulwark stretching hundreds of miles on a north-south axis, a rim of concrete bunkers, emplacements, pillboxes, tank traps, and unknown corollary mischief stretching farther than the eye could see. It conjured in the captain the image of a drowsy pit viper sunning itself along an Oklahoma river, and he remembered Capt. Shinn's August twilight warning of serpents. The rivers Our and Saar divided the two armies. The captain pondered what strategy could exist for either side to mount an attack without the river and its banks becoming a necropolis of worthy men who fell in pointless battle. Despite the reality, he ached to engage the Germans and their storied army without delay or rumination.

Hall stood on a parapet, glassing the German positions with his binoculars. "It's time to bring this shit to an end," he said to himself as he blew the air from his lungs.

That evening a beam from a solitary flashlight cleaved the dark like a nighthawk's call. It illuminated a book held open by Hall who sat in a wing chair of acid green at the cynosure of Baron-Vervoy Castle's private library. A worthy habitat of ghosts, the room wore its moldy scent with dignity and its high walls murmured a forgotten magisterial language to its lone inhabitant.

All was still. But the fortress itself was uneasy on December 15, 1944. Hall glanced at the clock, which showed eight thirty-three, although it seemed much later on this blue night so close to the winter solstice. With a brown army blanket wrapped around his shoulders and his black boots propped up, Hall resembled a six-foot tobacco pipe, bowl aglow, an image worthy of a Belgian surrealist. The captain was the giant pipe, recumbent on the chair and ottoman.

Rectangular Romanesque windows mitigated the room's heavy stone supremacy and, had they not been draped, would have revealed a brazen gibbous moon ornamenting the Luxembourgish and Germanic countryside with the play of yellow and indigo.

Few officers visited this refuge of books, and the captain usually had it to himself. One of the library's few English-language volumes was in Hall's possession, *Huckleberry Finn*, Mark Twain's fabled story of life on the Mississippi River whose faraway currents allowed his own father and uncle to cross forty years earlier, escaping the grip of the law and the bounty hunters who wished them harm.

"The War Department is damn brilliant," Hall told the walls as he opened the book with his nicotine-marinated fingers. "Army-issue flashlights with a gooseneck head! An invention of beauty and ingenuity." The shape allowed him to clip the flashlight to the top button on his jacket, shine it on his book, and turn the pages with one hand, while holding a glass of cognac in the other.

But his attempt at humor did not improve his mood. As the beam washed over the novel's tarnished pages, Hall's mind wandered. He set the book on a Guéridon table next to him whose legs were festooned with creatures wrapped in the throes of attack and defense. Extinguishing his flashlight, pushing the curtain aside, and opening a leaded window, the captain surveyed the moon drifting through the night, a radiant convex eye inspecting the earth and illuminating a mysterious snow drifting down from almost nothing. Wandering by were a few thin and mutilated clouds like stuffing torn from a celestial comforter.

The captain took a deep breath of forest air. The interwoven scent of pine, juniper, and cedar in his nostrils spoke to something unfamiliar. Opening the window further startled the old room with a salvo of cold and new oxygen. The walls awakened. They addressed the captain in the low language of shifting lathe and quaking mortices. Hall stretched, cleared his head, inhaled another draught of night and muttered something about old bones. Then he sealed the window, closed the curtain, and reclaimed his place in the chair with Twain.

Before he could get through the next page, Hall yelled at the room. "No enemy would dare go into battle in this damn deep freeze. We're gonna sit here and mold!" The captain lit a cigarette, calmed himself and continued his reading until a knock startled him.

Opening the heavy wood door he saw a familiar form in the dim entrance. The boy wizard of Durant, Oklahoma stood at attention.

"First Lieutenant Leo Graham reporting for duty, sir."

His presence stupefied Hall. A thousand-year-old fortification on the dividing line separating angry armies was the last place he expected to be re-united with his friend.

"Leo?"

"I have come to open the purple testament of bleeding war,'" Graham deadpanned, quoting Macbeth. "Great to see you, John William, er, captain."

"What are you doing here?"

"You are lookin' at your new executive officer, arrived to help you bring this pathetic war to its rightful end."

"How the Sam Hill did you….?"

"Ma arranged it. Friendship with a U.S. congressman from Oklahoma City and a case of fine bonded bourbon moved the mountain."

"You must have shit for brains," Hall said as he grabbed Graham, two inches shorter, and put him in a bear hug. The captain patted his friend on the back as if he were pounding away the dust of lost time.

The captain threw another log in the fireplace to warm the encounter and seasoned his greeting with a pouring of blackmarket cognac he had been nursing for ten days. Hall emptied the bottle, depositing an inch-and-a-half of fragrant liquid into a crystal tumbler and placing it in the lieutenant's hand. The captain, then Graham, leaned back into chairs.

"You're a salve for my tired eyes, Leo. How is your ma gettin' along? Still bakin' the best cinnamon rolls in the Oklahoma?"

"She's doing well. With me outta the house how could she be doing otherwise?" Graham leaned back into the chair. "But she isn't around Durant much."

Dorothy Graham had taken a job in Oklahoma City, one of hundreds of women on the line at Douglas Aircraft building B-24 bombers.

"Can you imagine a fifty-year-old housewife riveting aluminum fuselages and assembling bomber cowlings, John William? She's been doing this for two years."

"The U.S. was goddamn skinny when it entered the war. Your ma, Leo, is helpin' get us up to playin' weight." Hall rose and stepped to the bookcase where he re-shelved his book. A puff of old library dust thick as gun smoke ambushed his face.

"I 'spect it is great for her to be workin' to keep you alive," Hall coughed as he returned. "Your ma is of strong timber." He rested his feet on the ottoman and glanced at his empty glass.

Graham's arrival had brought memories to the surface that the captain wanted to re-inhabit. "So how are our old hangouts in town doin'? The Bijou still have Saturday matinees? Cattle auctions at Jimmy's still serve those massive beef san'iches with a splash of bootleg whiskey from under the counter? The Depression startin' ta' ease off?"

"Hard times are still there, John William, though now anyone who can draw air has a shot at a job. Lots of folks like ma have fled Durant like livestock from a dry rill. Moved to Oklahoma City, Tulsa, or Ponca City for work in the war industry. Most are billeted in old warehouses and gymnasiums."

"And you, how have you been, Leo? Army life seems to have burned off your baby fat pretty well."

"'Bout the same as ever'body. Tryin' to get through the bad times so we can party when they're over."

The captain looked long at his friend. "Leo. There's no future anymore. Not here. No past either. Just the present." He changed the subject, "Have you heard anything from your pa?"

"No," Graham said as he looked down at the floor. "What's our situation here?"

Hall got up, walked to the window, and pulled the drapes back. Graham remained seated, sipping his drink, observing his friend's body language. The captain stood at the stone sill and looked into Germany.

"I'm sure you've seen the maps, and there is a briefing at zero nine hundred tomorrow. The short of it is that we've been in forward positions since late September about eight klicks west of the river's perimeter. Across the water the enemy sleeps. Recon estimates it is a mid-size contingent."

Hall turned to face Graham and leaned his back against the stone wall.

He felt the chill penetrate his fatigue jacket.

"That's good," the captain informed Graham.

"Why is that good?" Graham asked.

"Because our men are spread so thin a larger force would swamp us." The captain's voice was sharp. "Some of our brass think the Nazis are finished. That they are posted along the river just to keep us stationary. Beginning to think that myself. The enemy isn't going to do a damn thing. I don't know what's holding up the show, but my preference isn't to let the Krauts die of old age." Hall lit a cigarette and flipped the dead match on the floor. "Of course, I'm not callin' the shots. So we wait."

Under the captain's instructions, Graham would review Headquarters Company positions in the field after the morning's briefing and prepare a report on readiness and morale.

"Then work with our recon guys and get yourself acquainted with what's going on with our friends across the stream," Hall said.

The captain threw his arm around his friend's shoulder. "Great to have you with me, Leo!"

"Now, let's leave this place," Hall grinned. They left for the castle's great room. Local farmers and townsfolk had gathered to celebrate the Yule and the American presence in their country.

"You'll see how gracious the local people are, Leo. They have little but want to share the best they have: wine, bread, cheeses, dried meats, brandy. Fair ladies may also be sighted," Hall winked.

"Like this place already. Won't stay long at the party though. Want to be ready at the crack of dawn."

Hall scoffed. "No need for that. Nothin' ever happens here, Leo. I'll see you at nine bells so you can get some rest from your trip."

They found the festivities joyous. The food and fires lent a savory burnish to the air. Men in long Belgian coats, black hats, and boots spun women in multi-colored skirts and frayed flying aprons into the evening.

Chapter 2

CALIBRATED PURPOSE

After leaving the celebration, Capt. Hall stumbled into his room about 1 a.m., removed his boots, pulled the covers back, and dropped into bed clothed. Accordion and violin continued to sing in his memory. It was December 16, 1944.

Captain Shinn who also attended, left early and travelled the three-and-a-half miles of empty road from the castle to battalion command post. Graham, sapped from his journey and with a clenched coil in his gut, retired to quarters before midnight. Anxious about meeting his friend's and commander's expectations, he laid awake while the rest of the officer corps and most of the 60th's ground troops slept. Unknown to any of them or their superiors or subordinates or drowsy sentinels, the unexpected came upon them.

At 3 a.m., German foot soldiers weighted with weapons and gear and ornamented with pitch on their faces and carrying talismans at their necks—crosses, rabbit's feet, and lockets holding images of loved ones or locks of hair—began crossing the Our River. Suppressing noise with tape, string and rags enveloping metal, they moved westward, protected by uneven and scarped terrain, and gathered not far from the 60th's porous front. Here they would engage a few companies stationed to interdict "remnants" of the weakened Wehrmacht on the Western Front including those near Beaufort commanded by Hall, Shinn, Lamb, Lazarus, and Rossetti. There to do the impossible, they waited like lightning in a bottle. For the second time in the long war, the Germans would attempt to conquer the Ardennes and those who held it by deploying tanks and infantry through the steep dense forest.

The vaunted Volksgrenadiers, German infantry cloaked from view, paused like sprinters awaiting the starter pistol. When the Nazi artillery unleashed its barrage, the continent seemed to quake. It negated all sounds other than its own and signaled the German ground troops and Panzers to attack with calibrated purpose. The last great battle in the Second World War's European theater, the Battle of the Ardennes, had been set in motion. The hood had been removed from the falcon. Hall, Col. Corbin Collier's Headquarters Company commander, was in a deep post-revelry slumber when the invasion began. Where Shinn slept, the concussion of German siege-howitzers powdered the ceiling plaster of the two-hundred-year-old home. Debris falling on his face woke him. Confused, he grabbed his carbine and rushed into the night. What he saw electrified him. *This is of another dimension*, he thought and felt in himself a deep primordial shudder. Along an eighty-five mile line stretching from southern Luxembourg, where the 60th huddled in foxholes and ancient structures, to northern Belgium, Hitler was moving a massive army though U.S. forces toward Antwerp and the sea.

****

At precisely 5 a.m., as the barrage began, Lt. Leo Graham bolted from his room and sped to his company commander's quarters. The sky and the countryside were alive with fire. He could see tiny shadows on the ground streaming below him. Hall woke to move his cattle out of a fearsome Oklahoma thunderstorm before realizing he had breached a different nightmare.

The captain rushed to his field telephones frantic to contact his men two-and-a-half miles away. Then talk to Col. Collier. Both phones were dead. Seizing his boots and gear, Hall started for the stairs. In the doorway he saw Graham rushing toward him.

"Gotta get to the cellar before we're blown apart," Hall shouted. But as he passed the portal to the high lookout, he ventured outside onto the parapet. His lieutenant followed. The bleary disoriented captain studied the land below lit brightly with bursts and flares dispatched by German artillery. The dried leaves on the oaks quivered in the eerie glow like pages in candlelight.

"For the Great I Am!" Hall whispered as he gaped at the German colossus in motion.

"They're on us, Leo. Rushin' up the long hollows on foot. Look! With every shell burst you can see their helmets churning in the draws. There's a thousand of 'em!" It was then Hall realized that the invincible German machine with its terrifying efficiency, the uncanny force that lay coiled in his dreams for months like a comatose beast, had finally awoken.

Graham studied the field of battle. Flashes jumped from the bores of the Wehrmacht rifles. To him they looked almost like lightning bugs blinking in the Southern night. Hall read the defiles that led straight into the heart of the 60th's position. "Goddamn. Brilliant," he muttered. "The bastards are like coyotes that stay nearly invisible at the far edge of their prey's vision."

Rushing to the door, he screamed, "We're fucked, Leo! Follow me!"

They dashed to the cellar. It was filled with women, old men, and children, a scene of panic and terror. The pounding German artillery had alerted them and the American force through its lust for noise and death that the Nazis were superior to nature. And to God.

"Leo, secure us a damn jeep while I head back to the room to check the field radios."

When he arrived both were ringing.

"We're surrounded!" one of Hall's lieutenants yelled over the phone. "We need artillery support or they'll swamp us!"

Hall shouted commands back over the wire to his platoon leaders. "Fire at muzzle flashes. Hold your ground." Shells fell thicker and faster. The German infantry was in a firefight with every forward company in the 60th.

Shinn was on the next call.

"Hall, er, Rover Boy this is Bad Boy," he blurted. "Three—surrounded by Germans. One—and Bravo—overrun him."

Hall's radio squawked. "Bad Boy, repeat! Couldn't hear you over the shelling and radio static."

"Three of our companies surrounded by Germans," Shinn yelled. "Your's , Charlie and Bravo. Billy Bones reports without division artillery support, the Germans will overrun him."

Hall's other field radio screeched. It was the ring of battalion headquarters. Col. Collier, 'Comfort Six,' was barking on the line.

"Rover Boy, this is Comfort Six. What are the conditions with forward companies?"

"Three are girdled by Krauts," Hall shouted, "fighting for their lives. All need Divarty support. Men firing at movement and muzzle flashes. Over."

"Have all companies hold their positions," Collier screamed. "No unit is to move from its foxhole. Then get your ass down here. Comfort Six out."

Hall and Graham tore from the castle and made their way by jeep through the shelling toward the battalion command post at Hotel Meyer, a stone building nearly four miles by road. The captain ignored the fury around him. As they bounced and swerved, he realized that he had failed. He had allowed his adversaries to gain the advantage and had caught this seasoned military man unprepared. Hall felt like crawling into a hole to die.

With their arrival in the town Hall and Graham met a torrent of resistance from the front and left flank. They could see the old hotel being eaten away by rifle and machine gun fire from a stampede of German ground troops.

Chapter 3

THE COLONEL UNFAZED

"The command post is fighting for its life, Leo," Capt. Hall shouted above the thunder as they approached. The faces of the dead and dying laid like discolored apples covering a white orchard floor. With the hotel under attack other German platoons rushed past like a sounder of boars to raided supplies, the mess hall, and ammo dump.

Through his binoculars, Shinn, who was separated from his company and helping protect the colonel, spied the jeep. "Hall is ripping up the road dodging German flak," he alerted Collier. "His executive officer is with him returning fire, but…." He stopped in mid-sentence not wanting to tell his commanding officer he doubted either would make it to the hotel alive. Shinn saw sparks from bullets ricocheting off the jeep's exterior. Hall swerved to avoid a bazooka rocket by a few feet. When the jeep was within a block of the Beaufort Hotel, the enemy's blistering gunfire drove Hall and Graham to cover. The captain whipped into an unoccupied alley between two prominent buildings at breakneck speed and hammered the brakes. Grabbing ammunition belts, they fled the vehicle undetected. At the end of the alley, both men stared at the rear of Hotel Meyer. Grenades, machine gun and rifle fire, and mortar rounds continued to cut through the space between them and the command post. The air was thick and bitter with fumes of burning tires and exploded ordinance. GIs were being cut down like wheat meeting the scythe. Abruptly, a lone American private crouched and, gripping his M1 rifle, broke across the plaza in a wild sprint past the hotel and away from the onslaught.

"Let's hope he makes it," Hall yelled to Graham.

Racing at full stride the soldier nearly reached cover inside an overturned horse cart when a glowing phosphorous tracer round from a German machine gun hit him in the shoulder. He staggered but continued to run as his body began to smolder. Then, twenty feet from the wagon, his torso erupted in flames. Shrieking, the man dropped his rifle, tore off his helmet and sat on the ground. His screams ended. His body jerked as he tried to take off his boots, as if preparing to jump into a cold spring-fed river. Hall raised his M1, aimed and pulled the trigger sending a round into the GI's head.

Hall knelt, looked up at Graham, who appeared to be in shock, and then fixed his gaze on the hotel's back entrance. "We got seventy more yards to go," Hall cried. "In this chaos we're as likely to be killed by our own men as the Krauts. Get in the jeep. We'll get as close as we can, then stop, use it as cover and belly crawl to the damn door."

Steering the jeep from flat on the floor, Hall slowly maneuvered it toward the rear of the command post. Riflemen inside the hotel couldn't tell if the vehicle was protecting Nazis or GIs and they kept firing. The captain braked the jeep between the shooters' window and the door. Graham hugged the ground and crawled up from the rear. Hall joined him and they made it to the hotel where the captain yelled a password then broke the door open with the butt of his rifle.

When they entered the building, Col. Collier, unfazed by the break-in or the onslaught, was on the phone yelling. He betrayed no trace of panic and was operating at top speed.

He turned to Hall. "Take these men; bring our tanks forward." The colonel pointed to three tank commanders from Ninth Armored firing rifles out of the front windows. "You're gonna give our forward companies artillery support from here. Shinn you're the forward observer. Move out and call in coordinates to Hall. Move!"

Graham thought, *I'm not sure leaving the hotel now is the smartest decision.*

Under covering fire, the tank commanders, their crews, and Graham advanced to American Sherman tanks hidden behind a stone palisade. Shinn moved in the opposite direction to high ground. He found a protected cleft where he had visuals on the surrounded American companies.

Hall and the tank crews were blind to where they would be firing. Shinn's coordinates would tell the captain exactly where to drop shells two miles in the distance.

Chapter 4

THE INFERNO

Prof. Shinn arrived in the empty classroom. A ring binder with reminders of his first days in battle replaced note cards on the podium, but once he started speaking he never referred to it. The academic flipped through the pages without focus as students took their seats, but his mind was not in the room. It still was on the precipice overlooking the frenetic December battlefield.

The professor had left the students hanging at the end of the previous class wondering how that first day of battle would be resolved. Today he picked up his story without a preface. It is still Dec. 16, 1944. Captain Shinn is standing on high ground with binoculars calling in coordinates of Nazi positions, guiding Hall to drop deadly ordinance on top of the enemy.

"Despite the cold, I felt like all my body moisture had passed through my palms. One wrong coordinate could bring our shells onto our own men rather than their attackers. I had to be perfect, you see, and Hall had to be perfect. The big steel guns on his tanks were ponderous but they had to be as precise as watch works.

"To break the tension and test our communications, I radioed Hall using my code name, uh, Bad Boy." The class cackled at the irony. "'Rover Boy this is Bad Boy. Come in Rover Boy. What are you reading this fine day? Over.'"

Hall, enjoying the unexpected humor, replied over the surrounding gunfire. "No books today. Just reading the names stenciled onto each of my tanks: 'Lucille', 'Helen', and 'Lucy Lee'. Short stories but interestin' histories. Nothin' can go wrong now."

After a moment while he cleaned the dust off his instruments, Hall yelled into the field phone, "Give me the coordinates, Bad Boy; I'm damn good at fire-direction control. Let's start the shelling at safe distance from our boys and inch it toward the Krauts. Out."

Shinn took a breath, calculated coordinates and range, then phoned Hall who checked the numbers and relayed them to each of the three tank commanders who dialed them in. Hall nodded to Graham who gave the order to fire.

Thunder and smoke jumped from the tanks as the shells flew from the barrels. Because of the high trajectory the projectiles didn't reach their targets for seconds. Shinn looking through the distance with his binoculars saw poofs of snow and debris when they hit but heard no sound. The first rounds landed behind the Germans. Shinn's next command brought the shells directly into the enemy lines. He could see the explosions—and the German's agitated retreat.

The effort stalled the German advance and bought time for the surrounded American companies. "Hall's tanks airmailed their particular brand of death onto the enemy two miles to the north and east," Shinn remarked without passion. "Our aerial attack injured none of our GIs. Over the next couple of hours, we had halted German infantry assaults on our forward units. Now we could put a rescue in place."

Shinn stopped. After a gulp from a glass of water, he looked around the class. Seventy-five percent were men. An image from an old film Shinn saw as a boy blanked out the present, and in an instant he reimagined a black and white scene. In it is a classroom of eighteen-year-old German pupils listening to their schoolmaster. Hearing a band and parade marching outside the window, he diverted from his original lecture to an emotional tribute to German patriotism. At the end, he asked who would volunteer to fight for the Kaiser. To a one they leap up in an ecstasy of nationalism. "I will!" they all bayed.

Taking another sip of water, Shinn looked out the window into the hallway. Watching the proceedings again was Prof Dagg. He waved for him to come into the room. But the old professor vanished down the hall. Shinn returned to his account and outlined the enormity of the offensive. Twenty-six days before Hitler launched the attack he began shifting his air force, the Luftwaffe, from the Russian Front in the east to the Western Front. The Nazi chancellor also moved ground forces to the eighty-five mile border separating Germany from Luxembourg and Belgium. "During the siege, the Germans had over 1.3 million men deployed against us," the professor said.

"How do you know this, Prof. Shinn," a student asked.

"We captured German troop strength reports."

****

Shinn told the class, "By late afternoon that day, it was relatively quiet." The German's superior position allowed them time to prepare for the next attack. Hall put four men and some communications wire in a jeep and sent them out to Bravo Company. However just a few hundred yards down the road they were stopped by a German sniper firing from the attic window of an old house. "Capt. Hall figured it would be a difficult job routing out the sharpshooter," Shinn recollected. "It might cost several GIs their lives. Nor did he want to expend tank shells to take out one man if he didn't have to, so the captain ordered his tanks to roll over the two-story structure and level it."

Shinn opened a worn hardcover book.

"The next day the rain of artillery hit us again everywhere and with such prolonged intensity some GIs developed emotional trauma. After returning to the states, I discovered Dante had described the event centuries earlier.

"Suddenly there broke on the dirty swell

of the dark marsh and squall of terrible sound

that sent a tremor through both shores of Hell…"

"As the German onslaught intensified, trees around us came down," the professor told the class.

"a sound as if two continents of air,
one frigid and one scorching, clashed head on
in a war of winds that stripped the forest bare…"

"What I witnessed in Luxembourg in 1944 had been tucked away in Canto IX, of The Inferno," he said. Students' eyes widened.

"ripped off whole boughs and blew them helter skelter
along the range of dust it raised before it
making the beasts and shepherds run for shelter."

"But all I could think of at that moment of perpetual noise and fire was the warning in Revelation,

"…and he cried with a loud voice:
'Hurt not the earth, neither the sea, nor the trees.'"

With the command post again likely to be overrun, Col. Collier abandoned Hotel Meyer and retreated to Savelborn, a tiny village to the rear. "It was all we could do even though our forward companies remained surrounded." The professor squeezed his fist. "To the north of us, it was worse. At Malmedy, Nazi soldiers machine-gunned one-hundred-and-twenty unarmed American GIs they had captured. In only three days German forces had driven deep into Belgium, creating the 'Bulge,' and would soon be on the Allied position at Bastogne, a critical crossroads city Hitler had to conquer and control."

By nightfall, on the second day, the shelling diminished. "Everyone was exhausted. We tried to catch a few hours of sleep."

Chapter 5

BLUE MOMENT

Just after 1 a.m. on Dec. 18, burrowed into the northeastern corner of a crumbling church in Savelborn, Capt. Hall was having a fitful night, his mind wandered the uneasy zone between sleep and consciousness, actuality and illusion. Finally, he sat up. His thoughts had drifted towards the months he had "bivouacked" in the "high castle" and his jaw hardened. Relative luxury and comfort in the calm eye of world war, he knew, had destroyed native wisdom. He had allowed arrogance to wall off his appreciation of the enemy's cunning. *I should have foreseen this German stunt. God help us. God spare the world of this captain's stupidity!* Hall thought. A rodent was scratching around inside the battered wall. He ignored it and passed into a sleep where the burning GI at Hotel Meyer waited for him.

Racket from Hall's field phone jarred him at 3:20 a.m. Collier was on the line. "All company commanders will report to me at zero three forty." The colonel's voice was hoarse.

Collier had learned from Allied intelligence that enemy troops, part of the German 276th Volksgenadiers, kept only three units in their sector, about seven hundred men. With heavy fog due to set in and three of his companies still surrounded, the colonel announced that the 60th was going on the offensive. "We are gonna counterattack the Krauts," Collier growled. "We're piecing together two task forces supported by tank columns. Task

Force Hall will move out at oh-five-hundred hours to rescue Shinn's Charlie Company and then connect with Task Force Philbeck dispatched from the 190th Tank Battalion to liberate the other two companies. Punish the Hun while you're doing it, gentlemen. Do not fail!"

As Collier reviewed Army topographical maps with his officers, the distant sound of machine gun fire and shelling called them like sirens' songs to a rocky shore.

"The mission here in Luxembourg and Belgium is goddamn essential to our victory over Germany." Collins spoke with a fury that unnerved his officers. "And we're gonna succeed! Eisenhower says Hitler unleashed his dogs to split our armies, driving his forces into us like a lance through the center of our belly. The Krauts won't stop until they reach the goddamn sea, and we're cut in half!"

The colonel plunged his bayonet into the table. The impact toppled maps to the floor, taking with them compasses, protractors, grid readers, company icons used like pawns, and other charting paraphernalia. "If the bastard succeeds, we'll probably lose the war! Or at best be stalemated," he roared.

Capt. Hall was alive with energy. He was still mortified by being caught off guard by the German offensive in his sector. *I can redeem myself,* he thought and rushed from the command post to muster his tank crew.

"Collier has patched together a hodgepodge of men from other units to be our infantry. We will rescue our surrounded companies," Hall told Graham and his tank crews. "Most of these soldiers were pulled from an engineering company. They're cooks, supply sergeants, bridge builders, truck drivers, mechanics, and maybe a few riflemen. None of 'em have ever worked together in this role and few have tasted combat. I've never seen such a sorry situation. But we will make do."

"Hope the cooks have a good recipe for shoe leather," Graham moaned.

The captain put Graham in command of the nervous ground troops from engineering. Sergeants were to instruct them how to follow tanks and use them for cover. They also would review the basic operation of their

Garand M1 rifles.

"Some of 'em probably haven't fired a damn weapon since boot camp," Hall spat. "I'll be in the lead tank and keep you briefed on how and when to deploy the foot soldiers."

Pointing to the map, the captain reviewed the route. Task Force Hall would lead from the Savelborn assembly area north to Berens to rescue Charlie Company while Task Force Philbeck, led by Maj. Tommie Philbeck, would attack to the east and northeast to liberate Headquarters and Bravo companies.

"After we have freed Charlie Company we'll hook up with Philbeck, clean out the rest of the Krauts, and drive what's left of the bastards into the drink." Hall pushed his finger across the map to the Our River.

"Who is this Major Philbeck?" Graham asked after the tank crew climbed into the tank.

"Met him twice," Hall replied as he folded the map and stuffed it in his jacket. "Excellent tank commander and helluva fella, so we'll forgive him for bein' a damn yankee."

"A yankee?"

"Yeah, he's from Iowa," Hall waved to the west. "Monona, Iowa. Not sure where the hell that is. Now let's kick the Krauts and free our people."

The captain's heart raced as he prepared his troops to move out. His body smelled of earth, rodent droppings, and blood which masked his human scent. His first test as a commanding officer in combat had arrived. Face to face with his adversaries. Leading soldiers on a critical mission and looking to swing the advantage in this sector to his battalion.

"I am damn pleased The Man put me in charge of a task force," Hall exclaimed to Graham. "He gave no other captain this responsibility. I won't fail him, you, or our men again."

****

At the front, German commander Gen. Kurt Möhring had drawn additional forces from other units. He would deploy two regiments, not the three companies Collier expected. Not seven hundred but about four-thousand German troops would attack the 60th and other battalions in Luxembourg and southern Belgium.

At 5 a.m. on Dec. 18, on the third day of battle, Hall took command of the lead tank he named after his sister Lucille and moved his task force toward the front. The conditions on the ground, as predicted, were terrible. The pre-dawn was cold and woolen with fog when the convoy proceeded down the road.

"Can't see my hand in front of my face," Hall radioed to his two other tank commanders, "so we'll be crawling the main road toward the battle lines. I'm sending an Intelligence and Reconnaissance jeep to serve as point vehicle. I should be able to keep on the road by following in its tracks. Keep your tanks in my tracks. Out."

Task Force Hall inched down the road. After four hundred and fifty yards, the jeep driver made an error. He veered right in the thickening fog and snow and traveled down what he thought was the correct route. Hall's tank stayed immediately behind him on the narrow artery. After another two hundred yards a column of German tanks and infantrymen approached Task Force Hall on the same road from the opposite direction. Out of the fog, the contours of Hall's task force became visible. The captain sat atop the lead tank. Half his body was outside the turret hatch. A bullet whirred within inches of him. Then an unrelenting salvo split the air. Hall ordered his men to return fire then ducked into the belly of the tank. Through his periscope he surveyed the German forces. By the number and location of muzzle flashes breaking through the fog and darkness, Hall realized he was in trouble.

"Damn, that's a helluva lot of firepower!" he muttered to his gunner.

Graham called for orders.

"Continue forward behind me! Rover Boy out," Hall shouted.

Within seconds, Hall's column and the German Panzer column were passing each other on the same one-lane roadway. Hell exploded. Tanks and half-tracks fired at each other from as close as fifteen feet. Bazooka anti-tank rockets and machine gun fire poured in from all sides, cutting Hall's unit to pieces in minutes. In the far rear, the living disengaged and ran for cover. Task Force Hall's lead vehicle, the captain's tank, and the remaining infantry on the ground did not stop but moved through the fire zone. The lead jeep and the front remnants of Hall's column continued through the murk another hundred yards until they reached Eselbour Woods.

The sky was hemorrhaging daylight. It looked like a bruised torso lying on the horizon. Hall was ready to revive his rescue mission and ordered the column around. As they moved they passed through a battle-scarred road littered with burning machinery. The remaining task force had moved toward the missed intersection and turned toward the river and Charlie Company's position. But as the lead jeep reached the convergence of two lowland routes, the Beaufort Crossroads, two German platoons, shooting from embankments, raked it with fire. The volley killed Hall's first-platoon lieutenant and the rifleman with him. The jeep tumbled off the narrow road into the ditch. Hall's tank, coughing black smoke and fumes, turned toward the river. At that moment, a German bazooka gunner rose from a foxhole, fired a rocket, and landed a direct hit on Hall's tank, setting it ablaze. It roared and stopped like a paralyzed rhinoceros. German bullets hammered and pinged the tank creating a terrifying uproar inside. The crew members went into screaming frenzy. Every sound the captain heard was alien to his space. Hall ordered the four out of the tank to avoid burning to death.

"Prepare to fight on foot! Dismount!" he bellowed, his voice ripping through the turmoil.

The crew glided from the hatches and used the tank to shield themselves from German lines of fire. No one was hit during the breakaway. Hall's men, hurtling head down, appeared apelike as they disappeared into the fog.

The captain hoped to save the tank and unhooked a fire extinguisher from the turret wall in the gunner's station. The cabin now was filled with smoke. He had but a few seconds to prevent the blaze from igniting the tank's exposed ammunition and likely its fuel supply. After pulling the locking pin from the extinguisher, he shot three long blasts of flame suppressant into the fire and it went into stinking smolder.

Hall quickly wiped the sweat from his face and hands with a mechanic's rag. The fumes from the extinguisher and the smoke from the burning tank galled his nose and lungs. The captain feared he would suffocate. Outside, hoping anyone left inside would burn or smother to death, the Germans continued spraying bullets on the tank's escape hatch. Hall tried to fire the cannon. All he heard was a dry "clunk," and collapsed in the gunner's seat. Time was abandoning him. The captain closed his eyes.

Chapter 6

REVERBERATION

"Come then, Sam, let's dance." Capt. Hall held out his hand. Samantha Waterford touched it and the soldier trapped in the smoldering tank was at once back in the Queen Mary's palatial ballroom. The Oklahoman stared. He had found it amusing that the luxury liner's ballroom floor had been crafted for the shoes of the wealthy and famous. But during its retrofitting for war, it was left intact for him and other outcasts of the Great Depression.

Music surrounded him. He heard Waterford cry, "'Tales from the Vienna Woods'! "You like Strauss waltzes, don't you, John Hall?"

"Can't get enough of 'em." He held her close and whispered, "A lot of tempo changes, kiddo, in this waltz and we're gonna end up goin' about ninety miles an hour in the middle. So be ready, Sammy, to keep up with me."

Her response was strange and echoed in his mind. "And you be ready for what awaits you in Europe, Capt. Hall."

He led and they were off. The accumulated patina of pops and scratches in the recording was exported through the speakers as if the past had created its own rhythm. The silken music coursed through them, a steady wave unaffected by the wail of the present. A few minutes into the waltz, when the music was at its most sublime, and the pace was of a beating heart, only Waterford and Hall remained on the floor; they, the only people on earth, spinning with grace and bravura inside the blue contours of a trance where their feet barely skimmed glassy waters.

"Jesus, Hall!" Rossetti shouted from the bar in disbelief. The captain convulsed and returned to the present.

Chapter 7

WE HAVE A SURPRISE FOR YOU

C apt. Hall ignored the relentless clang of bullets bouncing off the shell of his tank. He had to get air, join his men, get back in the fight.

"We're shot up, disorganized, lost in the fog, pinned down," he uttered as if an entity were present. "My command tank set on fire. We're outnumbered. Why the hell can't I get outta the damn startin' blocks?"

With the tank as his shield, Lt. Graham had belly-crawled to the smoking vehicle. He pounded his bayonet handle on the tank's exterior. It's tong-ting-tong pealed inside like dull a bell. "You dead in there, Captain?" the lieutenant hollered.

"Hell no! Get the crew back here. We're going to attack!" he coughed.

His junior officer gritted his teeth. "John William, the crew bugged out into the fog. Our remaining riflemen are scattered ever' which way, and you never saw so many Germans in foxholes in your life. They're just across the bow of your tank." Graham pounded on the hull again louder. The higher pitched signal was more urgent now. "A German bazooka gunner is about to blow the hell out of Lucille! You're not long for this world!"

"The minute I lift the hatch give me covering fire," Hall shouted. "Then drop back into the woods and round up the men."

The captain grabbed a bandolier of rifle shells, put a couple extra cartridges in his pocket, and opened the turret hatch slowly. Fresh air rushed to his lungs. He slipped his M1 onto the top of the tank. Lastly, he snatched his .45 pistol from the shelf by the periscope. Hall kept a shell in the chamber and a full clip in it. Having jammed it into his holster, he buttoned the flap to secure the weapon. Then the shooting stopped.

From a narrow slit, Hall watched the Volksgrenadiers. Some stood above their fox holes with rifles ready to fire. With only four of the five tank crew having exited the tank, they taunted the remaining crew member.

"Come out. Come out. Ve have surprise for you," one of them jeered in English to the hoots of the others.

Crouching inside the top hatch, the captain took a long deep breath. Calm now, he was ready to leap out over the side. He waited a few seconds and watched. As the bazooka gunner readied to fire, the German riflemen relaxed slightly, easing their rifles down to watch the rocket in flight. When Hall saw their eyes turn toward the bazooka, he leapt from Lucille and Graham began firing. The surprised German infantrymen shot at the captain in a panic. No bullet found its target. The bazooka rocket fired at the Sherman and missed. But its drag came close enough to suck Hall off the tank before he could jump. He landed on frozen ground. The captain's feet swept out from under him and his head bounced off the ice. The stunned man froze in place. His left leg was astraddle with its boot at his hip. Germans took him for dead. A bitter smell filled Hall's nose. His head throbbed and his eyes were open but they could not focus. The Germans ducked back into their foxholes as a few GIs in the distant woods fired at something.

Time was leaden. The captain maintained a dead man's repose and his body ached. The sun climbed and warmed his face. His sight returned. "Now is the moment" he said to himself and made two quick rollovers to get under the tank.

Hall couldn't see or hear the Germans. A foreboding overtook him. He felt sick. The tank, he sensed, was a death trap. The captain felt his body go into a near weightless state, and he scrambled into the open. Pushing himself off the ground with his rifle, Hall started his sprint for cover and slipped. His legs split wide apart as the German bazooka gunner fired another round at Lucille. She would have none of it and it curved away from her and passed between the captain's legs in a hissing fury. The shell exploded in the ground twenty feet beyond. The rocket flash had ripped Hall's fatigue trousers off his legs and he was toppled by the concussion of the exploding rocket. The captain skidded along the ice before securing his rifle and racing for cover. A score of German riflemen fired manically at the escaping figure.

"I ran to my right across a field. I felt no pain. Everything was working on automatic. Just picking up my feet and putting them down, but it felt like I was in air," he would write.

The bazooka blast was rough enough to put Hall in shock. "I didn't know where I was or what had happened. Just running, ducking and dodging like a scared jack rabbit. Bullets whizzed by."

Enemy fire against the fleeing, half-naked figure running horizontally in front of them was too hysterical to be accurate. The captain hunched low to the ground; his right hand clenched his rifle like a vice. He knew the weapon was his only chance.

Hall spotted an outcropping of stone formed like a cupped hand. Diving, he skidded across the ground into the cavity. Briefly he was invisible to his tormentors. The Volksgrenadier commander called for his men to cease fire. The captain breathed. Hall's cheeks puffed up before a sigh escaped. Peeking from his cover he saw dozens of Germans in foxholes gouged out of the terrain and set behind pyramid-shaped emplacements. He turned to look for his men. They had taken defensive positions more than four hundred feet behind him across the road at the wood's edge. Wanting to rush the Germans, the captain yelled. "Prepare to attack across the road! When I jump up and give a rebel yell, move over the road and attack!"

Having given the order, the captain jumped up howling. In a dash to the right of the dug-in Germans, Hall fired instinctively. Three Volgrenadiers dropped. He looked behind him. None of the inexperienced troops of his task force, paralyzed as much with uncertainty as fear, had followed his command. Hall dove for cover but shrapnel clipped him below the knee severing a vein and slicing cartilage. He fell and lay prone behind a strange upheaval of earth shaped as if by moundbuilders. In that moment Hall tied the wound, surveyed the field and totaled his assets. He was like a solitary figure exposed on the open prairie and battling the elements. His brother Roy was with him, "One shot. One rabbit or you go home hungry, John William." The captain peered above the embankment's brow, brought his rifle to his cheek and fired. A Germans soldier's helmet flew back like a stone skipped off water. Hall lowered himself to watch the enemy respond. He imagined Roy spotting when he hit eight bull's eyes in ten seconds from 50 yards.

"You don't have a chance!" Hall yelled to the Volkgenadiers. The captain rose above the mound and fired three more rounds; the shells did not advance past the figures in his sights. The captain had entered into an azure solitude. Nothing existed for him, not time, not space, not Zion nor earth, not gravity, or the grave. For him all that existed in that blue moment was the moment. And he filled it, excluding all else.

From behind the maelstrom, the German lieutenant spotted the elusive fugitive from the burning tank through his periscope and vowed to dispatch him. He ordered concentrated fire on the captain's position and pulled five soldiers from the ranks to close in and take him out. As the effort took shape, the lieutenant searched for others he believed were reinforcing the captain's sniping. For Hall, the Germans were easy to spot. Their rifle barrels twitched like chicken legs a split second before they rose above the threshold of their bunkers. The first three sets of eyes never reached the top of their foxhole. Another two were mortally wounded as they leveled their guns.

The German commander ordered five more to engage the lone American rifleman, who was moving a few feet left, a few feet right after each volley. The captain was striking most of the German helmets dead center now. The Nazi riflemen couldn't predict Hall's next location or find other shooters. This put them off balance. When the German lieutenant ordered the remainder of his men to move up and fire, Hall maintained his fluid rhythm just quick enough to conserve precision with mobility. His hands were steady and his breathing un-rushed and he reloaded his eight-round clips in twos as he could from shells pulled from the bandolier as smoothly as he drew cigarettes from a pack. Some of Hall's shots missed and ricocheted but this kept the Germans tentative. Each time the captain hit his target his men in the woods heard the echo, "Ich erhielt ein!"

****

When Graham arrived back at the rendezvous point and located the remaining contingent of Task Force Hall along the wood line, he was shocked. He raced to the first sergeant he spotted.

"What the hell you doin' here!" Graham yelled. The staff sergeant had been assigned to Task Force Hall from another unit. The lieutenant didn't know him.

"Cap'n seems to be taking it to the Krauts, sir," he said with pride, and a bit of glee, as he watched through his binoculars. "Almost every time he shoots he hollers 'I got one' in Kraut speak!"

"Why are you sittin' here on yer ass, you damn fool!"

The sergeant looked confused.

"Speed two good riflemen up to relieve the captain! Then we'll all move to his position with you leading the goddamn charge on my command. GIT!" Graham yelled, barely able to restrain himself from kicking the soldier in the rear. Two GIs finally moved toward Hall.

The shooting and mayhem continued until the Germans stopped popping up. Their momentary cease fire was important since Hall had ducked behind a mound but was out of rifle ammunition. An enemy soldier had moved by stealth within a few yards, and then rushed the captain's position. Hall yanked his .45 from his holster, pointed it, and pulled the trigger before the German could shoot. All he heard was the feeble click of the firing pin trying to find a bullet that wasn't there. Within that second the captain realized he had grabbed someone else's pistol from the tank. The onrushing German pulled a Walther pistol from its holster and aimed it at Hall's head. But he fumbled the grip and cried out, giving one of the approaching GIs time to shoot. The German soldier suffered a wound to the heart and fell dead onto the captain. Hall grabbed his throat and pushed off the soldier's helmet. Two vacant eyes looked up at him. Even in death they were opalescent. He was no older than fourteen.

The Volksgrenadiers went quiet and another GI arrived with more ammunition. Hall's trance broke and the cold and pain rushed into his body. He left the two GIs firing into the enemy position.

"Keep them pinned!" Hall shouted. Under their covering fire, Hall made his way back to the woods. He ordered the red-faced sergeant to drive the half-track. They would run over the German trenches and "feed'm grenades." As the armored carrier approached, Hall laid fire on the Germans with the machine gun while two GIs on each side of him prepared to hurl grenades into the foxholes. But before the halftrack reached the foxholes, the Volksgrenadiers waved a flag of surrender.

The captain surveyed them as they climbed from their holes. Most had removed their heavy stahlhelms. Half of them were but children and men too old to be foot soldiers.

The captured German commander, his hands clasped behind his head, approached Hall. "How many of you picking us off?"

"Just my brother Roy and me," he replied looking away from his adversary. On the ground in front of him more than twenty Volksgenadiers lay dead.

****

Professor Shinn had compressed his knowledge of Hall's December 18 offensive into a few paragraphs and ended his account to the students.

"He had survived, but his task force was in tatters and had failed to rescue my company," Shinn said. "Col. Collier cancelled the mission and ordered Hall and his remaining troops back to the command post. I got in my jeep and went out to meet him. After the enemy surrender, Captain Hall told me he looked at his watch. The time read 7:48 a.m. Task Force Hall had been in action an hour and forty-eight minutes."

Chapter 8

THE DAGG ENIGMA

Two days later, Prof. Shinn walked to Union from the bus stop. It was later than usual. Bundled up and moving briskly, he strode from block to block staring down at the sidewalk, shoveled to reveal its equidistant lines. Wrestling with anxiety, the scholar looked up only at intersections. Agitated by the metastasizing of war in Indochina, he failed to notice a bold blue sky and two defiant clouds signaling to earth the beauty of solitude.

At his arrival, his unvarying greeting ruffled the air. "Good morning, Eve. Any tea?"

"Eberhard Dagg was in earlier, Roger," Eve informed him as she nodded toward the tea pot.

"You know anything about him, Eve?" the professor asked as he poured himself a cup.

"I know he has Vietnam stuck in his craw! Other than that, not much. Meaning all that I want. He was nearing retirement when I came to Union. Never had a genuine conversation with the man. He doesn't talk to people outside his Era of Reign, I suppose."

"Yeah, he can be ornery. But his barbed demeanor is mostly theatrical."

"Sure. I'm not saying I don't get a kick out of him and the other half-dozen real characters around here. Since I was three, I have loved the circus."

Shinn plopped in the empty chair in Eve's office to talk about the emeritus professor whom he believed remained one of the keener intellects in New York academia. "And, for better or worse, among the most tenacious men I have ever met," Shinn said as he pulled his socks up.

"Yep, I am aware of the tenacious part." Eve mimed, pulling a noose up around her neck and gagging.

"The old guy's had it tough, Eve. Born in Bavaria in the 1880s. Emigrated to the U.S. as a child with his penniless family. Always had a passion for learning and charging into spiritual and secular thorn bushes."

"My take on him, Roger, is that he is drawn to thorns rather than fruit. Seems genetically miscast. He should have been a hyena."

Ignoring her comic hyperbole, the professor stood and leaned against the wall. "He is a fighter, yes, especially for the cause he puts above all others: America. The only thing that prevented his family from perishing was the work ethic of Eb's parents, and, according to Eb, the singular opportunity afforded them as part of The Great American Experiment."

"How did he lose his eye?" Eve asked. Shinn ignored the question and continued on topic.

"Dagg entered the University of Minnesota just after the turn of the century on scholarship and graduated with a science degree. Then the young man came to believe that spiritual development, not material wealth, was essential to America's future. So he enrolled at Union in 1915 to pursue a divinity degree."

"And how do you come to know all this about the professor, Roger? You two soul mates?" Eve grinned.

"Oh, I would have lunches with him from time to time," he smiled back. "We had some common interests. The Rapture. The Inquisition. Baseball," he continued with a straight face. "And we'd have an occasional drink together at day's end at West End Gate. He, his schnapps, I, my gossamer Spanish Amontillado." Shinn, not a drinker, gestured foppishly to accentuate his simulated pomposity. After a pause and a sip of tea, his eyes narrowed.

"I was an infantry officer in World War Two, Eve. Dagg's unshakeable friendship helped me get through a rough patch, a very rough patch, after the war. I had had the 'good' fortune of spending months in a Nazi POW camp. Forced marches, interrogations, German food, that kind of unpleasantness. Captured during the Battle of the Bulge, I am sorry to report."

Eve's face dropped.

Cutting short his pursuit of a divinity education, Dagg enlisted in the U.S. Army under Gen. John J. Pershing. The Army shipped him to France where he would enter the Great War as a medic. Private Dagg never fired a weapon or was in combat, though his experience in field hospitals with the burned, wounded, and gassed would provide him an ample view of the cruelty of modern weaponry and those who wielded it. After the war, he finished his degree, became a Lutheran pastor in upstate New York, resigned to get his PhD., and was hired at Union as a lecturer. In the fifties, Dagg mentored Shinn in his academic and personal life and the younger professor admired him.

"He's restless, always has been," Shinn said. "A soul inevitably inclined to forgo intellectual and spiritual comfort in pursuit of a new frontier, the thorn bush if you will."

"So why abandon his strict German-Lutheranism?" Eve had become absorbed in this mysterious academic.

"Two World Wars," he answered sadly.

"And in 1943 he committed 'heresy.'" Shinn smirked at the word. "He publicly renounced his belief in the benchmark affirmations of Protestantism," the professor told the dumfounded assistant. "Eb came to espouse self sacrifice as the only way to spiritual fulfillment."

"Bet that won him a lot of followers," Eve coughed.

"It caused a convulsion, a rift in his family that never healed."

Eve exhaled. Her manner bordered on contrition.

The office phone rang and she jumped. Eve put the heavy black receiver to her ear. Dagg was on the line.

"I'm sorry, professor, Dr. Shinn is in but he is with someone now," Eve said, straightening her back. "Can I have him call—"

She dropped the receiver with a clang onto the base from four inches above it. "He hung up on me."

"Soon after I took my post at Union, I witnessed Dagg's activism and supported it." Shinn removed his glasses and looked into his secretary's eyes. "In 1947, Dagg was instrumental in organizing an ecumenical project aiding refugees and others in Europe, Asia, and Africa whose lives were ruined by the Second World War. He worked fifteen-hour days. Dagg came to believe that our novel, 'incandescent' constitutional democracy was the only hope for global progress and human advancement." Shinn replaced his glasses and lowered himself into the chair. "Unwavering in his faith in this country, he later took on what some now consider unvarnished nationalism."

"Sounds like he became what he hated," Eve frowned.

Shinn nodded and Eve repeated her earlier question.

"How did he lose his eye?"

"It was during a march in Washington, DC."

The professor rose and stood in the doorway. Eve saw for the first time that he carried himself like a soldier.

"Dagg was a sign-waving supporter of Harry Truman's Federal Loyalty Program, a scheme designed to root out government employees 'disloyal' to the United States." Coming upon a dissenter, who was a staff member of the Library of Congress, Dagg exchanged words with him and got into a fight. During the altercation he tried to hit the man with his sign but instead caught a fist on his left temple.

"The blow carried such a force that Dagg's left eye emerged from its socket," Shinn relayed with a grimace. "Eb hit the ground in a daze and the mob nearly trampled him to death. His left eye was permanently blinded. From then on the man's injury, which purged the color from the cornea, was visible to everyone."

"Well, if it were me, I would have sued for a prosthetic eye," she huffed.

"Eb considers his pale eye a badge of honor, Eve, like the military's

Purple Heart. After that incident, his allegiance to country unruffled, he hardened his attitudes against certain liberal thinkers…"

"Even though they supported freedoms he once championed!" Eve asked. Shinn smiled, walked into his office and closed the door.

After opening the shades, the professor pulled out his war diary and more photographs. Destroyed Sherman tanks and a half-track used for transporting troops sit inert in a snow-covered field following a direct hit by a bazooka rocket. "They burn in minutes," he recalled, "and the tires melt into the earth." He unfolded his old military maps onto the desk. His division's December 1944 positions, the geography of battered expectations, were unmistakable.

"During the war I never appreciated the mapmaker's art," he said out loud. "So much of nature's art and allure conveyed in just two dimensions."

Seeing the maps twenty years later proved an epiphany to the professor. Even the arcane military overlays with their ritual iconography did not diminish their graphic elegance. Nor their capacity to provoke remembered doom.

In a fit of excitement, he rushed into Eve's office with the maps open and flapping.

"Look at this, Eve!" The professor laid them across her desk, disrupting her papers. "See these erased pencil marks. They show how my unit's command post lurched from place to place during the first three days of the German onslaught. It is a drawing of pure chaos!"

Pointing to their shifting locations, Shinn explained the alarm he felt for his unit. "We were the wounded field mice retreating from the hungry owl!"

Eve stared up at her boss, wondering what he wished her to say. Shinn gathered his maps and returned to his desk.

He picked up Hall's photo again. The captain was still balancing on the edge of the gorge, still on tiptoes. Still grinning. Still smoking the same cigarette.

The finished lecture notes for the day inscribed his thoughts between the red and blue lines of recipe cards. But more freely on the unlined side were jotted random words that would later prompt his memory if need be.

Afterwards the professor packed two books in his satchel, grabbed his cup, and started to exit. Again, Prof. Dagg intercepted him outside the entrance. The younger academic put his head down and coursed down the hallway.

"Sorry, Eb, gotta get to class. Let's talk soon over a schnapps."

Chapter 9

PHOSPHOROUS

February brought its full measure of cold to New York. The month froze the city to a near-impenetrable hardness. As Prof. Shinn looked beyond his classroom window, he saw hatted and capped and scarfed heads bouncing outside. Crystalline puffs of breath hung like low-altitude cumulus surrounding their faces.

At one minute past the hour, Shinn began, though the last students were still seating themselves.

"After the Volksgrenadiers surrendered to Task Force Hall at the Beaufort Crossroads, Lieutenant Graham put together a squad of guards to escort the prisoners back to our command area at Savelborn."

Task Force Philbeck had arrived at the Crossroads shortly afterwards. Shinn was with his master sergeant, Aldo Spies, a former bricklayer and tuck-pointer from Far Rockaway, Queens. They were in a jeep close behind Philbeck after reconnoitering the battle lines. Major Tommie Philbeck informed the captain of the rescue. Hall's Headquarters Company, Company A, and American survivors from other units were on the road back to Savelborn. But Lazarus's Bravo Company was still fighting. And Hall's task force had failed to liberate Shinn's Charlie Company.

"I knew this and wanted to launch my own rescue mission with or without tanks," Shinn told the class.

"Colonel 'Comfort Six' Corbin Collier had called and ordered Task

Force Hall back to battalion headquarters," Shinn recalled. "Hall didn't like the order. But he had no say in the matter."

"I don't understand his reluctance to get medical help," Rivera interrupted. "He was all messed up."

The professor nodded and told the class how Hall's men could see this barely clad captain shivering inside an Army-issued blanket.

"Sergeant Paz peeked into the bed of the armored half-track where Hall was lying. He couldn't believe what he saw." Shinn was pacing as he spoke. "Below his waist, Hall had only skivvies, torn ragged by the rocket blast. On each leg was a water blister nearly the size of a football. Both were red as the Nazi flag. Flying shrapnel had sliced open the right knee. Sergeant Paz asked sheepishly, 'Sir, where are your britches?'" The class broke out in laughter.

A twenty-four-year-old sharpshooting Californian, Paz was a hardened soldier, but selfless and well liked. He jumped into the truck's bed and rummaged through the locker where he found a pair of fatigue trousers. Hall took them, climbed out the back, and reached for his bayonet. Handing it to Capt. Shinn, he asked him to scrape grease from the axle onto the blade. Then Hall spread it like a field poultice onto his scalded legs and rear.

"Then Paz and I supported the burned man and eased him gently into his trousers. The outside temperature was well below freezing."

On the way back to battalion headquarters, where he was to catch a medical transport shuttling the wounded to a field hospital, the captain lay in a fetal position in the back of the open halftrack. Intense pain gathered around his burns and shrapnel wound. Paz wrapped him in another blanket and forced him to take water to ward off dehydration.

"Despite finally dispatching the Germans at the crossroads, Hall knew his task force was in dire circumstances. He failed to rescue, even reach my company. And the captain still couldn't reconcile how he let a wily enemy move invisibly like 'germs through capillaries' into our zone on December 16th."

Walking over to a chair he had placed near the lectern, the professor sat down. He scanned the room but saw through the students into somewhere else. "As Hall's 'disassembly' of men moved along the road, I scouted from higher ground on the flank. I saw a Wehrmacht Volksgenadier platoon, maybe sixty, seventy men, coming up on the remains of Task Force Hall from higher ground. I radioed down to alert them, but could not get through."

Volksgenadier units, remnants of ten German infantry and artillery battalions destroyed in the August invasion of France, had been patched together by Nazi high command. Included in their ranks were what remained of the twenty thousand German boys conscripted for the Hitler Youth Corps. Hall and Shinn knew this.

Less than two hundred yards away from Task Force Hall, the Germans waited behind the crest of a low hill. They had readied their rifles and bayonets and would attempt to destroy the remaining twenty-four GIs in the task force along with their captain.

"I saw this taking shape from short of a mile away, and we rushed to warn Hall. Sergeant Spies navigated the jeep through ditches to avoid German detection."

Snow was falling un- harried by wind. Suddenly the battle exploded with mortar fire booming like kettle drums.

"The moment we arrived at Hall's armored personnel carrier, the first German rifle shot hit a GI standing in the open near me. That one round entered our perimeter with a high, razor-sharp screech. I saw the exact moment when the projectile pierced the soldier's neck. The enormity of blood that rushed from the wound was sickening."

Two students left the room.

"The incoming volley of German fire was intense. Bullets and shrapnel thickened the air. The ground between the half-track, which I was using as a shield, and the dying American soldier was being pockmarked by the fusillade. I made a slight gesture toward the kid when Spies grabbed my arm. 'He's gone, captain,' he said."

If anyone other than the infantry captain and his sergeant saw the dying GI, no one attended to him, and he lay splayed belly up. More Germans commenced firing from the hill; the hysterical whir and ka-zee of slugs ricocheting off the vehicles disoriented the men. Spies maneuvered from the rear of the armored half-track to the side where he had visual advantage. When he departed, Shinn moved from his crouch and walked into the open where the dead GI lay. He stood straight up staring at the pooling blood. The shelling intensified. Around him the tormented, agitated ground hurled ice and grit onto his body. Something grazed his helmet and spun off into space. Victor Paz who was nearby shouted "get down!" Dropping his rifle he rushed from his cover to knock the captain to the earth. Shinn, recovering himself, pointed to the bleeding figure. Paz knelt by the dying man, wiped the residue from his face and dipped his fingers in the still warm blood of the youth. In a divot beside him that had exposed the ground, the sergeant worked the liquid into the earth. He wetted his thumb with the scarlet paste and drew it down the warrior's forehead as if sanctifying him with chrism.

****

"Dooley!" Hall bellowed.

Sergeant First Class Hercules "Dixie" Dooley, the unit's fiercest machine gunner, fired two more rifle rounds at the Germans, jumped out of his makeshift foxhole and into the half-track with his captain. Hall, sick with pain and lying flat on the truck bed , pointed to the automatic weapon perched on the deck like a malformed iron totem and directed Dooley to ready it to fire. Dooley studied the open ground before him. Grayish-blue smoke from ignited gunpowder begrimed the air. But his view of the terrain was clear enough.

"Load the .50 caliber with white phosphorous shells," Hall barked, now sitting up in the truck's hold. The Oklahoma captain glanced at Shinn who had moved behind the vehicle. The incendiary cartridge, if striking a man, woman, or child, could turn them into a torch and burn them to death from the inside out. In Hall's own words it was the "worst weapon in any arsenal," and he was calling it into action.

"Yes, sir!" Dooley boomed, displaying a gleeful smile and a willful disregard for the enemy bullets hurtling by him. "We have the position. We'll wipe 'em out!" Hall rose higher from the half-track to assess the enemy, then dropped out of sight.

Sergeant Dooley was a thick man and dirty. In the many months bivouacked in Luxembourg before battle, Shinn had not seen him clean once. Before joining the Army, Dooley had been a machinist in Kentucky and later in Louisiana. Shinn guessed the black sludge under the man's long ochre fingernails was grease and iron filings accumulated during those years. The sergeant had a pernicious voice that, at its loudest, sounded like exploding ordinance. Or it could rise and fall like a twelve-foot wave. One reason Shinn didn't trust him was his delivery. It reminded him of tent preachers. The New York captain with a divinity degree had wanted him muzzled to check his "twisted" evangelizing along with the litany of obscenities and racial slurs that was his sphere. Unfathomed by Dooley, he was not his own man. Years of parental ignorance and psychic abuse had encased his intellect like a sausage and occluded long ago whatever kinship he might have developed with humanity. Complementing that, Hercules Dooley had a tolerance for killing. Shinn surmised the sergeant had done yeoman service in the Klan.

Shinn, only eight feet from Hall's conversation with Dooley, was stupefied. "I couldn't believe what I heard," he confessed to his students. "It put me in a state of paralysis. That Capt. Hall would inflict torture on human beings—it was unlike him—I thought. It was pure sadism."

Quickly the gunner gripped the bandolier holding high caliber phosphorous ammunition. Dooley could almost smell the flesh of his enemy on fire and hear their screams. He yearned to see them burn before he sent them to roast hell. The Germans reached the ridge; Dooley cranked the first shell into the chamber and drew a bead on the Nazis at the front of the line.

Hall, still seated on the floor and invisible to others, gave Dooley the order.

"The Krauts are gonna charge our position in a few seconds, sergeant. When they do, fire the phosphorous rounds over their heads and well off to their sides. Force the enemy into a narrow frontal assault."

"No sir. Every one of these bastards are gonna go down by my hand!" Dooley removed the gloves and gripped the gun's firing mechanism with his bare hands.

"Finally, I understood," Shinn shouted. "Hall would use the *threat* of horrific death to work their surrender! But Dooley flew into a rage."

Ignoring the incoming fire, Hall jumped to his feet. "Do as I say or get the hell away from the goddamn gun!" he yelled in a voice that would grind bones. The captain's hand touched his still-holstered and re-loaded .45 pistol. Glaring at Hall, the sergeant nodded that he understood the order.

"What if Dooley's aim was off," Shinn pondered in front of the class. "What if he disobeyed the order and fired into the Nazis anyway? What if Hall's ruse was ineffective and we were overtaken? Destroyed?"

Dooley's fury seated itself in his tongue. As the German frontal assault began and bullets menaced the space around him, Dixie Dooley became a wild-eyed revivalist on an iron pulpit.

The sergeant ratcheted the first round into the chamber and wailed, "For wars were about him on evvv-errrr-y side until the Lord put the enemy under the bless-ud soles of his feet."

The bandolier of ammunition rolled flawlessly into the machine gun. One private fed the belt into the breach. Another husbanded the empty bandolier out the other side.

"And no longer stood an adversary or eeee-vvvvil purpose," Dooley shrieked from inside some primal cavity. Above all else was the berserk of the reverberating volley. The spent cartridges pinwheeled about him like roving prayers, dropping to his feet.

Dooley streaked the burning white phosphorus above the German helmets. The lofted shells cut through trees and bushes behind the soldiers and ignited anything on the icy slope that would burn. A sulfuric odor seized his nostrils and fortified him. Halting in their tracks, the onrushing force fell to the ground, gripped it with their bodies, and continued the assault on their bellies.

The junior Wehrmacht commander watched the maneuver from binoculars wrapped in hide and cloth. He saw his offensive about to crumble and bellowed to his men, "Angriff fortsetzen!" With the command they leapt up and resumed the charge. When the Germans were within sixty yards of the Hall Task Force, a second volley of phosphorous shells passed a few feet above them. They kept coming. But their fire was panicked even though no one was shooting at them except Dooley.

The third phosphorous salvo skimmed just inches over the enemy soldiers. They hesitated, staggered and to a man dropped their rifles. Lifting hands over their heads they continued advancing until surrendering in front of Hall's half-track and the smoking machine gun. The fuming German commander broke into a delirious run toward his rear lines.

"There's your man, Victor," Graham hollered.

A pop, a whistle, and then the faint sound of a door closing. The retreating German officer dropped heavily into the snow.

"Spear shot, Paz!" Hall yelled.

Shinn strode to Graham. "They are weeping, lieutenant!" he said, declaring what everyone was seeing.

"They thought the next volley would be on them and burn through their bones," Graham wheezed. "They escaped a horrible end. And they know it."

For a moment all was still. Paz didn't move from his position. Hall sat motionless near the gun. All the American GIs stared at the Wehrmacht soldiers kneeling like acolytes as if in an act of grateful contrition. Shinn's mind tried to absorb the scene. The dead German commander who had sunk into the snow was now a vague black form unable to journey into the next minute.

"The sanctimonious Dooley was at least partially right," Shinn announced to the class causing a stir. "Hall's task force had the advantage. Even with the enemy's superior numbers, Hall could have had the onrushing Jerries cut to pieces. He sidestepped what most battlefield commanders covet."

Chapter 10

MARK MY WORDS

"Hall's decision to let the Germans get close to their position was a sizable risk," Prof. Shinn confessed to his class. "Then trying to checkmate them into surrender even more of one."

"He was so confident in his judgment that the phosphorous ploy would work, I don't think Hall ever considered having to kill those German soldiers."

Belloc stood. "How did Hall respond to Dooley?"

"As Graham was getting the surrendering Germans to their feet, Hall turned to Dooley and told him to look hard at them. Dooley could see the group was young—in their teens— and interspersed with old men. Hall had seen who they were fighting at Beaufort Crossroads."

Shinn paced in front of the blackboard. "Hall yelled at Dooley." The professor mimicked an Oklahoma drawl. "'Any idiot ud know they'd surrender, sergeant!' I think they could hear the captain in Berlin. Then he said, 'You think they wanted to leave this earth burning to death?'

"Then I saw Hall get in Dooley's face. He whispered in his ear, but still loud enough for us close by to hear, 'You're damn close to shoveling guts in the medical tents for the rest of the war.' Hall's face was crimson with rage."

After the dressing down, Dooley cornered Paz.

"Mark my words, Mexican," Dooley said to the sergeant, "This Okie yellow belly's reckonin' will come."

"Dooley thought Hall was naïve," the professor related, "that he didn't know how 'the game of war' was played. And he didn't like Hall's taking the enemy alive while the Germans were spilling 'sacred American blood.'"

Paz's reply to the sergeant carried a warning. "He said something like, 'Don't threaten the captain with your shit, Dooley,'" the professor remembered. "'And my family is from Chile, you goddamn fool!'" Laughter from the students seemed to shake the windows.

****

Spies and Shinn got in the jeep and made it to Beaufort dodging enemy sniping and random shelling. Shinn needed a face-to-face with Col. Collier. He wanted orders to rescue his company.

Task Force Hall, with over a sixty German prisoners, arrived at battalion headquarters an hour after Shinn. One of the medical jeeps had a stretcher that carried Hall through Beaufort en route to an American field infirmary.

"The enemy hit the men in Hall's task force ferociously," Shinn told the students. "Many died or were incapacitated. Lt. Ruder, the captain's best platoon leader, was killed while on reconnaissance. It had been only two-and-a-half days since the German offensive began. Hall shouted to me going past on the stretcher, but I couldn't make out what he said. I just hoped his wounds weren't serious."

Chapter 11

THE SYLPH

The U.S. Army Field Hospital in southern Luxembourg where Capt. Hall convalesced was little more than scores of large camouflaged tents mushrooming up from the ground and heated by oil burners. Inside, the odor of bloody bandages, ether, and feces converged and soured the air. The compound was miles behind the battle lines and the muted din of artillery sounded as inconsequential as street noise to the soldiers. To the staff it was different. It spoke of their own mortality and chilled them. Moreover, this was death's low articulated whisper that seduced many of the wounded to return quickly to the killing arena from which they had just been extracted.

In the hospital, Capt. Hall's mind returned to the fiasco of Beaufort Crossroads. He closed his eyes and began to draw a blueprint to reach Shinn's still-imperiled Charlie Company, when a figure appeared above him.

"I kinda knew I'd find you here, captain. Saw your name on the Division Morning Report," a nurse said.

Hall opened his eyes and jumped up with a start, then gasped from the pain radiating through his body.

"It is best you stay in bed," the nurse said as she helped him back down into the cot. "I've seen your medical report. Appears like you took a beating, but you will recover. You may be the only soldier alive whose legs were the gateway for a bazooka missile." She paused. "It must have looked like high comedy to your German audience."

"Well, they couldn't kill me," the captain replied, trying to defend his honor.

"Of course not," the nurse said as she doubled-checked his bandages. "How could the Nazis even take aim laughing that hard?"

"Didn't know I'd see you here of all places, Sammy," Hall swooned, clutching her hand."

Without scanning for anyone watching, Samantha Waterford knelt by the bed and kissed the captain on the cheek. "It is good to see you, John. I wish, though, you weren't in this dreadful state." Waterford had spent months in residence at a London hospital being schooled on the treatment of battle wounds both physical and psychological. Then was shipped to the continent with hundreds of other medical personnel. "We are on our way north to Belgium. Lots of us. The casualties up there…the casualties, the horrific casualties, John. They are monstrous."

The captain gripped her hand; she was a sylph, inscrutable, an alloy of iron, saffron, and myrrh. "Great to see you, honey. But I'm sorry this isn't what you had in mind when you travelled to Cleveland…"

"You know that I abhor the violence," Waterford said, attempting to subdue her emotions.

"… and now you're nursing the broken and hopeless in hell."

"I thought by now humans would have evolved," she whispered. "And yet here we are, reduced to shit, still throwing stones at one another."

Waterford tucked the white blanket around Hall's body to secure it from drafts. "But I am here to heal, and for the others to gift them relief from pain if I can, a serenity, until their end comes. But I am not the same person, John, as I was on the bus to Ohio."

He peered into her face as if seeking a clue as to what she meant.

"Your colonel is here…"

The captain pulled her close and whispered, "I'm not interested in him."

"I have to get going."

"What has changed?" he pleaded.

"I had lived my life in a narrow spun-sugar box. I didn't look beyond it." Tears glistened in her eyes like crystals, and she kissed him. His grip on her hand tightened, but she released her's and walked away. A swell of emotion rippled through the captain.

"I meant what I said on the ship, Sam!" Hall called out. He tried to hide it but his voice carried the undertow of panic.

She turned, waved, and was gone.

While standing near the tent entrance talking to a doctor, Col. Collier spotted his captain among the rows of cots. Task Force Hall had failed its mission; Charlie Company remained isolated and surrounded. Even though he and his few remaining men routed and captured the 276th Volksgrenadier remnants, the captain expected the worst. Unsure of what his commanding officer would say, he didn't move until the imposing Collier stood at the foot of his cot.

"Good morning, sir." Hall's greeting was listless.

"How are you feeling, Hall?"

"Ready for duty, colonel."

"You've got today and tomorrow to get yourself healed up," Collier told him, sparing the niceties. "Then you'll take command of your company, and on my orders move north and torment the goddamned Krauts. They have eight divisions eating alive our two in Bastogne."

Hall knew this and the soldier standing above his cot was boring him.

"Hit 'em hard, disengage, then hit 'em again," Collier snapped.

The colonel was letting his West Point bluster leak out, and Hall didn't like the seepage. It smelled. He didn't require "pepping up" to fight the enemy and didn't appreciate anyone who felt he did.

"Keep them off balance and delay their advance," the colonel continued. "That's the sketch. I'll brief battalion officers, you included, tomorrow night. No ifs, ands or buts, we are gonna buy time for Third Army and you're ol' pal Patton to arrive from their vacation on the Mediterranean coast."

The captain could sense the colonel thought he was clever, rolling out his lame insults.

"Has my company been brought up to full strength?" the captain asked, leaving off the "sir."

"When the Third breaks through to Bastogne," Collier continued, as if he didn't hear Hall's ask, "it will move to reinforce our counterattack and we'll drive the Krauts back into their fucking 'Fatherland.' In the meantime, the Hun will not take Bastogne. Under any circumstances. Got the picture?"

"I need an armored infantry team at 0600 in the morning. We're gonna go back and extract Company C from the Germans," Hall said bluntly, not caring that he was giving instructions to a superior officer. "I'll be back for your briefing..."

"Jesus Christ, Hall, that's not your orders!" the colonel bellowed snorting fire. "Hell, you'd probably try another stunt like you did at Beaufort Crossroads and try to kill the whole fucking German army yourself. Past time you remember that you are supposed to be commanding men, captain. They are to do the fighting...."

Hall interrupted. "I wouldn't criticize those men. They rose to the occasion and put their lives on the line. Hell, for tank mechanics, pole climbers, and cooks not trained infantry, they did well. They did damn well. But they couldn't do what had to be done."

"You aren't a grunt rifleman anymore!" the colonel snarled, pointing his finger at the man on the cot. "Lead, for chrissake!" Collier knew that the loss of his captain would impede his plans.

"Besides, I sent Shinn to get his men."

A doctor hurried over to Collier. "If you can't keep your voice low, colonel, I'll have you take your leave. This isn't your briefing room, and the patients don't need to hear your orders!"

Collier ignored the physician and drew close to his subordinate. His tone changed. It was somber, distant. "I wanted to let you know that Maj. Philbeck was killed in action yesterday. Good man."

The captain expelled his breath.

"He had rejoined his tank battalion when he got in a hellish firefight somewhere near Pommerloch, interdicting the German advance."

Hall, fevered, unable to clear his mind, saturated with remorse and frenzied with worry over Sam, didn't speak but lay on the cot gazing at the thin twitching canvas of the tent, a fragile membrane protecting the scores of patients under it. He stared at water stains on the roof. They reminded him of layers of a chrysalis he had seen in his mother's garden.

Not getting a response, Collier stood, putting his hands on his hip. "Be prepared to attack the Germans in Belgium, Hall. Let's sting the bastards for Philbeck and Ruder. They deserve no less from us."

Chapter 12

THE CHALK LINE

From the front of an empty classroom, Prof. Shinn on a steel folding chair sat looking out at the rows of desks. In one hand he held a letter written on Christmas Day 1944 by his new bride. In the other, a stub of white chalk.

He found the faded missive in a box mistakenly placed among the miscellany of orders to duty, morning reports, citations, and discharge papers. Having discovered it just before class time, Shinn decided to read it now to himself.

In the letter Katharine recounted the modest Christmas dinner she shared with Roger's family in Ohio, her being greeted by a blaze of hoarfrost that blanched every tree limb and bush and telephone wire in town, along with news of friends and vexatious neighbors. It closed with an expression of her deep love for him. Katharine had written the three-page correspondence on the blank sides of old bank statements. Her war writing was always upbeat, never mawkish or gossipy, always Katharine. Shinn recalled how much he looked forward to hearing from her during his "time in this other dimension." He looked around the room. The students had arrived without his awareness.

"In our last period, we left Captain Hall lying in a field hospital. He had killed German soldiers. But he wasn't thinking about them, he told me after the war. The man was contemplating Waterford's peril, the loss of American lives, and his company's impending reentry into battle." The professor re-folded the letter and slipped it into the silky interior pocket of his suit coat. "Before we begin, does anyone have a question?"

Robert Newman raised his hand.

"Yes, Mr. Newman?"

"I see no real ethical dilemma at play here," Newman stated, directing his words as much to the class as the lecturer. "You are telling us about a comic-book-hero just fulfilling what he considers his duty. Wiping the land free of evil doers and saving American women from harm is an old canard of the military establishment, and your captain bought into it."

"Actually, Hall didn't—" Shinn, thinking Newman was finished, began to reply. But the student continued to nudge the professor out of the conversation in an effort to move the audience in his direction. His demeanor had changed. Unlike the emotional performance at the St. James Church rally, Newman spoke with evenness, adopting the pace and deliberation of one with authority. As if speaking to each nascent scholar, he pivoted in all directions.

"In the early forties, our government scooped up all the able-bodied adolescents and programmed them through deployed propaganda to fight for their country. The emotionally overwrought stuff worked! Just like today."

With a sweep of his arms, the student asked the class rhetorically what kind of civilization uses nationalist disinformation to "recruit farm boys and gas station attendants to be killers."

Shinn quietly watched the reactions. Newman's intrusion had annoyed several in the class.

"I think we've heard enough, Newman," Rivera interrupted. "The professor called for questions, not homilies."

"What does it mean?" Newman continued, raising his voice and palms in a gesture of incredulity. "Is it that our would-be warriors have such shallow morals that they are easy prey to bullshit?"

The class groaned at Newman's conceit.

"Sounds like you've drawn the contour of the battlefield captain on our blackboard and are now trying to squeeze him into your preconceived outline, Mr. Newman," Shinn challenged. "Does he fit? It appears you are attempting to characterize all soldiers as the same?"

"In a larger sense, yes."

The theologian in the professor studied Newman for a moment. "I would like to refer you and everyone in the class to Paul Tillich's writings. Explore the meaning of your own existence first, he tells us. Then, have the courage to receive the answers, no matter how painful."

Having a keenness for students willing to duel, if they can defend against a sharpened blade, Shinn walked away from the lectern.

"I appreciate the strength of your commitment, Mr. Newman. But wouldn't you agree that violence and war are essential for certain purposes? Worthy purposes, in fact?"

"No!" he coughed and scanned his classmates.

"Men and women need not love war to fight in one, do they?" Shinn pressed him. "Or perhaps they love something they think they can get only through war."

Newman offered no response.

"Some goals in war have an ethical dimension, such as protecting loved ones or preserving the rights of others, don't you think?"

Newman appeared uneasy but listened.

"Isn't Normandy Beach the very essence of the social contract Americans wrote themselves? That our nation will commit in final resort the blood of its men and women, as well as its fortune, to save other people and civilization from tyranny and torture?"

Shinn loosened his tie as if to ease the flow of speech.

"It is often said that a war-weary world longs for peace as though war were somehow an accident. Or the connivance of a few against the ardent wish of mankind."

The professor moved to the far right edge of the blackboard, which bridged the room's anterior. He touched his white chalk to the cinder-black surface and walked toward its far side making a continuous mark. As the chalk advanced along the route, it sounded like a purr until it crossed the seam between the two juxtaposed slates. There, it threw off dust and issued a "snap" as if excited to have reached the end of something and ready to move on further.

"Or, in reality, if such a 'thing' as 'reality' exists, don't most men desire peace, but solely on their own terms? Don't they 'thirst for peace,' only *after* they have confiscated their neighbor's land? Or they are about to be drafted and 'have a lot to lose'? Perhaps the line between moral and immoral, ethical and unethical, is impossibly thin, Mr. Newman. Unlike yours." The professor lifted the chalk as he ran out of blackboard and ended the pale eighteen-foot fault line, not with a question mark, but with a resounding "!".

Chapter 13

THE WANDERING SHADOW

With Task Force Hall failing to extract Charlie Company from the Nazi grip, Col. Collins ordered Capt. Shinn to fashion a plan. The captain rushed to battalion communications to try to make contact with his troops. After three unsuccessful attempts, the captain, unwilling to consider that the thirty-two men of Charlie Company were dead, estimated the field telephone wire had been cut.

He exited the building and grabbed his sergeant.

"What are your orders, sir?" First sergeant Aldo Spies asked as they left camp and disappeared into the night.

"Not gonna risk taking a battery of men out at night not knowing," Shinn started. "Uh, the colonel offered us some men who returned from Task Force Hall. I don't want to mess with GIs who don't know where the business end of the rifle is."

Spies, though he knew the answer, repeated his question.

Shinn let out a large breath and unfolded his topographical map of the battle area. Hidden in a high pinched ravine, Shinn struck a match, shielded it with his body, and threw light on a map. It showed estimated enemy troop strength and location.

"You and I probably will find our men here, sergeant." The anxious officer pointed to where his company had dug foxholes. "We'll lay wire behind us as we go. Re-establishing radio contact between them and our command post and verifying their position is our only hope of an accurate rescue."

It was midnight on Dec. 19th. Fog and light snow complicated visibility, but moonlight broke through intermittently and helped guide the heavily armed pair. After twenty minutes, Shinn and Spies were well into enemy territory. They moved at a slow, deliberate pace. Shinn felt this would make them sound like they belonged there.

Out of nowhere a soldier told the two to halt in German and English and approached with a rifle pointed at the captain's head. He wore an American uniform with one stripe on each sleeve.

"What is the password?" he demanded.

"Brooklyn," Shinn answered, which was the rifleman's cue to complete the phrase and prove he wasn't an imposter.

"Dodgers," the private responded, and they greeted one another. Shinn briefed him on the mission and asked for his advice. Separated from his unit and wandering, he was of little help, though the private said he picked up conversations in German two hundred yards to the east. Spies gave the rifleman the coordinates of command headquarters and sent him on his way. The captain and sergeant swerved due south hoping to avoid the enemy outpost. Shinn's head was pounding.

Nine minutes later the captain was expecting to find his company dug into the terrain where he would re-establish wire communication to battalion and affect a rescue. A voice broke out of the darkness, "Werfen Sie Ihre Waffen!" freezing Spies and the captain in mid-stride.

"Werfen Sie Ihre Waffen!" came the demand again. "Weapons down!" A soldier, wearing the German stahlhelm helmet, with his rifle slung over his shoulder, emerged from the woods. A flashlight was in one hand and a Walther P38 pistol in the other. He was rail thin, of low rank, and apparently alone, probably a sentry. No one moved until he started yelling again. Spies gripped his rifle and broke for cover. The sentry put two bullets in his back then turned the pistol on Shinn.

"I need to check on my sergeant!" Shinn shouted to the sentry, "Ich muss ihm helfen." The sentry's reply was terse. "Nein."

The cold crawled into the captain's bones and he began to shiver. Spies coughed and hacked uncontrollably. Shinn glimpsed him struggling to crawl. Another German, probably awakened by the gun fire, arrived. Shinn wept as the Nazi soldier crushed the sergeant's skull with a blow from the butt of his rifle.

"Why?" the captain screamed. "Why?"

Two Germans of low rank marched Shinn to the Our River, passing Wehrmacht corpses that lay quietly illuminated by the moon. Moving past them, no one spoke. In death, no ferocity remains, Shinn thought. They looked pitiful and helpless to him, the empty eyes staring across the cold tributary toward their homeland. At the shore, the exhausted captain huddled with eight other captives, inches from where filmy ice had formed on the water. Remorse for his sergeant and anxiety for his company nearly overwhelmed him. Shinn felt he was dying inside. A solitary boat that had seen many years was at the river's edge waiting to ferry him and the others into Hitler's Germany. They were wet, cold, and empty. As they looked over at the Siegfried Line, fortifications that loomed above them on the hills across the river, every sound was dissonant. Guards fixed bayonets. Men coughed. The forlorn echo of captives' boots on ice and rock and the faraway rumble of cannons invaded the captain's ears and he knelt and brought snow from the water's edge to his face to cleanse it . The leaking boat groaned as he stepped in. Shinn saw the silhouette of a single figure standing at the stern. He would negotiate the vessel across the dark river.

After crossing the river and a two-hour journey on foot, Shinn and the eight, and fourteen additional prisoners gathered along the way like stray cattle, were marched single file into Diesz, a disheveled town of deserted streets. Here, a stone barn performed as the Nazi military police redoubt. Soldiers of low rank forced the prisoners inside. A Nazi officer directed an underling to push a heavy wooden barrier to the side. Constructed on a sliding rail with iron supports and rusted Garrick hangers, the door screamed as it was opened. Shinn peered inside and surveyed the tiny cells. Dirt floors were matted with old straw. A sergeant nudged him into one, then closed and padlocked the entryway. The lingering aroma of cow manure filled the air. This the captain found comforting. His grandmother's stables in Ohio carried the same earthy pungency. The moment the captain's body hit the straw, he fell into a slumber more comatose than sleep. Less than an hour later, the door opened then closed. As the bolt glided into its holder with a crack, the captain woke.

"And who are you," he asked of the man, spent and foul smelling, who stood before him. Despite the frigid temperature, his arms were bare, his skin bone-pale.

"Aberanth Wronge, lieutenant, 01281948," the man offered with unusual spirit given his circumstance.

"Here," Shinn tossed him a rag he had used as a blanket. "Where is your jacket?"

"They took it. I'll get it back, sir."

"Rawn-guh," Shinn pronounced the newcomer's name. "How do you spell it?"

"W-r-o-n-g-e," he replied. "Friends call me 'Abel', sir."

"Is there a reason the Jerry's put you in here, lieutenant?" Shinn leaned closer to the soldier trying to get his bearings, including whether this figure was a spy.

Wronge swaddled the cloth around his chest and shoulders. "They won't put officers and enlisted men together, sir. This was the only space they had, I guess."

****

"How long was it, your interrogation?"

"This is my fourth," Wronge beamed, as if he had just rolled in on a warm ocean wave. "They questioned me seventy-four minutes today."

The lieutenant sat down and Shinn could see his lip was cut and clotted and his face had bruising. He had older wounds. Wronge was missing six fingernails. *Not likely a Nazi mole*, the captain deduced.

"Seventy minutes for name, rank, and serial number!" Shinn exclaimed probing this strange man.

"Mostly," came the reply. "They already know a helluva lot about me already. They know about you too, sir."

"How do they know about me?" the captain shot back.

"The German Feldwebel, a petty policy mandarin who keeps this dreary hole humming, has your battalion roster on his desk. He showed me your name. They know you are the commanding officer of Charlie Company, 60th Armored Infantry Battalion of the Ninth Armored Division, sir." Wronge's demeanor shifted; his narrow face went into a squint. "He said they captured all of your remaining men yesterday. Some were executed."

Though he was wary of anything the Germans might say about his troops, Shinn nonetheless choked on what he heard. And how would they know about him? Headquarters Company threw battalion papers into a burning half-track at Fort Meyers.

"Did they say how many of my men survived?" he asked.

Wronge shook his head.

"Where you from, lieutenant?" the captain asked the shivering man. He was drawn to the indigo tattoo on his neck peeking through the threadbare wrap circling his shoulders. Shinn recognized it as a sacred Hindu mark signifying the first sound of creation.

"Oh, I've lived everywhere," was his reply.

The captain wanted to know where he had joined the army.

"Oh, the place doesn't matter much, does it?" Wronge huffed. "In this place I like to discuss only what is consequential because conversation here is rare."

"Just trying to get acquainted," Shinn said as he blew warm breath into his hands.

"Let's start with paradise, the Arizona desert. Have you seen the color that explodes after a spring torrent?" Wronge stretched both arms to his sides and loudly snapped his fingers as if trying to wake the spiritually somnolent. "It is beauty incarnate."

"Have you any family?" Shinn continued.

"Oh, I have many brothers in the North."

"What happened to your unit?" the captain asked, suspecting the soldier was borderline insane.

Wronge's stretching switched into a jerky dance. His hands clapped out a complex beat. "I have been having these dreams, sir. I'm in my old job in the states. But I can't locate the people I work with in the office. Damned strangers shuffle papers at tables where my friends once sat. The old building had changed inside as if it were built a century in the future. The walls change colors; they pulse and sing, eerily. Could not find my way around," he cackled. "I was on deadline and my desk and my files are gone and a man…." The lieutenant stopped mid-sentence and seated himself gently into the corner.

"Well, it's clear you aren't getting much rest, lieutenant," Shinn offered.

"Nothing but a portal," the lieutenant laughed pointing at the cell door, "to a dead end, captain. We all realize there is no way out of this horror film but are afraid to…."

Wronge wore a twisted grin, but if he meant to say more, he couldn't. The cell door slid open revealing a youthful, spit-and-polish German feldwebel at the rank of staff sergeant. Though he carried himself like a patrician, to Shinn his low rank and gnarled hands betrayed a working class heritage. "Kapitän," the officious soldier said sharply. He waved his rifle upward, signaling Shinn to rise. The escort marched the American down a stone hallway to an open door. Squatted at the entrance of the interrogation chamber was a gamy Nazi sentinel, who was missing teeth and looked to have weathered more than seventy Prussian winters. He grinned at the captain with violet lips and purred, "Sing, Sing."

The room had greasy pocked limestone walls that appeared to have a skin the color of pickle brine. Its dimensions could not have exceeded ten by twelve feet. Centered on the wall across from the feldwebel was a Gruen clock that showed a quarter to six. No daylight was yet visible from the one clerestory window. However, a single light bulb dropped from the ceiling to within two feet of a disfigured table. It glared around the bleakness and threw shadows off insects crawling the walls. The noir cliché of the solitary bulb momentarily amused Shinn.

I guess Nazi sadists are not creative people, he thought.

The Germans had positioned one seat on each of the table's longer sides precisely equidistant from the ends. One was wood with soiled velvet cushions on the back and seat. The other a spare steel folding chair with a crushed back-rest.

The guard signaled Shinn to remain on his feet. The captain put his hands in his pockets and lifted his feet up and down to stay warm. He scanned the floor and perimeter where he detected iron-brown splatters, probably aging blood.

Once a knackwurst factory, no doubt, Shinn joked to himself to deflect thoughts of what was ahead. And attempt to shut out the numbness in his legs.

After standing for fifteen minutes—according to the clock—a porcine German officer entered in full uniform visible through a heavy unbuttoned overcoat. His eyelids were thick as dumplings and he carried a large satchel, which he dropped with a thud on the floor next to him. He gestured for Shinn to sit.

"Sorry to keep you waiting, Captain Shinn," the festooned officer rumbled as he removed his coat and took his seat. "I am Hermann Göring."

The absurdity nonplussed the American captain. This fool was not the head of the German Luftwaffe, Shinn knew. The Nazi stared at him. No one emitted a sound. Then the interrogator tipped his head back, dropped his jaw, and released a volcanic shriek of laughter. Shinn gaped at the roof of his mouth, the wobbling uvula and a horseshoe of perfect upper teeth. The laugh turned the Nazi officer's corpulent face a vivid carmine and his neck billowed beyond the rigid wool collar of a dirty gray uniform.

"What, you don't recognize me!" he shouted in English between his burbling. *Hustling American captains appeared to be lively entertainment for him*, Shinn mused.

"Okay, I am in reality Major Rainar Krüger. Now tell me about yourself," he exclaimed joyously as if he had invited the American to his study for cordials.

"Sir, I am Roger Shinn, captain, 08253294."

"Yes, I know all of that! Are you married?"

"I am sorry sir, but that is all I can tell you."

The major's face dropped quickly dousing his smile. "Hmm, if we are to be friends, we must be friendly to one another." His breath was purple.

Krüger re-positioned himself in the chair and began anew.

"Well, no harm," he said, but his stare had hardened. "I'll tell you more about myself. Uh, but first, is that the way you sit before a superior officer?"

Shinn had relaxed. In the American army when a soldier is given permission to sit that usually means "at ease." The captain straightened his back, locked his jaw and looked ahead.

"Much better," the major smiled and let out a loud raspy fart. "Now please excuse me, Roger, I must heed the call of nature."

Krüger left the room, as did the feldwebel. Shinn could hear them talking in German outside the door. A man to whom the major referred to as "lieutenant" joined the conversation. They spoke for a couple of minutes. Then their voices evaporated, and Shinn was alone. When the major returned another fifteen minutes later, the captain had nodded off.

"Achtung!" the major bellowed as he entered the room. Shinn woke and leapt to his feet.

"Are American soldiers so ill trained that they don't come to attention when a superior officer enters a room?" Krüger yelled, gesticulating wildly with his arms.

"My apologies, major, I didn't hear," Shinn responded.

"Shut up!" the major boomed, then breathed and lowered his voice. "Now where were we? Oh, yes! I was going to give you a report. You'll be pleased to know, I am sure, that that was one of my best shits this week."

Shinn could smell something rank on the major, but didn't know how to respond. He said nothing and held a straight-ahead stare. The major's tantrum had caused the light bulb to sway, sending Krüger's bilious shadow wandering around the walls.

"So, where were we before I had to excuse myself?"

"You were going to tell me about yourself," Shinn said blankly.

"Yes! But first I have a gift!" the major exclaimed with joy. He produced a bottle of prune brandy and two glasses. Then offered Shinn a cigarette.

"No, thank you, sir. I don't smoke."

Krüger frowned and lit one for himself. "Then let's have a drink," the major insisted, trying hard to be friendly as he poured brandy in Shinn's glass. Knowing this was part of the German interrogation regimen and more a draught of hemlock than plum nectar, the captain refused politely again.

"You disdain to drink with me!" the interrogator screamed.

"Major Krüger, I mean no disrespect, but I don't drink." At that the major jumped to his feet in a fury causing his chair to crash to the floor. Seeing the German's anger, Shinn nodded and took a sip of brandy.

The major gulped his and poured himself another. Then he saw Shinn's was only a third empty. "Drink the rest of it!" he demanded.

The captain, wanting to avoid drunkenness, swallowed it as slowly as he could. Krüger refilled it and ordered him to drink. The routine continued at an accelerating pace and both of them emptied their glasses a half dozen times.

Finally, Shinn burst out, "I can't tolerate anymore!"

"You will drink," the major demanded.

The captain's throat was tight. "I cannot."

Krüger reached in his satchel and removed a heavy wooden billy club.

Shinn had seen American military police use them to bludgeon uncooperative GIs into submission. Not wanting to be beaten, the captain swallowed another half glass then said, "I'm done."

"Hofmann!" the German officer screamed, and the feldwebel burst into the room. They said nothing to one another, but the guard immediately grabbed Shinn's arms and pinned them down behind the chair.

Krüger rushed to Shinn's side of the table and gave him three savage blows. The first to the head made the room give off sparks. The third one hit the captain's collarbone with such force a cracking sound reverberated around the space. Through the pain, Shinn thought his attacker had splintered his clavicle.

The major grabbed the captain, wrenched his prisoner's forehead back until his face was toward the ceiling. Shinn choked and coughed as the German poured liquor down his throat. The major picked up the club.

"I'll knock your teeth down your throat!" he bellowed. "Swallow it, goddamn you. If you vomit, I'll wipe your face in it. You call yourself an officer? A German corporal can drink more!"

Hofmann pried the captain's mouth and held it open with gloved hands that smelled of rancid meat. The room spun, Shinn convulsed, swallowing his vomit, and then gulping the brandy. Krüger emptied the rest of the liquor down Shinn's throat, smashed the bottle against the wall, and returned to his chair. Perspiration beaded on the major's face, and he glared across the table. The captain tried to suppress his retching but failed, soaking his shirt and fouling the floor around him.

Krüger rifled through Shinn's jacket pockets. He found a picture of the captain with Katharine and his Army ID card.

Chapter 14
SECRET FORMULA

Hofmann left the room without a prompt, as if this routine by the two Germans had been repeated so often it was convention. And they were actors in a comic theater reciting their lines and performing their wooden stage movements in some vile self-fulfilling amusement.

Shinn had use of his arms again, but as he watched a roach climbing the wall, his eyesight failed him. The room went black. He shut his eyes and breathed evenly to suppress panic. All he could detect were hypnagogic spots flashing in the darkness.

After minutes, the captain saw large sparkles behind his closed eyelids. He opened them slowly and light flooded in. Images emerged.

Sitting in his chair quietly for four long minutes, Major Krüger stared at the tabletop. Saliva dripped from his mouth and down his chin. It collected in an ugly pool near the table's edge. Whispering to himself, his only words were "Such a nasty business." Shinn, his wrenched jaw resting on his chest, was disoriented, nauseous, and racked with pain. He tried to discern whether the hurricane had passed or he was in the tranquil eye of it.

"What did you say your name was?" the inebriated Krüger grunted, renewing the interrogation. He glanced at the captain's identification card. "Roger, do you know where my wife is?"

Shinn shook his head.

"She's dead, Roger. She and my son were killed by American bombers. And she was an American girl!" he heaved.

"I am sorry, sir, I truly am," Shinn said, slurring his sympathy.

"Don't call me sir," he replied. "My middle name is Wilhelm, and we're brothers. Just call me Wil." With that Krüger broke down in tears. Shinn wondered if this Nazi hypocrite was just putting on a show.

"Do you have a child?" he asked through his weeping.

"No, Wil," the captain replied.

In his hand Krüger held the picture of Shinn and Katharine. "But you have a wife, and you know how I feel." As he stood and walked over to Shinn, the major wobbled. He put his arm around Shinn's shoulder and called him "Roger" and "brother" as he talked. They sympathized with one another as only drunks can do. "Roger, I am a major in the regular German Army, a professional soldier and officer. You're only a junior and a captain. It is never necessary for me to apologize. But I do apologize."

Krüger was adamant—he lost his composure and had not planned to beat Shinn. He laid his *Schirmmütze* on the table. As he spoke, his prisoner glared at the foreboding hat. Its front soared up into a wool crown as if the wearer was some kind a deity. *Deluded bastard*, Shinn thought while the major droned on in his Teutonic warp of English. Near the crest of the cap was the prescriptive Nazi badge. The heraldic Reichsadler eagle clutched in its claws not game plucked from the Rhine but a twisted cross. Just below was a human skull pressed out of silver. And in this image, as insignificant as it was, he saw from his alcohol-laden fog the enormity of the fascist cosmos, "Human sorcery has made wholesale murder acceptable to a democratic country!" The captain glanced at Krüger pissing on the wall and said with scorn, "Germany has the most extraordinary army ever forged," the major said. Shinn's mind floated around the room unfastened. He remembered tomatoes he had grown in hot Ohio soil, the ones he plucked and ate on the spot.

"How disconnected I was to the vast German military-political apparatus," Shinn confessed out loud. "What infantile creature would devote the time and, indeed, the ardor to adorn the caps of its officers with fetishes of death once sported by pirates?" Shinn vomited again.

Krüger sat down at the table with his zipper still open. The captain craned his neck and stared into the all but clear irises of the major's eyes. They looked like peeled grapes with a fly in the middle of each. Shinn laughed out loud.

The Nazi ignored the slight. "Whenever I think of my love, I lose control," he slurred and began again to weep. As interested in playing his abuser's counselor as eating insects off the wall, the captain nonetheless responded with a form of cardboard empathy, and they pushed on. Shinn refused any discussion of military affairs, unless he had convincing lies to confuse the enemy. But the major now cared little of Shinn's stonewalling. The history of his wife and family were what Krüger wished to convey to his captive. "My frau was born on the East Coast, and we lived in New Jersey for years," he began.

The major's recollection of New York City, the penny chocolate machines in the subways, the popular songs, Mayor Jimmy Walker's tenure in office, and dozens of other details, convinced Shinn that Krüger was telling the truth, though he didn't care.

Two days later guards marched Shinn to the interrogation room. He stood this time nearly a half hour before Krüger arrived. The pain, his weakened condition, and fever caused him to lose whatever interest he might have had in this game. He seemed at times to lack the energy to care about survival itself. The captain worried that the injuries he had sustained and the horrors witnessed had immobilized forever his capacity to be shocked or emotionally connected to anything in this sphere. Yet this episode chilled him to his core.

Krüger entered the room. "How are you feeling, brother?"

The captain jumped to his feet, directed his swollen eyes to the front, and said nothing. A rush of air from the opened door caused the dangling light bulb to sway back and forth. Shinn closed his eyes to avoid nausea.

"Come on," the major whined. "You aren't going to give me the silent treatment just because of the little misunderstanding from a couple days ago?"

Taking his seat, Krüger motioned for the captain to sit.

"Are you having headaches or dry mouth," he asked.

Shinn opened his eyes and glared at his interrogator but did not speak.

"If you are faking, you will be whipped," the major said casually. "But if you have legitimate head injury, we have new remedies. Probably the best in the world. To reduce discomfort and any serious impairments."

Krüger noted that only Germans could be treated, but he would make an exception in the captain's case.

"I find your offer hard to believe," Shinn whispered. "It is equally difficult to accept that you are interested in methods of healing."

"Oh, don't be surprised. We must keep our command staff in good health. And, of course, our soldiers in the field."

"And what is your secret formula…?"

The major cut him off. "Our laboratory Jews. Sometimes we use gypsies and queers. Papists…."

The captain peered at him quizzically.

"Let us just say that we use an advanced level of controlled experimentation. Including research on head trauma. Our German doctors and scientists do. On inferior subjects. To learn…." Krüger didn't finish the thought.

"Human vivisection?" the captain choked, his chalky complexion turning red. "You Nazis mutilate and kill innocent human beings in the name of what? You are nothing more than a vector of some unutterable disease…"

Krüger waved his hand viciously. "Hypocrite! You Americans are no different from us!"

"Humanity! Justice!" Shinn yelled. "They are codified in our founding documents, sewn into our national character!"

Hoffman was standing in the corner observing the exchange when Krüger glanced over at him. When their eyes met the two erupted into a fit of laughter. The captain's jaw tightened and the howling ceased abruptly.

"We took a page from your own book, brother," the major smiled. "The virtues of racial hygiene, human experimentation, even sterilization, we learned it all from your 'work' with American Negroes, the Red Man, and your mental defectives. What you couldn't enslave, you infected, tortured, and killed. Many for science."

Krüger stood, straightened his uniform, and signaled to Hoffman that he wanted a drink. "Now, Roger, let's have some schnapps. And I'll enlighten you about your human experiments on syphilis at Tuskegee."

The captain would endure three more days of freakish interrogation and meandering conversations. The German major continued his battle of wits to exact information out of Shinn, but the effort now was half-hearted. As a prisoner, he remained steadfastly evasive. "I don't know," and "I am not allowed to answer that," and "I prefer the sun and fun of Coney Island to this shit."

At least three times a day, the major would depart the session for long stretches. The razor-burned feldwebel nearly rupturing with zeal would conduct interrogations in his absence, and the German's questions were numerous and detailed. They wanted but did not receive intelligence on American forces from the restive, hungry captain, whose psyche wandered in ashes and blood.

"Vat do these damned insignia mean?" the feldwebel demanded, showing the captain pictures taken in France of shoulder patches on dead American soldiers. There was no more coercion or beatings or alcohol forced into his throat. But they continued to probe Shinn's stress points. And his bruised and fractured collarbone ached. He said nothing, though occasionally the pain would cause him to hurl.

Shinn was informed at the close of his fourth interrogation that he and the other prisoners would be moved from the compound. Krüger gave him a Red Cross parcel and described the supposed delights of living in an officer's stalag where Shinn was to be transported. Krüger put his arm around

Shinn's shoulder. "I hope to see you in America when the war is over, brother," he confided to Shinn.

"I would like to see you as well, major, under different circumstances," the captain replied without revealing that such a meeting might not be healthy for his inquisitor.

Chapter 15

PARTICLE OF HUMAN KINDNESS

"Phil, I can smell the aroma of trout cooking over the camp-fire!" Prof. Shinn said to Prof. Philip Sekou Chikelu as they crossed paths in the Union hallway. He rotated his arm and wrist like a fly fisherman cutting a graceful arc into the universe.

"Yes, Roger, me too, and good day to you," Sekou Chikelu said. "Walden Pond *is* calling. But I want to ask if you mind, uh, if I sit in on part of your class today?"

"I am talking about my life as a POW, Phil," he frowned. "That is more a warning than a chapter head."

"I would like to hear what you have to say."

"You always are welcome. No need to ask."

The hallways were full of students and the light-hearted commotion they create when talking over each other. "Why waste your time sitting in on '20th-Century Ethical Challenges,' my friend?" Shinn asked.

"Well, first of all, you're in this movie, and you are one of my favorite stars," Sekou Chikelu replied.

"Oh, you think I'm Cary Grant! Or Bela Lugosi?" Shinn stretched out the spoof. It reminded him of Hall's repartee with Samantha Waterford on the Queen Mary.

"Actually, Roger, if you want the nut of it, I heard about your previous session. I want to know what it was like. And maybe get a sense of why these great rich northern white empires, so 'civilized' and 'advanced,' are so hell-bent on ripping each other's appendages off, you know, this deep into their 'adult' stage." They reached the classroom door. Like the entrance to a surgical theater the brass fixtures gleamed the window was polished like a lens. Shinn opened the portal for Sekou Chikelu and slapped him on the back. "Phil, welcome to the show. 'The Modern Age of the Primordials and Homo Horribilus,'" he joked.

"In Professor Dagg's case, I think he *actually has* a love affair with the Bronze Age," Sekou Chikelu intimated, dry of mirth. The remark peeved Shinn.

The students were unusually quiet as they seated themselves. All eyes were pasted on the man in front. Shinn picked up the narrative from the previous session. "After my fourth interrogation I was thrown back into my cell, and I heard Lt. Aberanthe Wronge." The professor glanced to the right as if looking at the soldier now in the adjacent chamber. "I hadn't seen or heard from Abel in days, but it was apparent he was painfully ill. And he had diarrhea."

Throughout the night, Wronge struggled to persuade the guard of the obvious, that he needed a doctor, Shinn told the class. It did the lieutenant no good.

"I asked the guard if I could see Major Krüger. Perhaps I could persuade him to have Abel taken to the infirmary."

Shinn's "brother," if he got the message, did not respond to the appeal. Wronge died the next morning.

"I am not confident the guard even delivered the message to Krüger," Shinn confessed. "Abel was only twenty-four years when he passed. For me he remains spiritually alive. In here." The professor tapped his chest. "As for the guard who believed human life was worth nothing at all? He himself had been dead a long time. He merely wasn't aware of it."

The door at the back of the classroom squeaked. Turning toward the noise, the audience saw Eberhart Dagg enter near where Sekou Chikelu sat. He shuffled to the opposite side of the room where he took a chair in the last row.

"Weeks later, I talked to several Americans interrogated by the Nazis at Diesz," Shinn continued. "By combining our information, we concluded that four German officers had done the questioning." The American captives that spoke to their inquisitors, even if not about military information, avoided the roughest treatment.

"By their accounts, Krüger was the only officer of the four who handed out beatings." Shinn was unfolding the experience with an even voice. "He had a colleague of mine undressed and strapped naked onto the same metal chair I had occupied during my interrogations. But for him, at the major's insistence, a small stove was placed under the seat and lit. The pain from Krüger whipping his burning flesh coupled with extreme psychic trauma overwhelmed the soldier. He wailed and passed out."

When the prisoner regained consciousness, the major personally threw him, scalded and still naked, outside into the snow.

The students gasped and shouted. The professor waited for the reaction to die down.

"Krüger didn't offer my fellow soldiers liquor or ask to become their 'brother.' His only human gesture was to give this GI, who miraculously survived, the same Red Cross package all prisoners got before we left Diesz."

At 5 a.m. the next morning, German guards roused Shinn and the rest of the prisoners. Instead of ushering the men into a train's passenger cars as promised, the guards herded them into boxcars. A sharp wind blew unhindered through the porous sides. For six hours the captives huddled together before the train moved. The Battle of the Ardennes had begun just nine days ago. Time, once liquid, was now inert, paralyzed for the American prisoners.

"When we crawled inside the boxcar, none of us knew when we would depart, where we were going, or how long the ride would be," the professor recalled. "Our spirits were low. Very low. Unless we could escape, death, we had come to believe, would be the only end of our misery."

Belloc stood. "How long were you a prisoner?" he asked.

"I saw four days of battle and a hundred-seventy-one days in Nazi captivity.

It took six-days in the German boxcar to reach its destination. Stops were made for maintenance, loading new prisoners, and taking coal. Lettered on the boxcar's side, *Hommes 40, Cheveaux 8*. The freight wagon had normal capacity for forty men and eight horses. But the inside was razor wired, so the twenty-four prisoners were confined to barely a third of available floor space; six German guards, supplies, and armaments got the rest.

"Only half of us had real estate to lay down at one time," Shinn told the class. "So we stood in shifts. As for a toilet, no need to discuss that here."

The halting ride over decaying and damaged tracks caused motion sickness in many. Shinn had seizures of diarrhea and muscle spasms. He had eaten nothing in twenty-four hours before the departure and the day before had just enough to make him sick.

"The day's meal in our 'luxury passenger' train was a miserable soup, drunk from a German mess cup. With no soap or warm water to clean them, the metal containers were filthy with grease though we were too malnourished and miserable to care." Some students shook their heads at the professor's matter-of-fact demeanor as he described the misery delivered upon him. "Our meal always was a few dehydrated vegetables floating in brown water."

Two days into the journey, the captain stood awake at the side of the boxcar, facing east, when dawn arrived. The other captives were slumbering on the floor or asleep standing up. From his position at the barred window, Shinn could see white desolation rushing by. Occasionally, black birds would move through the cold sky like dry leaves. A German guard of low rank sat on a crate across the razor wire chewing his breakfast of hard bread. He was within three feet from where Shinn leaned against the coarse enclosure.

"I watched him eat it, every bite, every rise and fall of the jaw, every swallow," Shinn gestured as if blankly raising food to his mouth. "I was starving. Stymied trying to remember the last time I had eaten anything of substance. When the guard cut off a piece of bread I asked him for it. I didn't know at the time how pathetic his bread ration was. But he gave it to me anyway."

The professor walked to the front of the stage, bent toward the class and motioned with his arm as if handing the bread to them.

"'Here you are, captain', the aging guard whispered to me in perfect English as he threaded the morsel through the wire and into my twitching hands.

"'Dankeschön', I said to him, hoping it meant 'thank you very much' and not 'thank you, beautiful'. Though he did look somewhat angelic to me." The class let out a low chuckle.

The captain bit into the bread. It was black, hard, and bitter. His mouth was dry, and he could hardly swallow it, but he forced down half and stuffed the rest in his pocket.

"The German glanced over and thought I had eaten all the bread." Shinn broke into a smile. "He cut another wedge about the size of a man's ear. This he covered, as carefully as if he were stroking a newborn kitten, with a slightly sweet spread that I learned later was beet butter."

The guard again pushed it through the wire barrier. The viscous spread made swallowing easier and the food warmed his stomach.

"I'll never forget his kindness, this gesture of kinship, this particle of human caring, which for a brief moment interrupted this heinous war and moved a flicker of hope my way. I could not control myself and wept as I ate the bread."

Chapter 16

UNWANTED BALLAST

The train had twenty-six boxcars and freight wagons. About half had sides made of slats with narrow openings between them. They were colder than the enclosed cars though the inhabitants had more light. Others had a solitary open window, with two iron bars preventing escape. The Nazis packed thirteen hundred captives onto the train. As many as sixty men were crowded into one car. As the locomotive moved north and east the temperatures became more extreme. Many died en route, the crew tossing them off the moving train like unwanted ballast. A few of the guards made bets as to where the bodies would land. Flung corpses hitting trees would prompt a cheer from the German gamesmen.

"With our space so limited and the men in a wretched state, quarreling was almost continuous. I tried always to maneuver to the side for escape and to peek between the window bars to see what life looked like," Prof. Shinn said as he stared from a classroom window. "The terrain—I assumed we were in Poland—was flat, desolate. In a hallucinatory moment I thought the heavy snow cover was there to protect the earth from war," he paused still looking outside, "as if silk could stop a bomb."

The professor moved his gaze to Dagg and as their eyes met the old man shifted his body uneasily. "I saw many a decrepit wooden wagon drawn by horses under the mastery of a single driver. In the splits and ruptures in their sides all manner of rags and newspapers had been stuffed to block the rabid cold from reaching the soldiers inside." In the open carts, the captain noticed that frozen burlap or canvas was stretched over the wagon bed. Under these frozen tarps he detected ammunition boxes and wooden crates shaped as if to accommodate firearms. The Nazi Reichsadler eagle, the omnipresent trademark of Aryan military superiority, was burned into their ends.

"This primitive transport was how the great Nazi war apparatus supplied their armies on the front," Shinn exclaimed. "At least in January 1945. And I had a good guess at what the wagons would be carrying on their return trips."

The caravan paused at train stations where it would load more prisoners. POWs standing against the boxcar's sides could see German villagers between the slats.

"From brittle bodies hung clothes saw-toothed at the edges by age and wear, giving these souls the appearance of winter scarecrows." The professor halted to compose himself.

At one station, a skeletal young woman with one arm worked furiously. "Somehow she had managed to turn a fender, the front mud guard blown away from a Nazi truck, upside down. She had positioned the rough metal crescent inside a short stack of tires. In that icy cradle she laid down an infant. The child was wrapped heavily in layers of what looked like scraps of wool, broadsheet newspapers and old ribbons. I don't now what happened after that. The train pulled away. I have always hoped that she returned with milk."

The class shuffled in their seats as Shinn's vulnerability returned. Phil peered over at Dagg. His face twisted in anger.

As prisoner-of-war trains left stations, a mile or more of local citizens would often line the tracks around oily drumfires and peer at the human cargo in the stinking boxcars. "About all they saw were our faces and hands, we the foreign enemy pressed into the spaces of their cages. Yet, in both Poland and Germany, the townspeople, old and young, would lift their hands in clandestine gestures of empathy as we rolled past and out of sight."

Captain Shinn's train traveled seven days out of Germany and into Poland. The boxcars stopped with a deafening clang and lurch at Oflag 64, a prisoner camp near Bromberg, Poland. Boxcars were emptied of their captives. Guards carried those too sick to walk to a dilapidated shelter where a British doctor captured in France seven months ago strained to keep dozens of ill and wounded alive. Able-bodied American, English, and Canadian captives hauled dead comrades to an open grave. There they were thrown on top of a pale colony of lime-powdered corpses awaiting their final seal, closing them off forever from the living.

"During it all, my wife Katharine was living in my mind," Shinn closed the session. "By now I was sure the Army had telegrammed her a 'missing in action' notification. I worried how she might suffer from the anguish of not knowing. I learned after the war she miscarried our first child." The room hushed. A few muffled sobs rose from places unknown.

"And then there was Col. Collier. What did he think when I didn't return from my mission? Had the battalion recovered, I wondered? Had it continued on? Or had the Nazis destroyed our force, despite it all?"

Chapter 17

'CEASE, YOU FOOL!'

Following his release from the field hospital, Capt. Hall, legs bandaged, stood atop a tank with binoculars in an armored column headed towards Bastogne. Only traces of the chaos that had begun on Dec. 16th entered his consciousness. To him, it all seemed so long ago. Primeval. But the soul-freezing cold and relentless blizzard remained. Hall's nose and lips were raw where he wiped away drainage. The boots of the GIs, the tank treads, and the wheels of the trucks and jeeps mushed through new-fallen snow upon which pine needles lay like lost pointers from a billion compasses directing Hall everywhere and nowhere.

The captain's troops strained through the narrow roads and passageways all morning. The only sound was the chorus of evergreens orchestrated by the storm's restlessness accompanied by the distant groan of Panzers pushing through to Bastogne. After another half mile, Hall's forward observers detected movement. Ahead, through the falling snow, dark figures and bouncing Stahlhelms rushed like a wave of frightened voles up an embankment to higher ground. Hall ordered his tanks, machine gunners, and riflemen to engage. The ensuing firefight was one-sided. Without Panzer tank support the Germans were cut down and survivors were allowed to withdraw. Hall's company proceeded numbly past Nazi corpses.

Surviving the day without a casualty, despite two firefights that exacted a lethal price on enemy ground troops, Hall felt that he had finally taken control of events. He had outmaneuvered a near-certain disaster at Beau-fort Crossroads, and, at that moment, the wind changed direction. He had led his men into the heart of battle and won a victory. Despite straining his relationship with the colonel, the captain had reclaimed his confidence. "The honor of being depended upon inspired me. My fear of making unre-coverable mistakes disappeared like copperheads from a ragin' canebrake," Hall would write.

✳✳✳✳✳✳✳✳✳✳✳✳✳✳✳✳

Evening came. The soaring pines created a darkling cathedral of the blue-black forest. The air was still and fragrant and Hall stopped his column for the night in a clearing. They set camp a few kilometers west of Clervaux.

The captain ordered his men to form a circumvallation with fallen trees and limbs, metal debris, and anything that could hinder a bullet. "Lt. Gra-ham, move the company into the circle with guns ready," Hall ordered. "Po-sition the command and mess trucks at the perimeter's center."

For supper, the cooks prepared hot barley soup. A full ladle was poured into each man's steel mess cup. Half way through the meal, a scout ap-proached Hall.

"Wehrmacht infantry column less than two hundred yards from us in the next clearing, sir, all bedding down for the night." Dwayne Stuntz, a lieutenant assigned to Hall's unit after the death of James Ruder, was with the captain when the scout announced his discovery.

"Jesus!" Stuntz elbowed in. "How many, private?"

"I'd say they were half our size, give or take," the scout responded. Stuntz smiled.

"What should we do, captain?" Stuntz asked in anticipation, his dull eyes animated now. Hall moved to a rise and surveyed the German en-campment through his binoculars. The lieutenant followed.

"They know we are here, lieutenant," Hall drawled, continuing to observe the enemy. "They are aware we've got 'em outnumbered and that we need a good night's rest too. So have ever'body but the guards hit the hay.

"And Stuntz, tell Lt. Graham I want two extra sentries posted throughout the night watch. And inform him of the situation."

"What about breakfast, captain?" Stuntz asked.

"The men will eat breakfast as usual, Stuntz," Hall replied slowly, reflecting his annoyance at the question.

Ninth Armored assigned First Lieutenant Dwayne Stuntz, to Hall's company while the captain was convalescing in the field hospital. For Hall, the death of Ruder was a blow, and with it came an emptiness he couldn't overcome. The captain had come to love the funny, plainspoken, impish lieutenant. Ruder was a superb soldier; Hall didn't think he could be replaced. But he hoped Stuntz could, at least, steer first platoon through rough waters with competence.

Stuntz was twenty-four, 6'2", 195 pounds, a native of Montauk, Long Island. Only the captain knew his military background.

"I'm getting a liverish feeling about our new lieutenant, sir," Graham said that night after he and Stuntz talked. "I think he has delusions of competence."

"You think he's a bad moon risin', Leo?" Hall never referred to his executive officer by anything other than his first name when they were in private conversation. Graham in turn kept references to his superior officer informal which is what Hall wanted despite its shredding of military protocol.

"The guy is squirrelly. I don't know. Just think we should be wary, John William. Underneath, he's a guy that seems to despise himself, like our old friend Dunn Cardamon, and probably for good reason."

"When I was in the hospital I read Stuntz's dossier," the captain replied as he looked over at the new lieutenant eating his soup in the distance. "On paper, he seems to have the makings of a good soldier."

Like Col. Collier, Stuntz was a West Pointer. He qualified as a sharpshooter with both the M1 and the .45 pistol, not the best, Hall thought, but acceptable given the guy was from New York. And records showed Stuntz was an accomplished map reader.

"Yeah, there seemed to be a couple things outta kilter, Leo, but without knowing him I didn't want 'ta make further judgment."

One of the peculiarities was Stuntz's record at the academy. Though he was in the bottom half of his class, his West Point peers rated him in the upper third of "best cadets."

"Sounds like he could talk his way out of a lot of shit," Hall commented. "And had only one demerit in four years. Hard to trust somebody with a record that clean."

The captain also had raised an eyebrow over Stuntz's request that followed graduation from the nation's top Army academy. He didn't desire a combat branch. The War Department assigned him to the infantry.

"It surprised me that Stuntz wanted to be in Quartermaster Corps." Hall winked at Graham. "Not a good career move, comin' outta West Point!"

The captain took his last sip of soup and grumbled that he couldn't risk lighting a cigarette.

"Guess he preferred keepin' track of Army-issued blankets, handling prisoners, and buying Spam by the trainload?" Hall's derisive question met with a knowing look from Graham. "Important work, no doubt. But I hope he doesn't wanna command our ice cream platoon."

"I know you will give him the benefit of the doubt," Graham said. "But ice cream or not, I don't think Stuntz is one to shrink from violence."

Hall was tired, his day's energy spent. "That fits the bill here, I s'pose," the captain mumbled.

Early the next morning, a break in cloud cover allowed the sun to emerge. It sent a consoling message to the ice-blue Belgian countryside populated with burned out ordinance from both armies. Except for the sentinels, Hall was the only one awake. He peered with his binoculars across the landscape between him and the German contingent, which was asleep, save two off to the side. One was a guard gesturing to a driver atop an aged wooden wagon pulled by a team of two draft horses. Both were little more than dried hide bags with teeth and hooves. The ribs on them pushed out so far from their sides they appeared to be on the cusp of complete escape. The captain dropped his binoculars and scanned the scene. On a rise above the wagon he spotted a white form. As he focused his eyes it appeared to be another horse but a rank incongruity from the two hacks. So pale it was almost silver. Diaphanous but rippling with musculature. It cocked its ears and gazed down at the cargo, then seemed to stare at Hall. The captain raised the binoculars to his eyes and searched for the animal. But is was nowhere. Suddenly the German soldier on the ground stopped shrieked.

"Ausziehen!" he yelled to the civilian driver. Fearing his troops would see what the wagon held, he gestured wildly to the old man to move out and the bent wagoner whipped the horses. The rig jerked and moved from behind tree cover into Hall's view. The Reich still used horse and wagon to move its dead from the battlefields and here, compressed into a solitary image, lay the lurid reality of it all. Inside this former livestock wagon, its low sides formed by uneven cadaver-gray slats, was an enormous, translucent sac. It appeared to be a colossal larva and within its membrane, as if suspended in a kind of frozen amniotic fluid for the dead—water, saliva, blood, bile, cranial liquor, urine—were German bodies, the uniformed and the naked, and pieces of humans: arms, rib cages, feet, teeth, livers, lungs, larynxes, mandibles, colons; the humiliating residue of soldiers who were once machinists and teachers and students and stonemasons; composers and barbers and cheese mongers; bookkeepers and booksellers and bread makers and farmhands; fathers, husbands, uncles, sons making their last passage, homogenized inside an ignominious orb like hospital waste exposed for all to see. As the thing vanished into the haze, Hall pondered the mysterious horse and the little man urging the doleful conveyance toward those who would fulfill that last office for the dead. *In his earlier life, the driver must have schlepped animal carcasses for a German leimfabrik*, Hall mused, a glue maker with sizable rendering capacity. Only that or a career as a gallows gravesman, or perhaps a trader in hides, could have hardened him to the horror of which he now was a participant.

Within twenty minutes Capt. Hall's company was awake and taking breakfast; the Germans also were eating.

"Sir, what should we do, uh, to these Krauts, I mean?" Stuntz asked the captain in a challenging tone. "Clervaux was where the German Second Panzer Division destroyed our 106th on...."

"I know this loo-ten-ent!" Hall interrupted, sounding out every syllable. "What would you do, Stuntz, if you were in my slippers?" Hall asked calmly, with his eyes fixed on the enemy through binoculars.

"Well, I know the Germans would burn every last one of us if they had our advantage. So, uh, we should do the same to them."

"That so?" the captain drawled still peering through his glass.

"Give them no quarter." The lieutenant's posture was strangely unmilitary, slouching, as he spoke. "Moderation in war is an absurdity. War is violence pushed to its furthermost bounds."

"Spoken like a real Prussian general, Stuntz." Hall knew the lieutenant considered him a hillbilly. "Or maybe a parlor general."

The captain pulled the binoculars from his eyes. "The Germans are watching to see what we're gonna do, lieutenant."

He turned to Stuntz. "I'll think about what you said. Get your platoon ready to move out."

The German commander, a middle-age oberleutnant, saw Hall's company stirring and ordered his men to be on alert. "Aufmerksam! Bereiten Sie sich auf einen Kampf vor," he told his officers, preparing them for a firefight.

Hall watched the German movements with interest. Was he about to make the same mistake he made at the castle? Is he underestimating his enemy again? The captain pondered this a moment then called his lieutenants together.

"Well, gentlemen, I thought the German 'hospitality' was real good last night," Hall said jauntily. "So let's get the hell out of here, head toward Bastogne and all of you wave to 'em as we go by." His tone changed as he turned to Stuntz, "Understood?"

The muscles in the lieutenant's jaw hardened. "Yes, sir!" he responded with the others. As he hurried back to his platoon, Stuntz struggled to maintain his composure. His fists clinched like a constrictor suffocating a rat.

Hall's force began their march. Their path took them closer to the stranded German unit. He and his men waved to the oberleutnant and the German contingent. Both the Germans and Hall's force had their weapons at hand, but had lowered their rifles or slung them on their shoulders. Stuntz alerted his driver to keep the jeep moving in pace with the column. When Hall's company was about to complete their pass beyond the enemy unit, Stuntz moved behind the Browning machine gun mounted in his jeep. With a loud jerk he brought the bolt latch back cocking it to fire. The American column was no more than ninety yards away from the Germans. Everyone heard the lieutenant set the trap. Immediately, the German rifles sprung to life and took aim at Hall's force. Hall's heart leaped into his throat and a wave of sparks rippled through his body.

"Aufhören, du Narr!" Hall thundered at the lieutenant so the enemy would understand, "Cease, you fool!"

Livid at the command, Stuntz sent a blinding glare at his commanding officer. Hall's right arm became arrow-rigid and his index finger pointed at the machine gun. No German fired but the American troops kept their weapons trained on the smaller German force. Stuntz slowly disengaged the firing mechanism and returned to his seat in the jeep. Hall didn't remove his eyes from the junior officer until the tension subsided and the Germans lowered their weapons. Hall, standing in his vehicle, knew one thing. He would have been the second one killed in a firefight after Stuntz. The mission would have been destroyed along with many of his men.

After they had passed into safe territory, Hall stopped the column.

"Leo, get me the West Point Wonder," he ordered. "And post sentries."

The raw lieutenant knew his commander could court martial him for insubordination. As he jogged to the captain's jeep, third from the front,

Stuntz felt the eyes of the company's men burn into him. This filled him with self-importance. His arrival was deferential. He snapped to attention and saluted, then resumed a casual demeanor, putting his left hand in his pocket. "We could have taken out all those bastards, captain!" Stuntz made a sweeping pugnacious gesture with his free arm. He was ready to deploy the lessons his father drilled into him: real leaders don't back down. Stuntz would stand his ground with this "hick" while remaining short of further justifying courts-martial.

At first, Hall's words lodged like tacks in his throat. "Enough!" Hall shouted when he regained his voice. The captain jumped from his transport. His boots hit the ground like hammers, and he looked up at the taller lieutenant. "At what cost 'our taking them out', West Point?"

Everyone in the company could hear the dressing down. Ignoring protocols that officers were not criticized in front of enlisted soldiers, Hall had resolved to hold class, re-assert his command, and bring forth the contours of his decision.

"In advance of my removing your testicles, soldier, I'm gonna impart some wisdom. Stand at attention, goddamn it!" The lieutenant looked around at the men staring at him and came to attention.

"You remember the old Russian general? The one who came upon Napoleon's starving, half-frozen troops retreatin' to France away from the Russian front?"

"Never heard of him," Stuntz snapped.

Hall glared at him and waited. Then knocked him to the ground with a right to the jaw. The lieutenant wiped blood from his mouth and returned to attention.

"Never heard of him, *sir*," Stuntz shouted.

"Well, loo-ten-ent, the damn general was a fool. In fact he reminds me of you."

The captain was inches from Stuntz's face and the lieutenant felt Hall's spittle jumping from his mouth. "This Russian commander decided his fresh, well-armed troops were going to delay their assigned journey to the front. He wanted 'em to pick the bones of this defeated French regiment. Easy! So he ordered his men to charge. He watched, exotically plumed and eating a goddamn pomegranate or something, atop his horse at the peak of a hill." Hall stepped back and lit a cigarette.

"They didn't teach you about this brilliant maneuver at the Academy, loo-tin-unt?" the captain spat.

Hall's voice echoed off the terrain. He was not one to lose his temper, but witnessing arrogance married to gross stupidity did it. He imagined his men piled on the frozen ground in front of him like freshly scythed bundles of wheat.

"Don't recall it, sir."

"Well, this arrogant bastard's assault cost a thousand Russian and French lives. A military disaster, Stuntz. Nothing was gained. Nothing! Except more carrion for the crows." Hall ground his teeth.

"I wasn't about to make that same goddamn mistake!".

The captain had analyzed the depleted Wehrmacht unit. It was on its last legs. Nor did he want prisoners to impede his mission. Hall estimated that engaging the Germans unit could cost fifteen percent of his men killed or wounded.

"You know our orders are to move toward Bastogne don't you, Stuntz? We're supposed to take on the belligerents mounting an attack on Bastogne, don't you?"

"Yes, captain."

That a captain would hold an officer to account, and in front of them, dumbfounded the soldiers.

"There is nothing in the orders about killing or capturing strays looking to surrender, or anything that might bog down our advance, is there?"

"No, sir."

"You did notice that those Nazis eating hardtack for breakfast had fuel problems, didn't you West Point?

"No, sir."

"Well, they did! Those Germans will surrender without a fight to our quartermaster unit six klicks behind us. They will be much better at handling POWs than we, don't you think?"

Before he could answer, Hall turned to leave. The men, who were resting on one knee, stood. Hall stopped and faced Stuntz.

"If you were leading our quartermaster unit, Stuntz, would you have saved yourself the bother of prisoners? Just executed 'em all?"

The lieutenant hesitated. "Don't know, sir."

Chapter 18

FIND AND DESTROY

On December twenty-eighth, Col. Collier sent a courier to Hall with new orders: "Rover Boy, find and destroy camped and retreating Nazi combat units. —Comfort Six"

The German Siege of Bastogne had ended the day before, eleven days after the German offensive rocked the western front. Bastogne never fell into German hands. The momentum had shifted like waves responding to an unseen agency. The elite German armies shuddered, stalled, and commenced their retreat.

After receiving the message, Hall mobilized his company. One tank leading the column of men, and one at the tail. It travelled on rutted, crooked roadways, abandoned except for corpses and the massive litter of battle that emerged from the snow like ubiquitous nightmares.

The pronouncements of war heard in the distance were ceaseless, but Hall's force had not seen an enemy unit in forty-eight hours. Directing his men toward a crossroads near a tapering defile where he thought retreating German troops would likely pass, Hall altered his pattern.

At noon on January third, the captain ordered his men to halt and establish a redoubt above a sloping bank. Cover was ideal to surprise Germans in retreat. His company, he calculated, would have time to eat, dig foxholes, and set camouflage in time for the Wehrmacht's arrival. Hall's scouts had detected movement toward them and the Sauer River.

Hall's men used hatchets to chop away frozen earth and tree roots. Afterwards, they scraped and dug into the reluctant ground, digging deeper with entrenching tools they carried on every other backpack.

Within twenty minutes, Hall's field phone buzzed. "Rover Boy, this is Red Wolf. I am following Kraut troop movement," his scout said. "They could be on you within the half hour. Seventy strong. Mortars, machine guns. I see no armor. Over."

"Keep on 'em, Red Wolf. Rover Boy out."

Hall mustered his lieutenants. The German howitzers firing from miles away were no longer shelling around his area. This gave him confidence that the Wehrmacht ground troops would indeed move through the thoroughfare that lay before them. The only artillery sounds were coming from the West where the Germans were shelling around Bastogne to mask their troop withdrawal.

A stillness surrounded Hall's company in the forest. The only thing moving was the white breath rolling from every nostril. "They'll be in our snare in less than thirty." Hall armed his lieutenants with patience. "Keep your men quiet until I holler."

Battered and diminished during the defense of Bastogne, Ninth Armored ordered the 60th to split off company-size units. They were to engage in individual marauding actions, hitting the Germans by surprise where they could best disrupt their escape to Germany. Hall's company, down to seventy-three men, was now its own fighting unit and virtually untethered from its battalion. It had the attributes of a clever and capable youth who escaped a ham-fisted parent. Though unprotected by a larger corps, Hall liked this arrangement. It fitted his method. His company's agility could detect, overtake, and sting recoiling Nazi forces and dispatch them as best they could. Hall's men now called themselves Company O for "Outlander."

"These Germans are strays and interlopers, Leo. What do you think?" Hall asked as they watched and waited.

"I think we'll be fishing this summer, John William," Graham replied.

"Other than that, I'm moving to our right flank."

"Leo," Hall whispered. "Curious whether the old-time Greeks would have let their enemies pass through like I did back at Clervaux?"

"Hell, Heroic Age Greek warriors were brutally tribal, John William!" The nonchalance of his commander amused the lieutenant. And that he had such a wayward thought before battle. "Greeks dispatched their foes without mercy. As an ancient Greek, if you had wounded the commander of that Nazi unit in battle, you'd have run to where he crawled, killed the bastard, stripped him of his weapons and medals, hacked up his body, and showed off the head in a drunken victory celebration."

Running to his post the lieutenant shouted back, "Most of the Greek virtues lay outside of war."

When the Nazi forces entered the fire zone as predicted, the captain's cry started the firefight. The arc of battle opened with chaos and quickly worsened. Bazooka fire immobilized O Company's lead tank while American machine guns crackled and wailed. German soldiers dropped into the snow and colored it. Hall's machine gun platoons supported by the remaining American tank finally overwhelmed the Nazi detachment, and they disappeared into the Ardennes's embrace.

"Lieutenant, have the men hold fast," Hall shouted to Graham through the field phone. "Get Paz to reconnoiter and report back what the hell the Germans are doing. I expect them to return to reclaim the road from the right flank. Out."

Hall leaned back on a protective berm, inhaled a gust of arctic air, and scanned the surroundings. Snow-faced slopes formed a valley. From his spot, the tall trunks of pines were like black, unlit candles, perfectly vertical, stuck randomly into a peaked white cake. Hall lowered his gaze to his boots. The constancy of wet and cold had turned their creases into yawning splits. His feet were moist and numb.

"Wish I had time to take these boots off and hold my feet in my hands," he thought. "I'd warm 'em up." Beyond his outstretched legs the ground was pitted, disordered. "Wonder if this ol' earth'll grow anything again," he asked himself, "except bones?"

For a few seconds, his entire body disappeared into rest. He recalled an enormous cottonwood that powerful winds had disrupted on the family homestead. Uprooted, it leaned heavily on another smaller tree. The timbers met one another at an apex. Silhouetted in the sky with the earth as its base, the trees formed a scalene triangle. Hall had always wanted to be the shortest side of any uneven geometry: the one holding up the longer side preventing it from collapse.

Sgt. Paz radioed Hall. The Germans had set up mortars on a desecrated piece of ground carved out of the forest. Nine days earlier, Nazi panzers crawling toward Bastogne had flattened it.

When it came, the mortar shelling hit with a fury but was short of its mark.

"Leo!" Hall shouted into his radio, "The mortar shelling is about on us. Get the men out of their foxholes and have them fall back. Out!"

As Hall's men bolted up the vertiginous highland forest, German ground troops charged. And a lone panzer appeared out of nowhere, its shape lodged in the corner of the captain's eye. Bullets and shrapnel blistered the air. Screams from the wounded erupted and echoed. German mortar fire intensified on the company's new position, and the shelling brought pines and cedars roaring down on the quick and the dead like beams from a collapsing roof. The captain glassed the sweep of the enemy attack and chewed on his lip till it bled.

"How are the men faring? Over," Hall radioed Graham.

"Six wounded. Anxious, but their adrenaline is taking over. Dooley knocked senseless by the concussion of a mortar round, but not hit. Think he'll be alright. Over."

Hall spit tacks. "I'll move to the nest. Give me covering fire. And get Stuntz to move his bazookas and take out that goddamn tank. Out!"

The captain made his way to the company's machine guns. He had a private reset them, and then directed him to support the rifle platoons, which were enduring the assault. Almost immediately a GI, operating a Browning automatic rifle, was hit. In a dead run, Hall grabbed it and a pouch of twenty-round clips. He kept running and dropped where he could better establish the right flank. He tore off the bipod, slipped its asbestos glove on his left hand, positioned the heavy weapon, and laid a fusillade onto the enemy. Taking advantage of the volley Hall's men rose and advanced toward the Germans with sustained accuracy.

"Well done, you bastards!" the captain muttered to himself.

From the corner of his eye, he thought he saw movement behind and to his left. Hall glanced over his shoulder. Nothing. He resumed firing. When the Browning was empty, Hall signaled for help. Cobern Gance, company master sergeant, dispatched a soldier to Hall's position.

"Captain needs help!" To be heard over the roar, Gance yelled in the private's ear. "Keep yourself low to the ground. You are a lizard!"

As the GI made his way to Hall, a German rifleman the captain had failed to detect moved behind him. From eighty feet behind a stump, he aimed and fired. Hall heard a sound that cracked like close thunder. A bullet entered his left leg, tore into the femoral muscle, and Hall's rifle dropped from his grip. He felt a sharp jolt rippling up and into his lower torso.

"What the Sam Hill is this!" Hall yelped, fumbling to locate the wound. His hand found the warm viscous flow from where the bullet exited the leg. He wiped blood from his hand onto his jacket, rolled, unholstered his pistol, and looked for the shooter. The Wehrmacht trooper peeked from behind a tree and put a bullet into the lungs of the private running to Hall's position. The captain saw just enough of him to swing and fire a round that penetrated the Nazi's head. He dropped like a stone. Hall put a tourniquet on his thigh and switched to firing his rifle.

Within minutes, Hall's men overwhelmed the Germans, but did not pursue the Wehrmacht survivors, who again disappeared into the forest. Nor did they move until noon the next day when battalion issued new orders to march eastward toward Germany. A field medic treated Hall and splinted his leg. The captain stayed with his unit, traveling in an armored personnel carrier. The soldier killed trying to aid Hall was Private Tom or "Roach." Thomas Edward Rochambeau was a descendant of a French general who had fought with Washington during the Revolutionary War. A letter from the captain was delivered to his parents in Newport, Rhode Island eighteen days later.

Chapter 19

ROLLING THUNDER

Roger Shinn sat in his living room reading the evening newspaper. A southerly spring breeze had pacified the evening chill and the professor opened the window to enjoy it.

"What time are you leaving for the meeting," Katharine asked.

"Should leave in about twenty if I am to make it before eight." He looked at her waiting to hear a response.

"Do you know what you will say, or will you conjure it up on the bus ride?" she asked.

"Oh, the seventeen-minute bus ride will give me more than enough time to prepare remarks that will guide college students and working, single men and a few high-school seniors through the moral and ethical maze of an undeclared ground war in Southeast Asia." Roger patted his suit jacket. It made a soft crunching sound. "Not to worry, I have my outline in here, in my breast pocket."

He placed his newspaper on the side table and swigged a drink of water from a glass lifted from a coaster bearing the Ninth Armored insignia.

"I am thankful that I won't be the only one making remarks, K," he added. A retired attorney feared by prosecutors also would be there.

"He is unforgivingly smart and pissed off at the war," he muttered. The attorney would review filing procedures for conscientious objection and penalties for avoiding the draft without a deferment. "An alternative-service spokesman will outline how to apply and the annual quota."

A sigh escaped his lungs. He stretched. The professor dreaded seeing the collected anxiety on the faces of the crowd.

"And me, I will try to give them my take on this war along with some optimism. I hope they will listen…." Embracing Katharine he lamented, "…because the decisions they make now will be with them the rest of their lives."

"The reality is they are all screwed," Katharine remarked pointedly. "Many of them, anyway. The ones who don't want the course of their existence to wind into the jungles and Operation Rolling Thunder. It breaks my heart."

Her husband ambled to the bathroom and brushed his clean teeth. Then he straightened his already perfect tie, and reviewed the notes he had already mastered. This was a regimen he often deployed when trying to unplug his anxiety from a noxious reality ahead. It had worked in the past. Clearing his mind. And making it ready.

****

He arrived and found a dreary meeting room. It reminded Shinn of 1950s labor union halls depicted in black and white motion pictures, the ones where a balding weather-beaten baritone-voiced labor leader with heavy eyebrows tries to calm the rank and file before a callow, milky skinned youth stands from the crowd demanding vengeance and igniting pandemonium. But here in 1965 the professor had one foot on each side of the feud.

Here he saw over two hundred men under the age of thirty, their brown chatter frenzied and strident. Scattered throughout, like weakened but essential pillars: a few girlfriends, mothers and fathers. Shinn noted the others who don't seem to fit in this gathering but have tried to dress the part.

After the event ended and the doors were locked, the professor didn't return home. He walked a few blocks to listen to the "quiet" of the city. Its ever-present low evening mumble and honk put him in a meditative state. After a few minutes the weary figure entered a small neighborhood bistro, dim and sparsely populated. This evening, the former infantryman sat at a table carved with wear. He ordered an ounce of French cognac with water on the side. Shinn, who rarely drank, relaxed and readied himself for a vicarious trip to Paris. The waiter gave a generous smile and placed the jeweled mahogany liquid in front of him. It came not in a traditional snifter but in a low-ball glass of leaded crystal. A white embossed cocktail napkin had been positioned underneath.

I think my waiter is pleased with this glorious presentation, as am I, he chuckled to himself and nodded to his server. *No doubt he is fantasizing about this French marvel on his tongue.*

The barkeep returned to the counter. He glanced back at Shinn who lifted his glass to him in salute. Smoke hung in the air and the worn furniture was the comfortable, inviting kind. The professor heard the food was good. He would come here two or three times a year to relax in an uncommon space, watch unbuttoned people of all walks, and "learn about the actual civilization we live in." It was almost as if he could assemble their stories, personalities, and aspirations from facial expressions, body gestures, and the color of their voices. This lifelong student of social harmony and communal dissonance had come to believe that gesture and inflection were often more faithful than words, which he could barely make out anyway in this setting. A dating couple held hands in the corner booth. At the bar a garrulous interesting-looking gentleman dominated the conversation with two others. A few tables over a man of rough appearance had brought his two young children for a well-deserved macaroni and cheese dinner. All of these people would remain anonymous to the professor, but he would not forget the impressions they shelved like books into his heart.

But tonight, Roger Lincoln Shinn's inner attentions were on his war years, now inescapable. His first sip of cognac rushed to his head and delivered him to a Europe twenty years ago. The musty merry cafes of Paris he visited on furlough. The Baron-Vervoy Castle, the thirteenth-century mammoth that had lumbered with distrust into the twentieth. The magnificent aroma of the Ardennes. The kindness of destitute people.

A group of young men entered the bistro making noise. Shinn recognized them from the meeting. Two figures trailed, Robert Newman and Álvaro Belloc. They moved to the bar and ordered beer. Newman scanned the room and spotted Shinn. He said something to Belloc and waved to his professor.

"What kind of tea do you have in the glass, Professor Shinn?" Belloc asked as the two approached the table.

"Earl Grey. Do you know him?"

"Know him well enough to believe that isn't he," Belloc laughed.

"Please, join me." Shinn gestured for them to sit. "I would be interested in your take of tonight's meeting."

"Depressing!" Belloc exclaimed.

"Surprised you were there, and astonished at what you said," Newman replied, interested in avoiding small talk. "Sorry, Professor Shinn, but I thought you were kind of a warmonger."

Belloc lowered his head and peered down at his fingernails, embarrassed and knowing this conversation could turn unpleasant. Others who came in with Newman and Belloc came over and stood at Shinn's table.

Before the professor responded to Newman's "warmonger" epithet, he noted two men, late twenties, had come into the bar. They had also attended the meeting.

Shinn told the group of his scorn for war, his abhorrence of violence, his support of the peaceful settlement of differences, and his passion for nonviolent but, nevertheless, profound change.

Members of the group appeared skeptical. They readied themselves to engage in the debate.

"Change is imperative," Shinn recalled from Thomas Merton, the New York playboy turned Trappist monk. "Violence, however, will not really change anything. It will only transfer power from one set of bull-headed authorities to another."

Before Newman could jump into the conversation, Shinn presented a caveat. Groans from the young men echoed around the bistro. "I support peaceful resolutions, except when aggression is the only remedy to a crisis."

Newman started, but Shinn cut him off.

"Kindly let me finish my thought, Mr. Newman."

"Certainly," Newman conceded.

"That is my opinion. However, I am not pushing my opinion in our ethics class. What I do is present a set of circumstances, real events, and battlefield situations, as a means to construct a more complex view of war. Actual war at boot level."

Newman glowered. The five standing around the table gulped beer. They wished to hear the young sharp-tongued sage defend his position.

Shinn felt like Socrates about to be presented with a cup of hemlock."

"War is immoral, professor," Newman began. "I do not accept your exceptions. When people propose that war is okay as long as it is 'the only remedy,' we are just chasing our tails. We open ourselves to bad outcomes, can't you agree?"

Newman took a sip of beer. Foam clung to his upper lip. He erased it with the back of his hand. Only a few people remained in the bistro beyond those collected around the professor. Shinn's waiter leaned in at the end of the bar toward the conversation. Another, disinterested, washed glasses in the bar sink.

"All wars are the same," Newman concluded, "and they must end. Beginning now."

"If I felt an undeclared war in Indochina was the same as the Second World War or our Civil War, Robert, you probably would not have heard the remarks I made tonight in defense of conscientious objection or other ways to deploy one's sense of morality. But that defense comes with warnings. No one should ignore that for everyone who refuses to fight in Indochina or another state sanctioned conflict, another life must take his place."

Shinn reiterated that neither he nor history looks at all wars as the same.

"Kurt Jooss's *The Green Table*, professor," Newman interrupted.

"The ballet at City Center?" Shinn was perplexed.

"A work of genius. It shows how all wars begin with public and political failure. They regress the same. Smell the same. Spread decay the same. End the same. It is the dance of death in eight scenes. Repeating and repeating." Newman stopped. The barroom walls themselves seemed to gasp. Realizing his rising tone, Newman stepped it back. "Jooss's work is incontrovertible, professor," he concluded with evenness. "All wars are graveyards dug for the young by the old!"

Shinn leaned back and sighed. "A tidy maxim, Robert."

Someone dropped a tumbler in the kitchen and it shattered on the floor. But no one at the professor's table turned.

"But I fear it misses the point."

Belloc peered down at his hands again.

"The Second World War was a response to an existential threat to humanity and western democracy," Shinn continued, his voice relaxed. "In my view no small matter."

The professor rubbed his finger around the rim of his glass as if it was a Tibetan singing bowl.

"Had you been there, Mr. Newman, would you have missed that clear and lucid moment? Ignored the fascist vulture about to eat your liver? Allowed it to re-shape your western civilization into a military dictatorship led by deviants and sociopaths?" The professor fixed on the young man's eyes. "I have my doubts."

"After Vietnam there will be another war," Newman countered in a low voice. "Then another and another, all spiraling off into eternity."

Shinn stood up. "Yep, we have our work cut out for us." He grabbed another look at the bar. The two curious men were still at the bar. "If we are to prevent those ends."

He gripped Newman's shoulder, recommended the students not discuss politics with "J. Edgar's boys" at the bar, said goodbye, and left money on the table. Securing it in place was the crystal glass that held most of the poured cognac. The professor's first sip that evening had been his last.

Chapter 20

THE THROWAWAY HAMLET

At the next session, Prof. Shinn brought the class up to date with events on the ground. By late January, German soldiers surviving the Ardennes Forest offensive had retreated into Germany en masse. Hall's leg wound from the German sniper hadn't healed but festered black. Collier put Graham in command of the company and ordered the captain to a London hospital. He would not return to the battlefield until early March, a few days after the Ninth Armored had secured the Ludendorff Railroad Bridge spanning the Rhine River at Remagen. That the Germans had failed to destroy the bridge during their anxious retreat from Belgium allowed Allied troops and equipment to stream into western Germany. The Reich still husbanding the disorder of the old world could hear the breathing now of its executioners. One of them who crossed the bridge at Remagen was Capt. Hall.

He arrived at the 60th Armored Infantry Battalion command post in a jeep bouncing from rut to rut. Warmer weather, freedom from hospital cots, and Lt. Graham received him as he reached the American front line. "Welcome back, John William!" Graham cried.

Hall was thin, withdrawn. He wore a face as palid as the cigarette papers he rolled with cut tobacco. Wounds had weakened him to the point that the buttons on his jacket felt heavy. But his freshly cut hair and face shaved close by a barber's straight edge gave him the air of a courting bachelor.

"Thought you'd have had the war won by now, Leo. Kinda wanted to stay in the English countryside," Hall smiled distantly. He stepped from the jeep onto marshy soil in new boots polished to resemble black pearls.

"I don't believe that for a moment, captain. You want to get to Berlin just as much as I do. The schnitzel there is worth dying for."

"How are the men, Leo?" Hall asked, unresponsive to the lieutenant's black humor.

"Tired. But ready to end this thing. Remagen was brutal. We lost a lot of GIs over a few feet of steel."

Graham loosened the belt that held his pistol, buttstock pouch, canteen, and bayonet, then dropped it onto the seat of a jeep. "Hitler had the Wehrmacht officers responsible for the bridge fiasco shot in the head. They were buried in shallow graves where they fell," Graham told him with a rueful squint.

"Damn thankful Ike didn't treat me that way. You know, when I failed us back at the high castle and then again on the rescue," Hall mumbled with a weak laugh.

"The brass fucked that one up," the lieutenant countered. "Anyway we dine on our defeats and come out all the stronger for them." He pulled his coat collar around his neck. The March wind pierced the weak sun's warmth. Around them men in the encampment drifted like pack animals without a lead.

"Let's get you some coffee," Graham said, his boots making a sucking sound as he lifted his feet out of the mud.

The melting snow had left the bivouac area a wallow. Both men had trouble standing, and the pulsing whir of tires trying to move vehicles from the mire was all around them. Spinning wheels sent mud and chert flying like buckshot. Those caught in it cursed. Some bled.

"I'm gonna buy you three rounds of drinks the next time we find a functionin' tavern in this hell hole," Hall promised, looking straight at the lieutenant. Graham thought the captain acted dazed, strange, as if he had just crawled out of Oz. "One for your fine job leadin' this company while I was in the infirmary surrounded by fetching nurses and ugly doctors."

"Jesus!" Graham scoffed and changed the subject. "Has the colonel brought you up to speed on our next foray?"

"He was busy when I reported. We gave each other nods then I came over here."

Graham grabbed Hall's arm and moved him out of the way of flying mud and rock. On a minor piece of higher ground GIs were loading supplies into dozens of trucks. When the sun charged through clefts in the clouds, a round of cheers exploded like fireworks.

"Major General Leonard has brought the Ninth together again as a cohesive fighting unit," Graham said. "So he and his dogs will be calling the shots. No more renegade Captain Hall and his merry invisible Company 'O.'"

"We're gonna crawl up the enemy's ass all the way to Warburg then to the Mulde River and then on to Leipzig," Graham pronounced. When he heard the name of the revered city, Hall seemed to scramble out of his funk.

"Leipzig will be a bitch," he said. The great German metropolis, city of books, nurturer of Bach and Goethe, was no longer an entity. It was rubble. And ruins were easier for Germans to defend than open boulevards and standing architecture, Hall calculated.

The endgame had arrived, the captain realized. Yet, at that moment, he felt a strange off-center mood of neither joy nor relief, only dullness. Hall reached eastward. He sensed he could almost touch the end of hostilities like it was a chair or a lamp. He allowed himself no outward expression of it. This inevitable gratifying victory, he gauged, would be problematic. "The end will come larded with a mass of unwanted cousins, Leo," Hall muttered.

Pulling his boot from the muck the captain tried to stretch his damaged leg. It was unnatural and distant, almost as if it belonged to another body, though pain, at least a sensation of life, came with it.

"Cheer up. This war is about won, John William!"

Hall didn't reply to Graham's prediction. "I want them to make you a captain, Leo," Hall interjected. He already had submitted a recommendation to Col. Collier that Graham be promoted. "All the reports—yeah, I read 'em—said you did a helluva outstandin' job here. Helluva job. Your promotion and your savin' me at the rifle championship in '39. That's what the other two rounds of drinks are for."

****

As Hall's unit marched toward Leipzig, they met enclaves of heavy resistance. The captain maintained an unshakeable ache for victory even as his capacity for war was ebbing. The dead, whom he had ignored for so long, had begun to arrive, and they seated themselves on straight-backed chairs in perfect rows along a narrow vaulted corridor in his mind.

On an evening in early April, Hall's unit marched to an upland position in Saxony south of Leipzig and set camp. The sky dome was a clear Stygian black, the stars uncommonly luminous. From his perch, the captain could see the lights of a German hamlet about four miles distant. Hall summoned Graham, his four platoon leaders plus Gance, his first sergeant, and Dooley, his best gunner, into his tent.

The captain knelt on the ground spreading his contour map on a folded blanket. His face sagged as if he hadn't the strength to engage its muscles.

"Pieces of a German regiment failed to deploy to Leipzig to aid in the city's defense. They are holed up in that town down there," Hall told the six as he pointed east. "Prob'ly between five hun-durd and a thousand Krauts. Not that many fightin' men, though. Command estimates a lot of sick and wounded amongst 'em. And the remaining civilian population is mostly unarmed."

American high command had ordered Nazi havens "reduced to powder" by B-17 bombers flying sorties just after daybreak from the United Kingdom. On green felt English tables, upon which laid crisp paper maps the size of bedsheets, the destiny of every German town, village, and city had been prefigured, delineating the spared and the damned. And Lebensstadt, the hamlet on Hall's map, had been chosen for the latter because of its "infestation."

Before bombing the village, elements of the 60th were to dispatch by stealth its tanks and ground troops to surround and eliminate any Nazis trying to escape.

"Our orders are to hammer any Krauts fleeing the town and clean out any enemy survivors when we sweep the rubble," Hall told them.

"Lot of innocent civilians gonna go down with 'em," Lt. Longfellow gasped.

"As always," Hall said.

Longfellow continued. "Visited it years before the war, sir. All I know is it's a beautiful little town."

"I will enjoy kicking Hun body parts out of my way on the march to Berlin!" Lt. Stuntz cracked.

"Goddamnit, we're here to talk about our mission," Hall bellowed. "If you have anything to add before my decision, make it useful!"

"Sir, I think it a crime to destroy this town and every human in it," Longfellow shouted as he glared at Stuntz. "In the daytime, it looks like a piece of artwork from the top of this hill, something out of a fairy tale."

"You sound like an old woman, Longfellow," Stuntz snorted. "What would you have us do? Call off the bombing and do a suicide charge?"

Sergeant Dooley interrupted, "Agree with Lt. Stuntz on this one, sir."

"Agree with him on what, sergeant?" Hall asked brusquely, his patience thinning.

The same Dixie Dooley, fed by some hidden reptilian host and still angry that he couldn't scald the enemy at the Beaufort Crossroads with phosphorous four months ago, repeated his zeal for blood. The captain realized he had blundered by bringing him into the briefing.

"All I'm sayin' is that our orders is clear," Dooley coughed.

Stuntz tried to strengthen his case. "We're not here to preserve charming German villages, sir. We're all here risking our necks to win a war, and we win by destroying the enemy..."

"I don't think 'mercy' is what Longfellow is advocating—" Hall started.

"We gotta lay God's terror on 'em so future Kraut generations never forget us, captain, sir," Dooley sermonized.

The captain looked up at Leo Graham and Finn Dunbar as if to ask if they had anything to add. Neither twitched.

"Everyone dismissed, except the first sergeant," Hall said abruptly. Cobern Gance stepped forward as the others left the tent and stepped into the night.

Hall considered this man complex and able, and unlike any other soldier in the battalion. No matter how many readings he took of him, Hall could never quite assay the magnitude of his capabilities, though he knew they went deep. And he was about to test them.

"Here is the map of our troop strengths and positions. This is written proof of the upcoming bombing sortie. Good luck." Hall, who earlier had briefed Gance, pressed the paperwork into the first sergeant's hand.

"How old are you?" Hall asked.

"Forty two. Born in Pittsburg, 1903."

"Where d'you get so good at speakin' German?"

"Both my mother, who is Alsatian and my French father speak it. We spoke three languages in the household everyday."

"How'd you end up in this man's Army?"

"Worked in my father's optometry business until The Crash of '29. The Depression did something the Spanish flu couldn't do ten years earlier: All but ruin us. For too many, a fresh pair of spectacles was a luxury delayed. The family business couldn't support my wage. I left. Now I am here."

"Well, you're the right man for the bidness ahead of us, Gance. Make this work."

The first sergeant saluted. Rather than returning the salute, Hall extended his hand. "It is all in your court now."

In Hall's company, Gance was in charge of operations and a master of reconnaissance, including deploying patrols behind enemy lines. He was a studious, unflappable, confident man who spoke well. At times he seemed clairvoyant. He could decipher battlefield terrain and enemy exit points at the blink of his carbon-dark eyes. Most of the soldiers he worked with were young and they respected him.

After leaving the conversation, Gance hastened to a waiting jeep. Three GIs followed. "Where ya headed, sarg?" one of them asked.

"Going to visit the German commander," he replied matter-of-factly. Two of the three were intrigued and jumped in the jeep. "Leave your weapons," Gance said.

The vehicle spun away kicking up mud, lights searching for road, under a white flag of truce. It hesitated at the town's perimeter then moved on, passing a German outpost. The Americans waved as they went by. The jeep stopped in the village square.

Gance asked a German guard to alert his commanding officer.

"Guten Abend. Ich muss wissen, wo Ihr Kommandant ist. I must talk with him immediately," the American said, acting as if this was a friendly social visit. The young guard froze. Three other German soldiers converged on the jeep with rifles trained on its occupants. Except for Gance, they reacted like exposed quarry fearing to breathe.

The sergeant got out and walked to the front of the jeep where the German riflemen and the guard were fidgeting. To his right he saw a German major, partially dressed, rushing from a house. His trousers were intact, but the jacket was off and a white undergarment was all that covered his chest. Military-issued suspenders flapped around his knees like goose wings torn loose from their sockets.

"I have a message from my commanding officer," the sergeant began in German. The Nazi major was furious. But the sergeant quietly stood his ground, saying nothing further as the German officer got within inches of him, yelling epithets. *This is show*, the first sergeant suspected.

"My captain wants to avoid destroying this town at daylight," Gance said coolly in the major's native tongue, "and he kindly requests your surrender."

The major responded in English as he put his pistol to the sergeant's temple. "You are a dead American!" In the jeep the two GIs swallowed their panic. Gance's tremble was undetectable to them.

"You will want your colonel to see this map," Glance replied in German, opening the documents Hall had given him. "It is a map of our forces and their positions in relation to this village."

The edgy major snatched the documents and glared at them while the first sergeant, speaking in German, quietly pointed where two American divisions, 16,000 men, were ready to strike along a front that encompassed the hamlet and half-dozen other population centers. Then Gance showed the German officer documents confirming the schedule of bombers taking off from England. If Lebensstadt and its inhabitants were to be spared, he said forcefully, Allied commanders had to be alerted "am schnellsten."

"Major, you no doubt have men in your regiment who have homes and families here," the first sergeant pleaded softly. "I will await in my jeep for a decision. Also, I must inform my commander within a quarter hour that these documents are back in my hands or our offensive will be launched."

"And you will be dead," the major promised him.

The GIs in the jeep, still stunned by what they walked into, and not knowing the gist of the dialogue, peppered their sergeant with questions as they repaired to a murky spot outside the town.

"I can't answer your questions," Gance whispered. "All I can say is that we have a chance of getting back alive. Don't jeopardize it by acting jumpy."

After an interminable wait, all documents were returned, but another twenty-five minutes passed before a German corporal approached Gance. The soldier asked that an American officer come into the town.

"A German officer cannot surrender to you," the young corporal informed the first sergeant in German, "but he will surrender to one of your field commanders."

Glance called the captain. "Inside of two hours the Germans will have warehoused all their weapons and equipment, and Nazi troops would pass in review."

"I'll be there," Hall replied. "Make it 0700 hours for the ceremony. And tell them any damage to property will not be tolerated. Out."

The first sergeant made the arrangements, secured clearances by radio, and, later that morning, the German regiment passed in ritual parade in front of the American captain. Ninth Armored took custody of weapons, equipment, and every enemy soldier. When the major approached Hall with his ceremonial sword in outstretched hands, the captain gestured for him to keep it. "I want you to have it," the major replied. Hall accepted and the formal surrender was complete.

The dawn's red but this neck of the woods is bloodless, Hall considered as he walked east from the makeshift parade field. He had known that Gance would be in peril from the moment he departed camp. After the ceremony, he grinned as the former optometrist approached him. "Damn fine work!" Hall's words sparkled and his demeanor had lightened. A new vigor spread across his face; his buoyancy returned. "Proud to have you in our company, Gance. Colonel Collier'll know of your heroism. And of the damnedest guile I ever witnessed."

As the German regiment marched under guard out of the town, they heard the quaking of Allied bombers and, minutes later, the sound of distant explosions. The captain was watching the flares on the horizon when a messenger approached him. "Sir, Col. Collier wants you at headquarters."

****

At the 60th Armored Infantry Battalion command post, the colonel waited for his captain. Immediately, Hall caught the odor of scorched protocol blistering the air.

"You wanted to see me, sir?" Hall snapped as he entered Collier's tent and threw him his crispest salute.

"'Wanting' to see you is the least favorite thing in my life, Hall."

He kept Hall standing at attention, still trying to summon words he could direct like coffin nails.

"I have it on good authority that you presented our battle plans, maps, and bombing itinerary on a silver platter to some goddamn German major last night. To remind you, Hall, the Germans are the enemy! Where in Army training manuals did you find that goddamn tactic, captain?" Collier, close to combustion, spat.

Hall, though thrown off balance by this level of fury, nonetheless decided to remain resolute.

"No such passage exists, sir." Hall replied.

"For a pretty goddamn excellent reason!" Collier bellowed. "I think I will list for you all the ways this idiotic thing you pulled could have gone wrong…."

"No need, sir, I went over them more than once."

"Oh, did you remember the one about courts martial?"

"Near the top of my list, sir."

"Blast it, Hall, General Leonard is up my ass over this. Thinks I'm sloppy. Thinks my command structure is haywire. That I've allowed crazy shit to substitute for—"

"I felt I was the only one who could make a decision on whether and how to pursue this plan, and I made it, sir," Hall said firmly. "I believed no German commander would surrender without seeing the bona fides. It all worked to our advantage."

"Christ!" Collier sputtered. "The fucking Kraut commander could have relayed our whole goddamn command structure, troop strength, and positions all the way up to General Model or Karl Gerd von fucking Rundstedt!"

"That chain of events wadn't gonna happen, sir. Not at this stage of the war," Hall countered. "No way the enemy could have relayed the intelligence in time to take any action worth a damn."

"Anything else, Hall?" Collier snapped as he scanned maps and reports, avoiding any more eye contact with his leader of Headquarters Company.

"The German commander knew somethin' full well," Hall said, dropping military niceties, his voice betraying raw anger that rose when he was confronted by willful ignorance or conceit or someone challenging his native abilities. "He knew he would sign the death warrant for himself, every soldier, and a few thousand civilians if he refused my offer. My decision was correct. For many reasons."

"Get out!" Collier yelled.

The captain did a crisp about face, threw back the tent flap, and exited. Lt. Graham was waiting for him.

"Hell hath no fury like a West Pointer scorned," Graham quipped as they approached the jeep. Hall smiled but said nothing. He knew the risks had been greater than what he itemized to Collier. He knew this before he brought his team into his tent to divert them from the scent of a rogue decision. And he knew that not knowing the sanity of the command occupying the village was his greatest liability. Had they been like Stuntz or Dooley, who had doomed themselves to live in a freakish dimension of hate, the outcome could have been disastrous. Aches lit up in the captain's wounds when he pondered this possible miscalculation.

"As I considered this gambit, Leo, I could see canaries falling dead in a sunless mine," the captain confessed. He was certain one of those canaries could have been the numinous Gance. "But hell's bells, I just knew it would work!"

Chapter 21

THE WEIGHT OF OPTIONS

Philip Sekou Chikelu, his voice operatic even when using the spoken word, was discussing with Eve the difficulties of translating ancient Aramaic and Greek into a modern tongue when Shinn arrived.

"Good morning, Eve, Phil," Shinn trills as he walks past the coffee pot to where the tea is steeping, "what's the topic of the hour?"

"Just talking to Eve about The Vagaries."

"The Vagaries?" Shinn repeated.

"You know, the quirks of trying to convey meaning from languages thousands of years old into vernacular English, Sekou Chikelu said." Eve elbowed in, "Isn't everyone talking about this over coffee this morning, Roger?"

"Ah. You mean, how did the word 'Lucifer' which translated as 'light' and the star of morning somehow become a scarlet devil in snakeskin?" Shinn asked. He formed horns with his two index fingers and placed them on his forehead. "Yeah, I think that conversation deserves two cups."

"Your dilemma is similar, you know." Phil eyed Shinn. "You are trying to translate 'primordial' events from two decades ago into something that will percolate into today's twenty-year-old mind."

"That's like trying to cure blindness," Eve deadpanned.

"Well, I must get ready to do cataract surgery," Shinn sighed. "But, remember, when Greek poets and playwrights needed an oracle to spy into the future or decode the past, they usually cast a blind man or woman."

Outside, the early Manhattan spring morning accelerated the banga-rang of life already vibrating beneath the spring soil. Inside the classroom, the professor pushed tall vertical windows to their highest point. He used a seven-foot wooden pole reminiscent of a cavalier's lance. Oxygen rushed through the openings and fired in him memories of Ohio public-school teachers performing the same ritual thirty years ago. The outdoors made its way in and around the stuffy interior until it had visited every corner, cleansed the air and began its journey again. Shinn peeled off his suit jacket and ritualistically hung it on the back of a chair. He arranged note cards on the lectern. The students arrived, chatted, and fell still.

Picking up from the last session, the professor began, "Hall told me after the war that he 'didn't give a rat's ass' what Collier said to him. I think Hall did what he had to do. It was a moral calculation and a military one. But he felt compelled to save that village and not waste lives."

Before Lebensstadt, Hall had gotten wind that he was in line for a pro-motion to major and would receive medals for valor, Shinn continued. "Had the captain's strategy backfired, he knew his commission and any promotion or battlefield citations would have evaporated."

He nodded to Rivera. "Given all that, I find it abnormal that Hall didn't consider playing it safe," she stated.

"Well, Hall felt he had to pursue the Nazi surrender. He had to make it work. In his reckoning, this was the only option to avoid inestimable ca-sualties in his own unit and give civilians in the town a future. 'Abnormal' would have been the textbook approach, don't you think?"

The Battle of Leipzig was a different matter. German troops, remnants of Wehrmacht and Panzer divisions, had embedded themselves in the ruins of the city like wasps in carrion. "They said the feral dogs of Leipzig were the second enemy. Madness and starvation and shadows of lethality haunted the city's manifold recesses. As part of Ninth Armored, Hall's company—his tanks, infantry, anti-tanks squads, and machine gunners—roamed this flattened metropolis," Shinn said looking around the class. "They were easy prey. I have seen film clips from this action, which I never want to see again."

The professor cleared his throat.

"They went ruined house to ruined shop, through culverts and sewers, through the rubble of libraries and schools and the remains of hospitals. They were to kill or capture the lees of Nazi resistance. Which, frankly, they did with proficiency. But not without costs."

Chapter 22

STRANGE COMFORT

Before his unit's Leipzig operation and just three weeks after Capt. Shinn had arrived at Oflag 64, he and the rest of the prisoners were on the move again. From one landscape, its human warmth and mystic beauty long ago cremated, to another eerily like it. Nazi units were fleeing Poland to avoid imminent carnage at the hand of advancing Russian armies. Chained to the same destiny, Allied prisoners were force-marched along rugged tertiary roads that wound from Poland to Parchim, near Hamburg, Germany.

"It was January when we started our nearly two-hundred-mile walk," Shinn recollected. "We had no coats." The prisoners wrapped themselves in fetid blankets and scraps of cloth and paper to keep from freezing.

"After just the first hundred yards, my pack felt heavy." Shinn sat on a chair in the front of the class struggling to subdue his emotions. The students listened, astonished they knew so little of this man. "It was nothing more than a blue-checked pillow case with a few supplies." Shinn laughed mirthlessly. "Whenever I wanted something, it seemed like the pack had little to give."

The pillow case contained a thin mattress cover, a sliver of soap, knife, fork, spoon, a couple of cans of food, a razor, and two paperback books he liberated from the Oflag library. And a small Red Cross parcel. "It felt like I was carrying a hardware store with me.

No one noticed when Eberhardt Dagg and Philip Sekou Chikelu entered the room.

"We marched for weeks," Shinn went on. "It was early March when we boarded another box car at Parchim and traveled to Hammelburg, Bavaria. By this time, at least a hundred of us had died of exposure, sickness, wounds, fatigue, heartbreak."

At Hammelburg, the Nazis herded weak and starving American, British, and Canadian soldiers into a barbed-wired bog. Surrounded by piercing bleakness and seemingly perpetual night, their numbers dwindled. Thoughts of freedom they once harbored had all but vanished. "We seemed little more than spots of grease," the professor said.

When word broke through on March twenty-five that Americans had established a bridgehead less than sixty miles from the lock down, everything changed.

"Thoughts of survival and tending to the sick and desperate consumed us," Shinn explained. "Trying to endure, I read the same two books over and over in an attempt to ward off foolish optimism. Probably could recite them for you today. But when we saw American P-47 fighter planes overhead—they were so close we thought we could smell their exhaust—they entered our senses and our emotions escaped."

On March 27th, prisoners in the camp were awakened by American artillery. It rose like a white testament. The noise crowded out all darkness and flung a thunderous warning toward the German jailers and their protectors. "GIs, reinforced by Serb militia, attempted to rescue the inmates who hung on the fencing oblivious to danger, drained spirits eyeing the battle through dirty wire as if watching a game of rugby. And we were the prize."

A smile came to the professor's face. "For a moment, unlike the poet's warning, *I* felt young again. Whole." In the frenzy, a few men escaped. But the action failed, miserably.

"Gen. Patton had ordered the attack. We later learned that his son-in-law was a prisoner in the camp," the professor noted. First Army commander General Omar Bradley would call Patton's assault on the camp "a story that began as a wild goose chase and ended in tragedy."

"For some, even though the attempt failed, it lifted their spirits. For others in the camp, it was crushing. The Germans were still a force to be reckoned with." Shinn stood, took a few steps, and put his hands in his pockets. No one was moving. In one of his pockets, the professor rubbed a German bullet that had penetrated the crumbling facade of Hotel Meyer. It had passed through the body of an American soldier running for shelter. After the firefight, and two days before his capture, Shinn dug it out of the mortar with his bayonet.

"At seven in the morning on March 28th, the Germans rounded us up, and we began another forced march. Our destinations were Moosberg and then the town of Gars am Inn, a spartan, soulless place where we would linger. But the weather was warming and a measure of hope cracked our despair."

Shinn took the highly polished bullet from his pocket and laid it matter-of-factly below the note cards on the lectern. Over the years, his fingers tenaciously rubbed the totemic copper and steel slug as if seeking to erase it.

"I must reiterate that I was in a POW camp specifically for American, Canadian, and United Kingdom officers. As brutal as our conditions were, they were far better than the German camps that incarcerated our enlisted men—the privates, corporals and sergeants."

Moving toward the front of the stage, the professor studied Dagg before his eyes swept around the class. "During my days in captivity, as isolating and as miserable as it was, I began to take small solace in it. Strange as it sounds. I was not witnessing, like so many others, the slaughter on the killing fields."

American forces liberated the captives at Gars am Inn two months later in May of 1945. All were hospitalized.

"I wish I could express to you the joy at being freed, but I cannot. I will leave it to your lucid imaginations," the professor suggested. "But I can tell you this. I have never seen a more brilliant sky than on that spring day when the gates opened to us all. That sky was a place where no one cries. It was the blue of infinity."

As the students left the classroom the former infantryman gathered his note cards gently as if the memories on them could break. He slipped on his suit jacket from the back of the chair and secured the cards in its inside pocket. Lastly, he closed the windows.

Chapter 23

THE HORROR

It would be five days until Prof. Shinn's next class convened. During that hiatus he pored over his diary, official military accounts of the final days of the Third Reich, and letters he had exchanged with men in his battalion after the war.

"After Leipzig fell," he began his conclusion to his students. Some visiting students, a few faculty he hadn't seen before, Professors Philip Sekou Chikelu and Eberhard Dagg, and Eve Spektor had taken seats in the back. "The Ninth Armored ordered Captain Hall to split off his unit and engage in what the military called 'mopping up' action. This took him through Saxony in Southern Germany. A unit of the First Infantry Division would be on his flank. From Germany they were to relocate into Czechoslovakia, where separate German units had coalesced."

As Hall's troops marched through the Czech countryside, it was exploding with spring flora, their brilliance covering the earth's wounds. Passerines waltzed in the sky. Lt. Graham had hitched a ride on the outside of Hall's tank and was jabbering.

"Captain, was there even a war here?" the lieutenant asked of the man half out the top hatch. "It's like we stepped into another time."

That night, the captain got a crackling, barely discernible call over the field telephone. A disembodied voice like electromechanical coughing sought to break through the hissing static.

"Rover Boy, this is Golden Fox…civilians fifteen klicks…your position… need food…medical. Divert…town of Zwodau…zulu…whiskey…oscar… do you read…near…Karvoly Vary…urgent…Over."

Finding it on his map Hall re-plotted their next day's course to the town of Zwodau in Czechoslovakia.

Except for the sentries, Hall was the last to bed down. Aching with hunger, despite taking his rations, he lay on the ground looking up into the heavens, borderless except for earth's horizon, which reminded him of the divagating arc in an old man's hairline. His eyes fixed on the constellations and followed the vast contour of Cygnus. His lids drooped, and he fell into a slumber where white swans flew from iridescent ponds and took wing to the north. In the beyond, the slain, like an endless convoy of orphaned children, rose from the earth and hovered above the vista, gazing toward the birds in flight. Dogs marauded and bayed. A battleship, its bow piled with corpses, coursed westward across a dry wasteland.

At dawn on May sixth, Lt. Dunbar woke the captain.

"Sir, more chatter on the radio. Command wants us to move," Dunbar said softly, as he nudged him. Hall scrambled to his feet and within ten minutes the company broke camp. As they moved to Zwodau, they sang. At the second hour, an odor descended on the company. It had a pernicious and alien smell. Less than half an hour further, the men covered their mouths and noses, some with cloths soaked in canteen water. But it penetrated everything. At an outcropping of rock, Hall ordered his men to halt and take cover. The captain moved to high ground where he was masked by mountain-meadow grass growing from stone fissures. He set his periscope and saw the Czech spring unmade.

Before his eyes were three circles below all formed by barbed wire enclosures twelve to fourteen feet high. The outermost circle, which fenced in acres of the small valley, was erected as a final barrier to escape. Four guard towers were built equidistant around its perimeter. The small inner circle contained the Nazi command center, out buildings, and soldiers' quarters.

Inside the expansive second enclosure were hundreds of emaciated figures in rags. They appeared to the captain to be women. Movement was scant. A sign on the fence read "Zwodau-Flossenbürg." The air was an entity unto itself, like a rotting beast. Hall left a trail of vomit as he made his way back to his tank.

"I don't see a German anywhere, Leo," Hall hacked on his return, his face blanched and beaded with sweat. Vomit streaked his jacket front and sleeves. "And I can't describe what I saw—the people—somehow we've gotta approach the compound. Looks like it encloses about twenty acres or so of hell."

Hall verbalized some orders and leaned his back gently against his tank's tread. Unable to settle himself, he crawled under the armored chassis where he laid flat of the ground in the shade. Graham called First Infantry, seeking medics, gurneys, and personnel transports. And food and potable water, enough for a thousand starving people.

When provisions arrived, two-dozen-foot soldiers followed the captain and surrounded the camp in wide circumference, then moved cautiously toward the barbed-wire perimeter of the compound. Fearing ambush, Hall had placed armor and the remainder of his troops in an upland position overseeing the advance and ready to defend against an enemy snare. But the American troops heard only the sinister buzz of insects circling the starving and the dead.

As they approached, the men came face-to-face with the horror. A few of the figures lunged at the fence, grabbing its mesh and gawking. All were indeed women. Their tongues swollen, they wheezed through diseased mouths. Most had ulcerated skin oozing blood and an oily residue. Some had black and purple bubo-like growths at the groin as large as hens eggs. Behind them the Nazis had stripped the dead of their rags and left them to rot in high piles like waste collected at a building site. The corpses looked like large desiccated frogs decayed to a burnt umber. The vision of this underworld forged by human deviance paralyzed Hall's men. Most wept into their sleeves. The sun was bright that morning, yet powerless to diminish the shock.

Though untrained and unready for what they saw, the troops schlepped water inside the compound to the survivors. Some of the women seemed unmoved by their presence. When Graham saw Army Quartermaster and Red Cross units arriving with division medics, he ordered the gate opened. Over nine hundred mummified skeletons tried to rise. But only a handful of them—persecuted Roma, Jews, Catholics, lesbians, and "Aryan traitors" to the fascist cause—were strong enough to walk from captivity.

Hall, remembering his warning, stepped back from the horror and threw a message to the wind, "A thousand years, Shinn. A thousand years!" The captain could not assimilate what he had seen. Not in the room where he lived. Even battlefield carnage did not reach this proportion of human depravity. Not this. His self raced to escape, but there was no harbor.

With Quartermaster in charge of the refugees, he took his company forward late that day into northern Czechoslovakia in search of remaining German enclaves and the fugitive Nazi guards. The company moved through the rest of the day without incident and made camp. Only a few took supper. The soldiers turned in for the night.

"We are ready for our early start, captain," Lt. Stuntz assured Hall, who was reviewing maps by flashlight. "I think the men want to 'meet' the Krauts who fled that camp as soon as possible."

"We'll track 'em down right after daylight, as I said in the briefing," Hall replied without looking up. "I think the Germans are near Karlovy Vary, not but a few miles from here."

Before daylight on May 7, 1945, Hall summoned his lieutenants and reviewed their orders. The rest of the company cheered when their platoon leaders delivered the news they wanted.

The captain sent six men to return to the Zwodau camp, photograph it, and burn it to the ground. As the flames consumed the shacks, guard towers, outhouses, German quarters, and the dead, the remainder of Hall's company, their weapons ready, their bodies filthy, their uniforms hanging on them like torn souls, marched toward Karlovy Vary with a vigor that masked their depletion. The captain's instructions were explicit: on his command, the tank, mortars, and ground forces would destroy the enemy. Hall had delivered his order like a curse on the century. "You won't stop shooting until you are out of ammunition. Or no German has a breath remaining."

Afterwards, Lt. Graham caught up to his commanding officer. His eyes were blank. "You okay, captain?" Goodfellow was a few paces behind.

"The stain…we must wipe this filth from the land, these murderers of innocents, of women and children, the Custers of our time…goddamn it… goddamn these criminals who hide behind the shield of war."

The morning was hazy with low visibility as Hall's company came to a ridge. After calling an abrupt halt, the captain ordered absolute silence. Below them shapes materialized in the distance. Hall could hear faint German voices and directed Dooley to belly crawl closer to observe the figures. "Let me know what you see," Hall snarled through a whisper.

After a wait, Dooley radioed back. Above the steady hiss of his field phone, Hall heard the news. "One bastard is wearing a commandant's uniform, captain," Dooley told him "I swear these are the Krauts responsible for the women's camp. Bet my life on it. Over."

The guards and staff from Zwodau had joined another German unit. One hundred and fifty soldiers had finished eating and were preparing to move out.

"It's time for us to break up their party, sir," Dooley recommended to the captain. "No armor, not a Panzer tank in sight. Looks like they have six mortars, three stationary machine guns, uh, well-positioned to deliver enfilade and crossfire, three or four anti-tank weapons. Out."

Hall summoned Graham. He alerted him to the situation. The lieutenant levied a warning, "We will be exposed, John William! If we attack their position, the damn cliffs on the sides will prevent us from any flanking action."

"Not worried about that."

"Then we gotta hammer 'em with the Sherman and the mortars before we go in," Graham declared. "I think we can soften 'em up bad enough that they will surrender."

"Maybe you didn't hear. Their surrender doesn't interest me."

"Surrender is preferable to fucking up our troops for nothing, captain!" Graham reminded him, his voice like a stiletto. "Captain! Let me handle this."

"We're not finished here!" he cursed, stumbled and momentarily pressed his head to the ground. He remembered enemy infantry moving en masse up the Luxembourg coulees, his men being killed shot-by-shot, the anonymous GI destroyed by phosphorous, his tanks and halftracks burning in the field like giant iron torches, Ruder's body thrown onto a truck bed, the spectacle of long lines of mangled American soldiers laying shoulder-to-shoulder, framing the road from Savelborn to Christnach. His memory conjured again the private blown apart while attempting to save him, the screaming wounded, the dead walking out of Zwodau.

"Not finished here!" the captain's repeated exhortation defied his own order for quiet. Graham stepped back. Hall paused. "Make sure the platoon leaders have their men ready," he rasped. "Okay, we'll tender up the Hun. Start with our artillery, then go in full bore!"

As American gunners trained their weapons on the shapes forming from out of the fog, and spotters moved into position to call fire, the captain climbed to Dooley's cloistered location on the ridge. He glassed the German force through his periscope. A frozen river had lodged in his veins.

"They suspect someone's on their tail, sergeant, and have ceased prep for exit. They are gettin' battle ready. It's time."

"Yes, sir," Dooley crowed under his breath. He was like a fly rubbing his back legs together preparing to feast.

The miserable shadows of Zwodau staggered forward in Hall's consciousness. He was ready to insinuate his will. Lifting his fist aloft the captain alerted his unit. When his hand dropped the reckoning would commence. And the earth was still. Hall's arm remained raised. "Sir, give us the order!" Dooley urged. But the captain wasn't there. He had returned to the past and his father boasting on the ride to Lawton of clipping rubes and armed men standing in his doorway threatening his kin. Between the blink of his eye he relived the family's rupture, the death of his mother, his oldest brother's grotesque homily on the porch days later. *They were never meant to survive, Johnny Cakes. Not in the grand scheme 'a things. Hell, ever'body knows that!* Lucy Lee spoke from the grave. *You have original fire, son.*

Hall looked into the branches of trees under which his fist was raised, as if seeking an oracle.

"The order, sir!" Dooley pressed.

The captain stared through Dooley into the other side of death. Effigies untranslatable in any tongue flashed like glowing bullets. Then Shinn appeared on the deck of the Queen Mary. *Our mission is more complicated isn't it, captain? And how do you know what you dish out isn't going to be too much or too little?*

"I know because of who I am," Hall answered out loud, confounding Dooley. The captain took a breath and expelled it, raised his left arm, and crossed it with his right signaling his men to hold their fire. Slowly he brought his fists to his waist and turned to the sergeant. "We'll call for their surrender."

Dooley spat on the ground. "Too late for these fucks, sir. Past time to rid the land of these reptiles. We owe it to the prisoners—to our dead. To God!"

If he heard, Hall gave no response.

"This is our kill day, captain! Their requiem hour."

"Not our path!" Hall barked angrily. Goodfellow rushed to their position. "Captain, you got a call from battalion. Colonel Collins is on the line!"

"This is Rover Boy, over," Hall snapped into the lieutenant's field phone.

"We have a hun-durd—fifty Krauts here..."

The impatient voice on the line interrupted. "This is Comfort Six. Hold onto your sack, Rover Boy. Hitler is dead. German high command has surrendered. This goddamn war is over! Do you copy, over?" It was May 8, 1945. The Ninth had been at war in Europe for 248 days.

The captain couldn't speak.

"Do you copy, over!"

"This is Rover Boy. I copy. I copy. I copy. What are our orders?"

"Cease all hostilities unless fired upon. Repair your unit to the 60th rendezvous point in Bayreuth, pronto. Do you copy, Rover Boy? Over."

"Affirmative, Comfort Six. Rover Boy out."

The German surrender and the imprecision of victory stunned the captain. He had been on the precipice. Seconds earlier he could have fallen. Near him, Dooley convulsed with anger. He had heard little of what was said until the captain rang his executive officer. "Leo, have the men stand down. The war is over. Stand down. Do you copy? Over." With that the sergeant stood like a stone.

"Sergeant, what are the Krauts doing?" Hall snapped after he hung up. Dooley moved slowly. He glassed the Germans. They had left their posts and were jumping around "like crazy men" inside their camp. Some dropped to their knees making the sign of the crucifix across the breast of their uniforms. The sergeant almost swallowed his tongue.

"Those bastards!" he bellowed."

"The war is over, sergeant." The captain, still fighting to orient himself, repeated: "Germany surrendered."

Two hundred yards distant Hall's troops went into a frenzy. Some fell to the ground howling in ecstasy. Others screamed for the revenge promised them. A few locked themselves in prayer. The German soldiers moved forward out of the fog. On sticks they hoisted white flags made from their underwear.

Dooley now was ninety feet from Hall and in a stupor devoid of relief or elation. Approaching the American line the Nazis carried with their surrender a grating laughter. The miasma of the death camp hung on them. Dooley perceived that the Nazis considered their stench an article of pride. He wailed and his voice echoed off the hills.

"Get hold of yourself!" Hall yelled to the sergeant as he headed back to the jeep. "Have your men collect the German weapons and military ordinance, Sergeant Dooley, then round up the Kraut prisoners, post guards, and get 'em the hell away from us!"

Dooley cursed. As the captain turned, the sergeant drew his 45-caliber pistol, howled, and triggered his weapon. The blast gave off a booming vibrating rumble and the bullet whirred toward the captain. At the sound, the American troops froze in confusion. Off its mark, the heavy, wobbling round winged the captain's forehead and the shock felled him. As Hall toppled, he ripped his pistol from its holster. Dooley took another aim at his grounded quarry. Before the sergeant could fire again, Victor Paz discharged his rifle sending a bullet through Dooley's gut, dropping him instantly to the ground where he bled onto the rocks. Hall, confused and dislocated, gathered himself and rushed to Dooley's side to give him aid. When medics arrived and took charge of the wounded man, the captain approached Paz, gripped his shoulders, and, saying nothing, stared into his eyes.

"Yeah, I'm with you, captain," Paz smiled.

Chapter 24

THE DISINTERESTED MACHINERY OF ENDINGS

In June, the 60th Armored Infantry Battalion left the continent and was dispatched to London for medical clearance before the passage home. Like a patient mother, the Queen Mary was waiting in moorage. Surviving soldiers walked or were carried onto her upper decks to journey westward in the heat of July 1945. Stevedores, flanked by military escort, carried coffins of the fallen into the ship's hold. At the dock, a small gathering of English men, women, and children waved tiny American flags as the liner pulled out from the quay. Not long after the sun vanished like a red farthing into a slot machine.

She was different now, the ship. She still cut the waters with poise and resolve. But her silhouette on the horizon was more majestic, ascendant, as if she had the gravitas to arouse at least some measure of attentiveness from the immense ashen waters that surrounded her, but were otherwise indifferent to the affairs and fabrications of the human species. Unlike before, there was no frenzy in her gait. No rush to commence or conclude. The Queen moved with a particular decorum she had not evinced in her August passage a year earlier. For now she was also a funereal vessel, a crucible, a coffin bearer for some of the very soldiers she earlier had so expeditiously transferred into the eastern maw. And her crew, obeying edicts from American functionaries on shore, thought it profane, if not ill-fated, to locate the motionless, the silent dead in the hold, where resided the ship's vast, wanton, disinterested machinery of propulsion. And for the living, those whole and those fragmented, it was perceptible in their pauses between toasts and cheers that an uneasiness resided in the new and unknown reckoning that awaited them in their western mooring.

The men laughed and talked and drank and exchanged diverting stories and bizarre anecdotes of battle. "The Kraut bullet entered the front of Bjornstad's helmet, took a right turn, spun around the interior three times, exited out the side and didn't give the bloke so much as a scratch!"

Many dreaded the twilight hour for it was the forewarning of sleep, that anxious slumber which would endeavor to purge soldiers' psyches. But many were impervious to healing. And at twenty-three hundred hours, two Army buglers played "Taps," the slow mournful liquid elegy to the end of day and, for the dead, the end of their earthly enigma.

****

The first morning of the voyage was magnificent. On the deck a gaunt but smiling infantry officer just promoted to major approached a drawn, peaked soldier reclining on a weathered canvas chair. "What are you reading, major?" Hearing a familiar voice, Major John Hall stood and his hand surrounded Major Roger Shinn's in a long, welcoming greeting. That the London hospital had released Shinn and put him on this ship home was a heartening surprise.

"I got some letters from the colonel, Lazarus, Lamb, a couple of others," Shinn told him. "They could tell me a little about the escapades of the 60th and you Four Horsemen. I figured you didn't write after the surrender because your nose was in a book. It was Collier who wrote to me and said you made it through the war."

Hall wrote sparingly. It was a chore that didn't suit him, and he didn't believe his phoneticized and otherwise eccentric spelling memorialized on paper was something he wanted to defend. But when the mood was with him, he still liked to talk.

"Hell, major, you know writin' isn't my strong suit!" Hall exclaimed, his weak defense more of a jest. He pulled a pouch of tobacco from his shirt pocket. After rolling some blend into a cigarette paper, Hall sealed it neatly by licking the edge. A slight tremor in his hand caused him to lose some of his makings, which collected on his khaki shirt. The soldier used the exact movement and pace each time he rolled a smoke, and it reminded Shinn of a religious ritual. "Besides, I figured we'd meet up on this boat or in New York. Plenty 'a time to catch up.'"

"Ha! Crystal Ball Hall." Shinn sniffed at Hall's slightly absurd confidence and his dodge for not communicating. But they talked, each finally able to connect. Except for Leo Graham, this was Hall's only unaffected conversation since the cessation of hostilities. But the two newly promoted majors exchanged experiences as if they were observing them from a mountain. Details were few. And neither wandered into the horrors they witnessed. Except that Hall spoke in the most general terms of the rescue at Zwodau which was enough that Shinn would fulminate on it for years. Overall the conversation was as light and placid as the water around them, and they spoke of their families and what they might expect on their return to American soil.

"I had all my paychecks from the War Department mailed directly to my oldest brother, Irvin'. I gave him Power of Attorney so he could deposit them in my bank account." Hall wore a grim smile. "What'll ya bet I have the same balance as when I sailed for Europe!"

"You need to get more reliable kinfolk, Hall," Shinn teased, then changed direction. "I heard about 9th Armored while I was in captivity. Overheard some German officers talking about you guys."

This amused his friend. "If they didn't say we were whoppin' their asses, then they were tryin' ta' get under your skin."

"No, they didn't know I could hear them. German command called the 9th the 'Phantom Division.' They never knew where in the hell any of our units would appear. And where we did appear, it spelled 'schaden.'"

"'Trouble.'" Hall laughed. He flipped his cigarette butt into air. An edge of the paper had come loose and it descended, flapping like a wounded moth into the ocean foam. Shinn watched its downward flight. "To be truthful with ya, the Wehrmacht gave us an awful lot 'a hell, Shinn. Just not as much as the SS gave you."

Hall lit another cigarette as if to service a submerged anxiety. "We're sailin' out of a long nightmare, major. It's time for us to live a little. Before the next one rolls in."

"Hitler's gone," Shinn began in response. "Most of his henchmen are dead or standing trial or already in prison. We won't have them to worry about. The thing I'm looking forward to most is a small patch of garden and quiet."

"Yeah, I can't see Nazism or fascism ever comin' back," Hall remarked. "Not anywhere, not after what the world has seen of it. Those goddamn turds cannot be polished."

The Oklahoman talked about what he wanted to do as a civilian: learn golf, tango with dark-haired women, float down Missouri's Buffalo River, when his thoughts scattered like a school of fish fleeing a stone tossed in a stream. And he stopped himself. "This war, dammit, sent us a warning, parson."

"What is that, John?"

"Human decency is damn thin. Ice on an Oklahoma pond in spring is sturdier. Come to think, maybe it's more like eyesight. Once diseased it turns into blindness. Can't see right from wrong. And there is not a damn thing we can do about it."

"I'm as confident that we can win a lasting peace as you were sure of victory in battle," Shinn said emphatically. The warm sun was in his hair and on his face. He could breathe fresh salt air, and he knew that neither prison nor war could hold him, and this feeling had great width. He knew his God's gifts would endure.

"Humans can remove their own tarnish. We're pretty resilient. Look at history."

"History teaches. Problem is it doesn't have any pupils," Hall responded, remembering something he read.

"We have a lot to sort out."

"So we do," Hall acknowledged. "In between the sortin' I am gonna be down at the river. Wish you'd come down to Oklahoma and share it with me sometime, parson, the taste of fish and hush puppies cooked outside in the evening calm and washed down with a splash or two of bourbon. Beyond that, I hope there is a dance or two left in me."

Something caught in Hall's throat. He hesitated before he spoke again.

"You weren't with me for long after the damn Bulge commenced, but you really were, Roger. You really were. I had turr-bil moments, but I could still hear ya' speakin' to me. And it worked out. I think it all worked out, as well as it could have."

The sun was large and red now as they surveyed the west. "Still a harbor somewhere on these colossal deep waters, isn't there, Major Shinn?"

"'The bright wind boisterous ropes, wrestles, beats earth bare of yestertempest's creases," the major replied, remembering lines from Shakespeare he once performed.

Chapter 25

WATER'S ONLY PURPOSE IS TO REACH THE SEA

The green of Manhattan in early May had expunged all memory of winter. New life emerged in plots and patches and parcels framed by expanses of cement and stone and tar. Some crawled up façades and palisades as if attempting escape from the city's noise and merciless feet.

As the professor entered the last class to conclude his varied, tapered, and personal meditation on war and ethics, he was cheerful. He believed forty-one more people had encountered anew the foremost paradox of humanity. As had he.

Earlier Prof. Shinn had asked students for topics, issues they wished to review in the last class before examinations. Instead they asked for resolution on some uncertainties.

"Who freed you and the other prisoners of war," Mia Rivera asked.

"Last time into the breach," he whispered to himself. "Last time" and he gripped the lectern.

"Five days before the Third Reich collapsed, the American 86th Infantry set us free," the professor said. "And we got the hell out of Gars am Inn and Germany with haste."

Sekou Chikelu, in the same distant seat he always occupied, listened.

Shinn ritualistically removed his suit jacket and draped it over the back of a nearby chair.

"And what about the survivors of the 60th?" she continued.

"Hall was the best company commander I knew. Bar none. But so many soldiers had that vein of silver running through their human geology."

Ariel Jeffers checked her notes. She had saved a question from weeks ago and interrupted. "Your seminary training, Dr. Shinn. Was it an advantage? Did it prepare you for the moral quandary of armed conflict?" Newman, a few feet away, still believed she was missing the point of the class and scoffed. She returned an unalloyed glare.

"I did not get my education in morality until I was on the battlefield and a prisoner of war," he answered without hesitation.

This admission shocked the class. Newman saw it as an opening to swat at the professor's words as if they were house flies. "So-called moral warriors, whether clergymen or infantrymen, engaged in misnamed 'good wars,' do little except perpetuate the madness," he asserted again. "Nothing changes!"

Shinn shook his head. "No. Neither Hall nor myself considered the Second World War a 'good war.'"

"Rather than 'bad war,' 'good war,' we might be better defining armed conflict within two contrasting categories," the professor countered. "'Existential Wars' on one hand and 'Wars of Mockery' on the other."

"Mockery?" Fred Bushnell erupted.

"As in contempt for human purpose, intelligence, the family of humanity," Shinn said.

Sekou Chikelu smiled at where his friend was moving the discussion.

"Here is the core of it." The professor pushed his finger into the lectern. "I knew I could have been a chaplain in the Army. It supposedly would have been 'easy.' But that would have prevented me from confronting too many choices, you see, the hard existential material of moral decision-making."

He stepped to the middle of the stage, scanned the students, then focused his gaze on Newman. "In war, in this massive crucible of life and death, vicarious experience does not equate to being there. So-called 'moral authority' is hard to earn until your choices become concrete. When you must make a decision while in the storm of moral uncertainty. When you finally realize water's only purpose is to reach the sea."

His words were resonant. They filled the room, lingered, then disappeared. "Until we are tested with moral choice, whether it is to declare, avoid, or support a specific war or take a human life on the battlefield, we are little more than armchair moralists. Morality is rooted in experience."

The professor's arm swept slowly over the entire room in his summation and he snapped his fingers like his cellmate at Diesz. "Until we find ourselves on the precipice, we really don't know anything of morality. Until we face—personally—the vulgarity, the putrefaction of humankind. Until there is choice, Mr. Newman, it's only philosophy. We play around with abstractions and equations but we are without the references. Though we can judge people, without these 'references' we cannot rightly grasp an individual's moral quandary or plumb those depths."

Shinn returned to the lectern, shuffled recipe cards, and paused. The students were still. Sekou Chikelu's heart had lodged in his throat. "I hope my story leads you to at least one conclusion: that each of you must question both the sovereignty of others' opinions, including my own, and the validity of shallow answers to thorny mortal dilemmas. For future perils will challenge you all. We will need acts and forms of social organization that we've hardly begun to imagine."

"Now, have you any other questions?"

Álvaro Belloc broke the silence. "Did Hall ever see Waterford again?"

The professor tapped the lectern briefly trying to think of what to say. He rotated his neck slightly. "Before I saw Hall on the Queen Mary's return trip, he had—in the first hour of the first day—inquired about the register of nurses on board," Shinn replied, now walking again along the stage and looking down at the floorboards. "It wasn't available. And female quarters, as you know, were *verboten* to men. We ate on separate shifts."

Shinn had encountered Hall often on the voyage and was conversing with him on deck around noon the second day. "Mid-sentence, Hall spots a familiar form distant from where we stood," the professor recollected. "She was in medical whites and looking out to sea. She wasn't supposed to be there at all. We couldn't see her face but her black hair was loose and dancing in the wind. Hall immediately strode over, tapped her shoulder, and uttered something. I saw her when she pivoted to face him."

They spoke briefly but Shinn couldn't make out the conversation, though he recognized what had happened. Hall and the woman conversed a minute or two before the nurse hurried inside the ship.

"Hall staggered to the rail, gripped it, and stretched his arms out as if trying to pull them from their sockets, then lowered his head between them." The professor spoke heavily as he looked at Belloc. "After a few moments he straightened and scanned the eastward horizon toward Europe as if he were listening for something."

"'Sam Waterford didn't make it,' the nurse had told Hall. 'She's gone. She was killed on the front. During the siege of Bastogne.' It was a terrible blow to all in her unit. She was one of many Red Cross nurses who wouldn't survive the shelling. Hall informed me she had been 'wounded' long before that."

"And Captain Hall?" Jeffers asked.

"The War Department wanted him to stay in the Army. They had just promoted him to major but offered to make him a lieutenant colonel. As they did me."

"Did he accept?" Belloc followed.

"No."

"Do you know why?" Jeffers probed, sensing the answer.

"His reasons were…," Shinn hesitated. "I can only guess…" He was uncertain whether to proceed. "In war the captain had seen wantonness beyond his imagining. He stood looking into the eyes of his species and saw what it was capable of, out to its most shadowy and unutterable margins. Though that is not how he would put it."

The class laughed.

The professor surveyed the ceiling, searching for words. He walked to the lectern, lifted his notes again, gazed beyond them, and set the cards down. "I would say that the cold blue flame of war had found him alone and surrounded in the Ardennes Forest. But in him at that moment it had met its match." Shinn moved his gaze to Newman. "Facing almost certain defeat, the captain altered the course of battle. For him, that moment would be with him the rest of his life. That would be enough."

Chapter 26

TOWARD RIVERSIDE

After the students left the room and the professor slid the giant windows down and locked them, Newman reentered quietly. "I regret my incivility to you, Prof. Shinn," Newman stated, his back straight, his gaze direct. As he spoke, his thumb clicked a ballpoint pen. "I am not ashamed of what I believe. But I, uh, just wanted to say that I have come to—as contrary as it may seem—to value my time in this class. And, yes, to admire you and your counsel."

The professor smiled, remembering his conversation with Katharine and the possibility that Newman may have seen part of himself in him.

"It is important to me that you didn't give me an 'F,' Robert," Shinn grinned as he shook the student's hand. "Your opinion matters. Quite a lot to me."

Newman nodded, walked away, and then turned. "And I will be with you this evening at the rally, at Riverside."

The professor's face brightened. "My wife Katharine will be there. I want her to meet you."

****

Shinn packed books and materials into his leather satchel, causing its sides to stretch. He rubbed his hand over its collection of abrasions. They appeared to him now like parts of an Aramaic text trying to form itself out of broken script. Pushing a black button with a pearl top, he shut off the lights and exited the classroom. In the fall, he won't return, instead spending the semester as a United Nations fellow.

Student reaction to his first-person account of a fragment of war satisfied him. Two hours from now, he will address a gathering at Riverside Church. Presumably a mixture of frenzied and levelheaded activists, concerned citizens, and students. Some will want to proselytize, others condemn. But more than a few of those who searched, he hoped, would find a cause that would address that which harrowed them.

His notes as always jotted on blank recipe cards stolen from Katharine's stash in an anonymous corner of her kitchen cupboard are with him. They outline his respect for the power of good against Gordian human troubles. The former infantryman would also issue a summons, a metaphorical call to arms urging potent non-violent resistance to the country's military adventurism and, in its wake, a profound change of course.

"It is all in the cards," he cracked. "Three recipe cards."

As he moved down the hallway to leave, Shinn was jolted by the appearance of Eberhart Dagg, who reissued his shopworn greeting. "I'm glad I caught you, Professor Shinn."

"And how are you today, Eb?"

"The president of Union has granted me an audience."

"I find that, sorry, unbelievable," Shinn replied with disinterest as he moved toward the exit.

"Well, you shouldn't!" Dagg fired back.

"I consider it so since the provost tasked me to inform you that the university takes a dim view of your harassing alumni and donors with distorted complaints. I just haven't had the…"

"A number of people have joined me…" Dagg huffed before being interrupted himself.

"Who is accompanying you, Eb, on this visit with the president?"

"I am capable on my own of discussing the damage you are doing to this nation's pre-eminent seminary."

"What may I ask are you hoping to get out of all this, old friend?" Shinn asked, building fortifications with an even-temper while lighting torches between his words. "You want me gagged and censored? Bound up in some fascist straight jacket so I can't draw air? Expelled? Burned at the stake, perhaps? What?"

"I have heard from colleagues who are appalled by your counseling of so-called conscientious objectors."

"You don't speak for the faculty or Union, so it must be for yourself," Shinn sighed.

"You are here to be an educator not an activist, Roger."

Shinn's eyes narrowed. "With respect, Eb, you have been an activist all your life. More importantly, you have no idea what I am counseling young people about."

"Students wanting to avoid service on supposed 'moral' grounds," Dagg rumbled. "There will be consequences...."

"Consequences? Consequences!" Shinn murmurs and stops.

Dagg watched as the former soldier stared down at the granite corridor, dropped his satchel, and spoke with a pause between words, like breaths between trigger squeezes.

"I see you are unaware—of the blood."

"The what?"

Shinn stared into the remove. Beyond it stood the Ardennes. "It must come down to something, doesn't it?"

"What are you...?"

Peering into his colleague's eye, Shinn exacted a long silence, which petrified the old man.

"I was there, Eb. That bullet flew so damn true. I heard a pop then a wwwhhhhiiiit. It entered his neck, a perfect kill shot, and blasted out the other side. Blood doesn't ooze or drip, you know, not from a wound like that. It coursed out of the breach in that numinous nineteen-year-old soldier like some sacred scarlet arc. Must have been a four or five-foot surge before it bent toward the earth. At that point, he was abandoned on that dirty swirling ignorant stage where just a moment earlier he had tried…" Shinn could not complete the thought.

"The mountains stopped breathing and our soldier stood, stood straight up for the longest time. Then, like a corpse cut from the gallows, he crumpled onto the ice. In just that moment a boy of promise alive at the center of the epochal twentieth-century was extinguished by a primeval fire. It was the bite of Cain! And I couldn't comprehend it, Professor Dagg. I just could not get my mind, or whatever was left of my rational self, to accept what I had witnessed!"

Dagg's eyes widened. Shinn narrowed his stare as if boring into old armor.

"The soldier's body didn't convulse, Eb. But the blood. The blood. It flowed like a cataract." Shinn pointed serenely to an invisible body on the granite floor. "Even in death his heart kept beating, and from each beat another fountain. Can't you see it?" The younger professor raised his voice and pointed again to the floor. "The blood marking his spot. Just like a dog sprays its urine. It was all he had, you know, to declare his territory before vanishing. His final signature to a world already more than eager to step over him. Forget his time on this earth and his province and this, his last battle. So he just kept pouring it forth. His paean to war. His red sacrament. Streaming it into *our* space."

Professor Shinn stepped back.

"Right there his generational line ended." A third time Shinn directed his focus to the surface of the hallway. "Soul and substance passes from parents to child, parents to child for millennia." The professor knelt and moved his hand as if over consecrated the ground. "All that gathering of thousands of years of his many, many mothers enduring childbirth, of fathers and mothers and family sacrificing, suffering so the bloodline would endure and their progeny bloom. His ancestors rippled through him and then, with him, they were expunged! From a solitary bullet made by an unknown hand sent from an anonymous warrior. He had no siblings. No children. He was the end of the line. The terminus. His final summation—not by voice, but by vein!'"

Shinn stepped closer to the old man who had made no attempt to interrupt or challenge.

"And no voice stopped the hand of Abraham this time, Eb. The boy had no sacred poet, you see. No one to sing long his praises in mythic register. He must have feared being reduced to an integer, a tic entombed in vast statistical meaninglessness that swells around old wars like bloat and is trotted out in glorious anonymity on patriot days. His blood just kept flowing. Fighting the darkness! Why won't we get beyond this perpetual night, old friend? This damned insanity?"

Shinn faltered. He grabbed Dagg's narrow shoulders and looked into his eyes. Dagg began to chatter. His mottled skin was drawn taut around his skull and a milky film floated on his ancient blindness like paraffin. The dying boy would live in Shinn's mind as long as he drew breath. Hall would be there. The long-dead nurse would. Wronge would. Others would sing to him all his days. But Dagg would exist long after Shinn was dust. As would Dooley. And Stuntz. And Krüger. They would carry forth tirelessly in endless battles till the close of time.

Dagg prattled incomprehensibly, and it echoed in the hallways, but Shinn couldn't hear it. Waves of sound and voices and music filled his head. The laughter of soldiers, their cries at death, whirlpooling dancers, the cheering in liberated villages, the melancholy incantations of the forest before battle, the squall from his would-be executioners, the blows to his body, the thunderclap of artillery, the burnt odor of gunpowder, the careening, screaming bullets that surrounded but didn't divert him, and the dogs, the eternal barking of dogs as he traveled down the hallway silhouetted there in the terrible light walking toward Riverside.

THE END